WHEN THE MORNING GLORY BLOOMS

Cynthia Ruchti

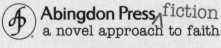

Abingdon Press fiction
a novel approach to faith

Nashville, Tennessee

Other books by Cynthia Ruchti

They Almost Always Come Home

When the Morning Glory Blooms

Copyright © 2013 by Cynthia Ruchti

ISBN: 978-1-4267-3543-1

Published by Abingdon Press, P.O. Box 801, Nashville, TN 37202

www.abingdonpress.com

Published in association with Books & Such Agency.

Scripture on pages 107-108, 148, 158, and 166 is from the Holy
Bible, New International Version®. NIV®. Copyright © 1973, 1978,
1984, 2011 by Biblica, Inc.™ Used by permission of Zondervan.
All rights reserved worldwide. www.zondervan.com. The "NIV" and
"New International Version" are trademarks registered in the United
States Patent and Trademark Office by Biblica, Inc.™

Scripture on pages 216 and 245 is from The Authorized (King James)
Version. Rights in the Authorized Version in the United Kingdom are
vested in the Crown. Reproduced by permission of the Crown's paten-
tee, Cambridge University Press.

Library of Congress Cataloging-in-Publication Data has been
requested

Printed in the United States of America

1 2 3 4 5 6 7 8 9 10 / 18 17 16 15 14 13

*For those I've rocked
and lullabied
and those who have rocked me*

Acknowledgments

In its embryo stage, this story first found encouragement from author Deborah Raney, who said, "I expect to see these characters in print soon," or words to that effect. Neither of us knew "soon" meant eight years or that I'd give birth to other books before this one. Thank you, Deb, for seeing something worth waiting for.

Before Barbara Scott moved from editor to agent, she prayed over story ideas I'd presented to her and then pointed to this one. Her radar detected something even I didn't know would be in the finished novel. Thank you, Barbara, for your well-honed listening skills.

My Abingdon editor, Ramona Richards, blessed me deeply during this process, championing the book and the way it was written, encouraging me when I needed it most, and introducing me to the joy of working with editor Jamie Chavez for the substantive edit. Much gratitude to you both and to all of the brilliant and talented Abingdon Press team. Thank you, too, for a book cover that tells a story by itself.

The true heart of everything I write is tended by friend and agent, Wendy Lawton of Books & Such Literary Agency. She works and lives with an elegance of spirit that calls me higher.

Thank you to early readers Andrea, Amy, Becky, and Jean. Your comments nourished my soul while my mind wrangled with the scenes. Amy, extra gratitude to you for reading the whole manuscript on a two-inch phone screen and for being the person whose voice first called me Mama. Thank you to my daughter, sons, son-in-law, siblings, and grandchildren for the privilege of loving you . . . and for loving me back.

Kathy, Julie, Jeane, NorthRidge family, Twila, Michelle, Shannon, Jackie, Diane, Robin—your labors and support are not forgotten. Becky, thanks for letting me borrow your name for a character and for modeling what it means to be a woman of excellence.

I'm grateful for my steadfast behind-the-scenes team of friends who pray for my stories without knowing all the details.

Thank you for your influence and education, ACFW.

Deep gratitude to my Beloved, whose magnificent invention—grace—shapes the ink strokes and what lies beneath them. And to my beloved, Bill, who listens to the constant clicking of the computer keyboard and hears the music of hope.

The sound of our falling is the call that sends Him to catch us.

1

Becky—2012

The hand on her cheek weighed no more than a birthmark. It fluttered, stirred by the breeze of a dream, but remained tethered to Becky's face.

Her neck stiffened. A neutral position was out of the question. She was trapped at an odd angle between the arm of the porch swing and the breath of the child.

With one foot planted on the porch's floorboards, and the rest of her a cradle, Becky kept the swing in motion. A smooth backstroke. Hesitation. Then as she lifted her foot, the forward stroke was accompanied by a two-toned creak the baby must have thought was white noise.

Becky guessed thirteen pounds. The bulk lying stomach-down across her torso like a seat belt might have come into the world a wisp of six pounds—less than a gallon of milk. But seven hundred bottles later, give or take, and he could hold his own against a Costco-sized bag of sugar.

A sweat bee buzzed a fly-by. Becky waved it off. Baby drool puddled at the top of her breastbone. She let it be, let it be.

The rich, woody scent of the neighbor's cottonwoods melded with the lingering aroma of her caramel latte, the one in her favorite pottery mug on the small table just out of reach. The mug, her book, sanity—so much seemed just out of reach.

The baby lifted his head. Feather lashes still closed, he nestled the opposite cheek into the hollow of her neck. She patted his diapered bottom with a rhythmic, unspoken "Shh. Back to sleep, little one."

The buzz returned, but not above them. Underneath Becky's right hip, her cell phone thrummed. She reached for it, motionless except for the espionage-worthy stealth of her retrieve arm and the unbroken choreography of her swing foot.

The phone buzzed again. She held it away from her, saw the familiar caller ID, and hit the "talk" button with her thumb. "What's up, Lauren?"

An opportunity, no doubt. Chance *du jour*.

A finals study group that included two brainiacs and a certified member of the National Honor Society had invited Lauren to a cram-fest.

"Please don't stay out late." Becky felt the vibrations of her words in her chest. The baby lifted his head and nestled, facing the other direction again.

Not late, Lauren answered. No. But Becky did realize the group would have to go get something to eat after studying, didn't she?

Becky disconnected the call. She may or may not have remembered to say good-bye.

The baby oozed awake and pushed against her chest until he'd raised himself enough to lock gazes with her. Those denim-blue eyes looked so like his father's, if her suspicions were correct about the child's paternity. She brushed strands of cornsilk hair off his cherub forehead.

"Your mommy called." Becky kissed one barely there eyebrow, then the other. "She says hi."

Dodging scattered mounds of clothes—distinguishable as clean or dirty only by odor—Becky crossed Lauren's room to the crib lodged between Lauren's dresser and her shoe jungle. Well-practiced, Becky eased the baby from her shoulder to the mattress. She pulled a blanket from the corner of the crib, but its sour smell told her it belonged in one of the piles on the floor, not wrapped around her grandson. Stifling a groan, she bent to the plastic storage tub tucked under the crib. One clean blanket, too thick for an Indian summer afternoon.

Laying babies on their backs? The "let's change everything we knew for sure" revised recommendation from the pediatric society or some other entity still disturbed her. Hard habit to break. Aren't they all?

Her dentist wouldn't appreciate her new habit of grinding her back teeth. She untensed her jaw, laid the blanket up to Jackson's waist, then exited the room with an armload of laundry she shouldn't have to wash.

Mid-hallway, she leaned against the wall. Baby socks and a pair of skinny jeans drizzled to the floor as she searched for a way to readjust her load. Not the laundry. The pieces that stuck to the rough edges of her fractured hopes.

Monica's well-intentioned voice thundered through the throbbing tunnels in her head. "Don't do everything for Lauren, Becky. You're enabling her. She'll never take responsibility if she doesn't have to."

Great advice, Monica. And who suffers if I don't bathe that child, if I don't put diapers on my grocery list, if I don't make sure he has something to wear that doesn't smell like curdled milk? Lauren won't even notice.

Drafting an apology for words her friend would never hear, Becky pushed off from the wall and aimed for the laundry room.

Jackson's cry stopped her before she recapped the detergent.

Mamas don't get to stay out past midnight.

How had pushing a baby through her woman parts given Lauren the right to abandon the house rules? And on a school night?

Becky steeled herself for a confrontation. She'd say, and then Lauren would say, and then she'd say . . .

No. That hadn't worked the last four times they'd had a similar conversation.

She drowned another tea bag—fragrant, impossibly smooth white peach—and forced her gaze away from the clock on the kitchen wall. But the digital displays on the stove and the microwave mocked her attempts to forget what time it was, where her daughter should be, the lure of her pillow, and the fact that Lauren's father was missing all the fun.

I hope you're enjoying California, Bub. She should probably use his real name. It wasn't Gil's fault his job demanded the kind of travel she'd find more fulfilling than he did. Wait. It was only a little after ten, Pacific time. She could call.

One ring. Two.

"Hey, honey. How's my angel?"

"She's not home yet."

"I meant you, Becky."

The sincerity in his voice was like ointment for a scraped knee. "I—"

"Are you okay, my pugalicious?"

"Gil. Not in the mood for nose-related terms of endearment, okay?"

"Sorry."

Of course he was. Good man. The kind she'd hoped Lauren would choose one day.

"Is Jackson sleeping?" he whispered, as if he could wake the baby from six states away, as the stork flies.

She swirled her tea bag through the steaming water. If it were her typical daytime choice—Black Pearl—it would by now be oversteeped, the deep molasses of Gil's eyes. "Jackson? Sleeping obliviously. Like I should be."

"I wish I were there."

"I know."

"What's Lauren's excuse this time?"

"Study group."

Gil's sigh traveled through the fiber-optic phone lines and tickled the hairs in Becky's ear. "Is she still talking college?"

A slosh of tea left a mini-puddle on the white countertop. She swiped at it with her palm, which turned the small puddle into a smear. "We want her to further her education, don't we? I mean, providing she gets through this last year of high school." She ripped a paper towel from its holder. "That's not a given."

"We knew this would be hard." Blistered. His voice sounded blistered, as though life's shoes had rubbed too long on a tender spot.

"He's our grandson."

"And she's our daughter."

"That's been confirmed, hasn't it?"

Gil chuckled. "You mean, how did two fully responsible, completely mature adults manage to raise a daughter who seems allergic to responsibility?"

"Something like that."

"She's not fully grown yet, Becky."

15

"Oh, that's comforting." The baby monitor let Becky know her not-fully-grown-yet daughter's infant son squirmed in his crib.

"Do you want me to call Lauren on her cell?"

"I tried that. It went to voice mail."

Gil huffed. "That'll be the last time."

"It's on my list." Becky turned away from the glare of the microwave's time keeper.

California said, "We're in this together, hon."

She should have replied instantly with something that meant, "We sure are." But six states of separation and full-time versus part-time parenting left an awkward gap she didn't have the energy or wisdom to fill.

"Becky?"

Somewhere beyond the walls, a car door slammed. "Never mind. She just got home."

—∞—

"Five, six, seven, *eight!*"

Monica's ever-present ebullience grated today like a hangnail on silk. So did the fact that nothing bulged over the lip of *her* yoga pants.

Becky retrieved Jackson's pacifier from the floor of Monica's lower-level exercise room, squirted it with water from her sports bottle, and stuck it back in his pouty mouth before returning to the video segment Monica seemed to enjoy far more than a normal person should.

"We didn't . . . use . . . pacifiers . . . with our . . . kids," Monica puffed out, proving she was working hard enough to make conversation difficult.

Mimicking a scaled-back version of Monica's arm and leg movements, Becky fought to catch the beat of the exercise video. "Yeah, well . . ."

"And none . . . of our . . . kids . . . needed braces . . . or had . . ."

"Cavities, either. Yes, I heard."

"I'm just . . . saying . . ."

Was she serious or teasing? "Two different schools of thought on it, Monica."

"And . . . slow it on down."

Oh. The exercising. No problem there.

"Beck, honestly, I don't know how you do it." Monica wiped a delicate dot of perspiration from her forehead with the back of her wrist. "You're an amazing woman."

"Even though I take full advantage of disposable diapers when cloth is more environmentally friendly and have been known to rock Jackson clear through his entire nap?"

Monica's arms flapped to her side. "You don't really— Oh. You were kidding."

Perfect mothers sometimes can throw a pall on the best-friend idea.

"No, I mean it," Monica said, lunging forward just for the fun of it. "I don't know that I could do what you're doing." She switched position and lunged again.

"Lauren needs to graduate." As if that explained it all.

With the video segment complete and Jackson temporarily content, the two women rehydrated and sat cross-legged on the floor near Jackson's bouncy chair. Becky knew her knees would give her grief for choosing that position, but she found herself drawn to eye-level with the cherub who didn't know any better than to love her.

"Doesn't it bother you that you had to quit work?"

"Bother me? Other than the loss of the paycheck and the fact that I loved what I did? No, not a bit."

Monica tilted her head as if to say, "Oh, you poor thing."

Thanks, Monica. That helps. Pity—every woman's deepest need.

Attitude adjusted with a Lamaze technique, Becky pressed out a smile. "We do what we have to do." With a Vanna White wave of her hand, she added, "This is all . . . temporary."

"He's gorgeous, Beck."

The two friends watched him breathe, watched his fists bat the air, his feet engage in a dance to silent music.

Becky caught a whiff of something other than a wet or dirty diaper. Sweat. Her own. Had she remembered deodorant this morning? She ran her tongue over her teeth. Had she brushed them? These were things new moms were supposed to fret about, not new grandmothers. No doubt Lauren had time to straighten or curl her hair, depending on her mood, and do a complete makeup routine before leaving for school. Becky reached into the outside pocket of Jackson's diaper bag, the area she claimed for herself, and grabbed a stick of gum. If Monica left the room for any reason, she'd dust a handful of Jackson's baby powder under her armpits.

She wouldn't, couldn't let herself think about what she would be doing at work today. The magazine layout she'd be supervising. The interviews other editors craved but couldn't secure. The adrenaline jolt from editing an article to its crispest, laser-sharp edge.

Becky rubbed her left elbow. Infant Seat Elbow, Gil called it. He joked about inventing collapsible legs with wheels for the infant carrier. Becky teased back that a little thing called a stroller had been invented long ago but the two items couldn't swap duties. Days ago, she'd dreamed he'd engineered the ideal answer. When she woke, the dream dissipated without leaving a blueprint. Dreams do that.

"Vitamin water?" Monica held one toward her.

Eww. She tipped her sports bottle in Monica's direction to signal she was good. The bottle's stainless steel sides kept its contents—unvitaminized, uninteresting, electrolyte-deficient tap water, with a hint of lemon juice—a secret. Becky didn't need another reminder about the proper way to do things. And hadn't she seen a segment on *Good Morning America* about vitamin water? Yay or nay? She couldn't remember the point. More than a few things lost their crisp edge with midnight feedings when Lauren had a test the next day. She rubbed her forehead. Brain fog could lift any time now without her objection.

"Beck, do you—" Monica hesitated, as if sifting her words through a tightly woven screen. "Do you regret not making Lauren go to youth group?"

Patience, get out of my way. I'm putting you in Time Out. "Monica, come on. You really think Gil and I could have prevented Lauren from getting pregnant if we had forced her to go to youth group?" *Blood pressure? Rapidly approaching nuclear meltdown.*

"Brianne can't stop talking about all she's learning under Pastor Jon's leadership. Did you know she's serving on the youth worship team now? We've always had an intentional family devotional time—we call it God Circle—at home, but the church is offering our young people tools to help them navigate the dangerous waters of—"

Is this the same church that didn't know how to react, where to look, what to say when Lauren came to the morning service in a skintight maternity top? The same church people who scheduled, then quietly canceled a baby shower?

Becky didn't know she had the oomph to go from cross-legged to fully upright at lightning speed. "Monica, we're done here."

The sitting one looked like she'd never been interrupted before. "This is only the first-round cooldown. We have four more tracks to go to complete the exercise series."

Becky took mental note of her internal temperature. She could boil pasta. *Cool down?* "I mean, we are done. You were the one person I thought I could count on for support."

Monica jumped to her feet. "You always have my support, Beck."

Her fingers fumbling with the safety belts, Becky unlatched Jackson from the bouncy chair, then propped him on her left hip, slung the diaper bag over her right shoulder, grabbed the front lip of the chair, which slammed against her shin, and headed for the door.

"Becky, don't go."

"We're done."

"I'll call you later."

Becky had no hands left to turn the doorknob. The burning sensation rose from her stomach to her throat to her jaw to her ears. Forehead to the door, her voice squeezed out, "A little . . . help . . . here?"

Jackson's pacifier hit the floor. The scream that came from his mouth was the one Becky thought she had dibs on for that moment.

Monica's hand on Becky's back felt like a branding iron. Apparently when an animal is branded, it reacts with tears.

"Please, hon, let's talk about this. That was insensitive of me. I'm sorry. Please stay."

Becky managed to grab the doorknob with the fingertips of her left hand. "Not now, Monica. I need a God moment. A God circle. God."

The contents of Jackson's diaper bag left a Hansel-and-Gretel trail from Monica's front door to Becky's Honda Civic. The contents of his diaper left a wet spot on her hip. She strapped him into the—to hear him tell the story—*straitjacket* car seat and dug a spare pacifier from the glove compartment to quiet the noise while she retrieved the crumbs of their morning's adventure.

Hot tears splatted the concrete paver sidewalk and driveway as she bent over the strewn baby paraphernalia. *Lauren. You should be doing this. You should be the one with urine on your hip. You should be holding that child to your breast, making room for car seats and high chairs, and losing sleep and shreds of sanity.*

She was probably in biology II right now. Biology class. *A little late for that.*

Becky slid into the driver's seat and glanced at the rearview mirror's reflection of the back window's baby mirror. Jackson's eyelids drifted shut over flushed cheeks.

Why am I doing this? Why am I doing any of this? Because I love that child.

She sighed as she turned the key in the ignition. *Jackson, too.*

2

Becky—2012

Love isn't Silly Putty. Thought for the day in the flip calendar that Becky's still-thinking-about-whether-I'm-calling-you-my-friend Monica had given her for her fortieth birthday.

Love isn't Silly Putty, it stated emphatically. *Even when it has to stretch far, it holds together.*

Really? Feels like ripping.

Stiffer house rules meant a sullen Lauren. Becky could take it. They'd been through that stage when Lauren moved from twelve to thirteen. And thirteen to fourteen. But babies have radar that responds to sullen with a dose of cranky. Jackson deserved all of Lauren's heart, all her love, not just when it was convenient or when she was in the mood to parent. Moms are always on call.

Few things about mothering are convenient, Becky thought as she filled out the parent section of Lauren's financial aid application for Westbrook's community college.

Her fingers hovered over the computer keyboard. The cursor waited for her to enter a response to "Gross Income." Grossly inadequate since she'd had to quit work to care for Jackson while Lauren finished high school.

Not just when it was convenient or when she was in the mood to parent. Always on call.

"Lauren?"

"What?" The girl didn't look away from the television. She sat on the floor, bent over with her elbows on her knees and her chin in her hands. So like she did at ten. Her son lay on the floor next to her, chewing his fists.

"Come here a minute. Please."

"I just changed him."

In the mood to parent. Becky moved to the couch. "I know you did." She patted the cushion beside her. "I want to talk to you."

"So, talk." Still no movement.

In the mood . . .

Lauren turned while seated, break-dance style, and faced Becky. "Sorry, Mom." She joined her mom on the couch. Her eyes glistened. "Even I don't like me lately."

Becky reached to draw her into her embrace. Lauren still fit. A too-young mom, but she still fit in the valley of Becky's heart. Her hair, as silken as Jackson's, smelled of mangoes. Sweet as a kiss of summer. *Oh, my baby!*

"Everything okay at school?"

"What do you mean?" Lauren pulled out of the tight embrace. "I'm doing as good as I can."

Becky considered correcting her grammar, but restrained herself. "Are you getting along with your teachers?"

Lauren shrugged.

"With the other kids?"

Lauren pointed at Jackson. "*That's* a kid. Nobody knows what to call someone like me." She twirled a hank of hair that had flopped out of her pseudo-ponytail.

"The other students, then."

"You mean, the other teen moms? Or did you mean normal students?"

"Lauren . . ." Should she whip out the consequences lecture? The "well, you should have thought about that before" PowerPoint presentation? The remedial health class DVD? Becky forced an empathetic smile. "Even I don't like me lately."

"Cute, Mom."

They sat side by side on the sofa, watching the only happy person in the room wiggle his baby toes.

"Mom, I don't know what I'm doing." The confession was accompanied by a sob that Becky felt down to her toenails.

"Neither do I, honey."

"I don't know how to be a mom."

"I don't know how to mother a teen mom."

Lauren laughed at that, the kind of laugh that acknowledges the sometimes comic alter ego of pain. "You weren't supposed to have to."

"What do you see for his future, Lauren? For your futures?"

"I'm not planning a future. I can't think past today."

"Why not?"

"I don't know the difference between a breast pump and a sump pump! What if I can't even keep him alive?"

I've wondered the same thing.

They held each other until Lauren pushed away and said, "Mom, you're burning up. Do you have a fever?"

So that's what a hot flash feels like.

Jackson rolled over for the first time that night. Lauren didn't *play* the proud parent. She *was* a proud parent. The video of the event hit all her social networks.

She flunked her French quiz the next day.

Monica's voice mail messages to Becky remained unanswered for three days. It felt like the emotional vacuum between Good Friday and Easter Sunday. Sunday. How was Becky going to avoid Monica at church? Avoidance hardly seemed a Sunday thing to do.

Gil's plane landed at 9:03 Saturday night. Becky pulled the Civic to the curb outside Baggage Claim the moment he walked out of the terminal. Jackson slept slumped in his car seat, unmoved even when Gil slammed the trunk shut. Gil whispered an apology when he slid into the passenger side. "Didn't know Jackson was coming along." He leaned tentatively toward Becky, as if testing the "It's appropriate to kiss in front of a sleeping baby, right?" waters.

She grabbed him by the shoulders and leaned in to his lips. The cars in line behind her wouldn't wait for much more than one kiss, so she put the Civic in gear, pulled into traffic, and repeated, "I'm so glad you're home," as if they were the only words she knew.

"How's he been?" Gil nodded over his shoulder at the still-sleeping child. "Where's his mom? And I use that word loosely."

Becky's heart clenched. "Homecoming."

Gil nudged her leg. "Oh, you guys. I've only been gone three weeks."

"Not *your* homecoming, Captain Important. The football game homecoming night."

"Oh."

"I know. I could have said she couldn't go."

"If she were an adult single parent, we'd have no say on choices like that."

"If she were an adult, she wouldn't be playing in the band for homecoming. What do you call this netherland?"

Almost a mile ticked by. "My fault. I call it my fault."

Becky took her eyes from the road long enough to glance at his shadowed face. "*Your* fault? What are you talking about?"

"I read a lot on the plane. And on the layover. One article, *New York Times* if I remember right, gave stats on the number of women who are reproducing without the 'nuisance of a spouse.'"

"You're not a nuisance, Gil." *You're not home enough to be a nuisance.*

He shrugged out of his suit coat and tossed it into the backseat, barely missing his grandson, and then rebuckled his seat belt. "And I read an editorial about teen mom reality shows."

"Did either of us encourage her to watch those? No."

"And I got partway through an essay about the importance of a dad's relationship with his daughter. It's my fault."

"You've always had a great relationship with Lauren."

"It didn't stop her from . . . from this." He gestured again to the backseat. "It didn't stop Mark from going to Iraq."

No. We're not talking about Mark today. Not today. Becky flicked the turn signal and changed lanes. She pointed over the seat with her thumb. "*That* is our amazing grandson. Ten years from now, we won't remember this part."

"Yes, we will."

"You're right. We will."

Silence drove them the rest of the way home.

"I wonder how much money the church spends on cleaning up the debris from other people's mistakes." Gil's low voice rumbled, even in whisper mode. He pointed to the overhead digital screen's preservice messages with announcements about a variety of addiction recovery programs, divorce care, get-out-of-debt classes, and Teen Mothers of Preschoolers.

Becky leaned toward his ear. "I signed her up for that."

"Your tithes at work," he whispered back.

"Lauren won't go. Too stressful to fit that into her home-work schedule. And her social life."

"Which is why teens shouldn't get preg— Hi, Lauren. Is he all settled in the nursery?"

Lauren slumped into the padded chair beside Becky. Talking without unclenching her teeth, she said, "Why does everyone else think they know what's best for my kid?" She crossed her feet at the ankles, legs extended far under the row in front of her, flip-flops flapping, and folded her arms over her chest. "That Cramer lady said, 'Just go. He'll be fine.' She insisted."

"Sophie. Sophie Cramer. Nice lady."

"Whatever. 'Just go,' she said. 'He'll stop crying as soon as you're out of sight.' Like *that's* supposed to make me feel better."

Becky reached an arm around Lauren's shoulders. She would have said something comforting except she'd been told the same thing and felt the same way the first time she took Lauren to the nursery seventeen years earlier.

Becky glanced around the sanctuary. How many other people in the room had to work up the courage to walk through those doors today? Different problems. Different consequences. Different reasons for sleepless nights.

Oh, joy. Brianne was on the worship team this morning. Brianne with the flat stomach and no stretch marks. Brianne with the angelic face and no residual diaper odor clinging to her skinny little sweater. *Forgive me, Father, for I have sinned and hath coveted my best friend's daughter's regret-free life.*

"What's she doing up there?" Lauren's tone dripped with the jealousy Becky felt. Like mother, like daughter.

"Monica said she sings on the youth worship team now," *which you would know if you went to youth group.* "I imagine they needed another backup singer and she was the logical choice. Lauren, we're standing. At least lip-synch the words to the songs, okay?"

Becky turned her attention to the lyrics on the screen. The letters blurred. Church used to be a sanctuary. Now it felt like an exhibit hall with their family on display in the "What Not to Do" section. The section with the broken people.

And she couldn't even whine about it to Monica.

Lauren's exterior posture more closely matched Becky's internal posture than Becky wanted to admit. Great day for a sermon about the Bible's Rachel, who "refused to be comforted" over the loss of her child. Even Lauren seemed to soften a little, brushing at a tear when the final song started with something about mercy finding people at the side of a broken road and lifting them out of the debris of their failings.

Who said an out-of-wedlock pregnancy was no big deal anymore? Twenty-first century and all that? Cultural acceptance. Reality shows spotlighting teen moms notwithstanding. Regret still destroys futures, changes relationships, rewrites dreams.

While Brianne bounced off the platform at the end of the service and into a gaggle of girlfriends, Lauren headed to the nursery to retrieve her son. Gil chatted with two men from his Tuesday night accountability group. Becky bypassed the conversations and sought out the privacy of a bathroom stall. Just like junior high.

She recognized the shoes of the woman in the next stall to the left. Monica's *what-were-you-thinking?* eggplant patent leather ballerina flats.

Becky noiselessly slid her own Walmart feet to the right. How long would she have to stay in the stall to avoid facing the woman with the perfect family life?

Oh, that was ridiculous! Had she learned nothing since junior high?

God grant me the something-something to accept the something else that I cannot change.

Serenity. Yeah, that was it.

Pull up your big girl panties, literally, and leave your hiding place, Becky.

Side-by-side sinks. A shared soap dispenser. Lavender— supposedly stress-reducing aroma. Automatic paper towel dispenser. *No, you go first.*

"Good to see you here, Becky."

"You, too."

"I don't mean, in the bathroom."

"Yeah, me neither."

"Let me get the door for you."

Noble, considering how you dissed my daughter, my parenting, my . . . "Thanks."

Monica searched the crowd in the narthex.

Wow, not even a lame comment about the weather.

Another few seconds ticked by before Monica asked, "Do you want to grab some lunch and talk?"

"Yes." Becky drew a steadying breath. "Someday. Not today, if that's okay with you."

Monica opened her mouth as if prepared to proffer the perfect response. Nothing.

Where was Lauren? Daughter of mine, this isn't your fault, exactly, but it's part of the fallout. "I'll see you next week, Monica." Becky tucked her Bible under her arm and caught Gil's eye with a "meet you in the car" hand signal. No doubt Lauren and the baby were already there, trying to make each other smile.

"Can I call you tomorrow, Becky?"

"I won't be home."

———✦———

Who was she kidding? Of course she'd be home. Where was she going to go? The spa? Work? The Ellison Corp. didn't have a gram-ternity leave plan. She'd had to quit to take care of Jackson when the school year started. If Lauren graduated on schedule, maybe she could work part-time next summer. If the new editor who'd taken her place didn't pan out.

"Burgers or pizza?" Gil alternated glances at Lauren in the backseat and Becky in the front.

"Let's just go home, Dad."

Becky nodded.

"I'm offering to take my two best girls out for lunch. What am I hearing? Okay, okay. Seafood. As long as it's deep-fried."

Jackson voiced his protest over that idea. With a vengeance.

"Home it is."

More howls from the backseat. Becky offered, "Lauren, try—"

"I've got it, Mom!"

And she did. Quiet returned except for the faint sound of a Kutless song bleeding from the earbuds of Lauren's iPod, one bud of which rested on the upholstered car seat near Jackson's ear.

Becky calculated decibel levels versus fragile eardrums, but landed on gratitude that Lauren had discovered a way to comfort her son. All by herself.

3

Becky—2012

I leave again on Tuesday." Gil's words slid into the conversation like too many raw onions on a fast-food burger slicked with special sauce.

"Where to this time?"

He drew his rake through another chaotic convention of sun-crisped oak leaves, stirring that unmistakable "autumn's here" aroma. The leaves rattled as they bumped against one another in an effort to escape Gil's tines. "Cincinnati."

Becky pulled a desiccated tomato vine, knocked the dirt from its roots, and threw it into the four-by-four garden trailer hooked to the riding mower. Gil didn't like traveling this much any more than she did. But with jobs this scarce, refusing to get on a plane was a death knell to collecting a paycheck.

She'd waited too long to respond. He'd know she wasn't happy about the trip. "It's . . . it's not so far. How long will you be gone?" At one time she'd been more skilled at imitating lighthearted. She brushed garden debris from her fleece work pants as she waited for his answer.

One second. Two seconds. Three seconds.

That long? You'll be gone that long?

"Becky, why don't you come with me?"

Her turn not to answer.

"I know," he said. "Jackson and Lauren are why. But maybe you could get Monica to help out for a few days? Please?"

"She works."

"Volunteering. Maybe she'd see it as an opportunity to serve. Ministry."

The hope in Gil's voice clashed with what Becky knew about Monica's interest in "ministering" to the aftermath of an unplanned, untimely, unblessed pregnancy.

Unblessed?

The arrival of the child changed everything. A blessed, wanted, adored, cherished child. Pulsing evidence of God's grace. A redemption object lesson.

A game-changer in so many ways.

The rhythm of Gil's rake stilled. A gust of a fall wind's rebellion tugged at the neat piles he'd created. He leaned his chin on the pad made by his crossed hands on the handle end of the rake. "Maybe when the little guy's a few months older."

She looked up into eyes that didn't resemble Jackson's. Middle Eastern dark, like she expected of someone born in, say, Bethlehem. How long had it been since she'd taken time to study the nuances in those irises? How long since she'd not left his side in the middle of the night to check on their grandson? How long since she felt comfortable surrendering to the fire of his touch?

She could have put a capital *H* on "his" and asked those same questions.

"Becky?"

"Yes?"

"Are you lost somewhere?"

"Lost in gratitude for you."

Gil's eyebrows arched. "Sounds like an invitation to me."

Becky's hand reached for the baby monitor tucked in the pocket of her windbreaker. "It's about time for Jackson's nap to end."

"Oh. Right."

Longing left its dusty residue on their words. Longing for each other. For life to be different, less complicated.

The monitor breathed deep, grunted, then started to make "I'm no longer happy here" noises, proving her timing accurate and Jackson's unfortunate.

She peeled off her garden gloves without losing eye contact with Gil. "I'll . . . I'll change him, feed him, and bring him out here. The sun's nice and warm. If I bundle him up, we can keep going."

And they would. Keep going. Like it or not.

"Want me to get him?"

"It's not your responsibility."

"Yours, either."

It was easy for Becky to assume Jackson's care as if he *was* her responsibility. Maternal instinct and guilt shared many of the same traits. Add to the mix her unquenchable love for him, and the concoction smoked and boiled like a showy science experiment. Baking soda—maternal instinct. Vinegar—guilt. Love—catalyst for anything good that came from it.

Catalyst. Cattle list: Angus, Hereford, Holstein. One of the lame jokes Gil shared on their first date. It reappeared every anniversary, like wooly caterpillars before the first snow.

She reached into her pocket to turn off the monitor. "I'll get him."

"Want me to pull these dead things over here while you're gone?"

Becky aligned her gaze with his. "No!"

"Just trying to help."

"Sorry to snap. It's my morning glory vines."

33

"Yeah? You're not expecting them to bloom anytime soon, are you? I believe their season is long past." He crumbled a crunchy vine into powder between his fingers.

"Don't . . . don't touch them, okay? I'll take care of them later. I'm saving the seeds."

Gil straightened, his chin tucked against his windpipe. "Yes, ma'am." He saluted.

"I'm not trying to be stinky about it."

"Sometimes you don't have to try." He winked.

She'd let that go. He did lighthearted better than she did. His smile seemed genuine. Plus, she hoped to catch Jackson before his babble turned to tears.

Or hers did.

Tiny black-brown seeds housed in a papery brown pod. Why did saving them mean so much to her? Most years, the plants would come back on their own. Or she could purchase a packet of morning glory seeds next spring from any number of suppliers—Walmart, the grocery store, the Westbrook Greenhouse. Even the gas station had a seed carousel, if she remembered right. She was no master gardener—that was Monica's department—but preserving those morning glory seeds each fall stirred something in her.

If she thought too hard, her dedication to the task might take on an obsessive taint. So she wouldn't think. She'd collect the dry pods, the remnants birthed from what was once a Microsoft-blue flower, rub the papery covering in her hands until the seeds separated from the chaff, and save them in the baby food jar reserved for that purpose.

The jar she'd used since her Mark first tasted pureed pears. Her heart lost another beat. How many could she afford to lose?

The jar she'd used since the first morning glory bloomed in the side yard. Since the sight of that startling, delicate, unfurled sapphire blossom with its glistening white center lifted her postpartum depression by an inch, then another inch the next day when another bloom appeared.

She fixed Jackson's bottle and toyed with another thought. How does a person recognize postpartum depression in a surly teen?

Becky pushed open the door to Lauren's bedroom. "Sweet boy, did you have a good nap?"

His hair, sleep-damp, stuck-in-the-50s pin-curl shapes around his baby doll face. The first Trundle with naturally curly hair.

Jackson Trundle. He should have had a different last name.

———

The paternity discussion long stale, "a'moldering in the grave" as some long-ago poet would have expressed it, Becky still cringed whenever Lauren's study group included Noah. Noah, the Eddie Haskell smooth-talker—*Good evening, Mrs. Trundle*—with denim-blue eyes. It brought no joy to her heart that Lauren insisted she couldn't be sure who the father was. Every mother's dream. And that she didn't want any help from the birth father anyway. Would Lauren feel differently about that if Gil and Becky weren't footing the bill for formula and diapers? And groceries? And a roof over their heads? And health insurance?

They should have forced the issue. Lauren wrote a name on the birth certificate in the line for "child's father." It was all

Becky could do not to search Lauren's room for a copy of that piece of paper. Did the backseat male have to file a claim in order to force a paternity test? That issue joined a laundry list of others about which Becky had no answers and sometimes avoided searching.

Lord, I used to be the one sad to have lost a son in Iraq but happy to have a daughter who loved me and filled my life with joy.

Splayed on the changing table, Jackson pinched his eyes shut and giggled from his belly, an outrageously soul-satisfying sound. Becky tickled his knee again as she held the front of the disposable diaper in position. The new diaper warmed beneath her hand. Wet already, and she hadn't even gotten the tabs closed yet. She replaced it with a fresh one, tugged a pair of sweat pants over his tickle-friendly legs, and pulled the clean-enough-for-now knit shirt into position.

He reached for her—*reached* for her—and a remnant of joy stole back into her heart, like refugees crossing the border into safe territory. He'd done that to her since the moment he took his first breath in a birthing center that was shy one man.

The missing man could be the one in the family room right now, part of the acne-ridden think tank conjugating French verbs between bites of Becky's caramel corn.

Caramel corn! She was an enabler! She might be, at that moment, giving sustenance to a hormonally charged teen who refused to man up and confess he had fathered the child now nestled into her neck with his fingers entwined in her hair, his love laced through the muscles of her heart.

She didn't like the suspicious side of herself. If Noah were innocent, she was worse than those whose eyes widened a few months ago when Lauren's belly entered the room before the rest of her. "It's not a giant wart. It's a baby!" she'd wanted to say to them. And what did that say about her? She owed an apology to all the people in the world with giant warts.

"Mom?"

Becky turned. Lauren stood in the doorway, Noah behind her.

"We're taking a break. Can we have Jackson?"

I don't know. Can you? Did you? Did the two of you—?

"I want to show Noah how he rolls over." She shifted from one foot to the other as she held out her arms.

"Carrie and Dane, too?"

Lauren shot her a searing look and leveled, "They had to go home." She took Jackson from Becky with an exaggerated tug.

Love isn't Silly Putty.

If I were the perfect mom, I'd say . . .

No idea. None.

"I'm going to run a load of darks. Mind if I grab yours while I'm here, Lauren?"

The lines of Lauren's jaw turned from freezer meat to refrigerated. Partially thawed. "That would be great. Thanks."

Maybe Noah was just a good friend. Bless him for sticking by Lauren in spite of everything. How many high school guys would do that? Maybe Jackson's eyes were more indigo than denim. Maybe he and Noah didn't share the same chin dimple.

Becky kicked at the piles of Lauren's clothes, half-expecting something to slither out of the shadows. With two fingers she picked up a nearly stiff charcoal sweater and pulled two pairs of jeans sticking Wicked-Witch-of-the-West style from under the unmade bed. Nothing slithered, but something rattled. The piece of plastic must have been snagged by a belt loop.

She bent with jerky, robotic motions. No.

No.

No. Please, God.

Becky stumbled to Lauren's overflowing wastebasket, dumped its contents on the floor, held it under her dimpleless chin, and threw up.

⟨⟨⟨ ⟩⟩⟩

"Mom! You were just holding Jackson. If you knew you were getting the flu, why didn't you say something? Now he's all exposed." Lauren held the baby on her far hip, as if shielding him with her body. "And gross. You owe me a new wastebasket."

"I don't have the flu." She sat on the edge of Lauren's bed—the basket on the floor at her feet—waiting to gain the strength to clean it up.

"My room stinks. No offense, Mom, but I'm not sleeping here tonight."

"It's not . . . the flu. Get your dad."

Lauren backed another step into the hall. "He's taking Noah home. Noah's sensitive to the sound of puking."

"Didn't Noah drive?"

"His anal parents took his keys. Total misunderstanding."

Headache. Throbbing headache. "When your dad . . . gets . . . home . . ."

"Mom, are you okay? Are you having a stroke or something?" One more step back into the hall. "Should I call 911?"

One of us may need 911 before this night's over. "Take Jackson to the family room. You can get the portable crib out of my closet, if you want. I'll be out in a few minutes. By then, your dad should be back."

She chuffed. "I—"

"Lauren, if you ever wanted to not cross me, it's now."

⟨⟨⟨ ⟩⟩⟩

Two teeth-brushings and a mouthwash later, Becky held a cold washcloth to her eyes. She heard the garage door opener grind open, then close. She timed her entrance into the family room to coincide with Gil's. She wouldn't face Lauren alone. Not this time.

Obviously prewarned—thank the Lord for cell phones, sometimes—Gil kept a respectful distance.

"Feeling better, honey? Can I get you anything?" He lowered himself into his recliner before she had a chance to answer.

Sweet man. "I'm okay. My stomach's okay. Relatively."

Gil reached to turn on the end-table lamp.

"Dad!"

"What?"

"Jackson?" Lauren pointed to the portable crib, as if it needed an introduction—an explosion of rainbow colors in a room of deep caramel and light cream.

Gil held his hands up, surrendering. "Ah. Indoor voices and low lights. Still getting used to having a baby in the house."

Becky's stomach spasmed.

"Mom, you're looking weird again. Why don't you just go to bed? Whatever it is can wait until—"

"Lauren, *it* can't wait." She dropped the piece of plastic onto the coffee table. "Care to explain this?"

Gil leaned forward, forearms on his knees. Becky caught the movement in her peripheral vision, but her eyes stayed focused on Lauren's face.

Gil reached to touch it, then withdrew his hand. "Is that—?"

"Yes, dear. A home pregnancy test."

"Becky, are you—?"

She dropped her lock-gaze with Lauren. "Oh, Gil. Come on."

"The vomiting. The irritability."

You want irritability? "This is not mine." She turned back to Lauren. "Want to explain to your father what this was doing in your bedroom?"

Lauren studied the threads in the side seam of her jeans. "Not really."

"That's . . . that's the old one, right? The one announcing Jackson?" Gil dipped his head as if trying to make his daughter look him in the eye. "The old one. Why you saved it is kind of bizarre."

Becky ran her tongue over her freshly cleaned teeth as she worked to temper her response. "Not the old one, honey. That was a different brand of test."

"How do you remember these details? I'm in awe."

"Gil!" Becky picked up the handle end of the plastic rod. She tapped it on the coffee table surface as if beating out a parent's Morse code of desperation. "Lauren, what does this mean?"

"Why are you looking at me?" Lauren drew her floppy sweater across her front, lapping it like two-layered armor.

"Well, let's see. Your room. Your bed. Your history."

"Hey! This is so not fair."

"Lauren, are you pregnant again?" Gil's voice was uncharacteristically throaty.

"No, Dad!"

Becky stopped tapping. "That's not what *this* says."

Lauren bent at the waist and rocked back and forth.

"Lauren?"

Gil slid out of his chair and knelt in front of Lauren. He lifted her chin and said, "Lauren, we love you. No matter what."

Becky wished she'd thought to do that.

"I am not pregnant!"

Jackson wailed, as if disappointed to hear he didn't qualify for a "Big Brothers Rawk" T-shirt.

"You made me scare him! Will you get off my back?" She stood, picked up her sobbing son, and clutched him to her chest, rocking all the harder now.

"Is it Noah? It's time we knew, Lauren."

Gil's laser-beam look told Becky this might not be the time to reopen that case.

She glared back. "What? We need to know." She turned her focus back to their daughter.

Lauren's eyes narrowed. "I can't believe you guys would think that of me."

"Kind of an odd statement coming from a seventeen-year-old whose curfew is earlier than her baby's bedtime."

"Mom!"

"Becky, cool it down." Gil made a hand motion that looked like a basketball coach trying to slow the pace of the full court press.

I can't raise my child to make good choices. I can't teach her how to be a good mom. And I can't even confront her correctly when she makes another dumb mistake. "Lauren, we do love you, honey. More than you'll probably ever know. It's because we care so much about you that we—" Her throat tightened. *Breathe in. Breathe out.* "Because we care, we're concerned about you ruining your future, to say nothing about what it will mean for these babies."

"Baby, Mom. One baby."

One inconsolable baby to match the other inconsolable people in the room.

Lauren tilted her head, chin lifted and jaw set in a line so tight her lips turned white. "That's not mine." She nodded toward the object of derision on the coffee table.

"Then whose is it, Lauren?"

"Brianne's, okay?" The tears coursing down her face matched her son's. "But it's not a problem anymore. She took care of it."

A groan started at the edge of the universe, dodged all the black holes in outer space, and rocketed to earth, to the Midwest, to one grotesquely silent family room.

Jackson laid one hand against Lauren's damp cheek. Becky knew it weighed little more than a birthmark.

4

Ivy—1951

How could Ivy take him seriously with that dot of toilet paper stuck to his chin knob? It bobbed as he chewed his corn flakes and stared at the nothingness with which he was obsessed. She would have made him a more substantial breakfast if he'd waited until she'd finished getting ready for work. Or if she'd set her alarm to go off a half hour earlier than dawn. He'd succeeded in swelling her guilt without a word.

"Dad?"

He picked up the newspaper. The word "Korea" always caught her eye. *Promising young Democrat John F. Kennedy from Massachusetts offers views on Korean War armistice talks in Kaesong.* Her father waded deeper into the paper. Editorials? Obituaries? Why did she even bother waiting for the courtesy of a "What, honey?"

"Dad, we're out of potatoes. It's Wednesday."

Meatloaf and mashed potatoes. Canned peas. Fruit cocktail. Like always.

He put down his cereal spoon and ran the palms of his hands forward and back on the overripe-lemon-yellow Formica tabletop. His wedding ring clinked on the metal edge at the near point of each trip.

She couldn't think about the meatloaf—squishing her fingers through the greasy meat and raw egg, globules of chopped cow and bread crumbs stuck under her fingernails.

Potatoes. "The ad says they're eighty-eight cents for five pounds this week. I could pick some up at the Piggly Wiggly after work."

He nodded. Once. That was something.

"But . . ."

Ornell Carrington braced his hands on the aluminum table edging and pushed off, his chair legs scraping like dulled claws on concrete. He shrugged into the faded blue work shirt he'd hung over the back of the chair and she shrugged out of her apron and into a holding pattern. Six buttons later, he dug into the breast pocket—the one embroidered with his name and Goodman's Hardware, not in that order—and pulled out an overworked dollar bill.

He held it out to her, gripped between his index and middle fingers like other fathers might hold a cigarette. "Wish I could give you more, Ivy."

Me, too, Dad. No matter what the subject, me, too. She swallowed against the recurring thought of raw meatloaf.

What's the word halfway between *thanks* and *okay*? Ivy needed it but couldn't retrieve the elusive word from where it hid. She took the bill from his fingers and held it in her left hand while she cleared the table with her right, depositing the bowl, spoon, and gas station juice glass into the once-white, chipped enamel sink.

"Ivy?"

She turned at the sound of defeat in his voice.

He latched the buckles on his coal-black lunch box, tucked it under his arm, and held those same two fingers in the air. "Two months."

Raw eggs. Crawling up her esophagus.

"Two more months. Then you're on your own."

He took a step toward the door, paused, then resumed walking away from where she stood.

A dot of toilet paper stained with a drop of dried blood floated to the speckled green linoleum in his wake.

She felt his every footfall as he descended the concrete stairs from the apartment units on their floor to the street level. For such a slight man, he walked heavy.

Ivy pulled the apartment door shut behind her and tested the lock. The cloying smell of dry-cleaning fluids and steamed wool filled the stairwell and short hall, closing its fingers around her throat. Living above a dry cleaner had its advantages in the winter with rising heat that kept their floors warm and their radiators relaxed. Now, with Minnesota summer humidity thick enough to make a decent soup, the location lacked benefits.

From the top of the stairs she could see daylight beckoning through the open doorway. He had left the door open. He'd known she'd soon follow.

He'd turned left, toward the center of town. At the bottom of the stairs, she would turn right for the six-block walk to the old folks' home.

Her feet were damp already in her rubber-soled shoes. But they thumped softly in her rapid descent, cushioning the spots where her father had clumped.

She turned sideways to allow Helene from apartment C to skirt past her heading up. Helene's youngest straddled his mom's hip. Mothers must develop a permanent hitch in their spines, carrying toddlers.

Ivy pressed against the wall, stiffening at the ammonia smell. How long had that child been in that diaper and those rubber pants?

Children should be seen and not smelled.

Ivy lurched out the doorway and onto the sidewalk. Half a block and half a thought later, she leaned over the low bushes at the edge of the empty lot and threw up.

Ivy cupped her hand over her mouth, blew a puff of air, then took a breath. More spearmint than the other. The chewing gum was working. Her stomach settled from tidal wave to rough seas, but the heat didn't help. She passed the red soft-drink cooler outside Farraday's Rexall Drugs and considered spending a nickel for the benefit of something cold to press against her forehead, the back of her neck, to tuck in her brassiere, crowded as it now was in there.

The walk to work seemed longer every day. She looked down. Her feet conquered one square of cement sidewalk after another, crossed at one corner after another. The cement was not wet and heavy, as it felt.

The downtown became neighborhoods, the kind that wagged their fannies as Ivy passed, reminding her she'd never have a yard like that, a regular house, a whitewalled DeSoto in the carport, kids riding bicycles with playing cards clothes-pinned to the spokes of the wheels and rainbow streamers flying from the handlebars, kids with skates strapped onto their Keds.

People like her lived in sweaty apartments with hollow, crusty stairwells and rutted linoleum. People like her got evicted at twenty-one by their own fathers.

People like me should stop coveting porches and be grateful for a saggy iron bed and a closet door, even if it doesn't shut all the way. Where would she be in two months?

A breeze teased the once-tight, now-limp curl of her bangs, but abruptly died out. Hope did that, too. Showed a little promise, then evaporated before she could enjoy it.

Drew came into her life. Korea took him away.

On a quiet street just a block from work, for no known reason, she smelled bus fumes like those from the wheeled monster that took him from her on the first of April. April Fools' Day. Miserable irony. She'd clung to his drab-green wool lapels, buried her face in his army-issued shoulder, marked the spot with her tears. He'd dampened her hair with his own. Then he'd pulled away, threw his shoulders back like a good soldier, and—as if she could live without him—climbed the stairs into the belly of the monster.

She'd pressed her white gloved hands over her mouth to keep her heart from clawing its way out as the bus belched and growled and overcame longing's inertia. Drew kept his gaze riveted to the arched ceiling of the vehicle, or somewhere beyond its roof, so Ivy's last view of him was his profile only, as if she'd already lost eye contact forever.

Three months ago.

She could still smell the bus fumes.

The idling bus had coughed noxious fumes in their faces as Ivy Carrington and Drew Lambert clung to each other and to their last few moments together.

"I'll write you every day, Ivy."

"No, you won't."

"I will. I swear it."

Ivy loosened her grip on Drew's uniform lapels, fearful of wrinkling the coarse wool, but more afraid of losing her grip on him.

"Don't swear it, Drew. You can't write every day. The war?" Ivy's sarcasm twisted the tourniquet of an already tense scene.

"Conflict. The government frowns on our calling it a war." His eyes teased.

If he wanted to lighten the mood, it wasn't working.

Ivy's reply gathered speed and volume as it readied itself in her throat. "Tanks and helicopters and guns and minefields and H-bombs—"

He tucked her hands tighter in his. "There won't be another H-bomb, Ivy."

"And men dying on both sides. What would you call it?" She regretted the harsh edge to her voice. This isn't how she wanted him to remember her.

"I'd call it . . ." His coy smile faded as he trolled for an answer. "I'd call it the only thing that could come between us."

She fought to pinch back tears, her efforts as futile as a facial tissue against an open hydrant. *No, Drew. The war isn't the only thing that could drive a wedge between us.* She carried the other possibility deep within her.

Within weeks of Drew's unit's departure for the alternating dust and damp of the hills of South Korea, Ivy Carrington's "possibility" became a certainty. She mourned not having told Drew her suspicions. Now it was too late. How could she put news like that into a letter?

Ivy couldn't risk it. She might as well paint a bull's-eye on his uniform, as vulnerable as he'd be if distracted by her bomb of information and its consequences. Staying alive. That was his focus. She'd have to keep quiet and deal with it alone.

And that meant leaving town and moving in with her father. She couldn't risk running into one of Drew's friends from the paper mill or his gossip-glutton mother or sisters. The only thing worse than Drew's finding out would be his hearing it from someone other than Ivy.

The deception repulsed her. Like castor oil—a necessary evil.

So many eventualities might eliminate her need to tell him . . . ever. She hadn't ruled out the idea of "disposal." Illegal, but not out of the question. She could find a way. Not an option that gave her any peace. But then, maybe peace was too much to hope for.

If the baby died on its own, if she miscarried . . .

What kind of person saw that as an *answer*? A dead baby? Why couldn't she think straight? Nothing made sense anymore. It was the baby's fault. No. It was her own fault for letting the passion of a moment override her common sense.

Ivy knew Drew would blame himself. All the more reason not to tell him. He'd already apologized a dozen times for that night. It wasn't fair for him to bear the weight of responsibility. She was a willing partner. A few minutes of what she thought was happiness. And it would cost her a lifetime of regret.

Half a continent, an ocean, and thousands of rice paddies separated them now. But the secret created the greater distance.

⸺◦∞◦⸺

She stared at what she'd written, cringing at the omissions and half-truths that stared back at her. Inventive by necessity, Ivy's airmail letters to Drew lacked the risk of vulnerability.

Dearest Drew,

I moved! I've been so lonely since you left that I thought a change of pace might do me good. So I'm on an adventure. I found a

49

job as a nursing assistant at a really nice old folks' home in Clairmont. My supervisor has rental properties all over town and gave me a good price on a small apartment above the dry cleaner (note my new return address). It's warm most of the time, from the steam and the mangle (that's the machine for pressing the clothes, in case you didn't know). I'll appreciate the steam more midwinter. It'll cut down on my heating bill.

You'll like Clairmont. There's a great diner just a couple of blocks from my apartment. I eat supper there on days I work late. Only ninety-five cents for the special. Depends on the day. Monday's usually spaghetti. Tuesday's pork chops. Wednesday's meatloaf. Thursday can be chicken chow mein (looks disgusting but tastes pretty good) or sometimes Swedish meatballs, depending on the cook's mood. Friday is always fish . . . for the Catholics, but I like it, too. I suppose I shouldn't have mentioned the food, being as you're probably choking down cold beans and canned meat every meal.

I don't have a problem walking to work. It's only six blocks. I sold my car—poor, sad thing—to pay for the first month's rent, since I won't get a paycheck until I've been at the home for two weeks. I don't miss the car much, except on rainy days. I might change my mind come winter. Maybe I'll take the bus then. Seems silly, since it's such a short distance. We'll see.

She'd filled two pages of onion-skin stationery and successfully avoided the one subject that occupied almost every waking moment. No mention of the fact that the smell of dry cleaning chemicals made her nauseous or that she'd moved in with her dad. Or that writing the word *meatloaf* gagged her. Or that the six blocks to work sometimes caused her ankles to swell, even this early in her pregnancy.

> Have you decided yet what you want to do
> when you're discharged, Drew?

What were the odds his response would be, "Start a family"?

> I hope you'll be able to finish college, like
> you planned. Clairmont isn't far from the
> Minnesota State Teachers College. You could
> commute. I bet my supervisor would have
> something for you to rent. She owns a couple
> of apartment buildings—one here and one
> in Westbrook. Do you want me to ask her
> about it? No commitment or anything. Just for
> information?
> It's probably hard for you to think about the
> future while you're over there. I think about it
> a lot. I miss you. I pray for you every day.

She had no confidence that God was interested in her prayers but trusted He cared about a young soldier willing to lay his life on the line for his country.

> I have to get to work. I'll tell you more about
> that in the next letter. I like the old folks' home
> better than waitressing, even though my wait-
> ressing is what brought us together. Remember
> how clumsy I was when I served you that first

time? You had me so flustered, I couldn't put one foot in front of the other.

Your letters keep me going, Drew. I miss you so much!

All my love,

Ivy

How different Ivy's letters sounded compared to Drew's! Sticking to safe subjects made her letters more like a round-robin written by a cousin dispensing family news and weather reports. Drew seemed to dip his pen in his heart to find the ink with which to write.

My darling Ivy,

I woke this morning with a pain in my chest. Our company medic examined me thoroughly and came to the same conclusion I'd drawn. Missing you has eaten a hole in my heart! There is no cure for me until I see you again.

I'll always regret our not having gotten married before I shipped out. I don't know why that would make any difference to me right now, but it would. I want you to be my wife, Ivy. My wife!

You said you didn't need a big, fancy wedding to satisfy you, even though I know you've probably been dreaming about one since you were a little girl. I wish I'd listened to you. When I got called up, I couldn't imagine our just running off to a justice of the peace in our street clothes with no ring, no plans, no reception, no family around us. Now those things seem like small concerns. I just want you to be mine . . . forever.

We haven't always done things right. I mean, the way we should have. But when I get back to the States, I swear the first thing I'm going to do is get you the biggest ring I can afford. When you see me, I'll be down on one knee.

Ivy moaned. Don't swear it, Drew. You don't know the whole story.

The thought of putting my arms around you again makes me a better soldier. Honest! I want to push the North Koreans and the Chinese back where they belong and end this thing so I can come home to you. Did you hear there are rumors of peace talks? Hurry up, Truman!

Every night I fall asleep with your picture pressed to my heart. Your face shows up in all my dreams. That sounds sappy, but it's true. Some of the other guys in my platoon complain they can't sleep for my calling out your name in the night.

When the Greyhound pulled up in front of the diner the day I left, the jukebox played "Moon River," remember? There's a sorry-looking river in my line of sight where we're dug in. As muddy as that worthless piece of water is in the daytime, it glowed when the moon-light hit it tonight while I was on watch. That's what you've done to me, Ivy. My life was pretty dull before it felt the light of your love.

Yours forever and a day,

Drew

She refolded the letter and swallowed hard. His tenderness should have thrilled her. Instead it made her uncomfortable. How would the fragile web of his love hold up under the anvil weight of what she couldn't bring herself to tell him? How would his dark eyes—coffee, no cream—respond if she could tell him face-to-face? With disappointment? Anger? One thing she knew. They wouldn't register gratitude. A baby was the last thing he needed right now.

Drew's sense of honor would press him to do "the right thing." They'd be married. And every day, Drew would resent the child's intrusion in his plans. That was the way of reluctant fathers.

That's what Ivy learned from her own reluctant father.

Ivy clutched the letter to her heart, willing it to grow arms like Drew's and envelop her with forgiveness.

He loves me, but for how long?

5

Ivy—1951

Ivy fingered the envelope in her uniform pocket, the paper representing both closeness and distance. As long as Drew remained unaware of what else she hugged tight to her soul, she could live in the fairy tale that things might work out. If he came home. And if he forgave her.

She opened the staff entrance to the Maple Grove Nursing Home. Lemon and cinnamon. A fastidious housekeeping staff and a creative cook—two things that made Clairmont's Maple Grove Nursing Home different from other facilities caring for the elderly and infirm. She'd heard the horror stories of places that didn't deserve the word "home" in their name. Glorified prisons in their starkness, smelling of untended bedpans and warmed-over cabbage soup.

The cinnamon fragrance drifted from the kitchen "on warm waves of wonderful," as one of the more lucid residents once described it. Ivy stepped farther into the facility, appreciating waves like this after her near-collision with Helene's soaked-through little one.

She clicked open her metal locker in the nurses' lounge and dropped her purse onto its floor. Shutting the locker door was impossible without another clang of metal.

"Hey! A little sympathy for the walking wounded!"

Ivy turned toward the voice. Jill.

An unlit cigarette bobbed and danced, stuck to the woman's limp lips. "You trying to make my headache worse?"

"Sorry," Ivy said. "Rough night?"

"The night was great." Jill leaned against her own locker and rubbed her forehead as if to erase whatever memory it held. "It's the morning after that takes its toll on a person."

"Wouldn't know."

Jill raised her narrowed eyes. "You wouldn't know what a hangover feels like?"

How far into this conversation did Ivy dare wander? "I have an idea. Look, I need to punch in."

"Yeah, me too. Time to pacify the ancient and the addle-brained."

Ivy's back stiffened. "Jill!"

Jill pulled the cigarette from her mouth and gestured with it. "Don't tell me you like working here."

Working was better than sitting alone in the apartment above the dry cleaner day after day. Did Ivy like working *here*? It had its rough moments. "I enjoy the residents. Most of them."

Jill snorted her response and took a long drag on her now-lit Camel.

She eyed her coworker. "What made you choose nursing?"

Jill bent to retie the white laces on her polished white nurse's shoes. "Didn't want to be a teacher." Her pinched sentence ended in a *whoo* of exhaled smoke.

Would the day ever come when a woman could choose a job she was suited for?

Ivy fingered last week's limp airmail envelope in the pocket of her uniform with her hand as she slid the stiff card into the time clock with her other hand and heard its sinister metallic clunk.

Punched in.

Without needing to remove the envelope from her pocket, she knew exactly what it looked like. The familiar, boxy handwriting. The heart-pounding postmark: Seoul, Korea, July 7, 1951—only a month in transit this time. A return address with power to rearrange her internal organs. Navy ink, paled slightly by the ocean crossing, by the sun and air and humidity, by the Army transport and freight plane and ground truck and on-foot mailman that brought the paper treasure to her door.

Drew's latest love letter. They didn't come every week, but often enough to testify to his sincerity. He was too good to her. Better than she deserved. Was it just selfishness that kept her from telling him the truth? The longer she postponed the news that was sure to bring their relationship to an end, the longer she could wrap herself in the warmth of his devotion.

She wasn't just lying now, she was *using* him! How long would her sins pile up before the ground opened to swallow her?

Ivy stood behind the wall of medicine cupboards and discreetly adjusted her stockings so the seams were straight in the back. The garter clips holding them dug into her thighs, a button of dented flesh forming already under each one. Regulations demanded hose, even on sweltering summer days. A few years prior, they'd been forbidden because of the previous war's rationing.

The clunk that imprinted Jill's time card startled Ivy. Her fingernail snagged her stocking. By the day's end, the tiny hole would be a full-fledged run, thigh to toe. Could she never be put together for a whole day? Did her scars always have to show?

Show. Soon her biggest scar would show.

Jill slid her time card back into the steel holding slot not far from Ivy's. "Welcome to another shift at the funny farm."

"Do you have to call it that?"

"What are you flapping your lips about?"

"Never mind."

"No. What did you mean?"

"It's just . . ." How badly did she want to stay on Jill's good side? Riding a wave of distractions, the moment passed.

"You're going to have a time with 117 today."

"Anna? What's wrong with her?"

"Stubborn old coot."

"Jill!" Ivy tsked.

At the percussive sound, Jill looked up. "Don't flip your cap. She couldn't hear me if I was standing on the edge of her ear lobe."

"What happened?"

"Refuses to take her medicine. Yesterday, she'd have spit it on me if I hadn't ducked."

"Honestly?"

Jill's rubber-soled white shoes squeaked as she pivoted to leave the nurses' lounge. "I've got to get that review report done. And I do not relish the tongue wagging I'll hear if our illustrious head nurse finds out I failed to get that biddy to take her morning meds again today."

"Let me talk to Anna."

"Good luck."

"I can't administer her meds, but I'll see if I can get her to cooperate."

"More power to you. Don't let her nab you with one of her rambling stories. You'll never get any work done. The senile imagination. Isn't it a hoot?" She shook her head. "No explaining some people."

—∞∞—

Anna Grissom's eyes lit up like a flashlight with fresh batteries when Ivy entered her room.

"Mrs. Carrington! You're a sight for sore eyes."

Ivy let the misnomer—*Mrs.*—go uncorrected. If the staff and residents didn't believe her married, she'd soon be fodder for the rumor mill.

"Doing okay this morning, Miss Anna?"

"Been better. At my age, is there any other reasonable response?"

"How old are you now? I could look it up, but . . ."

"I was born the day Lee surrendered at Appomattox."

"And that was . . . ?"

"The end of the Civil War." The look of incredulity on Anna's well-lined face said, *How could you not know that?*

"I mean the *date*, Anna."

"Oh. Yes. April 9, 1865."

"Eighty-six."

"Sixty-five, dear."

"No, I mean you're eighty-six years old, Anna."

"That's right. Am I confused, or are you? Silly question." Anna reached a gnarled hand to brush a stray hair off her forehead.

Ivy adjusted the lap robe around Anna's legs, tucking her securely into the wheelchair in which the woman would spend most of her day. "Anna, your nurse tells me you gave her fits about taking your medicines this morning."

"I gave *her* fits?"

"You saw it differently? I thought you might."

"It's my teeth."

"Excuse me?"

"I've still got all my own teeth, or most of them."

"That's wonderful, Anna, but—"

"Did I ever tell you about Puff's teeth? Now, there was a man with less than a full complement."

Another train of thought derailed. "Your medications, Miss Anna?"

"I didn't take them."

"I know."

"Because of my teeth."

Ivy wondered how much searching it might take to find a container with a secure enough lid that it could keep Anna's musings from spreading where they didn't belong, like egg whites on linoleum. "What?"

"I've got my own teeth, still."

"Yes?"

"And I can't abide cold."

"Anna, I'm sorry, but I don't understand—"

"That Jill person." Anna's sigh seemed to rattle her skeletal system. "She gives me ice water to swallow my pills with. I've told her my teeth are sensitive. Doesn't seem to care. Every day she works this wing, she hands me my pills and a glass of icy water. And yesterday I decided to hold out for room temperature."

"Oh."

"Does that make me ornery?"

Ivy bent to lay her too-warm, fleshy hand on Anna's bird-bone arm. "No."

"Cantankerous? Jill said I was cantankerous. I remember having a pig once that was cantankerous. I know the difference. Did I ever tell you about Ham?"

"Ham?"

"The pig. Try to keep up, dear."

Ivy smiled. Only Anna could chide her without guile.

"I called him Ham. His real name was . . . was . . . oh, I forget what Puff called him."

"Anna, I'd love to stay and chat, but I have eight other patients today, some of whom are *genuinely* cantankerous. I'll stop back a little later. Can I tell Jill that you'll take your medicines without a fuss if she brings you room-temperature water?"

"Of course!" Anna's eyes sparkled with a precocious child's delight. "I'm not here to make waves. I'm too old for that."

Ivy wiggled her toes inside her shoes. She arched her back. What would it be like in a few months when the baby weighed more than a whisper? The only good thing about heading home to that stuffy, friendless apartment at the end of the day was the prospect of getting out of her uniform and shoes. She'd punched out already but poked her head into room 117 one last time.

"Anything else I can do for you before I leave, Anna?"

"I can't remember his name."

"Whose?"

"The pig. What was Ham's real name? I'm losing the pieces."

"It'll come to you. If you're like me, you'll wake up in the middle of the night and *Eureka!* Don't worry yourself about it."

"I'm losing the pieces of my story, Ivy." The older woman looked up, as if tilting her head back would keep the threatening tears from spilling.

"It happens to the best of us, I guess."

Anna leveled her watery gaze at Ivy. "But I want them to know."

"Who?"

"My girls. I want them to know how it turned out."

"Your daughters? But your chart says—"

"A hundred and twenty-seven of them."

"Miss Anna . . ." Ivy fought to remove the hint of condescension from her voice. "I just read a magazine article about a woman who had the most children born to her of any woman on earth. From Eastern Europe, I believe. Sixty-nine. That's the record."

"Well, I had a hundred and twenty-seven of them." Anna's gnarled hand reached to rub the spot on her cheekbone where the map of Africa age spot rested. "And that must make close to four or five hundred grandchildren by now."

"Now, Anna . . ."

"Maybe more. Oh, how rude of me not to ask. How are your morning glories, dear?"

"My morning glories? I don't have any flowers outside my apartment."

"You call it morning *sickness*, I'm sure."

Ivy's knees lost their mooring pegs. At least half her previous height melted into her white nursing shoes.

"What?"

"Is it getting better now? Usually does. Not for all women, but most."

"Anna, I . . . I don't know what you mean."

"Didn't you tell me you were expecting? Oh, maybe not. I guess I just knew. Or maybe the Lord told me."

"How could you know?" Ivy retraced her conversation with every living soul at the home. No, she hadn't breathed a word. "I mean . . ."

"Experience. I can usually read it in the eyes. But that green pallor to your skin these past weeks gave it away. Funny you haven't mentioned it to me. I'm sure you have your reasons. Is your young man excited?"

"My . . . my husband? Yes. Of course."

Anna grew a sympathetic pout-spout on her lower lip. "Too bad he's got to be so far away at a time like this."

"How did you know that?"

"The letters."

Ivy sat down hard on the idle steam register along the wall. "I haven't shared his letters with you."

"I see their outline through the pocket of your uniform. Red and blue border. Must be airmail. Really far away?"

"Korea."

"Oh, child."

"His name is Drew."

"Drew Carrington. A stately name. Finding a fitting first name for your baby will be a challenge, won't it?"

"I don't know how you—" Was the room spinning? Ivy's mind whirled. She knew the day would come. Someone had to be the first to know. But this dear, almost ninety-year-old woman with "less than a full complement" of sensibility left to her? If *she* figured it out, how long before others knew? Or did they already? Had the break room gossip started without her?

"His name is Lambert. Drew Lambert. I . . . I kept my own name when we . . . married."

"Whoever heard of such a thing? I don't know. Young people today. Not you, of course, Ivy. You're one of the reasons I still have hope. Which brings me back to Ham."

"Your pig?" Any subject was safer than the one with which they were toying. "Yes, tell me about your pig, Anna."

"Actually, he belonged to Puff."

"Your husband?"

"Oh, mercy, no! Now, what did Puff call that pig? Ivy, I'm losing the pieces!"

What am I getting myself into? Just walk out the door, Ivy. You've put in your time. Spare yourself the grief. You've got larger concerns

than an old lady missing a piece of her memory puzzle. Maybe Jill's
got the right attitude.

No. No, she doesn't.

"Tell me more about him, Anna. The name might come to you."

Anna slapped her hands together in a single burst of mis-shapen applause. "Where do I start?"

"When did you first see the pig?"

"Soon after Puff moved in."

"Puff . . . lived with you?"

"Yes. Well, not in the way you might be thinking. He helped me run the place."

"The place?"

"Morning Glory."

"I'm sorry. I don't follow."

"Do you think it would help if you jotted a few things down? If my hands weren't so crippled with the *ar-thur-itis* I'd write this myself. I need to tell my girls how it all turned out."

"Your daughters."

"Not really."

"Now, Anna . . ."

Anna folded her disfigured hands and rested them on her lap. "I should start at the beginning."

6

Seems you're flirting with foolishness, if you ask me," he said, flicking cigar ashes over the side of the carriage and onto the blessedly damp, ash-snuffing lane.

Flirting was far from my mind. And I wasn't asking.

His speech gurgled. The man was drowning in his own spit!

He cleared his throat with a grinding sound. "Sure you ain't bit off more than you can chew? What're you planning to do with it? You can't be thinking too ambitious, considering the shape it's in."

People of various ilks and motives have wondered whatever possessed me to make what I did of the house. Aunt Phoebe's lawyer—a greasy man with extra chins and a deficit of manners—was among the first.

On the carriage ride from his office in Westbrook the day I took possession, he peppered me with questions about my intentions, as if he felt obligated to protect me from a nefarious suitor, as if I were proposing marriage to the structure. In a way, I suppose I was.

My hesitance to give clear answers must have frustrated him. His brow furrowed and he breathed sausage-scented sighs. Unconcerned whether or not he understood me, I clutched my thoughts close to my heart. His constant probing was like a squeaky pump handle. For all his flailing efforts, he was rewarded with no more than a dribble of information from me.

Tenacity sometimes steps over the line into stubbornness, but I won't apologize for that. It got me through more than one pickle.

His clothes smelled of yesterday's bullhead dinner and cheap homemade cigars. As we rode side by side in the carriage, I worked my shawl up around my shoulders, frail protection that it was against everything offensive about him. Being polite is not often a struggle for me. This day it was a canyon crossing . . . barefoot . . . with a fifty-pound pack on my back.

"You sure you thunk this through?" he asked as he urged the horse across the bridge at the entrance to Aunt Phoebe's property. Poor grammar seemed a good fit for his demeanor, a mismatch for his profession.

"I've given it a great deal of thought, Mr. Rawlins."

He grunted, then spit over the side of the carriage. We rode in blessed silence the last few hundred yards.

"You ain't but, what, twenty? Big place for a little thing like you," he said, turning the key in the padlock on the ten-foot, double front doors.

A little thing? Did he think I'd consider that endearing? "It suited my aunt, and she was no taller than I, Mr. Rawlins."

"I didn't mean because you're short. Just . . . well . . . being alone."

"As was Aunt Phoebe a good portion of her life."

Our footsteps left footprints in the dust on the hardwood floors. A bit of plaster from somewhere high on the foyer wall crunched underfoot. The air inside smelled like a damp cellar.

"Lots of upkeep in a place like this." He rattled the loose newel post on the banister in the entry, as if punctuating his point.

"I'm not afraid of hard work."

"That may be all you have going for you." I'm sure those were his words, though he'd turned his back to me and lowered his voice. "Don't suppose you need a tour."

"No tour. Just the keys, please." I refused to drop my outstretched hand, determined not to be the first to flinch. "Mr. Rawlins?"

"I must remind you that the bank'd be more than happy to relieve you of this albatross."

"If you would be so kind as to help unload my trunks from the carriage, Mr. Rawlins?"

"I don't think you've taken into consideration all this here house is going to require in the way of maintenance and—"

"I will save you the energy of delivering the remainder of your speech. Be assured I will inform Mr. Blakemore at the bank that you did all you could to persuade me. You discharged your duty as instructed. But I was and ever will be immovable on this subject. I'm keeping the house."

The veins at his temples beat frustration's pulse. He did not bear defeat well, which showed in his rough handling of my trunks and the fact that he left them on the porch. I was glad to be rid of him and his greasy odor, even if it did mean wrestling the beasts across the threshold myself.

After the dust of his departure settled, I walked back out through the front door and down the steps, turned, and approached on my own, with no irritation at my elbow. I reentered the house as I'd wanted to, with a sense of awe rather than restrained anger.

Aunt Phoebe's home was now mine. It came to me along with her walnut rocker, her silver tea set, and six hand-painted porcelain cups and saucers—the extent of her earthly possessions she felt worth mentioning in her will. The truth of the matter is she outlived her husband and his modest savings. Medical expenses whittled away at her worldly goods until, at the time of her death, her bank account and her house were as empty as her spiritless body.

I hadn't expected to inherit the house. I suppose that was naive of me. She had no other living relatives. When she died, I, also, was left with no one to call mine.

The key yet in my hand, I surveyed my new home. Empty, drafty, colorless rooms. All of them. As awkward in their emptiness as a missing front tooth on an otherwise distinguished politician's wife.

A stubborn hint of elegance remained in the architecture. Lofty ceilings. Ornate carved mantels and woodwork. A staircase that swept like a swan's neck to the second floor. The house whispered, "You should have seen me in my youth."

Now, every inch was bare and unadorned, unless one could count the layers of dust and the crisscrossed trails of rodent droppings. On that first encounter, my footsteps echoed hollowly as I walked the barrenness of the once grand Federal-style home. My inheritance? Or my liability?

I had only a handful of items to my name. Everything else had been consumed by debts, which I also had inherited. I was as unprepared to furnish a house as was an immigrant whose life savings covered the expense of the ocean crossing but not a penny more. I stood with my feet on foreign soil but having no resources with which to move inland away from the shore.

The cramped room at Mrs. Hazelton's boardinghouse took what little I earned but gave me the gift of closeness to the sanitarium where Aunt Phoebe's days drained to the dregs. She needed companionship, a kind face in the midst of a cruel disease. And I needed to be near her.

So now, these years later, I stood dumbstruck and dreamless in her home. As if chiding a petulant child, I asked the barren house, "What am I going to do with you?"

Rather than envisioning richly textured oriental carpets with which I longed to cover the floors and yards of Venetian lace hung at the windows, that first day of official ownership I walked through the house making note of which rooms could be closed off completely. No need to heat emptiness.

Within minutes I decided to ignore the entire second story for a time and convert one of the downstairs parlors into a temporary bedroom. That left four massive rooms on the main floor to consider. The formal parlor to the left of the entry. The library directly to the right. The dining room with its startling rich mahogany-paneled walls. And the kitchen, which stretched the full width of the back of the house.

At my mother's knee I learned to make do, to use creativity where money failed. But that first gray day, with the sun fighting a losing battle with the cloud cover, I could not rouse creativity from its untimely slumber. The emptiness kept its smothering hand over any thoughts wanting to be born.

How uncharming the house seemed, even as Aunt Phoebe became in the later stages of her illness. Sunken cheeks and sallow, parchment-thin skin. Relentless, suffocating cough that stopped only when her fight was over and her spirit lost its need for breath.

I closed my eyes and willed myself to remember her before she became sick. Rosy cheeked. Gracious in speech and movement. Full of vigor. Full of faith that patched all the holes in mine. Floating through those rooms, her skirts brushing past velvet settees and walnut lamp tables.

I opened my eyes to the vacant spaces around me. By the calendar, spring had a good foothold, but I felt chilled and as alone as a sane person dare feel.

How, God? How am I to do what You've asked of me? I've nothing but imagination left, and even it is threatening to resign. How am I to furnish this place—much less manage it—on a few remaining threads of misdirected ambition?

Before I finished formulating my complaint, the answer stole across the floor of the room. Ignoring the film of dust, sunlight fought its way through the beveled glass in the windows of the parlor in which I stood, laying a carpet of color on the floor and papering the walls with elegant, translucent shades of red, orange, yellow, green, blue, indigo, violet.

Clouds reclaimed the scene soon enough, extinguishing the splash of color. But the deed was done. I had my answer . . . and fresh hope.

Isn't it amazing how hope can so quickly grow stale when it is exposed to doubt? I vowed not to let that happen again.

God called me to the task. He'd accompany me through it.

Ivy—1951

Ivy laid down her pencil and flexed her fingers. The pillow Anna had suggested for the small of her back helped, but no cure existed for a hand cramp except to stop writing.

"What task, Miss Anna?"

"Hmm?"

"To what task did you feel called?"

"Oh, I'll get to it."

The longhand story already filled several pages of the steno pad Ivy had purchased at the five-and-dime. How far would they be into the notebook before Ivy knew where the tale was headed? How long before she even knew if the words were true or a brilliant work of senile fiction?

Did it matter?

Anna's face boasted more color than Ivy had seen in a long while. Her eyes danced with her memories, real or imagined.

Ivy could think of worse ways to spend her late afternoons and occasional evenings. Trapped between the broken springs on the seedy, tweedy davenport her father liberated from the alley-dump behind the dry cleaner. Stuck to the chrome and vinyl chair at the table in the perpetually humid kitchen. Writing airmail letters she didn't dare send. Taking out all the truth and writing them again.

If she kept Anna talking, rarely a challenge, she could forget what was happening in her body and on the side of a Pacific Rim mountain or in a rice paddy across too large a body of water.

"Weren't you afraid to stay in that big house alone, Anna?"

"Hmm? No. Alone, I was used to. An expert at it, you might say."

"And how old were you then? When you first got the house?"

Anna smiled. All her own teeth. Beautiful. "Mr. Rawlins was a poor judge of just about everything. I was all of twenty-seven when I took over Morning Glory." She hoisted her body straighter in the chair. "But don't you write that! It'll throw people off. It wasn't Morning Glory when I got it. That came later. *They* came later."

"They?"

"The morning glories. You been getting adequate sleep, Ivy? You're having a hard time following a simple story."

Ivy pressed her lips together. Swallowed a reply. Picked up her pencil and wrote.

7

Anna—1890s

Even now, when I think of it, my shoulders and back and knees and hands ache with the effort it took to scrub away the neglect in the house brought on while lawyers argued and paperwork floundered. A thousand trips to the pump in the backyard for yet another bucket of water. A year's supply of tallow soap.

Many nights, I crawled onto my straw tick near the fireplace in the day parlor too exhausted to pull the blanket over my body. Rebellious muscles then began the nightly ritual of releasing their tension, searching valiantly for a comfortable position in which to sleep. I awoke as stiff as a woman three times my age, but plowed back into the task as if I had more than a self-imposed deadline.

The color came every afternoon when the clouds were busy elsewhere. The rich bands seemed to appreciate my efforts to keep "their" windows sparkling clean. An onlooker would think me daft, but I often dropped my washrags and scrub brush when the prisms of light visited. I stood in the middle of them, in the middle of God's promise to me, gaining strength for the next chore and the next and the next.

One of those days, a knock sounded on my front doors at the very moment I returned inside from tossing the last bucket of scrub water into the yard behind the kitchen. I dried my prunelike hands on my work apron, then quickly removed it on my way from the back of the house to the double doors in front.

"Heard you was movin' in," the man said without even a how-do-you-do.

"Yes," I said, offering an outstretched, waterlogged hand in greeting. "I'm Anna Morgan. And you are . . . ?"

"Percival Lincoln Crawford, ma'am."

I cannot tell you how far my mind traveled in those few moments, inventing explanations for the circumstances under which a newborn, now a full-grown man with tattered coveralls and a sweat-stained hat, would have been given the name *Percival Lincoln Crawford*. Did he sense my rabidly wandering thoughts?

"Lincoln ain't my real middle name," he explained, as if that were the most curious part of his story. "I give that to myself, being as I never did like the name Clarence, and being as Mr. Lincoln was someone I'm proud to share a name with." He whipped his hat off his head as if he'd just remembered he was speaking with a woman.

"A pleasure to meet you, Mr. Crawford."

"Most people who call me something decent call me Puff."

"Puff?"

"That's right, ma'am."

"Do you smoke? Is that the reason you're named—"

"Oh, no ma'am! God done broke me of that! You can be sure!"

His agitation startled me. I hadn't meant to rile him. I was looking for a rationale behind his nickname. "Forgive my asking, Puff."

"Oh, you got a right. You got a right, that be sure."

"I do?"

"Well, now, you don't want to be hiring someone with a tobacca habit, I don't imagine."

"I'm sorry, Mr. Crawford." And I genuinely was, strangely enough. "I'm not in a position to hire anyone right now."

"But you surely do need help, if you'll pardon my pointing that out." He wore a grandfatherly expression. "You got outbuildings that seen better days. If you don't get some paint slapped on this house you might as well hang a sign inviting insects and such. And I might of killed myself coming up these steps, what with them rotten boards, which if they ain't tended to could drop a person clean through to kingdom come."

I smiled, which he seemed to take as an invitation to continue.

"Your garden out back ain't about to produce beetle manure if it don't get planted." His voice trailed off after the word *manure*, his eyes dropping to the hat he held in his hands. Was he concerned that he'd offended my "sensibilities"?

"Puff, I would like nothing better than to have some help around here. And I can see that you are a man of vision as well as energy. But I am simply not able to pay. Currently. If my circumstances should change, where might I contact you?" I added the question to give him a shred of hope. He looked as if he could use it. Subconsciously, I must have spoken the words to give *me* hope that my financial picture might indeed one day accommodate a hired man.

"You can ask around about me."

"Where, Puff? Do you live in town?"

"Just ask around. People knows me. G'day then, ma'am." He doffed his hat to me and bowed slightly before turning to leave. I couldn't help but smile when in his descent he gingerly avoided the rotten boards on the steps. He glanced back. I nodded that I'd noticed.

I say that an answer knocked at my door that day. I just didn't know it at the time.

⸙

I slept a weary but satisfied sleep that night, ignoring the emptiness, enjoying the fact that the emptiness was clean and smelled delightfully fresh. Left to my own devices, I would have stayed nestled in my makeshift bed far longer the next morning. But one can hardly sleep through the sound of hammering right outside one's door. I'd slept in my clothes, so I bounded up immediately, without the need to dress.

"Puff!"

"Yes, ma'am?" He removed a fan of nails from between his front teeth. "Did I start too early for you?"

I surveyed the work he'd already begun on the steps. The old boards had been removed. I slept through that? The first of several sawmill-fresh planks was well on its way to becoming a permanent fixture on my front porch.

How could he have misunderstood? Didn't I make it clear to him? Was he—the precious soul—unable to mentally comprehend what we'd discussed the day before?

"Puff, I cannot pay you!"

"Yes, ma'am. I know that."

I knelt on the top step and took the hammer from his hands as gently as I could, praying that my actions and words would not be perceived as condescending. "Puff, please understand. I haven't money enough to feed myself, much less hire you to do this work."

"I understand that. Yes, I does." He took the hammer from me and resumed using it to pound nails into the wood. Two

75

mighty blows per nail. His strength would have been frightening if he hadn't been humming at the time.

"Mr. Crawford!"

He looked up at the formality.

"How much for the lumber?"

"Man at the mill needed a couple of chickens. I had me one or two to spare. You got your new steps."

"But . . ."

"Now, listen . . ." He stood to his full height—well over six feet—slapped his hammer into a loop in his belt, and crossed his tree-trunk arms across his chest. "Are you tellin' me that if God 'structed me to do something good-deedlike for someone who needs it, you're gonna stand in my way?"

The fact that I was still kneeling at the top of the steps made his question all the more humbling.

Did I intend to stand in God's way? My heart longed to be generous with Puff, not take from him. But it appeared I was being called to receive. Would I do so grudgingly or graciously? One response would bless Puff. The other would not.

"Then, I thank you for your kindness, sir."

His grin threatened to carve a permanent fissure connecting his ears. I didn't count them, but couldn't help noticing that Puff was missing a few teeth. He filled in the gaps with joy. Beautiful.

He helped me to my feet. Sighing with an unusual, unexplained contentment, I left him to his work.

Coffee was all I had to offer him. I'd not taken time to bake anything for many days. But I do make an acceptable cup of coffee.

By the time I carried two cups of coffee to the porch, Puff was sweeping the repaired steps free of sawdust, his job completed. He received his cup with a nod of appreciation.

The sun had just pulled free of the treetops, brushing the eastern edge of every leaf and limb and blade with spun gold. It moved me that words were not necessary to bridge the space between us. The scene itself spoke loudly enough.

Too long I'd failed to fully appreciate that—in addition to the house that screamed its barrenness—I'd also inherited responsibility for the land on which it sat. The land—richly upholstered, all forty acres of it, with a narrow band of woods along the sides, a neglected orchard across the back, and profuse fields of wildflowers in front. The tree-shaded house itself sat three hundred yards back from Stony Creek and its namesake, Stony Creek Road, which ran parallel to the creek and then crossed it on a rough, slightly more than wagon-wide bridge.

"When the original shingles were laid on this many-gabled roof fifty years ago, two decades before Lincoln's war"—I emphasized the connection—"the house towered over the griddle-flat landscape, Puff."

"I can picture it."

"This imposing building was as out of place as people like me feel in the community."

He looked askance at me. "People like you?" His chuckle shook his shoulders.

"But the maples and oaks and pines and cottonwoods Aunt Phoebe and Uncle Raif planted on this once-bald property have certainly matured, haven't they? Branches, not shingles, claim sky-brushing dominance."

"You got a way with words, Miss Morgan."

His own forced a smile long absent. "Aunt Phoebe's journals and reports from the town's self-appointed historians tell me what the place looked like before the wagon tracks at the end of the lane were pressed into a semblance of an actual road, before the town took root where the creek joins forces with the river."

"Four miles downstream."

He must have walked all four miles before dawn.

As Puff and I sat sipping coffee and drinking in the scene, I let my imagination take me to the early days, when the wind blasted unimpeded against this grand house, when relief from the sun's rays came only in the form of infrequent clouds. "No wonder Aunt Phoebe and Uncle Raif were in such a hurry to get shade trees established, as well as the orchard, even at the expense of the wheat fields Raif intended to farm."

"Wheat?"

"My uncle expected to raise wheat here."

"I heard that. I did."

My tongue was as loose as the shutters on the west side of the house. It occurred to me to watch how much I said. But something about Puff prompted me to trust him as I had few others. He turned my way, as if waiting for the next chapter of the story.

"The day came when, to the clucking of neighbors' tongues, Uncle Raif chose to leave the arable acres fallow and divide his time between his orchard and art."

Puff nodded. "Art's a fine thing."

"That plan lasted six months, from what I gathered in Aunt Phoebe's journals. In order to eat, he sought work in town in his original profession as a bookkeeper. The orchard that awaited him at the end of the day balanced his disappointment at being bound to a desk."

"Desk wouldn't be my choice either."

Songbirds and insects played among the weeds and grasses. I hadn't listened before that moment. "For all the buckets of water my aunt and uncle hauled from the creek to quench the thirst of panting saplings, for all the effort it took to protect their 'young' from marauders—leaf-hungry insects and curious deer—I wish I could have thanked them."

We sat on the porch of a house less vulnerable with its thick-trunked sentries and leafy parasols shading it from what would soon be relentless summer heat. I imagined the full cycle of seasons in that setting, as entertaining to watch as an infant learning to crawl.

The spring wildflowers that hugged the feet of the bridge seemed to enjoy the morning that Puff and I shared over coffee. They danced and sang.

"Did you hear that?" Puff asked with wonder, his voice almost whisper soft. "I believe them wildflowers is saying to us, 'Look what God done all by Hisself! Ain't we something?' Now, a God as creative as that must surely have a plan, don't you think, to take good care of any of His childrens living on this propity?"

I looked at the back of Puff's head, as he sat several steps lower. His hat lay beside him so the quickening breeze could blow a breath of kindness on the beads of sweat that dotted his thick neck. Not the image of an ordinary angel. I supposed his halo was safely tucked in his pocket, to keep it from sliding off his damp, bald, ebony head.

"How old are you, Puff Crawford?"

"Can't tell ya 'zactly. Somewheres around the other side of fifty, I believe. Why?"

"You're almost twice my age, but four times wiser."

We carried the conversation this far before he turned to face me and said, "Got an hour or two tomorrow I don't know what to do with."

A claim a person could read clearly through fog at dusk!

"Sure would like to spend some time clearing brush out of that orchard. 'Course, I wouldn't want to take that pleasure away from you, if you had your heart set."

"Do you really think those trees are worth saving?" I was not prepared for the look on his face.

"Ain't we all?"

If anyone could breathe life into that exhausted old orchard, it would be Mr. Percival Lincoln Crawford.

"I seen blossuns out there."

"You did, Puff?"

"That's all you need to feed your hope. Ain't going to see all the fruit itself right away. Just a few blossuns. That be enough."

For you, Puff. But enough for me? Clearly my faith had room to grow.

Puff returned to wherever it was he lived. I spent the rest of the day pawing through the meager supplies in my kitchen in an effort to create something filling and worthy of Puff's appetite.

I was grateful for the handful of dried apricots I'd saved from the previous Christmas. I'd been living on very little. Too little. But now it was important to me to try to keep up with Puff's generosity.

That proved impossible.

When I opened the back door the next morning to draw from the backyard pump water for the day's needs, I nearly tripped over a headless chicken and a basket of eggs on the back steps. The chicken was fat and healthy-looking, except for being dead. Puff obviously knew something about raising chickens.

Meat for supper. And eggs for breakfast. The apricot braided bread resting under a towel in the kitchen was a widow's mite by comparison.

When Puff entered the yard from the orchard path behind the barn, I was sitting on the steps, ankle-deep in scalded, damp-smelling chicken feathers. He tipped his hat to me before removing it and pouring his first ladle of pump water over his glistening head. Two more ladles for his throat before he spoke. By that time I'd divested myself of the majority of stray feathers clinging to my work apron and hurried into the kitchen to cut Puff a slice of bread and pour him a cup of coffee.

"Might I trouble you for—" He stopped at the sight of the butterless bread on the plate in my hand.

"I should have asked yesterday, Puff, if you wanted sugar for your coffee. I'd offer cream, if I had it to give."

"No need. Your coffee don't need no doctoring. That for me?" He nodded toward the fruit bread. He'd taken a bite before I finished answering. "You're a fine cook, Miz Morgan."

"Thank you."

"I wonder if I could trouble you for a needle or something." He held out his left hand to me, palm up. In his lion's paw hand there was a splinter as big around as a knitting needle.

"Oh, Puff!"

"Looks worse than it is."

"Do you want me to pull it out, if I can get a grip on it?"

"That be best. I tried. But my fingers is on the clumsy side for chores like this."

I'm curious now why I would remember some of these details. I clearly recall how the man's blood flowed down the ravine in his hand and halfway down his upraised arm after the splinter was removed. I could almost see a rough nail where the thorn had been and feel the awesome force of Blood spilled for me almost nineteen hundred years before. I didn't deserve it . . . but there it was.

It shook me to see the blood. I've never been squeamish, a fact that would serve me well, down the road. But knowing

Puff's injury was a direct result of his wanting to help puts me in awe to this day.

I returned to the oddly comforting task of plucking feathers off our supper. Every stubborn pinfeather—so thornlike and intrusive—reminded me of the price Puff was paying in the orchard. I had nothing but my gratitude to offer in return. How could he be content with that arrangement?

It's a wonder I didn't harbor a moment's fear in Puff's presence. I suppose, in light of my vulnerability and the remoteness of the property, some might think me foolish for not having been afraid of a show-up-at-the-front-door-unannounced man of his size and strength.

But there was the look of heaven in his coal-black eyes. No denying. I always felt safest when he was on the "propity," as he called it.

"You planning to take on boarders?" he asked one day between strokes of the ax as he split and I stacked firewood.

"In a way."

"Be mighty tough away out here. A far piece for someone who works or is visiting in town. Don't know as you'll get many takers."

"I believe the setting is appropriate for my purposes."

He stopped, buried the ax head into the end of a piece of old apple trunk, and leaned on the handle. "You on a mission, ain't you," he stated, rather than questioned. His perception unnerved me. "A mission from God, ain't it?"

"Now, Puff, how would you know that?"

"Your hands are on your stacking work but your mind and heart is someplace else entirely. You got plans for this place, I'll bet my shirt, not that I'm a betting man . . . anymore. Big plans."

I started a new row of cordwood, my work gloves saving me from the rough bark and splinters. "Sometimes my dreams gallop like a racehorse, and reality follows unconcerned as a snail."

"You going to tell me more?" he asked, choosing an unsplit maple log on which to sit. "My back'll thank you if it's a long, long story that requires my full attention."

I laughed, as I often did in Puff's comfortable presence. Though I hadn't intended to, I confessed the whole preposterous scheme. He nodded along the way. "Uh huh. Is that right?" He scratched his stubbly chin from time to time. But he never once ridiculed my idea.

That endeared the man to my heart forever. That and the one tear that accompanied his closing comment: "I'll help you all I can."

Good thing I had no close neighbors to witness and wag about what happened next! Before I thought about my action's wisdom, I gave him a bear hug that "purt near snuffed the life right outta" him. That's how Puff told it.

He was the first person from whom I received encouragement rather than resistance.

In days to come, it would often feel as if he and the Lord were the only ones on my side. But considering how powerful they both were, I guess the odds were still in my favor.

—∞—

Ivy—1951

"Puff sounds like he was a wonderful man, Anna."

She smiled as serenely as age would allow. "One of God's favorites, I'm sure."

"Was he your . . . your beau?"

"Puff? Heavens no! He had his own sweetheart. And I had mine." She reached one knobby hand toward the other and twirled the simple gold band that rested loosely on her ring finger, held captive by the protective distortion of a swollen knuckle.

Ivy wondered when Anna would be ready to tell that chapter.

She turned her pencil eraser-end down and tried to rub out a smudge in the margin of the notebook page. The action chewed through the paper. Someone would have to convert these scribbles to a legible form if anyone but Ivy were to read Anna's story.

"Now, where was I?"

"Puff encouraged you to keep going. Was he right to do that?"

"More often than not."

8

Anna—1890s

The orchard cleanup took several days rather than the hour or two Puff didn't know what to do with.

He stood at the back door. "Miz Morgan?"

"Are you all finished?"

"Good as I can get it for now."

"I can't thank you enough. I took a walk out there yesterday afternoon before it rained. You've done wonders!"

"If it gets a little attention, an orchard'll perk right up, just like people do."

"I hope we'll get some fruit this fall."

"Maybe sooner. I believe that one row of trees is plums. May see some of them before summer's spent."

"Wouldn't that be wonderful? Oh, look at me. What kind of hostess am I? Would you like to come in?"

He hesitated. "I probably should head on home soon. Just wondered if you needed help hauling in the furniture."

"What furniture?"

"That what's out in the barn."

"There's furniture in the barn?" I brushed past him and out the door, heading across the yard before I realized how rude that must have seemed. Puff pounded right at my heels.

He reached around me and lifted the heavy iron bar on the double-wide barn door. It swung open with a sigh, as if an ample woman's flesh had been released from a corset. It took our eyes a few moments to adjust to the dark.

Big and empty and padded with many years' accumulation of straw dust, cobwebs, and pigeon droppings, the barn smelled of age and disuse, of old hay and long-absent animals. I was almost relieved not to find tables and chairs and beds in such an environment. Imagine eating breakfast on a table recently cleared of bird refuse!

Sunlight found its way into the barn in tiny, intense rays that squeezed through cracks between the barn boards. The windows—those on the ground level and those high above in the peak—were either shuttered or caked with what might turn my stomach, were I to speculate.

Puff was yards ahead of me in optimism, heading for what I assumed was a tack room beyond the horse stalls.

Another door creaked open at Puff's touch. It was pitch black in this internal room, affording me no clues to its contents . . . or its inhabitants, either.

Something squeaked and scurried farther into the dark abyss. I was grateful I didn't have to beg for light, since Puff was already lighting a lantern.

It was a moment or two before I was conscious of what the light illuminated. All the items were covered with yards of heavy canvas tarp, but many of the outlines were unmistakable. A camelback sofa. No, two. Several chairs. A long, heavy-legged table. A tall, flat, wide piece—perhaps a headboard. And many mystery pieces, disguised both by the tarp and an assumed layering of items.

Puff swept back a corner of one of the tarps, revealing a beautiful wine-colored velvet settee. His smile was that of a confident salesman proclaiming, "I think you'll enjoy this little number."

The way my heart stirred at the sight of the settee, one would think I could see into the future, that I could see how much of my life would be lived out on that piece of furniture. The tears spent, the hours of waiting, the wrestling with God, with my own fearful and rebellious thoughts, with the residents of my home.

I mark that moment in the barn as *The Beginning*. But its genesis was much earlier, not in a cobweb-draped barn or stable, but in the love-draped heart of God.

Ivy—1951

"That's beautiful, Miss Anna."

Silence.

Ivy looked up from the steno pad in her lap. Anna Grissom's knobby hands rested on the faded cardigan draped across her chest, one hand over the other, as if placed just so by a mortician.

Whose hands rest naturally in that awkward arch?

"Miss Anna?"

"Did I doze off? I apologize. Where were we?"

Ivy's breaths resumed a rate closer to normal. "Would you like to take a break? Rest a bit?"

"Why don't you fill me in on life south of the thirty-eighth parallel."

"What?"

"I can hear news about the war from the gossips in the hall or when Bernard next door has his radio cranked so loud Tokyo can hear it. But that's not the real story. It's far more interesting to hear about it from the soldiers on the ground, from the men walking that sour soil and facing the enemy."

Ivy could bear Drew's circumstances if she kept the enemy out of focus, fuzzy, like when her dad's television antennae wasn't adjusted right and the picture looked snowy, indistinct. Or when the horizontal hold went crazy and the picture lost intensity. She shook her head, but the encroaching thoughts remained.

"No? You won't tell me?" Anna's face expressed mock shock.

Training her mind back to the question at hand, Ivy forced the edges of her mouth into what she hoped passed for a smile. "I don't know much news that you haven't heard, Anna. Drew—" Saying his name stopped her for a second. "Drew doesn't share many details about the war itself, the 'police action,' as the government calls it."

"Some say the fighting's been different since MacArthur lost his job."

Ivy buttoned her uniform bodice where it had popped open. "Wouldn't know about that."

"It won't be a long war, Ivy. Can't be."

"You've known a few."

"Too many. You have to dig through a lot of debris in war to find the good things worth hanging onto—the songs, the ingenuity, the heroes."

"This war has no songs."

Anna cocked her head. "I wonder why that is."

Ivy tapped her pencil against the notebook in her lap. "Nothing to sing about."

"Does your Drew talk about battles he's been in, acts of heroism he's witnessed? Or is he the hero everyone else is writing home about?" Anna's eyes twinkled.

"He doesn't share those things."

The older woman winked. "So he only writes about his love for you?"

Warmth crept up her neck and ears. "He talks about the men in his platoon."

"Has he made friends there?"

"Brothers. He's met brothers. He talks about how devoted they are. They look out for one another."

"That's comforting, isn't it? How many men in his platoon?"

Ivy smiled genuinely this time. "I know the answer to that one. Thirty-six. Twelve soldiers, foot soldiers, per squad. Three squads per platoon. Three platoons per company . . ."

"Such romantic letters he's writing!"

"I asked him. My dad isn't a veteran. Neither were my uncles. Flat feet deferment. So I didn't know much about the military before I met Drew."

Anna's eyes misted. "This is a hard way to learn, isn't it? With someone you love on the front lines?"

"With all the talk about a stalemate, he says there's still combat. The worst are the night raids, he says. No one in Korea sleeps with both eyes closed if they're close to the action."

"You're blessed he writes so often."

"Sometimes it's old news by the time it reaches me. And my letters to him arrive in clumps, he says. Nothing for weeks. Then three or four in one day."

The tears tumbled down Anna's cheeks now. "I can imagine him waiting for mail call and not hearing his name."

Don't, Anna. Don't add to my guilt. I'm an expert at applying it. "I'll say hi from you in my next letter to him."

"You haven't heard, then?"

"Heard what, Anna?"

"About my discharge?"

Ivy jumped up and did a quick search of the bedclothes. What kind of discharge was she talking about? The longer

Ivy worked here, the more sure she was that nursing duties couldn't feel as awkward and unpleasant to others as they did to her.

"My discharge!" Anna repeated, as if Ivy were hard of hearing. "I'm being discharged, of all things."

"You're not happy about that?"

Anna's gaze traveled the perimeter of the room at ceiling height then returned to hold Ivy's in its magnet-strong, pillow-soft grip. "Ivy, have you ever been homeless?"

Counting my senior year of high school, two years ago, and a few weeks from now, three times. "Why?"

"My insurance ran out. That's what they tell me. I don't remember having bucket insurance."

Oh. Kick-the-bucket insurance. It unnerved Ivy a little that she'd started thinking with Anna's logic. "Your insurance won't let you stay here, Anna?"

"I'm too far from kicking the bucket, apparently. Not well enough to live alone. Not sick enough to live here."

Who proposed that plan, I wonder?

"So—" she took a deep breath, "they're kicking me out soon. I hoped we'd have more time with the stories. Can't afford the luxury of a nap, my dear. Unless your baby needs one."

"Anna!" Ivy shot to her feet from the vinyl chair. Her pencil clattered to the tile floor. She flew to the doorway and glanced in both directions down the hall, pushing aside how the fast movements reignited the nausea she still fought some days. All quiet on the western front and on the eastern front. The only people in the hall lived in wheelchairs, in other eras, and too seldom in their own minds. If they'd heard the word *baby*—unlikely—and remembered it to repeat it—unlikely—and connected it to her, would they be believed? Unlike—

Ivy, you're no better than Jill. You judged those residents on the virtue of their memories, their hearing, and their mental function. The way others treated, or rather mistreated, Miss Anna.

She leaned her back against the door frame and drew in a few stabilizing breaths. Was Anna about to become homeless? Where would she go, at her age?

No relatives? Hard to believe.

If Ivy's father kept his promise, Ivy would be on the streets right beside her. Maybe they could share a bunk bed down at the mission. Wouldn't that be a sight? Ivy and Anna arguing over who got the top bunk. Right now, Ivy could still take her, but in a few months neither of the women would create a pretty picture climbing a ladder. How long had it been since Anna's scarred legs had moved more than to scoot her closer to the edge of her bed or chair? Why had Ivy never taken the time to ask about the scars or about Anna's life shortly before becoming a resident?

Because Anna cherished only one topic of conversation—a story sixty years old.

Anna—1890s

The furniture crowding the tack room found more than enough elbow room once transferred to the house. We had to burn several pieces, their "innards" shredded by families of overly busy, nest-building mice. A few other pieces were salvageable but in need of sanding or paint or wood glue. Puff's department. I was in charge of reupholstering, as money allowed, and cleaning, endless cleaning.

The sun and breeze cooperated, blowing away stale and musty odors. Puff tied a stiff rope between mature maples. On it we hung two aged oriental carpets we found rolled up in a corner of the tack room. I beat them tentatively at first, unsure that their faded threads would endure the punishment, then more fiercely as great clouds of dust and airborne grit escaped from deep within their weft and warp.

Even as the Lord spread His grace-gift over the worn and tattered parts of my life, once the carpets were stretched over the floor, careful positioning of the furniture hid most of their scars, most of the broken places.

If I didn't know about Puff's kinship with his Maker, I would have wondered from what deep, secret, sweetly flowing spring he drew his patience. Not once—not once!—did he object or grumble or even sigh when I asked for his help moving a chair or table across a room or an inch to the left.

"This where you want it?"

"I . . . I don't know, Puff. Maybe closer to the window."

"Good idea."

"No. No, that's not right either."

"Pick another spot, then."

"You're an angel, Puff, to be so tolerant."

"If I ain't working in here, I'm working out there in the hot sun. I ought to be grateful these things ain't found their proper place yet. My other chores'll wait for me. That's the thing about work. It won't disappear if you turn your back on it."

Eventually, I stopped worrying about not being able to pay him. He seemed to derive such intense pleasure from serving that I feared robbing him of the joy! And I determined to be like him, because he was so obviously like Jesus.

Unashamedly, and without making a dent in the supply, I saturated the house with wildflowers. Promising myself that I would one day give them homes in worthy vases, I used what-ever I could find—old food tins and broken-lipped glass jars salvaged from the dump area behind the barn, hollowed-out chunks of wood, dented buckets . . .

The flowers—humble as they were—lent dignity to their even more humble containers, and filled the house with the beauty my soul craved.

I felt like the queen of England herself the first night I had a real bed beneath me, although I doubt that Queen Victoria was ever so grateful for such a simple pleasure. I let my tired body sink luxuriously into the mattress as if it were filled with pure goose down rather than stiff straw. It would have taken the feathers of almost a dozen good-sized geese to stuff a tick. Puff had two geese now on the property. They were a start.

Loss and lack are efficient, skilled teachers. At their knee, we learn to appreciate the smallest favors, the briefest joys, the crudest provisions, the simplest blessings. The wildflowers. A bed underneath me. A breeze on wash day. Stillness at sunset. A table in the kitchen. A chair by the window. A dead chicken on my back stoop. A friend . . . one friend.

Ivy—1951

While Anna took the nap she said they couldn't afford, Ivy vowed to enter the apartment that night with a new appreciation for its doors, though scarred; its walls, though peeling; its floors, though scraped raw.

Moving to Clairmont had been easier than explaining to Ivy's friends in Westbrook that she was in a family way with no family. Moving in with her dad almost guaranteed the absence of new friends.

Could Ivy envision someone like Jill seated beside her on a red vinyl and chrome stool at Butler's Soda Fountain? In the next blue velveteen theater seat, watching Spencer Tracy and Elizabeth Taylor's *Father of the Bride* at the Grand? Challenging the waitress at the diner to earn her dime tip? Throwing Ivy a baby shower in the basement of the Methodist church?

Who was she kidding? People like Ivy didn't get baby showers. They got stares and whispers wrapped in yards of shame, tied with a *loose* bow. The divorced woman in one of the ground-floor apartments would soon have competition in the glares and stares department. Except Ivy would soon be gone from the building.

And Jill as a friend? No. Friends make you stronger, happier. Jill made her itch.

She'd found a friend in Drew. Where was he right now? Bouncing down a dirt road in the back of a jeep? Hiding in a ditch, motionless, while so-called stalemated North Korean boots stirred dust as they marched past where he lay? Dodging enemy fire? Burying a friend?

Her stomach roiled. She swallowed excess saliva and closed her eyes against the swirling striped wallpaper in Anna's congested room.

"Ivy?"

Short nap.

"Will you read back to me where I left off?"

She looked at the page. The crowded lines of writing blurred. "I need . . . to take . . . a break."

"Well, certainly, dear. You go on home. I've only gotten halfway around the world praying today. I have some catching up to do. Will you come back tomorrow?"

Ivy knew without Anna saying it that she was part of Anna's "halfway around the world." So was Drew. Back tomorrow? How could she not? Addled as she might seem to others, Anna was the closest thing Ivy had to a real friend.

Ornell Carrington waited for her in the worn chair he called his, although it came with the apartment. A six-inch-tall John Cameron Swayze delivered the news from the curved screen of the television her father owned. Or did it own him? Its gray screen of shadow images and static held him. They fascinated him. They would have caught Ivy's attention too, if they hadn't commanded so much of his.

A fraction of a glance from him told her he was hungry and not pleased that supper hadn't been on the table when he'd walked through the door an hour or more ago.

"I had extra work at the home tonight, Dad. Helping an old lady." The term caught in her teeth like a celery string. *Old lady*. What a crude way to describe Anna Grissom.

"They pay you more?"

Would he believe she didn't hear him? "I'll get supper started." She reached for the apron hanging on a hook near the archway between the kitchen and living room.

"Don't bother," he said, pushing himself out of his chair. He snapped the knob on the television to the left, silencing Swayze's commentary. "I'll eat at the bowling alley."

Bowling league. She'd forgotten what mattered more to him than the television.

"I can make something quick. Warm up last night's chicken à la King."

"It wasn't that good." He shot a one-eyed look her way, as if testing to see if he'd sufficiently shamed her for getting home late, for neglecting her responsibilities.

Nice shot, Dad. Strike. Right down the middle.

She woke when the apartment door scraped open. What time was it? The luminescent face of the Big Ben alarm clock on her nightstand let her know it was a little after ten. Her face and arms bore the imprint of a thousand chenille tufts. She'd fallen asleep in her slip, sprawled diagonally across her single bed, her stockingless ankles and feet dangling over the edge. She rolled over and stared through the shadows formed by the light that stole under the closed door of her bedroom.

The pace of her father's footsteps indicated he'd had a good night. Bettered his 240 average? One strike after another? Maybe he should eat at the bowl-a-drome more often.

"Ivy?"

She should be grateful he never came home drunk. Never. His voice through the door was no threat. "What, Dad?"

"You left a light on out here."

No threat at all. *I love you, too, Dad. Sleep well.*

She listened as he went through his bedtime routine. Brushing his teeth. Gargling. Flushing. Clicking his bedroom door shut. The slice of light under the door eclipsed by the darkness, Ivy reached to turn the toggle on the milk-glass lamp at her bedside. She pulled her sweat-soaked slip over her head. She'd have to rinse it and her stockings in the sink and pray the humidity didn't prevent them from drying within the next few hours, when she'd need them again.

The oscillating fan made an annoying clicking noise when it changed directions to turn left. But if she hung her under-garments in front of its weak breeze, maybe . . .

She draped the rinsed items over the back of a kitchen chair she'd carried into her bedroom. After two tries, she succeeded in positioning the fan to rotate far enough toward them to aid in their drying and yet catch her in its return trip to stir the summer humidity into tolerance. The cigar box inside the orange crate she used as a nightstand held a growing stack of

Drew's letters. But rather than read through them all, she left the box closed tonight, flipped her pillow to the cool side, pushed the chenille bedspread to the foot of her iron bed, and draped just the top sheet over her tired body.

A bubble rippled through her lower abdomen at the spot where she'd long felt a hard knot forming. Then another ripple. Was that it? Is that what movement felt like? It's the kind of thing an expectant mom should ask her mother, if her mother were still around.

—⁂—

Another day. Another round of routines and practicals. No room and no resident mattered as much to her as Anna.

"Anna?"

"Oh, don't worry. I didn't follow through with my threat."

"What threat?"

"I thought that's why you came in here so soon after that Jill person left."

Ivy opened the blinds and exposed Anna's view of the blank space where a pair of elms once stood. She used a tissue to wipe the windowsill of dead flies. "Want me to open the window, Miss Anna?"

"You wouldn't ask that if you knew what I did."

Ivy turned her full attention to the slight woman sitting on the edge of her bed, slippered feet swinging. "What did you do this time, Anna?"

Despite the heat, Anna tugged her nightgown down to cover her legs to the ankles, a habit Ivy couldn't understand. Who would care if her bare legs showed in this environment?

"I threatened to make a break for it."

"What?"

"To scram. Skedaddle. Skip town."

Ivy chuckled at the thought. At Anna's speed, a turtle on morphine could outdistance her.

"What brought that on?"

Anna pursed her lips and cocked her head to the side.

"Silly question," Ivy added. "What happened *today* to bring that to mind?"

Anna stopped swinging her legs. She rubbed her hands over her knees, as if her knees ached, which they probably did. "My heart isn't strong."

Ivy drew closer to the bed. "I know, Miss Anna."

"But my mind is full, not feeble."

"I know."

Anna smiled at that. "Want to join me?"

"Join you?"

"Dig a tunnel to freedom?"

Ivy clutched at the fabric of her uniform skirt. She inhaled until it hurt, then exhaled until her lungs emptied completely. A stuttered new breath gave her air enough to say, "There's no place I could run that would give me what I really need, Anna."

"One place. There's one place." Her gaze drifted toward the head of the bed. Or was it the bedside table? The Bible lying open on the table?

"You threatened to escape, Anna?"

"Not a wise move, huh?"

"Well . . ."

"I know. How far could I get before someone turned me in?"

Ivy lifted Anna's legs at the ankles, startled as she always was by the feel of the ruffled, ridged skin. She swung Anna's legs onto the bed and watched as the older woman relaxed them nearly flat against the sheet.

"You act as if I'm staying a while, Ivy."

Ivy's hands worked to position the pillow comfortably under Anna's neck. "You don't really want to escape this place, do you? What would I do for entertainment?"

"Come with me." Quicksilver eyes held longing and hope. "I have to leave anyway. I suppose it's pure bullheadedness that would make me want it to happen under my own terms. Ought to know better by now. Making my own choices never works as well as letting God do the choosing."

"Tell you what. If you take a good rest and let that heart medicine settle, I'll let you choose whether you want yesterday's lime JELL-O with pineapple in it or today's red JELL-O with pastel marshmallows. Oh, let's get crazy. You can have both, if you want. How's that for choices?"

Anna laid her twisted hand against Ivy's cheek. It felt cool, despite the heat in the room. Anna's eyes searched Ivy's for a long moment. "Is your life missing good choices, too, Miss Ivy?"

I had a few, a couple of months ago, that would have left me some options. Now I can't even choose a flavor of JELL-O. Today's Friday. Dad will expect ring bologna and fried potatoes. Creamed corn. Chocolate pudding. He probably thinks it's too much to hope for an obedient daughter who stops making his life miserable.

Missing all the good choices.

Ivy tucked Anna's hands and arms under the bleached top sheet. "Let's pretend we have all the choices in the world, but we'll save them all for lunch, okay?"

Anna closed her eyes. "I see more than you think I do, Ivy. I know more than what comes out of your mouth. And you may not believe it yet," she opened one eye to peer at her, "but both God and I care a lot more than you realize, too. And we're both telling you it's going to be okay. Not today. Not tomorrow. But someday."

The woman nestled into her Anna-shaped depression in the mattress and smiled as she faked the early stages of a nap.

9

Becky—2012

Gil stuffed a pair of socks into an empty space in his luggage and sealed it shut with an unsmooth *zip-zip-ziiiip* motion.

Why couldn't he for once zip it with one tug? Why couldn't he for once not leave?

He set his luggage on its wheeled feet and draped his jacket over the extended handle. Then he turned his full attention to Becky. First, his hand on her arm. Then, his upper body completely engulfed hers. "Are you going to call Monica?"

Becky pressed her pain deep into Gil's stronger-than-hers chest. She felt his arms grip tighter, holding her so firmly that she couldn't be sure her legs offered her any real support. She took a supersized breath, but the words she hoped would accompany her exhale died convulsively in her throat—a noisy, spastic convulsion.

"It doesn't have to be today," he said.

"I'll . . . call her."

"It won't be easy." Gil's open palm on her back, swirling like a too-light massage, spoke a wordless comfort she'd known for more than twenty years. It had sustained her, maybe Gil too, when Mark announced he'd enlisted, when he announced

100

he was being deployed, when news of a clumsy but deadly improvised explosive device shot through them like shrapnel.

That open palm on her back. It rarely changed anything, except her courage.

"Do you have to go?"

"No," he said. His thick fingers moved aside the bangs that would forever frustrate her with their obstinance. Too long before a scheduled haircut. Too short after. As Gil stroked them, they seemed the perfect length for once. "No, I don't have to go . . . unless we want to keep paying the mortgage. Not a big deal."

If his words had been any louder, any cheerier, any more casual, she would have felt justified giving him a swift kick in the shin. But they soothed with the brief comedic relief that brought her legs back under her.

"You have to go. And I'll be fine." Her vision misted over. "Poor Monica."

Gil kissed her forehead. "I'll be praying."

"Thanks."

He glanced at his watch. She knew what that meant.

"You really don't mind taking a cab to the airport this time?" She followed him out the bedroom door.

He paused midstep. "Becky, you don't need one more thing on your plate right now."

"And that's one of the reasons I love you." She tweaked his barely there love handle.

"Besides," he said, resuming his walk toward the front door, "you need to put on your detective hat and find out if Monica knows the fully story of what Brianne did before you call her."

What Brianne did.

Two rooms away, Jackson let out a lusty cry. Her grandson. Alive.

Poor Monica.

"Secrets kill, Lauren." Becky held Jackson on her hip while Lauren stuffed a graffitied notebook and an apple into her backpack, a toaster pastry dangling from her lips.

Lauren slung one backpack strap over her shoulder, partially chewed the bite of pastry, and mumbled, "It's none of our business."

"Honey, Monica's my dearest friend."

The cross-eyed look Lauren shot at her said, "Yeah, that's been obvious lately."

"We haven't talked much recently. But she needs to know I care."

Lauren drained her glass of orange juice, puckered at its tartness against the taste of powdered-sugar frosting, and tweaked Jackson's knee, as if that were enough of a parental good-bye for the day. "Maybe it's none of Monica's business either."

Becky shifted the baby onto her other hip. He smiled as though oblivious to the reason for the sudden tension in Becky's spine. "None of Monica's business?"

"Mom, I don't want to be late for school."

Since when?

"Can we talk about this later?" Lauren grabbed the doorknob.

The open kitchen door let in a chilled gust, a portend of frosty conversations.

"Promise me we will talk. If Monica knows, she has to be hurting like crazy. If she doesn't, she deserves to know, and *then* she'll be hurting like crazy."

Lauren's sigh pushed the icy gust deeper into the room. "She knows, okay? She's been, like, crying for days. Brianne's a mess. But that's what happens when good girls fall."

The door banged shut. It must have gotten caught by the wind.

—◦◦◦—

As she waited on Monica's stoop, Becky looked at the reflection of herself in the glass storm door that protected the fancy wooden double doors. If that wasn't a sight. She was the suburban version of a bag lady. A diaper bag slung over her left shoulder, knock-off purse on her right, left hand clamped onto the handle of a massive infant carrier, right hand gripping an insulated casserole holder.

Casserole. As if that would help anything. She took a quick look at the bushes on either side of the door. Were they dense enough to hide a marine-blue covered casserole dish? She bent to try. The diaper bag slipped off her shoulder and knocked into the infant seat, waking its occupant. Crouched into a chiropractor-unfriendly pretzel shape, Becky dropped the dish behind the arborvitae. Her purse slid down her arm and joined the casserole just as the door opened.

"Becky? What on earth?"

Forget the purse. Forget the wild rice shiitaki oriental bake. Becky stood upright and steadied both herself and the infant seat. "Can we come in?"

"With the baby?"

Yeah. Bringing the baby was a bit of a stinger, but I didn't have an option. "If it's okay."

"I don't know." Monica's eyes showed the puffiness of recent flooding. Becky wished she could offer her friend flood insurance, but moms can't qualify for coverage. She knew that for a fact.

"Just a few minutes?" Becky shifted the weight of the infant carrier. The baby giggled. *Oh, Jackson, not now.*

"How's he doing?" A flatline question.

"Fine. Monica, I'm here because I want to know how *you're* doing."

"I'm sure you do." She turned and entered the depths of the house but didn't close the interior door.

Becky propped open the storm door with the infant carrier, retrieved her purse, then followed the trail of grief-crumbs Monica left for her. She found Monica in the formal living room, perched stiffly on the edge of the middle couch cushion with her palms down on the adjoining cushions. The signal was clear: *if you choose to sit, it won't be near me.*

Settling into a nearby wing chair, Becky noted, "We picked out that couch together. At the Hanson's going-out-of-business sale."

"Well, that makes everything all better."

A shroud of silence dropped over them—not gauzy but suffocating, like felted wool, a weave so tight no light or breath could penetrate.

All of Becky's rehearsed words died for lack of air. She'd dropped her arsenal of hurt over Monica's judgmentalism the day Monica's pain surpassed her own. Not the most noble reason. It would take her a while to work that one out to a godly conclusion. But even her "Monica, I'm here for you. Monica, we'll get through this together. Monica, how can I help?" words couldn't overcome the stifling lack of oxygen in the room.

She didn't intend to wait for an apology. *God, thank You for healing that in me. Monica's my friend. She needs me. I lay it all down, all the cutting, galling pain of her betrayal, her air of superiority, her accusations about how my inadequate parenting skills led to Lauren's fall from grace…as if grace has no guard rails. Now help me find the words to—*

"How could she do such a hateful thing?" Monica's lips stretched across teeth that didn't separate as she spoke.

"I'm sure Brianne was just scared, Monica. Unsure of what to do."

"I'm talking about your Lauren."

Instinctively, Becky reached for the infant carrier on the floor at her feet. She set it rocking. "What does Lauren have to do with this?"

Monica snugged her arms around herself. The action didn't stop her body's trembling. "Her hateful lie."

"What lie?" Becky's skin rippled.

"You don't seriously believe that story about my Brianne, do you? Becky, think about it."

Jackson squirmed, arching his back against the protective restraints. *Quiet, Jackson. Please be quiet.* He voiced his little-boy impatience.

Monica turned her head away from the sound. "Don't you think that pretty much says it all?"

⸻

Becky had never been kicked out of anything, much less the living room of her best friend. Not a movie theater. Not art class (although if she'd been the teacher she might have found the excessive giggling exit-worthy). Not even the Bible study she attended with the purpose of tormenting the facilitator with unanswerable questions. That was BA—before her awakening, before she dared to entertain the idea that the Bible was truth and anything she didn't understand about it was her lack of insight, not God's.

The drive home from Monica's was as painful a trip as she'd ever experienced. If she could have explained . . .

Explained what? Her theory that Brianne was not the girl Monica thought she was? That Monica's worship-leading, halo-sporting, clean-as-the-immaculate-Mary daughter wasn't?

Explain that Monica and Becky should have been closer than ever, that they now shared a common—all too common—sister-pain. Broken dreams for their daughters. Regret they'd never outlive. Deceit clouding the birth of their first grandchildren.

Ah, and that's where their stories diverged. Becky's grandchild lived. Monica's was gone.

But how could Monica assume Lauren made up the story? How could she think such a thing? How could she transform from a lean-on-me friend to a get-out-of-my-house— What? Not an enemy. *Lord, please not an enemy.* A friend temporarily dislodged, disillusioned, despairing, disenfranchised.

I thought Lauren said Monica knew.

A bubble of bitterness burst in her stomach. *Monica, how could you doubt me? How could you leave me when I most needed you? And how could you lock me out when you most need me?*

Becky could well understand denial. Denial had planted itself firmly in her gut when Lauren's "flu bug" turned into something more. It had seen that first home pregnancy test as the newest model of turkey thermometer. It had whispered, "Not my daughter. Not my daughter. No, not my daughter."

Lauren didn't understand, and voiced as much with her persistent "What's the big deal?" Second-generation denial. Twenty-first-century morals notwithstanding, Lauren had bypassed not just the traditional or God-honoring method but also the most-likely-to-bring-lasting-joy method of becoming a mom.

Becky sensed a sigh originating near her navel and working its sad way through her chest and lungs before exiting through her nose. Jackson dozed in the backseat. They should have been home by now, but the eviction from Monica's had reset Becky's internal GPS—*recalculating*—and had made the normal route home seem wrong. Everything was wrong. She'd crawled over piles of her own hurt in order to make an effort to comfort

Monica. Not only had she failed at that, but the breach now gaped wider than ever. The conversation had derailed so badly, it had been like a smoking, runaway locomotive with no track underneath it at all and a years-long friendship dead ahead. Dead. Ahead.

The parking lot by the city pond was vacant. Russet-, flame-, and mushroom-colored leaves skated across the asphalt like the weak-ankled children who would soon skate across the pond's surface. Another few weeks.

Becky pulled up to the edge of the parking lot barrier, with the car facing the water. She left the motor running for Jackson's sake and leaned her forehead against the steering wheel. These are the very scenes God must have wanted to prevent—a child with a too young mother and no known father, a baby and his mom with iffy futures, a grandmother with a broken heart and a broken friendship because her judgmental friend refused to believe the truth.

Without lifting her head from the steering wheel, she reached for the console between the two front seats and popped it open. Her fingers pawed through the sunglasses, breath mints, and paper napkins until they rested on her pocket-sized Bible. She drew it out, closed the console with the back of her hand, and opened the Bible on her lap where she could see it without moving her throbbing head.

The print was so fine in a Bible that small. Her eyes worked hard to bring the words into focus.

The book of Lamentations. Perfect.

Chapter three, verse forty-nine.

"My eyes will flow unceasingly, without relief, until the LORD looks down from heaven and sees. What I see brings grief to my soul because of all the women of my city."

Whoa. Spooky-accurate.

Verse fifty-two. "Those who were my enemies without cause . . ."

Double whoa!

Her eyes drifted to the bottom of the column of print. "LORD, you have heard their insults, all their plots against me—what my enemies whisper and mutter against me all day long."

She stopped there. The text veered off into, "Pay them back what they deserve, LORD." She didn't want to go there. Lamentations—written before Jesus came to give grace new meaning. Grace that started with disappointment and ended with forgiveness. Grace that took what happened in the backseat of a guy's car—just guessing—and turned it into the cherished child whose soft breaths told her he might be a snorer someday. Grace that now cradled her uniformed son. Grace that gave the kind of second chances Lauren had been offered.

Tears fell on the pages. She leaned back and rested the back of her head against the stiff headrest.

Lauren.

Monica couldn't be right, could she? Lauren wouldn't have lied. What would be the purpose?

Except to throw a little of the gossip limelight off herself.

She wouldn't!

Becky's cell phone buzzed. Caller ID told her it was Gil. She answered with, "My eyes will flow unceasingly, without relief, until the LORD looks down from heaven and sees. What I see brings grief to my soul because of all the women of my city."

"Becky? Becky?"

"Yeah, it's me."

"I take it the talk with Monica didn't go well?"

Oh, Monica. One of us is a fool. And either way, it stinks.

The call lasted until Jackson woke from his nap . . . two minutes later. It was long enough for Gil to ask a couple of questions that would stick to her soul like fresh tar to a dress shoe. Did it bother her more that Lauren might have lied or that if she did it meant she was pregnant again? Did it bother her more that Monica didn't believe Brianne had ended an unplanned pregnancy or that Monica didn't believe Becky? Was she more upset that their friendship seemed over or that Brianne's relationship with her mother was in serious trouble?

The temporary answer was all of it. She hated all of it. Equally distressing. If she had time to think about it, she might answer differently. But the smell of a soiled diaper and the cry of a hungry child ended the call and all hope of thinking.

Gil had one closing question: *What now?*

How often had they asked themselves that in the past months?

What do we do now?

Best-case scenario—someone would come forward on her own with the truth.

Worst-case scenario—Becky would guess wrong about who was right and either alienate her daughter or her best friend forever.

As she pulled into the driveway, she stifled a curse word—a word she never would have thought of using before the current crisis. If Lauren were pregnant again, she'd once more stolen Becky's "right" to celebrate hearing the words "Mom, Dad, we're pregnant!"

There was supposed to be a video. Becky and Gil, side by side on the couch, would open a small box while a glowing Lauren and her ultraresponsible husband looked on, filming, elbowing each other and holding back goofy grins. In the box, a tiny pair of crocheted booties and a note in kid scrawl: *I'm so glad you're going to be my grandma and grandpa! Love, Little One.*

There was supposed to be a shout heard 'round the world, echoed in a flurry of phone calls to every extended family member, neighbor, church friend, college roommate, hair stylist . . .

"We're going to be grandparents!"

"We're so happy for you!"

There was supposed to be unbridled joy with no smudges.

And now, there was supposed to be a Jackson-sized undershirt with the words "I'm the big brother" announcing an addition to the family. A too-soon addition, granted, which would generate a few raised eyebrows and sympathy for the new mom's energies. But the congratulations would be encouraging. "Kids that close together will be great playmates for each other. Lauren and her husband will get through it. Why, I had a cousin whose kids were nine and a half months apart. That's right. And the second child was triplets!"

Becky would post ultrasound pictures on her social network profile page. Gil would carry laminated copies in his wallet and on his cell phone and show any flight attendant who asked, "Do you have grandchildren?" Not that he looked old enough for a question like that.

These days, Becky felt old enough for people to ask, "Do you have any *great*-grandchildren?" Concern ages people. She wondered if the youth-serum scientists knew about that component.

What's the big deal, Lauren? It changes everything. It saps most of the joy. *All* of the joy except the sweet warmth of a baby's hand against your cheek.

And now what?

Wisdom, don't fail me now!

She didn't need to know today. God promised there was nothing hidden that wouldn't be revealed. At one time, that made her squirm. Now she counted on it.

Lord, reveal the truth . . . in Your timing. I'm not the center of this, the reason for it, or the only one affected by it. I'm going to need Your hold-me-back grip to keep me from trying to fix this myself. It's unfixable, isn't it? No good answer. Someone's going to be hurt. Someone already is.

Lauren dropped her backpack and shoes just inside the back door and tossed her jacket over the shoulders of a kitchen chair. "Hey, pumpkin face. How are you doing?" She tickled Jackson's belly just above the waist belt of the bouncy chair in which he was safely strapped while Becky browned hamburger for spaghetti. She grabbed a ginger snap from the cookie jar. "Hey, Mom. How was your day?"

Becky stopped stirring the hamburger. Such a ridiculously normal conversation. A few glorious seconds of normal. "Tell me about yours, first."

Lauren poured herself a glass of milk, grabbed another cookie, and pulled her cell phone from her jeans pocket. "Sorry. I gotta take this text."

Perfectly normal.

"Purse Suede. Get it?"

"What?"

"Mom, think about it. Purse Suede. Say it fast. Sounds like *persuade*, doesn't it?"

"I guess." Becky kept one ear tuned to Lauren's exuberance while she listened for the oven timer to signal that the garlic bread was done. Judging by the divine smell of buttery garlic, the ding would come any time.

111

"It's perfect, Mom. I wouldn't even really have to finish this last year of high school."

Becky thumped her fist to the middle of her chest—two punches—to restart her heart.

"Superdramatic, Mom, but just listen, will you? If I can make enough of these Purse Suede purses—and you know I'm creative because art's, like, my best grade—I can work from home and sell them online, and then I could help out more with Jackson. And then, by maybe spring, I could get an apartment and you wouldn't have to watch him at all."

The bullet points of how many ways Lauren's career plan spelled disaster lined up neatly in Becky's mind.

What would grace say? Well? I'm waiting, Lord.

"I'd . . . I'd love to see a sample of a Purse Suede."

Lauren's eyes widened. "You would?"

"Do you have a selection, or . . . ?"

"Well, not yet. Some sketches. Do we have a sewing machine that will handle suede?"

Great plan, Lauren. If you charge a thousand dollars per purse, you may be able to "persuade" a landlord to rent an apartment to you, and you can buy groceries and diapers and get a car and pay taxes and buy insurance and pay for a website on which to sell your thousand-dollar purses that you will ship in boxes you can't afford with postage you can't afford to customers who've never heard of you and oh, Lord God!

"How can I help, Lauren?" That's not what she intended to say. It slipped out like a preemie.

"You really want to help?" The look on Lauren's face was softer than it had been in months. Becky saw remnants of the little girl Lauren had been moments before a bad decision made her a mother. Likely a *series* of bad decisions. None of the mistakes Becky had made over the years could be attributed to one single wrong move. They'd usually compounded to the point of awful, like a litter box—not bad the first day, but disgusting if left to build up.

"I want to see you succeed, Lauren. But graduating is not optional. We'll start there."

Lauren slumped. "But what if . . . ?"

No. No. You're not pregnant again. You can't be. You won't fight morning sickness during midterms. You won't deliver before you graduate. No.

"Mom, did you hear what I said?"

"Sorry. Spaced out for a minute."

"What if my grades don't cut it?"

The baby food jar of morning glory seeds sat on the kitchen counter on their way to basement storage. Becky picked it up and rotated it, watching the tiny brown nubbins move at her will, lifeless now but with the potential for next year's blossoms. She'd heard hope—a seed of hope—in Lauren's concern for her grades. "I'll help there, too. We'll get through this together."

10

Ivy—1951

We'll get through this together." The words tasted unfamiliar to her as she said them, and sounded at least as unfamiliar to her ears.

Your mom's gone, Ivy. We'll get through this together.

Oh, Ivy. No! Well, we'll get through this together.

Things aren't turning out as we'd hoped. But we'll get through this together.

What if she'd heard words like that from anyone who cared about her? Drew might have been the one person to say them, if she'd given him a chance. She hadn't because of the burden she was and the burden she carried.

"What's that, dear?" Anna scooted herself higher in the bed. Ivy hoped the action wasn't as painful as it appeared.

"We'll . . . we'll get through this together."

"My being evicted isn't your concern, Miss Ivy."

"You're not being evicted. Discharged is different."

Those pewter-gray eyes turned to slits. "How?"

Ivy straightened the blanket at the foot of Anna's bed. "You're right. Not much difference."

Anna's crooked smile hinted at a less-than-fully-satisfying victory.

"I assume your home was sold to pay for your time here?" How far did Ivy dare nose her way into Anna's private life? But who else did she have to talk to about it?

"Long ago. Not to pay for my rent in these deluxe accommodations." She winked. "But, yes. The house is gone." Pewter turned to glass. "The morning glories. Gone. Except for those in my treasure box." She turned to face out the window, as if suddenly mesmerized by the view.

Treasure box? Oh. Her mind. "Let's not give up hope." Another unfamiliar line bubbled up Ivy's throat and escaped through her open mouth. Where were these things coming from? Not give up hope? What had hope done for her lately?

Ivy drew her chair closer. "How much time do we have?"

Anna's silver head turned back to the scene at hand. She eyed Ivy's middle. "I'd guess four months. Am I right?"

The growth Ivy fought all workday to ignore fought all day to be noticed. So far, Anna's powers of observation proved stronger than Ivy's coworkers' and supervisor's. How long would that last? Her dad's two-month deadline crept closer every day. Ignoring postponed the inevitable but increased the cramp around Ivy's heart. The day was coming. Her sin, unlike others', had a visible component.

The narrow white belt on her uniform was notched in the hole closest to its tip. The fine-gauge sweaters she wore to hide her swollen breasts and swelling stomach seemed ridiculous in this weather, even to her. What was she expecting? That some magical solution would waltz in and make everything all better? That society would overlook her unmarried-but-bloated state? That the church people who tsked and gossiped about other girls "in trouble" or "in a family way" would suddenly develop a sense of charity toward her alone? She'd given them no reason to be sympathetic.

Somewhere in town, at this very moment, a couple bent over a booth to slurp a chocolate malt from matching straws without losing eye contact. Somewhere, a couple held hands in a car at a drive-in movie, spacing bites of popcorn with quick kisses. Somewhere, a married couple lay side by side on a davenport, watching *Truth or Consequences*, his hands gently resting on her tummy, waiting for the flutter that said, "Hi, Daddy."

Truth or consequences.

Ivy sat on a folding chair in an old folks' home, taking dictation from a woman old enough to be her great-grandmother, in a 10 x 10 room only temporarily hers, plotting how she could save the woman from homelessness when she herself had no place to call home.

Anna—1890s

It was inevitable I would face "the scoffers," a name the townspeople earned for themselves. Had I been the banker, I too would have most likely laughed at the cockeyed scheme of a woman such as me. Imagine the gall of walking right up to the man with the money and asking him to share some of it. For a good cause, mind you. A cause, though, he neither understood nor applauded.

The cause was similarly of little interest to the shopkeeper and his wife—Mr. and Mrs. Witherspoon. I will forever repent of the urge to call them the Witheredprunes. *Oh! There it is again! God, forgive me.*

Denied the courtesy, I stood inches away from customers who were granted credit for the goods they carried smugly to their homes. Aunt Phoebe had been one of them, a member of their own community. I was a newcomer, an outsider. A stranger with a suspect idea.

The rejection that cut deepest came from the church. Would the reaction have been different if I could have had a chance to ease my way into the people's favor? Could I have gained their support if Pastor Kinney hadn't invited me to stand and introduce myself to the congregation that first Sunday, if he hadn't asked me, "And what do you plan to do here in our fair community, Miss Morgan?"

If it had been a courtroom rather than a sanctuary, Pastor Kinney might have held them all in contempt for the murmuring that followed my answer. How he managed to carry on with his sermon, I don't recall. I spent the remainder of the hour wrestling with God.

Lord, what have You asked of me? I can't find even a whisper of encouragement among Your own people! Am I all alone? Have I misunderstood Your leading? Is there no one who will stand beside me?

As I prayed, before me rose a vision of a balding, ebony-skinned man with scars on his hands. There were two of us.

I squirmed through the service like a five-year-old with an impatient bladder. I removed my gloves, then pulled them on again, feeling too exposed. Even with my line of sight locked on the pulpit and the man behind it, or on the hymnal I was forced to share with the person next to me, I felt the searing heat of the stares and glares of those who refused to understand.

To escape as quickly as I wanted would have meant pushing rudely through the crowd. Resigned to being swept along with the current, I kept my eyes focused on the hem of my flannel skirt.

A soft hand rested on my shoulder. "Anna?"

Propriety forced me to reply. "Yes?"

"I'm Lydia Kinney. Pastor Kinney is my husband."

"A pleasure to meet you, Mrs. Kinney."

"We would love to hear more about your plans."

"You would?"

She and I both heard it. Someone or several someones near us clicked their tongues in disapproval. Lydia Kinney grasped my hand in her two. "Please consider joining us for Sunday dinner. There's always an extra chair and a spare plate."

The temptation to refuse was great. But the root of my refusal could not be excused. I was afraid. Of what? Of being laughed at, ridiculed, persecuted? Jesus had walked that road before me to take the sting out of it.

Like a beloved aunt, Lydia Kinney raised my chin—I'd dropped my gaze again—with one silken finger. I caught the gentlest whiff of lavender.

"I see in you, child, great pain and great love."

She called me *child*, as if I were not a grown woman not that much younger than herself.

"The pain needs healing, which I intend to help along. The love needs a little mothering, if I'm right. Someone to tend to it, like a seedling needs tending."

In that epiphany moment, I was unaware of the rest of the congregation filing past us. They faded off, as if trapped on a blurred tintype. Lydia and I stood alone in a pool of sweet-smelling sunlight. Was its source the window, the sky, or something even higher?

"Do you have plans?"

Did she mean plans for the future or plans for dinner? "I'm not sure." A watery answer, but fitting for both angles of the question.

"The table was set last evening with the thought that God would draw to it a special someone. I believe that's you, Miss Morgan."

Our circle of sunlight grew to hold another. Pastor Kinney joined us, draping his arm tenderly around Lydia's shoulder.

"Has she agreed?" he asked his wife, smiling in my direction.

I wondered when they had spoken to each other about me, when they had communicated about the dinner invitation. To my knowledge, no words had passed between them since the service ended. It seemed as if they spoke a wide vocabulary with their eyes, and that their hearts pulsed as one. The thought was precious but created within me a longing just shy of physical pain.

Did they realize how dust-dry was my well of courage? Did they know what it would cost me to share a meal with them and relate the story of my heart's journey? Judging by their innocent invitation and the simple warmth of their smiles, they did not.

It was all I could do not to attack the succulent roast beef like a hungry dog. The browned potatoes, the glazed carrots, the thick slices of dark bread, and the sugary pink applesauce Lydia served in pink glass sauce dishes—if I'd allowed myself the rein, I would have groaned with satisfaction after each mouthful. But I'd been taught better than that. Small bites, long savored. And oh, I did!

We took our coffee and lemon cake in the parlor, where the conversation deepened from the shallow pool where we'd waded during the meal.

"What resources do you have, Anna . . . other than the house?"

Setting my dessert fork on the white china plate in my lap, I dabbed at my mouth with a napkin, delaying my answer a few desperate moments.

119

"None. I have none."

The look that passed between my hosts was unreadable. Pity? Concern? As shepherd of this local flock, was Pastor Kinney obliged to see that the authorities locked crazy people away, out of harm's reach?

Lydia stood to her feet and exited the room. I listened for the creak or thump of a door, which would tell me she had been assigned to enlist the sheriff's or doctor's help in dealing with the deranged person nibbling on lemon cake in their parlor. But she returned and rejoined her husband on the sofa, smiling and clutching an envelope.

Pastor Kinney's countenance and voice took on a light but rich quality—like good meringue. "Has this always been your dream?"

I almost laughed aloud. My dream? Far from it! If I had my way, I would be tidying a little cottage following a meal such as this one. I'd be telling my little ones not to run indoors and fixing a second cup of coffee for a devoted husband who adored me and wasn't ashamed to say so. I'd spend my days tending the house and the garden and the children—five or six of them—and making quilts and chatting with friends over tea and staying in the shadows.

"What God is asking of me is a complete and utter surrender of my own ideas. I still find myself battling Him about it."

Pastor and Mrs. Kinney produced mirror smiles.

The couple rose from their positions and knelt on either side of me on the floral carpet. Lydia took the plate from my lap and set it on the table near my chair. They each took one of my hands in theirs and began to pray—Pastor Kinney giving voice to the words, Mrs. Kinney agreeing with groans too deep for words.

I was being commissioned. Sent. Lydia's tears dotted the fabric of my skirt as they prayed. Through my own tears, I viewed the dark, wet spots on the gray flannel as evidence of love, which I hoped would never evaporate.

Pastor Kinney's grip on my hand was crushing; my fingers grew numb as his prayers grew more intense. I rose above the earth, above the obstacles, above the scoffers, above the lacks too numerous to mention, above the ridiculousness of the notion that a woman of my stature and limited education could carry off such a project.

Like a paralyzed man borne on a straw mat, I was placed before the Healer, the Provider, by my hours-old friends. Their faith moved heaven. My own was swept along in the flood tide, unable to resist. Able only to release my fears and questions, I watched them float away as if stripped from my weak hands.

With the final amen offered, my hands were freed, the blood rushing back into my grateful fingers, accompanied by a startling new fearlessness that flooded into my soul.

Before Lydia allowed her husband to help her to her feet, she pressed the envelope into my hands. "Seed money," she said.

They resettled on the sofa, brushing life back into their clothes . . . and knees. I fought my way through a jungle of unsuitable words, searching for something appropriate to say. Nothing surfaced.

"We will do all we can to help you, Anna." Pastor Kinney's words resounded as an echo of Puff's. Though more polished, they were no less sincere or welcome.

With my left hand, I held the envelope. With the index finger of my right, I traced a circle around Lydia's teardrops on my skirt, still searching for a fitting response. "I don't know what to say."

"We share your heart's burden, Anna. In fact, we have long wondered if we should abandon the pulpit ministry to do such a work as yours."

Such a work as mine?

Lydia picked up where her husband left off. "We couldn't understand why we were hampered. Now we know. We were not to take on the project ourselves but to assist you. And we will, to the best of our ability."

The money in the envelope smelled of sacrifice. I imagined its fragrance tickled God's nostrils and made Him sigh with satisfaction. As hesitant as I might naturally have been to take money from them, I didn't dare snuff the incense of their love.

"Seed money," Lydia repeated, watching me fiddle with the envelope. "To help you get started."

"It's not much," Pastor Kinney added, "but we will pray that it will grow like sourdough mix when it is stirred and fed, bursting out of the bowl until you have no choice but to give some away."

Relaxing a little more into the joy of the moment, I wondered how often this learned, suited man had stirred down sourdough. And I wondered when and how the Kinneys had been told to set aside money for a stranger whom they would entertain in their home. They didn't profess to read minds but asked questions and made comments that would have fed evidence, if I believed in such a thing.

We talked through another pot of coffee. The afternoon quickly advanced. When they offered to take me home in their buggy, I reluctantly but appreciatively agreed. They both accompanied me on the four-mile journey. It felt only natural to invite them into the house and let them in on my dreams as we walked from room to room . . . as we *prayed* through each room.

When they finally left, pressed for time by the setting sun nipping at their heels, I noted that I was both drained and refreshed—an odd combination, but as real as the floorboards under my feet. I found myself wishing Puff lived on the "propity" so I wouldn't have to wait to share the story with him.

And so another thought blossomed, a crocus of thought pushing its way through snow.

11

Anna—1890s

With the Pastor and Lydia Kinney's blessing, the seed money was used to buy linens and other household goods and to stock the pantry. On Puff's advice, I bought a milk cow and a sorry-looking but dependable horse to pull the wagon that had been sitting idle in a corner of the barn.

Also with Pastor and Lydia Kinney's blessing, I invited Puff to live in the tack room in the barn. How could I offer him such crude accommodations? I would have been quite comfortable having him in one of the upstairs rooms in the house. But propriety wouldn't allow such a thing. I was no doubt still inviting wagging tongues by having him on the premises at all. But it was obvious God had His hand on that man and had laid His plan on Puff's heart. Who was I to argue, no matter what it cost me in gossip?

With a little fixing up, the tack room was "near close to cozy," as Puff described it. He had a comfortable bed, a small table and two straight-backed chairs, a rocker for "resting his bones," a bookcase of rough wood for his surprisingly large collection of books, and a woodstove small enough not to overwhelm the room with its size or its heat.

Puff cut a hole in the outside wall for a larger window, which we scavenged from a pile of discards in back of the barn. The additional light in the room, coupled with the rag rugs I made for the floor and the patchwork quilt Puff brought from his old home, warmed it up.

He wouldn't let me go with him on his trips back and forth from his old place. I never did see it. He seemed so tickled with the tack room that I was tempted to ask if he'd had a roof and walls where he'd lived before.

As a bonus in the deal, Puff's chickens came to live with us. And the pig we called Ham. I guess in choosing that name we wanted to remind ourselves that he wasn't a pet but the promise of meat for the smokehouse and larder. I had other names for the animal. *Trouble. Stinky. Bother. Mudpuddle.* Puff now reminded me to call him Ham.

The comfortableness of our unspoken but heaven-assigned duties each day made for pleasant living. Puff cared for the animals, although I was happy to gather the eggs. He kept busy enough for three people, making repairs on the house, the outbuildings, and the fences. I clanged a rusty old cowbell hanging off the back stoop to call Puff to breakfast and dinner. He most often ate light for supper, taking leftovers or a bowl of soup to his room. I suspect he read a lot in the evenings. Times when I needed him for something, I always found him in his rocker with a book in his lap or resting on his chest.

It warmed me to my toes to see his big black Bible always sitting out on his table. Never sitting in exactly the same place or open to the same page, it was used enough to get ragged around the edges. I purposed to see to it that mine grew ragged from use, too.

Some might question, but I knew it was a miracle that Puff's hens started producing more eggs than we could manage. It was as if they wanted to contribute somehow. Once a week, I had enough eggs to take to town to trade for flour or sugar or chicken feed at the mercantile. I knew, of course, that the "seed money" wouldn't last forever, and that we couldn't sustain ourselves for long on egg money. But it was a start.

When I had extra cash, I spent it on paint and wallpaper for the upstairs bedrooms. They all needed it. Elbow grease wasn't enough to perk them up without paint. I chose colors that raised the store clerk's eyebrows, but I figured she wouldn't have to sleep with it, so what did it matter?

"I'd recommend basic white," Mrs. Witherspoon offered. "It's clean. Versatile."

And institutional, I said under my breath while reaching for the topaz and persimmon.

I painted one room deep lavender, in honor of Lydia Kinney. Not in the least to pacify Edna Witherspoon, I painted the woodwork white, pure-as-the-driven-snow, though-your-sins-be-as-scarlet white. I was finishing work on a quilt with appliquéd violets when, of all people, Lydia drove into the yard.

The quilt frame Puff had built for me, bless his heart, was set up in one of the front parlors, the one I considered an office of sorts, because the light was so good in there, and because it allowed me to leave the project to tend other duties without having to climb the stairs so often. So I had a clear view when Lydia's buggy pulled up in front of the house. I was at the door before she reached the bottom step.

"What a delightful surprise!"

"I hope I haven't come at an inconvenient time."

"Not at all. You're always welcome, Lydia." She balked when I called her Mrs. Kinney. "I'll make us some tea."

I recognized humbly that it was because of the gift she and her husband had given me that I was able to offer my guest tea. Somehow the thought framed the moment in holiness.

Lydia walked with me through the house to the kitchen and sat at my table while I fussed at the stove. I was grateful, so grateful, to have biscuits left from breakfast and fresh wild strawberry jam. Another divine provision. The ditches along the road were a jewelry case of wild strawberries waiting for an appreciative hand to pick them.

I stirred a dollop of honey into my tea. Lydia preferred sugar. Her spoon clinked delicately around her cup as she stirred and stirred and stirred and stirred, her gaze lost in the caramel-colored liquid.

At long last, she laid her spoon aside, clasped her hands in her lap, and let out her breath in what appeared to be a courage-summoning sigh.

"Anna, how near are you to being ready?"

"Ready?"

"For a . . . houseguest."

"Oh."

"There's a young woman . . . a girl, really . . . who is in need. The niece of a friend of ours from our old church in Selena. A darling girl who thought she was in love."

"And her family?"

"They . . . cannot . . . cope. They are not open to her staying with them."

"How old is she?"

"Fifteen."

"Oh, my."

"I shared your story with my friend after she wrote to me of her family's struggle, trusting you would approve."

"Of course. Is she showing?"

"She will be soon."

"Then I'm ready."

She arrived in the middle of the night, like a fugitive cloaked in shadows. Her knock at the door was timid, uncertain. But it pierced my sleep and awakened every sense in me. With my robe wrapped tightly around myself, I slipped down the stairs from the servants' quarters I now occupied, lit the lone lamp in the entry, and held it high as I opened the door to her.

The girl, named Elizabeth, lifted her eyes only long enough to receive my nod inviting her in. She turned, but the couple in the moonlit wagon at the far end of the drive did not nod or wave to her or blow kisses or in any way acknowledge she was their child. Once they saw that the door was opened to her, they tapped the reins on the horse's haunches and left the premises.

It was a scene revisited many times through the years. One to which I would never grow accustomed. One that would haunt my sleep and feed my grief and keep me willing to open my door in the middle of the night.

My welcome routine changed later to accommodate record-keeping and house rules and a covenant agreement. But that first night with my first girl was filled with awkwardness and uncertainty. As uncomfortable as she must have felt in a new environment, so did I in my new role. Looking back, I only did one thing right, to speak of. I loved her.

"Come on in, dear. Don't be afraid. You're welcome here."

I took the small satchel from her hands and set it on the floor at our feet. Then I wrapped my arms around her and drew her into my embrace. The way she cried into my shoulder, I wondered if she had been allowed to cry at all to that point. Her sobs shook us both. Down to our toes.

On second thought, I did two things right. I cried, too. I cried for the circumstances that brought her to my door. I cried for the dreams immature passion had shattered. I cried for the losses she was experiencing. I cried for the estrangement of her family. I cried for the ridicule she would bear, for the labyrinth of trials that lay ahead for her, and for the babe she carried in her womb.

How had Puff heard us? It was quite some distance from the front entry clear through the house, across the yard, through the barn to the tack room. And with Puff's self-confessed locomotive-like snoring, too! But there he was, lighting more lamps. Carrying the satchel upstairs to the lavender room. Turning back the covers. Lighting a chill-chasing fire in the white-washed brick fireplace while we women stood in a puddle of tears. He laid one big, shudder-stopping hand on our shoulders for just a moment, then disappeared back out into the night. How could he not be an angel? Who else would have known we needed him?

Sleep came, only because I'd exhausted myself with concern. When I checked on Elizabeth in the morning, I was grateful to see that she, too, slept. The violet quilt was tucked tightly under her chin. Her burnt-sugar-colored hair spilled recklessly over the pillow. Even in sleep, fear and pain and despair were written across her milky complexion.

I closed the door soundlessly and did what I would so often do. Kneeling outside her door, I prayed with stomach-twisting fervency for her and her child.

It was two full days before she spoke more than one-word answers to my questions.

"Are you comfortable in your room?"

"Yes."

"Do you need anything?"

"No."

"Is there any way I can help you get settled? Launder your clothes?"

"No. Thank you."

On the third day, she began to ask questions.

"Why are you doing this?"

"Doing what?"

"Why did you take me in? Even my family can't stand to lay eyes on me. Are they paying you? Is that it? Are they paying you to take me off their hands, to get rid of their 'problem'?"

"No, Elizabeth. They're not paying me. I'm not asking for money."

"Then what?"

Good question. What was I doing? And why? And did I have any hope of succeeding? Were my motives as pure as I wanted them to be? How could I explain what even I didn't fully understand?

"Elizabeth, all I can tell you is that God said I should open my home and my arms and my heart to you."

"Why would He do that? He knows what I am."

"What are you?"

"A whore!"

"Elizabeth!"

"That's what my daddy calls me now."

House rules about language and expressions of anger flashed through my brain faster than I could process them. "Elizabeth, please refrain from using that kind of language."

"But that's the kind of person I am."

"Are you?"

"That's what people think."

"*Are* you?"

She chewed her lower lip, looked toward the ceiling of sky, and studied it for a few moments. "No."

"What happened? Do you want to tell me? It might help."

She and I were walking the lane, partly for the fresh air and partly for the introduction of conversations such as this. At the bridge over the creek, we stopped to lean over the rail and watch the endlessly burbling water.

Elizabeth brushed a stray leaf off the railing. It floated slowly to its new resting place on the water's surface, then twirled in the eddy until a flash of current picked it up and carried it far downstream.

"It wasn't like we weren't in love."

As if that lessened the impact of the changes happening in her body . . . and in her life.

"Tell me about him." I kept my voice even.

"He's older. Eighteen."

Oh, child!

"We would have gotten married last summer if my parents would have let us. They insisted he have a job first. But it's not always that easy! Nobody was hiring. And he doesn't have much for skills yet because he sometimes is hard on himself and then he gives up trying. But we could have made it. I can work . . . or at least I could have."

For the first of what I believed would be many, many times, I chained my tongue to the roof of my mouth and forced my heart to listen when it wanted to talk.

"So we started sneaking off," she said. "If my parents hadn't been so stubborn—!"

Elizabeth broke off her sentence and cringed, revealing her conscience. She knew it was foolishness to look anywhere but to her own actions for blame.

"Where is he now?"

"My folks run him off."

"They did? Does he know about the baby?"

"I told him."

"How did he react?"

"He was mad at first. I can understand that."

You can?

"And then he got real quiet." Elizabeth pressed her lips into a trembling line, then sighed. "I never saw him after that night.

I'm sure my dad told him not to show his sorry head around there anymore. That must be it. Or he would have come for me."

Lord, my head is reeling with the weight of what these girls will need from me! How can I help them bring healthy babies into this world and make life-changing decisions and teach them about men and prepare them for an uncertain future and train them to care for themselves and—

"Miss Morgan?"

"Yes?"

"Ain't you gonna say something? Yell at me? Tell me how disappointed you are and that you wonder if my brains all leaked out?"

"You've probably heard that enough already, haven't you?"

"Yes'm."

We walked a few more paces, kicking at bits of rock and picking flowers that caught our interest. "Tell me what you know about God, Elizabeth."

Her beautiful hazel eyes clouded over. She snapped petals off a blossom, then answered. "He's the most disappointed with me of all. I done wrong. And I don't blame Him for turning me away."

"Where did you get the idea that God was turning His back on you?"

She didn't answer, but covered her face with her hands.

"Elizabeth, look at me. You, my dear, are about to step into a world of discovery about the Lord God. You are going to learn about His grace and mercy. You're going to learn how different His love is from the kinds we see around us sometimes. You're going to be swept along in His grace like that leaf carried downstream. And I'll consider it a privilege if you'll let me accompany you while it happens."

I didn't sleep much at all that night. My mind churned with ideas that wouldn't leave me alone. How could I have thought giving these girls a safe place to live would be enough? There was so much more. So much.

Their hurts needed tending. Their sins needed forgiveness. They would need education and training and encouragement. They would need skills—both parenting skills and job skills. Some, if not most, would need to support themselves after they left me.

They needed doctoring! I hadn't even thought of that yet. I began to pray that night for a kindhearted doctor who would give his time to young girls with babies in their bellies and nothing with which to pay him. A doctor who didn't mind waiting for payment until he reached heaven's gates.

Close to dawn it struck me that I was making plans as if certain there would be more girls than Elizabeth. I had no guarantees of that. Only a gnawing sense that I believed had been planted in my heart by the hand of a God who cared.

12

Ivy—1951

You still believe that, Anna?" Ivy doodled in the corner of the notebook paper. "That God cares about . . . about people like Elizabeth?"

"More than ever."

"Whether they deserve it or not?"

"That's what's so compelling—we don't deserve it. Oh, honey, God wouldn't have any friends at all if they were limited to only the deserving."

⸺⸻⸺

"Only the deserving." The phrase formed a rhythm for Ivy's footsteps as she walked the hall toward her supervisor's office. It changed the closer she drew to the blond wood door. "Oh, the undeserving. Oh, the undeserving."

Jill must have snitched. She must have guessed the truth—someone had to be the first—and felt it her obligation to report to their supervisor that Ivy was pregnant and unmarried.

Mrs. Philemon—*Mrs.*—beckoned her to the aqua plastic chair across from her own. "Are the rumors true, Ivy?"

Truth or consequences. Truth *and* consequences.

"The rumors about . . . ?"

"Do I need to spell it out, *Miss* Carrington?"

"No, ma'am. I mean, yes, ma'am. What you've heard is true." Ivy's throat clenched then unclenched. The truth burned on the way out but left a strange, Alfred Hitchcock-like calm in the middle of chaos. She'd told the truth, for once.

"That's unfortunate."

Ivy watched the peroxide bouffant bounce as the woman's ballpoint pen tapped divots into the desk blotter.

"Your application lists your status as married, Ivy, an application you signed as true to the best of your knowledge."

The envelope in the pocket of Ivy's uniform crinkled as she uncrossed her legs. Drew. "Wishful thinking, Mrs. Philemon."

"You're engaged, then?"

"No."

Peggy Philemon leaned across her desk and dripped condemnation as she whispered, "Divorced?"

"Goodness, no!" What did she think Ivy was, a— Oh. *God, forgive me.*

"You admit that you lied on your application, Ivy?"

"Yes, ma'am." The room shrank. Ivy smelled her own perspiration and felt it puddling in the center of her bra.

"Even if there weren't the matter of your . . . indiscretion . . ." —she glanced at Ivy's stomach and let the word hover— "falsifying your application is automatic grounds for dismissal."

No emotion linked the woman's words. None, it seemed. Peggy "the Perfect" Philemon waited. For what? An explanation that would turn a lie into a simple misunderstanding? A blink that would erase the last several months and allow Ivy to make wiser choices and avoid moments like this?

Dismissal.

Discharge.

Disgrace.

How would she tell her father? How could she ever tell Drew?

"You have two weeks, Ivy. I should send you packing immediately. But I'm not heartless." The word echoed unnaturally in the small room. "Besides, we can't afford to be any more shorthanded than we already are. Two weeks. I hope you have some savings."

Ivy peeled herself out of the sticky plastic chair and staggered down the concrete and linoleum hall to Anna's room to begin the trail of her good-byes.

"Two weeks?" Anna smiled. "We have time, then."

"For what?"

"Imagine what God can do with two weeks if He could make the world and everything in it in half that time!"

"Anna, it's hopeless."

"When you're done with your shift today, you be sure and stop in, okay? My story's getting to a part you need to hear."

If she survived her shift, if she didn't split before the day was over, if she didn't throw her name badge at her locker—or at Jill—and vow never to set foot in the place again, Ivy didn't intend to hang around after hours for another installment of Anna's drama. It was doing funny things to her heart.

"We'll see." A noncommittal response appropriate for dealing with children and the elderly.

But at the end of the day—a miserable, uncomfortable day—going to the apartment held less appeal than spending time with someone who cared. So she pulled up a chair, flipped open the stenographer's pad, and laid her sharpened pencil to the paper just as Anna began to reminisce.

Anna—1890s

My Elizabeth was as round as a Rome Beauty by the time apple harvest began. Her back bothered her, I knew, so Puff and I tried to give her chores that would keep her busy without taxing her unbalanced body.

She sat at a battered old table in the backyard, coring and slicing apples for drying from the bushels Puff laid at our feet.

I helped in the orchard as much as I could and still keep up with running the house and Elizabeth's lessons. Some days we hardly spoke over supper, we were so tired.

"Tired's got my tongue," Puff was fond of explaining.

Delighted as a Spanish explorer with a new find to report, Puff unearthed a root cellar near the springhouse. Its entrance once hidden by a tangle of blackberry bushes, the root cellar's cool interior now boasted crates of our beautiful red and yellow apples . . . far more than we would need to sustain us through the winter. It pleased me to think about hauling a crate of apples to the mercantile midwinter to trade for necessities. God was providing as only He could . . . although I noted that He got considerable help from Puff.

Puff taught us how to string dried apples on cotton thread and store them in the attic for safekeeping. He advised that I hang a sheet a few inches above the garlands of apples to keep dust or mice from settling on them.

Apple perfume scented our work clothes. Our hands were stained rust-brown from apple acid, and stayed that way until wash day, when hours of scrubbing clothes in hot soapy water bleached our hands clean.

Elizabeth's lessons stuttered at first. I jumped from one thought to another, one discipline to another. One minute we talked about diaper care, the next about grammar, the next about baking bread, the next about home remedies for childhood ailments and how to watch for infection, the next about understanding men . . . as if I knew a lot on that subject. I marveled that Elizabeth was so patient with me.

She didn't seem to mind that we were learning as we went along.

Sweet-tempered, Elizabeth was easy to love. She soaked up Scripture as if she'd been living in a desert. As her baby grew within, so did her understanding of grace. It registered on her face and in the timbre of her voice.

But she was just a child. We had to discuss her plans for the future.

"Elizabeth, as much as I would like to, I cannot let you stay here forever."

"I know."

"You and your baby will have to find a place of your own, lives of your own, not long after he or she is born."

"I know."

"Or . . ."

"Or what?"

"Or you will have to decide if you should let the child be raised by another family."

Silence stretched halfway to town. I knew she had considered the thought.

"My wanting this baby isn't enough, is it?"

I weighed my reply. "It is very hard for me to counsel you on this issue. My heart has a tendency to run ahead of wisdom at times. But we have to think carefully about this. Talk to Pastor and Mrs. Kinney . . . and to Dr. Noel. But ultimately you need to follow what God tells you to do."

"He isn't being very clear about it."

"He will be."

She laced her fingers under the roundness of her belly. "I'm not sure my parents will take me back . . . or if I want to go."

"I understand."

"I could go live with my Aunt Rhoda, I think. But she's too old to have me and a baby underfoot. I couldn't ask that of her."

"A lot to be considered in the next couple of months."

But it wasn't months. It was days. And it was almost more than I could bear.

Elizabeth's screams woke me from a deep cavern of sleep. I clawed my way to the surface and found her standing doubled over in the hall, holding her swollen belly with both hands while a river of blood and water flowed down her legs and between the floorboards.

I ran to the end of the hall that faced the backyard, banged the window open, and yelled at the top of my lungs for Puff to come help us.

Elizabeth fell into my arms when I reached her. I stroked her fear-matted hair and held her tight while we waited for Puff to help me get her into bed. It wasn't more than a minute before his strong arms were carrying us both, it seemed, and the girl was laid onto the already blood-soaked sheets.

I did everything I knew to stop the flow, including a dose of ergot, while Puff went for the doctor. The look that passed between us as Puff left on his mission acknowledged that, devoted as they were, our efforts would not be enough. But we had to try.

I was holding the stillborn child in my arms when Puff and Dr. Noel arrived. A tiny boy-child. Perfect and beautiful, but too small to survive.

As was his mother. Perfect and beautiful, but too weak to survive.

⊶∞⊷

I could have understood Elizabeth's parents' anger. It was their indifference I couldn't fathom. They came for her body, but left the baby with me. Not a word spoken. Not one word. They simply drove off with the broken body of their broken daughter.

Puff and Dr. Noel and Pastor and Mrs. Kinney and I stood in a circle of grief over a miniature grave on a windswept hill behind the orchard. We cried for our loss. And we cried, too, knowing this would probably not be the last time we gathered this way.

If I could go on, that is. If I could let myself love and lose so deeply again. The debate would not let me rest. It screamed its arguments—for and against—commandeering my thought-life.

Until little Robert Matthias—Elizabeth's predetermined choice of names—was buried, I'd not allowed myself to seriously consider whether I could go on. But the last shovelful of dirt had not been pressed into place on the achingly small mound before the doubts began to torment me.

Who would now entrust their daughter into my care? Would I trust myself? Was there more I could have done? What was I thinking to tackle such an enormous project? How presumptuous of me to think I could care for other people's children and their children!

I slept more than I should have in the days that followed. I woke late, troubling Puff, I'm sure. He often fixed and ate his own breakfast before I roused. I had to be reminded to eat.

My chores were done without thinking, which caused some consternation. Puff followed behind me, cleaning up my messes and mistakes, catching potential disasters before they happened, closing the ash door on the woodstove before I set the house ablaze, and latching the chicken-yard gate before our eggs and suppers escaped to the woods.

Pastor and Mrs. Kinney's loving words floated high above my head. I needed them deep in my heart, but couldn't seem to retrieve them from where they hovered. Their kite strings were just beyond my reach.

Puff tiptoed around me. Offering few words, but always a steady presence.

I visited the tiny grave too often, I imagine. It was probably not wise of me, but I needed the reminder that there was a logical reason for my pain.

It was the snow that taught me that I could—and would— go on.

For some unearthly reason, the first snowfall that year was not a light dusting but bucketsful that lay like downy quilts over all of nature's defects. Wrapped in my wool coat and a scarf so long it threatened to trip me, I trudged through the wet white to the top of the windswept hill.

The little mound was flat. It lay even with the top of the snow. I knew the grave was still there, under the white, but it was covered as with a thick, healing ointment.

After many snows, spring would come. Wildflowers would find the mound a most accommodating home. And life would go on.

By God's grace, so would I.

13

Becky—2012

The first snow of the season made Becky squint through the windshield as she drove Lauren and Jackson to school. Jackson was Lauren's show-and-tell. Not really, but Becky entertained the thought for a twisted, immature moment.

Career Day. The *guidance*—and she used that term loosely—counselor thought it would be a good idea to illustrate the concept that motherhood is a career, which it is, by having one of the teen moms bring her child to school. Just the fact that the counselor had to choose *one* of the teen moms was grief enough, in Becky's book. Was it on *Good Morning America* where she'd heard that 46 percent of current fourteen-year-old girls worldwide will have a child out of wedlock? Wait. Was that worldwide or just in the United States?

She remembered hearing her sister Eva, the birthing center nurse, moaning over the changes in hospital dynamics since she'd started her nursing career. Husband-and-wife team was no longer a given. Married, no longer assumed. That the male birthing coach was even the father of the child emerging from the laboring woman, not a given. It changed charting, birth certificates, language, and—according to Becky's compassionate sister—the atmosphere. How could it not?

"Almost there, people." She heard no response from the drowsy pair in the backseat as she signaled her intent to swing into the drop-off lane.

With Jackson all cute and adorable, and Lauren relieved of most motherhood responsibilities by the one—currently playing chauffeur—who waffled between enabling and hyper-enabling, Becky wasn't sure the Full-Time Parenting booth at Career Day would have its desired effect.

But it offered her a day to herself for the first time in months.

———

Becky considered calling Monica and inviting her to lunch at their favorite café downtown. No agenda. Just normalcy for a change. But how would she convince Monica that she wasn't either looking for or preparing an apology? They'd left the unclaimed pregnancy test in limbo while they waited for somebody—*please, somebody*—to tell the truth. Or for the passing of time, like the changing seasons, to make the truth obvious.

Lauren's PMS was as regular as digital clockwork, even allowing for daylight saving time, which led Becky to believe her daughter's story, sad as that sounded in light of her previous deception, currently sealed lips about Jackson's father, and the upheaval it would mean for Monica's family.

Lunch? Maybe not the best idea.

So with the snow accumulation covering the last blades of grass, Becky decided to spend her free day reorganizing the basement storage shelves. The "re" of "reorganizing" hinted that the shelves had once enjoyed a state of organization. That might have been true two decades ago. Since then, she'd aimed and tossed in the general direction of the shelving units.

On and under the narrow table near the basement door, she'd collected a fair number of items to take to the basement "the next time I go down there," which in hindsight might not have been the best plan. She needed three trips to haul the last six jars of homemade applesauce, the paint supplies from touching up that spot behind the bathroom door, and an odd assortment of little things like cardboard boxes and the baby food jar of morning glory seeds.

When she got to the seeds, she set them in the middle of the kitchen table instead and poured herself a cup of coffee the color of the seeds.

Quiet. She hadn't heard it for too long. It made her think.

Why do I do this every year? Why go to the trouble of saving these ridiculously small and insignificant seeds? How much would a new packet cost in the spring , even if they didn't reseed themselves one year? Two dollars? Why this compulsion to reclaim the seeds from each year's spent blossoms?

Because Grandma always did. And Mom did because Grandma did.

And that was reason enough?

Tradition. A lot to be said for tradition. Tradition means memories, and memories mean somebody cares.

Reason enough.

Cornbread stuffing at Thanksgiving. Hot cocoa at midnight on Christmas Eve. Oyster stew on New Year's Day. Breakfast at sunrise, lakeside, on their anniversary. Pick a lake. Any lake.

Becky's heart warmed at the memory of a sunrise breakfast in front of their computers with lake scene screen savers the year Gil was grounded in Detroit. As they talked on the phone, he ate continental breakfast—scrambled eggs and a bagel—while she sipped orange juice and nibbled an over-toasted English muffin with honey, missing him and knowing that a guy who would go to that kind of effort to hang onto a tradition was a guy worth keeping.

For all his quirks, Captain StrangeSocks was a keeper.

She twirled the jar and watched the seeds tumble over one another. In another setting, they would have been swept into a dustpan. Or tossed onto the compost heap. Or left on the vine through the brutal winter. A shiver rippled up her back.

Why did it mean so much to her to plant those seeds each spring, watch the impossibly fragile vines find their way up the tripod iron trellis, and wait for the day when the first tightly twirled blossom unwound itself and turned, unblushing, with petal-arms outspread to the sun? And the next day, another blossom. Finally, in early summer, a jungle of vines and a floral fireworks display of gossamer-thin, glistening flowers showed their faces on a strict schedule. Wound tight until the sun coaxed them open, shining for a while, then refurled for siesta in the heat of the day.

Some inexplicable draw—was it just that odd connection with the lifting of her postpartum depression?—made the morning glories her favorites among the flashier, pricier, hardier, more luxurious flowers in the garden. Simple in their elegance, with an untold tale buried in their centers, they seemed to whisper a history she had yet to discover.

The basement could wait. She'd spend at least part of her free day on the Internet, searching for a logical reason for the morning glory's appeal. Ah, the joy of a good rabbit trail, something artsy to keep her from her underdeveloped left-brained organizing efforts.

"Morning glories can grow fast," she read aloud, "reseeding ten feet in as little as two months."

Sounded like Jackson and his race to outgrow baby clothes.

"Morning glory blossoms often look like they're glowing from within."

The comment she read stopped her. Maybe that was it. That was the appeal. Tightly curled-upon-itself buds that looked as if they had no potential for beauty untwisted under the sun's light and warmth to reveal startlingly charming blossoms that looked as if they glowed from within.

A poetic concept.

If she were still working for Ellison, she might assign a writer to explore that idea for an article. Or an illustrated quotation. She envisioned it. Saw it on the layout board in what was once her office. But she no longer had the clout to dole out assignments or turn visions into reality.

She did, however, have the capacity to love needy children, and with an extra dose of God's grace, glow from within.

"Morning glories don't need soil that is too fertile or moist."
Good to know.

"For best results, scarify the seeds prior to sowing or soak overnight."

Scarify? Another way she identified with the flowers. She'd been *scarified* plenty over the past couple of years.

She did a side search for the definition of *scarify*. "To slightly nick." She needed a bigger word, then, than *scarify*.

The phone rang just as Becky had read a fine-print note about the state of Arizona considering morning glories noxious weeds.

"Mom?"

"What's up, Lauren?" Even Becky's loosely formed plans disintegrated in the split second that she waited for a response.

"Can you come and get Jackson? He's, like, mondo-crabby. I don't know. He might be cutting a tooth or something. How would I know? Oh, great! Mom, he just puked. Hurry, will you?"

Career Day. Parenting 101.

Between Jackson's flu, followed by Lauren's, followed by Becky's, followed by Gil's—all four of which involved Becky as caregiver—they'd missed three Sundays before Becky gave serious consideration to her earlier reaction: *We have to change churches.*

She'd entertained the thought before—when the world discovered that the extra weight Lauren gained was an embryo named Jackson.

Gil talked her out of it that time, insisting the church should be a bastion of forgiveness, a forerunner in the race to show mercy. Yeah, right.

This time Becky's reasons were a combination of embarrassment and altruism. If Lauren was lying about one too many pregnancy tests, the family could start over at another church that didn't know their history. If they were careful enough with their introductions, others might assume Lauren was a very young-looking new mom whose husband was . . . was . . . teaching English as a second language in a small but strategic-to-the-national-interest country. And how sweet of Becky and Gil to take her into their home until he returned.

If Brianne was the one keeping a secret, the kindest thing Becky could do for Monica was disappear from their daily lives.

Right?

Remove a layer of their embarrassment. Let their family handle it without the added guilt and remorse from the way Monica had treated Becky and Lauren.

And . . . without Becky and Lauren's unconditional love.

Okay. Bad plan.

Silence wasn't working. Assuming new identities wouldn't mend a relationship. *Monica, I wish you'd just talk to me!*

God, I wish You'd just talk to me!

That, Becky could do something about.

With Lauren back in school, Gil on the road, and Jackson napping—not quite his cherub self yet—Becky located her Bible—under too many things.

Somewhere in there was a verse about the danger of planning to be deceptive—a new church, a creative story about Jackson's daddy serving his country in a makeshift classroom. God bless America. Too bad she didn't know where that reference was. And who would believe that after they told them about Mark and Iraq?

In the pages somewhere was a verse or two about casting stones.

And chapter after chapter about a God who loves those who don't deserve it . . . and instructions to follow His lead.

I want to, Lord. But how?

The pages that fell open to her seemed unrelated to the cry of her heart until she read them a second time.

Ephesians 5:8-10: *"For you were once darkness, but now you are light in the Lord. Live as children of light (for the fruit of the light consists in all goodness, righteousness and truth) and find out what pleases the Lord."*

Truth and secrets. Light and darkness.

No more secrets. No more darkness. No more waiting for light.

Becky booted up her computer, logged onto the Internet, and sent Monica a gift—a pair of hand-dipped candles connected at the wick—with a note: *From your forever friend. We really need each other. No matter what. Becky.*

She paid the exorbitant extra fee for overnight shipping, but slept soundly that night for the first time in weeks.

Four days later Becky called the local flourist and ordered a Thanksgiving centerpiece for Monica—a cinnamon-colored pottery pumpkin-shaped container with rich autumn-colored mums and a hurricane-lamp center. With a candle. To light. To throw light.

Two days of silence later, she pulled Monica's Christmas gift from the hall closet shelf where she'd stored it since finding it on sale midsummer, before . . . before everything. It was one of the lighted village pieces Monica didn't yet have in her collection. A flower shop with—*what do you know?*—morning glories trailing up the side of the ceramic building. She tucked it in a neutral, non-Christmas gift bag, surrounded it with cornflower blue tissue paper, and left it on Monica's doorstep, under the overhang, away from stray snowflakes.

On Friday that week, a package arrived in the mail. A pink flashlight with rechargeable batteries, and a simple note: "Brianne said it was a girl."

With Jackson playing at her feet, Becky clicked the flashlight on and off, on and off, tears flooding her cheeks and making her nose run. That's how Gil found her.

"Hi, home! I'm honey!" His standard lame but endearing greeting.

She looked up from the couch and crumpled at the sight of him.

"Becky, my deliciousness, what's the matter?" His arms were around her before she was conscious of his crossing the floor to her.

She waved the flashlight at him.

"Is it broken?"

"N-no. *She* is."

"Who?" Gil pulled back just far enough to shed his coat.

"Monica. And sh-she needs me. I have to go to her."

"Go!" Gil said, rubbing courage into her back. "I'm here for Jackson. Take as long as you need."

She leaned into his strength. "I love you."

"Love you, too."

"What are you doing home so early?"

Gil stiffened. "We'll talk about it when you get back."

"No secrets. No darkness. Just light."

"What?"

Becky swiped at her tears, then framed his familiar, bristly face with her hands. "No secrets. Why are you home so early?"

"The good news is I'll be around more often to help out now."

"Oh, Gil! You were laid off?"

14

Ivy—1951

Dear Drew,

I was laid off today.

Next sentence. What's the next sentence?

What was Ivy's next step? How much of the truth could she share without destroying any hope of Drew still loving her? Mistakes made love disappear. A fact of life. It was not the life Anna preached, but the reality Ivy knew from the day she made the mistake that sent her mother away, the mistake that shriveled her father's heart.

She erased what she'd written. Even "Dear Drew" didn't seem right.

Showing up at work, going through the motions, and crossing paths with Jill wouldn't be easy for the next couple of weeks. Training her replacement would take the kind of courage it took Drew to poke his head out of a foxhole.

If you'd gone to college, Ivy, you could have majored in melodrama.

What was wrong with her? Maybe she was as selfish as people said. It shouldn't be this hard. Other girls had babies out of wedlock. *Those* kinds of girls.

If she didn't care what Drew thought, she'd outright tell him the truth and let the chips fall where they may. She'd figure out what to do with the kid when it came. If she had a job. And a place to live.

Getting rid of the baby hadn't really been an option, not even in the beginning when she could have taken care of the problem and no one would ever have known. Because she was so noble? That wasn't it. Could she even define the reason? The baby was a part of Drew. That sweet man who treated her better than she deserved, who looked at her as though she were beautiful, who held her hand as if it were something precious, who talked to her with words that fell on her ears like music and melted in her heart like butter on hot toast. *Oh, Drew!*

His seed had grown into a seedling in her. She carried part of him with her as she walked through her miserable days. The problem had a face, ears, hands, legs, toes.

And when the truth came out and Drew knew what she'd done, even if he walked away from her, she'd still have—

A flutter! She held her breath waiting for another. There! Life inside her. She held her hand over the spot. A faint tickle against her palm said, "I'm here."

Dear Drew,

I lost my job today. And felt our baby move.

The tears she'd been sandbagging let loose as she tipped her pencil upside down and erased every word.

Anna—1890s

The dawn of my grief-healing over Elizabeth and her tiny son came not a day too soon. Dr. Noel caught my arm after church and pulled me to the side to speak with me privately.

Have I told you about Dr. Noel? Noel Milbourn. Another of God's gifts to us. He registered a bit crusty on the outside but soft as down on the inside, like a good loaf of peasant bread. He knew up front that we had few resources with which to pay him. Looking back on it now, I cannot believe my brashness! First Puff and then Dr. Noel. *Could you please give of yourself, long hours, intense labor, day and night, with no hint of reward except my gratitude?*

Who but God could have motivated these men to say yes?

As we visited after church that Sunday morning, Dr. Noel stood at my elbow, half whispering his request. A young woman, late teens, had been found asleep in the alley behind the hotel, scavenging food from the waste pails. The sheriff, responding to the hotelier's request to remove the girl from the premises, noticed that her thin coat bulged with more than pilfered goods. Dr. Noel was called in. And now, he called on me.

As sweet-tempered as was my Elizabeth, Corrie was foul and uncooperative. The birth of her baby was imminent. I took comfort in that. Corinda Blake's presence in my home fogged the air, but it would not last long.

There was no question whether she would keep her baby. She made no bones about her view that "it" was a parasite she was eager to be rid of. I have never been closer to violence against another human being than with Corrie. More than once, my heart reached up to slap her, though my arms remained at my sides.

Corrie spat on my house rules and refused to work. I considered refusing her food in exchange, but relented for the sake of the baby. Had I a similar opportunity today, I'd tie her breakfast to the broom handle, her dinner to the laundry tub. I've learned much about being taken advantage of. I don't believe I helped her by letting her sulk and pout and poison our air with her foul words and attitude.

Puff kept to himself while Corrie lived with us. I don't blame him. Some nights I wished I lived in a corner of the barn rather than in the house where her complaints resided.

"I'm only here because the sheriff said it was this place or the orphan home."

"I know, Corrie. But since you're here—"

"I don't have to listen to your lectures. Nobody said I did."

Need I explain why I was so troubled that Corrie's baby was born as healthy as a horse, and that the mother herself slipped quickly from labor pains to relentless complaining about the loss of her figure?

On the hill behind the orchard lay a snow-covered mound. And now an *un*wanted child lay squirming and love-hungry under a borrowed blanket in a room down the hall.

Corrie refused to care for the child. Frankly, and ashamedly, I was grateful. Though my own workload mushroomed because of it, from the start the robust boy heard good things whispered in his downy ears. Gentle, though work-worn hands tended his needs. A voice laced with tenderness sang his lullabies. An appreciative heart noticed that his baby breath was as sweet as clover honey. Love diapered his bottom and prepared his bottles and eased his tummyaches in the middle of the night while the woman who gave him birth caught up on her beauty sleep and regained strength enough to walk away forever.

Because Corrie's baby lived, and because she did not want him, we were forced to enlist the aid of an attorney.

And so I faced another crisis of faith. With memories of Mr. Rawlins as nose-stinging as ammonia, I was not eager to work closely with any attorney. But that was the least of my concerns. Where on God's green earth would I find a lawyer willing to handle the paperwork for adoptions without collecting his customary fee? Where could I find a lawyer willing to work for eggs and dried apples? Ludicrous!

Pressed by a sense of urgency, fueled by doubts that Corrie would remain with me long enough to sign the necessary papers, I enlisted the Kinneys' aid. Before the week's end, they had secured an appointment for me with an attorney in Newcastle. The extra miles seemed a small price to pay, under the circumstances.

Because Corrie would not volunteer to watch the infant, I feared leaving them together while I kept my appointment in Newcastle. I couldn't trust her to change or feed the baby— or to care that he needed either task performed. It sounds as though I'm being especially hard on her. But I'm not exaggerating her lack of interest or cooperation.

So the child, whom I called Thomas, for lack of an appointed name, rode with me when Puff drove us to Newcastle. The child remained in my arms when I walked through the doors of the office building and introduced myself to Mr. Grissom's secretary.

The child, rooting hungrily at my breast as if I could feed him from my own barren body, made his presence known with loud protests as Mr. Grissom welcomed into his office our sorry duo—a woman who was anything but prepared to beg for help from a sophisticated lawyer, and the days-old babe who did not understand that his future lay in the hands of the man and woman who shared the office space with him.

"Miss Morgan. A pleasure to meet you. Please, have a seat."

I shifted Thomas to my shoulder, covering the infant's mouth-sized wet spot on my blouse with the baby's body, and lowered myself into the offered deep leather chair. Thomas nuzzled his face into my neck and cheek, his rosebud lips searching for what he could not find on me. My embarrassment nearly sent me fleeing from the room.

"A baby's hunger knows no propriety, does it, Miss Morgan?"

"I have a bottle for him."

"Please. Take your time. We can talk as he eats, can't we?"

The bottle I retrieved from the bag slung over my other shoulder was mercifully still warm enough. Puff had suggested I nest it in newsprint to insulate it. Where had he learned such a thing?

Thomas settled into a comfortable pattern of sucking and swallowing. Mr. Grissom and I settled into a more comfortable pattern, too.

The man's face registered a kindness that startled me. I assumed I'd be up against a fight for the rights of the child in my care. But Mr. Grissom's fists were not raised for battle. His hands were relaxed and outstretched on his paper-strewn polished oak desk.

"How can I help you?"

"I was led to believe you might consider giving legal counsel in regard to adoptions?"

"The Kinneys have talked to me about your ministry."

That was the first time I'd heard my feeble efforts called a *ministry*. It both humbled and thrilled me.

"And, yes, I would consider being of assistance. Is this child being put up for adoption?"

"Yes, sir. As soon as possible. The mother is with me at the present. I can't guarantee her whereabouts for long, I'm afraid. And then what would happen? I know nothing about legal matters. I have heard it has become more complicated. There are rules to follow and adoption agencies with good intentions that sometimes run aground. If the mother disappears, who decides the child's future?"

Thomas gulped too deeply and choked on the milk for which he was so hungry. I lifted him to my shoulder again and patted him on the back.

"Raise his arms over his head," Mr. Grissom suggested. "That often works."

It did. I was grateful and growing more indebted to the man across the desk.

"You have children, Mr. Grissom?"

"Yes. A son and a daughter. Both nearly grown now. My son is away at the university. My daughter will graduate this spring and head to Europe to study music, if she has her way. Since her mother died, she has been comfort, companion, and caretaker for me. A blessing I'll sorely miss when she is gone."

"You can understand, then, how important it is for a child to be given the advantage of a two-parent home, if at all possible."

"Oh, yes."

"And you must have dealt with families over the years who had not been blessed with children but who longed to provide a home for children who had none."

"Yes. Are you endeavoring to win me over to your cause, Miss Morgan? Your efforts are unnecessary."

The infant swallowed contentedly. I sought for words to introduce the financial questions swirling through my mind. That, too, was unnecessary. Mr. Grissom relieved me of the dilemma.

He leaned back in his wheeled desk chair, his vest and shirt stretching over a sturdy chest. "I understand that you are not involved in a money-making venture, that you do not charge the unwed mothers who find shelter with you."

"True."

"I also understand that you've yet to find a team of permanent backers, that you have had only seed money and God's grace off of which to live these months of operation."

"Also true."

He leaned forward, resting his forearms on papers representing cases far more significant than mine, of more interest to the courts than a small bundle curled against me, content to be held and loved, even if not by the woman who gave birth to him.

Mr. Grissom smiled as he inhaled. "It's been laid on my heart to consider tithing the hours I spend behind my desk."

"Excuse me?"

"I give financially to my church. But the Lord has impressed upon me the good that might be done if I also gave Him a percentage of my time here in the office. I handle an occasional pro bono case, but am interested in expanding to include other service opportunities. Can you be of assistance to me in this capacity, Miss Morgan?"

How gallant of him to turn my need to make it appear I was somehow capable of helping him! I stared down into the face of a child and up into the face of a saint.

"What is the standard fee for adoption legal work? No, please don't tell me. I would pay too high a price in guilt if I knew. Until I see where God takes me, until I know if I will care for two women a year or twenty, and how many of them will need to consider adoption, I can't begin to guess how much this might cost you, Mr. Grissom."

"I will not give to the Lord that which cost me nothing."

He quoted King David at the threshing floor. It moved me to hear a man of such education weaving Scripture into his conversation as smoothly as "Pleased to meet you" and "Good day to you."

"As I said, I am not at all familiar with adoption proceedings, Mr. Grissom."

"Before we're done, I am confident you will be, Miss Morgan."

So began our working relationship.

⸺⸺

I believe the word *bittersweet* was invented to describe the emotions that accompany adoption. Bitter-tasting bile pushed against the back of my throat as I witnessed Corrie's signing away her child. Would she ever regret the way her hand determinedly gripped the pen? Would she live to regret the decision to pretend she was not a mother? As calloused as she then appeared, would years and longing and disappointments and wisdom sand the edges of her slate-cornered heart?

Corrie and Josiah Grissom and I attended the moment, with Lydia and Pastor Kinney serving as witnesses. With different mothers and sometimes fathers, we would play the same parts too many times. It was always bittersweet.

The young women who shook like willows in an earthquake and cried with wrenching sobs and smeared the legal documents with their tears and needed my hand to steady theirs as they signed their names . . . their sour grief sweetened with the golden nectar of the family they knew waited in the wings to care for their child.

The women who wavered at the last moment, clinging to the fragile thread of hope that maybe, somehow, oh could there be a way . . . ?

But no. They knew the answer. Before signing, the women were experienced wrestlers, having wrested from God's hands the answer they needed, convinced in their heart of hearts that the choice was the only real choice they had.

159

"Please don't put your name to paper until you've heard from God," I counseled, always conscious that theirs was a decision no mother should have to make.

It was grievously difficult for me to hold my tongue sometimes. I advised. But I could not choose for them. Some gave up babies I thought they should have tried to keep. Some kept babies against my better judgment. I prayed the more diligently for them.

Corrie's Thomas was our first. Not long after the screen door slammed behind Corrie's "don't look back" body, an eager man and woman walked through my front door, fell in love with him, and pledged to care for him as their very own. I knew they would. I read faithfulness and gratitude in their eyes.

A lovely young couple. They sat so close on the sofa that I entertained the thought that they might be conjoined twins masquerading as a married couple. Once the child was brought into the room, neither Mr. Grissom nor I could draw their attention back to legal or practical concerns for more than a cursory nod or brief word of agreement.

"Yes. All right. Certainly. We will," they said, without glancing up from the face of the child.

The love they felt in an instant was so deep and profound, I knew it had celestial roots. The bile retreated. I tasted what I imagined manna must have tasted like the very first day.

I never saw the couple again after that, but I suspect their entwined hands tucked the love gift into the envelope that appeared in my mailbox every year on the anniversary of Thomas's adoption.

Do we really live before we are loved? I ask because I was often tempted to mark a date of birth according to the moment when the child first knew love. For some, like Thomas, it was not his birth date. The real beginning of his life fell on the day an eager couple wrapped him in their arms, intentionally choosing to love him.

Other children born under my roof could mark much sooner the day they began truly living. The day the young mother-to-be touched the bulge of her growing abdomen with the tenderness of a caress. The day she spoke soothing mews to her unborn child to still his or her hiccups. The day she confessed she would sacrifice everything to ensure the little one was cared for.

I'm wrong. Even Thomas was never unloved, not for a moment. I loved him, yes. But before I knew he existed, God did. God saw him and loved him long before his body was fully formed. The child might have been neglected and unwanted by his natural mother. But he was never unloved.

15

Becky twirled the pink microflashlight in her fingers.

"A baby girl? Monica, I'm so sorry." The whispered words into Monica's too quiet living room seemed inadequate at best, acidic at worst.

Monica held her hands pressed together in her lap, her spine rigid, rocking back and forth as if an internal pain took her full focus to control.

"So the baby was . . . far enough along to . . . to tell?"

Monica didn't respond.

Becky's veins ran hollow. Vacuous brain cells failed to supply her with words remotely comforting, healing, soothing. So she slipped from her chair and joined Monica on the couch. Mirrored her posture. Put one arm around Monica's trembling shoulders. Slid into the same rocking rhythm as if they were twin sisters. Silently prayed the only word she could remember, the only word that mattered: *Jesus. Jesus. Jesus. Jesus. Oh, Lord Jesus.*

Monica made several attempts at conversation. Nothing more than a consonant or two survived.

As the room darkened in response to the lateness of the hour, a single flame from the hurricane centerpiece the only illumination, Becky spoke. "Monica, I don't know what to say. Nothing's right. Nothing can match the pain you must feel right now. So I'm going to stop trying. I just need you to know I'm here. I'm here."

With a wracking breath, Monica turned a few degrees in Becky's direction. "Brianne . . . Brianne thought she was getting rid of a problem. Simple as that. She says it didn't occur to her that she was getting rid of my grandchild."

The word stung. A beautiful word. One of the most emotionally evocative in any language. *Nipotina. Petit-enfant. Nieto. Enkel. Child of my heart.*

"That's what got to her," Monica spoke into the deepening darkness, "what made her confess the truth. That it was, had been, my grandchild. Imagine. She felt . . . she felt bad for *me*. What will happen the day she realizes you can't erase a child? The child will . . . it will wake her . . . in . . . the night . . . and call out to her. Like mine does."

"Yours?"

"My first. Before Brianne. Long before Brianne. Long before I knew I had other choices."

Becky sniffed, then dug into her sweater pocket for a tissue.

"I wonder. If I'd told Brianne about my experience, would she have realized she had other options, too?" Monica looked into Becky's eyes then, for the first time since she'd arrived. How many days since Monica had blinked? Or eaten?

"Where is Brianne now?"

"She spends a lot of time anywhere but here."

Monica stood. Erect. As if letting blood that had too long pooled in her inefficient heart refill her arteries. She walked to the table lamp and lit a small corner of the room. Cozy. Warm. Homey. On any day other than this one.

She wandered, as if uncertain where to land, as tentative as a hummingbird. Becky watched as Monica moved around the room, wiping at invisible dust with her hand, straightening already straight pictures, fingering the chrysanthemums in the autumn centerpiece on the coffee table. "Thank you for this, by the way."

"Oh. Oh, sure. I thought—"

"I owe you an apology and I—"

"Monica. That's for another time."

Her eyes expressed her gratitude. "Can you stay a little longer?"

Becky thought of the mess she'd left at home—Jackson and Lauren and a husband without a job. "As long as you need."

"I tried to open a can of soup but my hands were shaking so hard, and I couldn't get the opener to work and . . ." Her words dissolving into tears, Monica turned to head for the kitchen, Becky at her heels.

"What kind?" Becky asked.

"Excuse me?"

"What kind of soup?"

"Clam chowder."

"My favorite."

"I know." Monica seemed relieved to be conversing on an ordinary subject.

"Our go-to comfort soup."

"Always has been."

"Okay if I call home and tell them I'm staying for supper?" Becky slipped her cell phone out of her pocket.

"Sure. And tell them . . . tell them thank you."

"For what?"

Monica leaned against the kitchen island. "For taking care of all the things you usually do so you could take care of me."

"Monica, we're in this together."

"Crackers?"

"Yes, I am."

Monica's sideways glance and merest of smiles told Becky her pun was intentional.

"Haven't heard that term used in a long time. Would you like crackers with your soup?" Becky asked, tentative about the waters of normalcy.

"Yes. Thank you. Middle shelf in the pantry."

Monica's butler's pantry was only one of the things about Monica's house that Becky had always coveted a little. It was a fabulous historic home with original hardwood floors and exquisite woodwork, including the swooping Gone-With-the-Wind-esque staircase in the front foyer. She loved how the house had been updated over the years, mostly Monica's genius, to provide her family modern comforts and high-end upgrades without destroying the historical integrity.

Becky's assessment sang like a voice-over on a home-improvement television program. It was more appreciation than envy, right? She ran her hand over the smooth, cold, granite work counter in the butler's pantry and thought about the copper-colored stain and hairline knife marks in her counter at home ("People, we HAVE a cutting board!"). She'd joked more than a few times that she'd trade houses with Monica any day. Without saying it aloud, she might have entertained the idea of trading lives within the last year. For brief moments. No more.

Somewhere in her past, something she'd read or heard told her that if we knew the hidden pain of others, we'd never agree to swap problems. We'd opt to keep our own.

Becky reached for the antique tin of oyster crackers and thought about the other adage she'd heard often: no mother can be any happier than her unhappiest child.

And no friend, she thought, can be any happier than her unhappiest friend.

Joy.

Like a blast of flash powder from an explosion, the stenciled words above the arch between Monica's kitchen and dining room blinded her as she returned with the crackers. *The joy of the LORD is your strength.* A verse from Nehemiah.

Strength and joy. About as related right now as cement and feathers. She wondered what that phrase did to Monica these days when she read it.

Monica looked up. "Took you long enough."

Becky set the cracker tin on the island near the two mugs of soup and two goblets of Welch's grape juice. "I'm easily distracted."

Monica's expression sobered again. "Me too."

"Grape juice, huh?" Becky swallowed a spoonful of the hot soup.

Monica shook out a handful of oyster crackers and laid them on the edge of the plate on which her mug rested. Then she took one cracker for herself and gave one to Becky. "It felt a little like . . . Communion."

<hr />

"That was awkward." Monica put her mug and spoon into the dishwasher, then reached for Becky's.

"What? Brianne's coming home in the middle of communion?"

"Brianne's ignoring you."

"She said hi." Becky added their plates to the lower rack.

With gentleness thick with meaning, Monica put her hand on Becky's shoulder. "We both owe you a lot more than that."

Becky patted her hand. "Let's agree we'll probably experience more than a few awkward moments before we get through this."

Monica sighed, a familiar sound. "I don't know what I'm supposed to do, how I'm supposed to act."

"What's your instinct?"

"You mean, regarding Brianne?"

"Yes."

Monica closed the dishwasher and touched the start button. A barely perceptible shoosh told Becky *that's* what a dishwasher is supposed to sound like.

"Am I a bad mom if I want to wring her neck?"

Becky chuckled softer than the dishwasher sound.

"And then I want to hold her tight to me and cry with her until there's no distinguishing which tears are hers and which are mine. But she's not grieving."

"How does a teenager grieve, Monica?" Becky caught her sob before it escaped. "I wonder if some of Lauren's choices are her twisted way of grieving the loss of her brother. Is that possible? How does a teen grieve?"

"Denial. Anger. Depression. That sounds like—"

"Us. It sounds like us, doesn't it?"

Twin sighs shuddered through the room. Becky swallowed the last of her Communion juice. "I guess I'd better get home." She set her goblet on the counter next to the sink. "You'll want to hand wash this, right?"

"How long have you known what it took me forever to admit, Beck?"

"I didn't know for sure until your message with the flashlight."

Monica hunched her shoulders and grasped her elbows with each opposite hand. "Not that. The fact that love is sometimes the source of our greatest pain."

The Trundle house lay as quiet as Monica's dishwasher when Becky walked through the door from the garage. Where was everyone?

Only the night-light lit the kitchen. She dropped her purse and keys on the counter and headed through the house looking for evidence. Nothing littered the family room. How unusual. Lauren's bedroom door was closed and a duet of soft snores spoke of two children asleep in that room.

What was that fragrance? Lemon? More specifically, lemon furniture polish. Gil had dusted?

He sat in the wing chair in the corner of their bedroom, the reading light leaning over his shoulder, illuminating the book he held.

Which question should she ask first? *What are you reading? You dusted?* Or a wrenching *Oh, hon, you lost your job?*

"I'm glad you waited up for me." She kicked her shoes off in the general direction of the closet. "Are you okay?"

"Are you?"

"No."

"Me neither. We make a good pair, huh?" He set his book on the end table and beckoned her to his lap.

"I may have gained a few pounds since I last sat on your lap, Gil."

"So have I."

She leaned her head against his shoulder and nestled into his neck . . . just like Jackson did when he was tired. Gil's arms encircling her and his exhales rustling her hair almost made her forget the massive herd of elephants in the room. Hundreds of them. Thundering. Trumpeting. Knocking down mature trees and partially formed dreams.

She'd let a few more exhales pass before—

"Hon, I'm so sorry." Gil sounded as tired as she was.

"None of this is your fault."

"No. I mean, I'm sorry. My leg fell asleep. You're going to have to get up."

Becky couldn't help it. The laughter effervesced from some long-bottled container deep inside. She crawled off his lap and slid to the floor at his feet, shaking with the effort of suppressing the noise that could awaken a baby but that also awakened her in a comedic yet tragic way.

Life. Pain and joy. Deep ache and deep laughter. Inexpressible concern and irrepressible gratitude.

And an amazing, honest, unemployed man to share it with.

"I made tea," Gil said, as if needing to explain the teapot and cups on the tray in his hands.

"Thanks, honey." Becky accepted the cup from her new perch on the bed, propped by what Gil insisted were too many pillows. Tea weather. The furnace kicked in, its reassuring warmth accompanied by the faint smell of fried dust. Need to clean the vents one of these days. Maybe Gil would now have time to . . . "So, no hope the company will reconsider?"

"It's a done deal."

"Any explanation, other than the obvious?"

"From what I hear, this is a last-ditch attempt to stave off bankruptcy."

"Who else was let go?"

Gil settled against his own collection of pillows and took a sip of his tea before responding. "It might be easier to list who wasn't."

"Oh, honey. Now what?"

He set his teacup on the nightstand. "Doesn't it seem as though we're asking that question a lot lately?"

"Nice fake smile, Gil. One thing we know: you don't have a future in the theater."

"The severance package is . . . "

"Hefty? Significant? Mind-blowing?"

"Puny, considering all I've—all *we've*—sacrificed. But it will help us through the next few months, maybe. We have a little in savings."

In the space of one day, the size difference between Monica's house, Monica's mortgage, and Becky's and Gil's flipped value. At a time like this, their modest house, careful spending, and lack of other debt more than made up for the lack of a butler's pantry and a noiseless dishwasher.

Still . . .

Gil's odds of finding another job at all in this economy, much less quickly, were slim.

She didn't need tea as much as she needed his arms around her. Divested of her cup, she snuggled into his chest, her ear against his heartbeat. Steady. Stable. Sure. And a little bit broken.

He smelled newly showered with a lingering hint of lemon. From his dusting. Bless him. The perfect man? No. Perfect for her? Maybe more so than she realized.

"Beck, my peach cobblerness, can we make a pact?"

"I married you, oaf. We've already made a pact."

"About this current crisis. Can we agree not to get consumed by how we're going to get out of this mess for . . . for three days?"

"Why three?"

His heart beat a drummer's timekeeping intro before he answered. "Because it's less than four?"

How humiliated he must feel. Jobless at his age, when finding other employment wasn't automatic and switching careers carried more risk than a high-risk pregnan—

"I need time to process what happened without the pressure of needing to have an answer right away. Does that make sense?"

"It's called a gestation period, hon." She reached up to stroke the curve of his jaw. "And yes, it makes perfect sense."

She and Monica were themselves only in the first trimester of their shared grief. The nauseous stage. Lauren, Monica, and now Gil. Becky was expecting fraternal triplets. Or troublets.

16

Ivy—1951

Is it true what they say, Anna?"

"What?"

"That trouble comes in threes?"

Anna raised up on one elbow so Ivy could flip her pillow to the cool side. "Not at all."

Ivy sighed, unconvinced.

"No," Anna said, "sometimes they come by the dozens." Her broad grin confirmed—all her own teeth.

What would Ivy do without Anna in her life? Who would have thought she'd be the one bright spot? Ivy's baby punched a fist into her kidney to remind her there were two bright spots. The latest airmail letter in her pocket voiced its vote that there were three.

Bright spots come in threes.

"Another love letter?"

Anna must have noticed her fingering the envelope. "Yes."

"Is he a good man, Ivy?"

Her thoughts traveled thousands of miles to a drooping olive-green tent under a dripping gray sky and a soldier on the edge of a sagging cot, bent over the letters he wrote to her. A faithful man. Serving his country. Planning for their future together. An uninformed uniformed man with unbending love for her because he didn't know any better. "He's a good man. More than I deserve."

"What does he write to you now?"

"Bits about the war. Soldiers stationed there longer than he has been talk about the night raids where the Chinese banged drums and shrieked and blew whistles and pounded on gongs as they attacked."

"Sounds like a circus."

"Disorienting, I'm sure. Turns out some of the ruckus was because the Chinese communication systems were so bad that they used the noise to signal their other units about their location and tactics."

Anna thought for a moment and then said, "Babies must operate under the same system. They make a lot of ruckus because they don't have the communication skills to say, 'I could use a new diaper!'"

As dear as Anna had become to Ivy, it seemed every subject held a danger zone. Drew, work, war, babies . . .

"Drew said the men work hard to keep their rifles clean and their knives sharp."

"Oh, dear. Such a necessary evil."

"And that they don't waste time because they can't afford to have their weapons out of commission for long in certain areas. I can tell he doesn't want to scare me, though. Those kinds of comments aren't frequent. He said the biggest surprise for him was that the whole country smells like an outhouse."

"What?"

"The Koreans use human . . . excrement . . . on their fields. The whole country smells like it. Others warned him on the ship over. He worked on his dad's farm as a kid, so he laughed them off. Until they landed."

Anna pinched her nose. Then she held her hand to the side of her mouth and said, "I half expected the same thing here."

"Me, too. I'm glad we were both wrong."

The pause between them hinted of the separation to come.

Ivy skipped telling Anna about the friends Drew had seen cut down by the enemy, about the minutes-old orphans crying through the smoking villages, about the villagers so wracked by starvation that they ate—. Time for another subject. "He draws."

"Sketches? Of people?"

"Other soldiers. Jeeps. A Sherman tank disguised with rice straw. An amphibious duck."

"Aren't all ducks amphibious?"

"This one was half tank, half boat."

"Oh."

"Their camp. The mess tent."

"Is he a good artist? Could I see some of his drawings?"

Anna played the role of mother and grandmother and favorite aunt and much older sister in Ivy's life. Friend. Her only friend. Friends shared things like quotations and sketches from love letters.

Ivy slipped the thin pages from the envelope, unfolded them with reverence, and flipped through to a series of sketches on a page by themselves. "I think he's as good as a lot of the war cartoonists I've seen in the newspaper." She handed the page to Anna and held her breath.

"Oh, my. You're right about his talent. These are wonderful. Oh, to have a treasure like this from—" Anna's eyes glistened, but she stopped talking.

"I like the one of the soldier sitting under his poncho, with his back against that broken-down shack . . ."

"His boots and socks on the ground beside him."

"Soaking his feet in his helmet."

The two shared a moment of laughter in an otherwise humorless scene.

Anna squinted and pulled the paper nearer. "He's writing a letter, it appears."

"I guess so."

"To his sweetheart? I wonder."

"Drew says . . . "

"What?"

"He says so many of his buddies worry about the women—wives and girlfriends—they left in the States, worry that they're not being faithful to them. It drives them a little batty."

Anna pressed her hands to her heart. "How difficult not to trust the one you love, not to be assured that their word is true." Her gaze drifted to the window.

Too much talking. Ivy hadn't allowed her mouth so much exercise since . . . ever. And for good reason. Look where talking could lead—into inescapable corners. Now she'd have to use more words to climb out.

"See the benches and the rough podium in this sketch, Anna? That's where they have church. No walls. No stained glass. Their chaplain is a character, from what Drew says."

"Aren't we all?"

"And this one." Ivy pointed to the lower right-hand corner of the paper. "I . . . I can't look at this without getting choked up."

"A child."

"One of the Korean children from an orphanage his unit visited. The little face seems to say so much, doesn't it?"

"It says a great deal about your Drew, too, Ivy. That the face of a child would so capture him. That he would sketch that face with such a tender touch and such vibrant expression. Mmm. A good man. He'll make a good father."

Words. Too many words. Ivy's long-braced resolve dislodged. "He . . . he doesn't know."

Anna held the sketches toward Ivy. "Most men doubt their abilities to be a good father. That's only natural. It'll come to him. He has all the signs."

"Anna, he doesn't know I'm carrying this child."

The older woman plopped her hands down along her sides on the bedcovers. "Oh, Ivy, you've been working so hard to hide the truth. You must be exhausted. Honesty takes so little energy. Dishonesty can wear a person out."

The smell of Salisbury steak and creamed corn signaled Anna's supper was on the way into the room, which meant Ivy needed to be on her way out.

"Get the letter written tonight, Ivy," Anna called out as Ivy collected her purse, the pieces of the letter, and the notebook with Anna's latest story. "We all must risk rejection in order to live honestly. A man like that deserves your whole, true heart."

17

Anna—1890s

It became routine for Mr. Grissom and me to share tea or coffee and sometimes a light meal after an adoption signing. His volunteering to come to the house, rather than our making the trip to his office, was much appreciated. The Kinneys stayed on occasion as well. But more often than not, other duties called them, leaving Mr. Grissom and me to reflect on the proceedings and speculate on the outcome.

Puff always seemed to be otherwise engaged. I assume he was not comfortable with anyone observing how the loss of our tiny houseguests registered on his face. I, on the other hand, had too little shame. I didn't even attempt to stop the flood of tears when they pressed.

Defying explanation, Mr. Grissom always waited patiently for my tears to subside before launching into discussion. He busied himself with paperwork or leaned his head back against his chair and closed his eyes. I imagine he prayed. I suspect he often prayed for me.

A team of permanent backers. That's the phrase Josiah used in describing the phantom people yet to reveal themselves. As grateful as I was for Puff, Lydia and Pastor Kinney, Dr. Noel, and Josiah, I had yet to discover those with the means and the desire to invest financially in homegrown acts of redemption.

The church was slow to be convinced. Wouldn't one think that the forgiven would be quickest to forgive others? That the redeemed would fall over one another in their rush to carry the song of deliverance to those who had yet to hear its calming melody? That those who had found refuge would do everything in their power to light the way for others?

But despite Pastor Kinney's best sermonizing on the subject, the church people seemed to see only sin and rebellion, bulging bellies of disobedience to God's plan of purity. They raised their chins and crossed the street to avoid us, as if their own white robes of righteousness might turn gray if they walked through the same patch of air. As if He whose hands had fashioned their robes had reached His limit of sinners to love. As if He'd exhausted His supply of grace.

Puff assured me the townspeople were not hopeless, just stubborn, steeped in traditional taboos, bound by fears that they couldn't love the sinner without being tattooed with her sin. Imagine what they thought of me! I must have seemed a carnival freak, every inch of my skin branded by the stains of the young women who sought refuge in my home.

The congregation might have run me out of town if they could have seen the stains on the inside of me, the pain I'd caused.

I recall an afternoon's conversation with Lydia that almost forced a confession.

"Your face is as gray as a November sky, Anna."

I wasn't hiding my disgust at the latest snubbing from the president of the Ladies Aid Society. Insightful to a fault, Lydia would have noticed even if I had successfully masked my disappointment.

"Anna, I know the joy is there, somewhere behind the clouds. But at present, you are casting shadows."

"Lydia, I don't understand how you can be patient with these people."

"Our parishioners? They need grace, like anyone else." She crossed her arms as if that were the end of it.

"They're pigheaded and rude and self-righteous and—"

"And your words just now were . . . were what, Anna?"

"But their hearts are Siberian! They're cold and unfeeling toward these unwed mothers. How can they not see that the girls don't need more judgment and shame, but love and careful guidance and encouragement and . . . and understanding that when people are in trouble, they need more grace, not less."

Lydia, always the wiser of us, waited a moment before she spoke, allowing the poignancy of what I'd spoken to seep into my own soul.

"They can't see, Anna, because we haven't shown them."

"But—"

"We have talked *at* them, not with them. We've responded to their disgust with disparaging looks and remarks of our own. Their arrows of prejudice against these hurting women are returned by our poisonous darts of judgment against their judging others! How can that honor God?"

"Lydia, I know He wouldn't want my girls to be shunned by His people."

"Nor would He want us to grow bitter toward those who have yet to plumb the full depth of His grace."

Had I plumbed the full depth? Obviously not. I'd seen it. I lived because of it. And my mother died at its hand.

Lydia's comment stung in a healing way. Medicinally. Like iodine. "They deserve the very kindness I'm asking from them?"

"Yes, Anna."

"My most challenging assignment yet."

"But might it also be among the most rewarding? Few things are as beautiful as the scene when the Son parts the clouds."

The dinner party almost a year into it was Lydia's idea.

I'd always answered honestly when asked about the financial picture for the home. "God is good. We have no reserves. But God is good."

I often tacked a faith statement onto both the front and back of our needs, like a train with a locomotive at each end. There were times, many times, when the cars in between reached far down the track, around the bend, beyond my sight. But I was often reminded that where God is concerned, there is always a locomotive at each end.

Lydia suggested a formal dinner party with a table full of prospective contributors. She'd handle the guest list if I'd see to the food and prepare a compelling appeal about the value of my home for unwed mothers.

Its value? I wasn't yet convinced of its wisdom. I wavered like a newborn colt, eager to run but handicapped by my own weaknesses and clumsiness. The meal would be the less taxing of the two chores.

For some reason, Lydia felt it necessary to keep the guest list from me. I was informed there would be twenty of us dining together on the chosen Saturday evening. That was all I knew.

Puff helped me put all three leaves in the thick-legged table in the dining room days ahead of time to allow me the opportunity to fuss and fiddle. A snowy damask tablecloth served as foundation. And upon it I would put what? The dishes we were content to use any other day seemed as coarse as burlap for this event, and woefully mismatched. Six milky blue. Seven bright cobalt. A handful of white bread-and-butter plates. All hand-me-downs for which I'd once been grateful and now found embarrassing.

But not for long.

Dr. Noel paid an unexpected visit the afternoon of my fretting over the dishes. He was on his way home from setting the broken leg of a neighboring farm boy whose hayloft acrobatics cost him a bit of time off his feet. The family paid Dr. Noel in the currency in which they were accustomed to dealing—gooseberry preserves, pillow slips, and an odd assortment of china. Two of this, one of that, three of another—bowls and cups and saucers and plates. White, pale blue, and silver-rimmed.

"The preserves I intend to keep for myself," he said. "But I have no use for the pillow slips or the plates. Could you use them?"

As so often happened, I'd been unable to create an answer to my need. Why had I assumed it was up to me? Why did I repeatedly falter when my own imagination ran dry of ideas? Didn't I know by then that the Lord delights in surprising His children with answers beyond imagination?

Each of the twenty place settings was unique, a quality I hoped my guests would find more appealing than symmetry. From the scrap box, I pulled a generous remnant of soft yellow cotton fabric. Measuring carefully, I cut from it twenty equal squares for dinner napkins. Bachelor's buttons and marigolds in milk-glass vases would help the setting look intentional, I prayed.

The flatware would accompany Lydia. Her mother's. She promised to arrive early enough to have it safely tucked at each place before the first guest arrived.

My attention turned to the meal itself. Had I the foresight, I long ago would have recognized that Puff's insistence on inviting his pig, Ham, to live with us was the divine preparation for this very meal. Ham's hams were well smoked and ready. Potatoes and beans from the garden. Pickled beets from the root cellar. Creamed cucumbers. Herbed biscuits with blue violet jelly. And apple-something for dessert.

The kitchen was a laboratory for apple experiments. When the harvest is plentiful, the laborers must be creative. Caramel apple cobbler with thick clouds of whipped cream seemed just the thing to sweeten and soothe the guests' stomachs before they were subjected to my financial appeal.

When young women lived with me, they worked beside me because their help was needed and because work is both healing and character building. At the time of the dinner party, I was alone in the house, more particularly in the kitchen.

Until Josiah Grissom arrived.

I never asked what prompted him to show up at my door two hours ahead of schedule. I was learning not to question the miraculous. As organized as I thought myself to be, the enormity of the task was overwhelming, a fact made evident by the flour-strewn but aromatic chaos in my kitchen.

Josiah shed his tailored jacket and silk tie, rolled up the sleeves of his crisp white shirt, and tucked a linen dish towel into his waistband for an apron.

"What can I do to help?" Six beautiful words! I may have wondered at his prowess in culinary endeavors, but I did not doubt his sincerity.

"Peel potatoes?"

"Are you asking if I can or if I will?"

"Both."

"Yes. And yes." He brushed a smudge of flour off my cheek before tackling the mound of freshly scrubbed potatoes. I think . . . yes . . . I can still feel the sweet pressure of that brief touch.

We worked in silence, for the most part. Puff joined us from time to time, lured by the heavenly aroma of the smoked ham and the hope that he might help taste test. He offered to start the coffee, a task I would've forgotten in my fervor to get all the food hot and ready for the table at the same time.

Puff and Josiah collaborated quietly as we neared the end of our efforts and as the clock crept closer to the appointed time for guests to arrive. Josiah took the pan of biscuits from my hands and shooed me upstairs to pull my frazzled self together, claiming that the two men had things well in hand.

One glance in the upstairs hall mirror told me I should have allowed more time for primping. My face was flushed and glistening. My hair hung limp and windblown, although the only wind I'd faced was self-generated as I'd flown from project to project. My work dress held evidence of every dish to which I'd put my hands.

I could hear the Kinneys' buggy wheels in the drive as I stepped out of my dress and into the navy skirt and white blouse Lydia always said was too "school marmish" for me. She was probably right. But my choices were limited, as was time. I wrestled with my hair, frustrated with its cumbersome weight and stubbornness. I quickly redid its braiding and let the braid hang down my back, fearful that I would miss the arrival of my guests if I took the time to pin it up. The wide navy satin ribbon from a hand-me-down hat held strays in place at the top of my braid. A small silk sunflower from the same hat became a brooch at my neck. Not until I began my descent down the stairs did I realize that I'd dressed myself to look like the dining table.

Josiah—fully dressed and none the worse for wear—and Pastor Kinney were conversing in the front parlor when I reached the bottom of the stairs. The faint clink of silverware and china let me know where Lydia was occupied. Puff had disappeared. Pastor Kinney called to us from the parlor, inviting us to share a brief season of prayer before the other guests arrived. Prayer, balm I needed.

Grateful again for divine timing, I raised my eyes following Pastor Kinney's decisive "Amen!" to see the dust clouds of an approaching carriage that was turning into my drive.

Puff had shaved! I'd never seen his face clean shaven. Or the black suit coat and collarless white shirt he wore over his best wool pants.

I'm certain some of our guests were startled that Puff did not slip into a servant role but into the chair Lydia offered him at the table. Had any of them voiced a whimper of complaint, or even raised an eyebrow, I might have embarrassed myself with rage. The room grew noticeably quieter, but Puff nodded toward the other seated guests, who nodded back, and the moment passed.

Around the table with me sat my Mount Everest. Five of them were already friends: Puff, Josiah, Pastor and Mrs. Kinney, and Dr. Noel. Each of them already gave to the effort more than I would ever have dared to ask. That reduced the number of potential donors to fourteen. The unconvinced out-numbered the convinced.

Some moments are etched in our memories as if chiseled there, not just written in pale ink on a colorless, thin page. I have lost much of the conversation of that evening. I can't tell you what comments were made about the food or the weather. But I clearly remember two incredible moments. Pastor Kinney rose, as if to pray for the meal we were about to enjoy.

"Anna, with your permission, I'd like to ask Josiah to lead us in prayer."

It seemed to me an act of pure-hearted humility for the spiritual leader of our community to recognize and defer to his brother in Christ, his friend and mine, such a key figure in the success of this endeavor. And oh, the words that came from Josiah's mouth—no, heart—that night. I was certain the ceiling was raised several inches by the power of his prayer propelled heavenward.

Shortly following Josiah's robust but reverent "Amen," Lydia nodded toward the doorway. I followed the path of her sparkling eyes to find two of "my" girls standing ready to serve. They wore shy but grateful smiles. Beyond a gentle roundedness that defined them as women, their work-trimmed bodies bore no tell-tale reminders of the babies they'd birthed here less than six months earlier. But I read it in their faces, in those beautiful, humble faces. They were mothers now . . . and it had changed them forever.

Both Meg and Dania had chosen to keep their babies . . . with my blessing. They were not flighty, fantasy-minded young women. Their decisions were carefully weighed. They chose to share a small house in town, and to share caring for their children—Meg watching Dania's bright-eyed little son while his mother worked part-time for the Witherspoons, and Dania caring for Meg's darling daughter so she could fill orders for sewing and alterations . . . skills she'd learned under my roof, I noted with joy just short of pride.

Life did not hold the promise of ease for them. I couldn't let myself think long on the hardships that lay ahead, but I admired their determination to love and care for their children.

And now they stood in the doorway of my dining room, prepared to serve me and my guests—guests I hoped would help fund the next few months of operation, the next few young women who needed shelter. A cyclic gift. A moment I keep tucked in a pocket of memory near my heart.

It crossed my mind to wonder who was tending their little ones. Then an intersecting thought—Lydia would have seen to that detail.

As they bent over the guests, serving us graciously, bringing platters of food from the kitchen, refreshing water glasses, pouring tea and coffee, removing plates, and serving dessert, it struck me that the home and its work was not the reason for the dinner party.

Certainly I was not. *They* were. These reclaimed lives. These grace-bought women who would go home to healthy children at the evening's conclusion. As they brushed past me, their very presence strengthened my resolve.

The dinner party retired to the front parlor following dessert. Meg and Dania stayed behind to clear the table. I took them aside for a brief moment.

"How can I express my gratitude to you?"

Both girls objected and attempted to throw the gratitude back my direction.

"Please leave the mess in the kitchen and go home to your babies."

Dania answered me with a lingering hug, and whispered that they would be praying for me. I would need it.

It has been my observation that those whom the Lord calls to an unusual task are rarely blessed with a passion for drumming up the dollars to support that calling. I then had (and still have) no stomach for fund-raising. I understand the need and the value, but it is a joyless, unnerving task for me, no matter how noble the cause.

The night of the dinner party—the first of many to follow, I now know—my heart raced, as frantic and directionless as the water bugs skating on the surface of the creek backwater. My stomach relocated ten inches north, pressing rudely against my throat, hampering my ability both to speak and to swallow. Hospitality was easy to feign. A calm spirit, impossible.

"Breathe, Anna." Josiah's whisper and smile could be hawked as nerve tonic. "No one here was forced to come. They're here because they care, or they are at the least curious. They didn't respond to a gun barrel pressed to their backs, or merely to Lydia's sociable invitation, but to the wooing of the Holy Spirit and the pull of compassion for the women who flee to this city of refuge."

City of refuge. The picture Josiah painted with his words eclipsed the illustration I'd planned to use. With the clink of silver on china and the music of companionable conversation swirling around me, I mentally rewrote my plea.

"Until just a few minutes ago," I began when I'd gained my guests' attention, "I was unaware that God wrote about this house in His Word. Thousands of years ago, He established the concept of cities of refuge to which His children could run when their passions or inattentiveness or carelessness or clumsiness got them into trouble. The Lord designed cities of refuge not for the innocent but for those whose actions caused pain, even death. In these designated refuges, the guilty found safety, help, and hope. It was God's design.

"Even before Adam and Eve sinned against Him, God set in motion the plan by which He could offer them forgiveness, redemption. In this birthing home, forgiveness is reproduced.

"I don't pretend that the women who come to me are innocent victims of circumstance, although some are. Most made foolish choices. They broke God's laws. This house and my arms are offered as a city of refuge for them, a place where they and their babies can find what they most need. Healing. Protection. Love that makes it safe to explore the possibility of forgiveness . . . and self-forgiveness. Within these walls they

187

gain tools to help them face future temptations fully armed and equipped to resist rather than fall prey to their deceptions.

"I can't turn my back on these girls. The world will swallow them up like a wolf hungry for the taste of fawn. It is my prayer that you will not be able to turn your backs, either."

—————

Did the table groan that night with the weight of gold bullion and silver coins my guests pulled from their pockets? No. But over the course of the next few weeks they all gave what they could. I was humbled by their trust.

And this is the wonder of wonders. Those first dinner guests became advocates for the cause. Other community members began to share their resources at the persuasion of those Lydia handpicked to attend. Never, in all the history of that home, did we have an excess. But we turned no one away for lack of provisions.

I misspoke. We knew a brief period of abundance. As did the Old Testament Jacob's discerning son Joseph, we stored it away in anticipation of lean years ahead. What would we have done without it when the locusts came?

18

Ivy—1951

An echoing, rhythmic shuffle in the stairwell let Ivy know her father was home early from the bowl-a-drome. Was he ill? That rarely happened.

She closed the cover of the notebook that held Anna's story, and from her place at the table watched the apartment door open and her father enter, more stoop-shouldered than normal.

He looked around the kitchen, as if exceptionally reluctant to make eye contact with her. Ivy followed his gaze. Sink empty of dishes. Counters clean—as clean as possible, given their age and wear. No extra lights left on. No overflowing wastebasket. What?

She stood and turned down the radio dial. Dinah Shore— "My Heart Cries for You." Ivy's musical choices were a good twenty years younger than his and somehow irritating to his ears. Still, no word from him. She turned the radio off. A deeper silence.

He set his black and pearlized vinyl bowling-ball bag just inside the door and moved through the kitchen to his chair in the living room. Was she expected to follow? Ask about him? Leave him alone?

Something in the curve of his shoulders said his current burden outweighed hers.

She sat on the corner of the couch, only the lamp table separating them. He hadn't turned on the television, though his eyes were trained in that direction.

"Dad, are you okay?"

He looked at her then, his face a puzzle. "I got a promotion today."

That was his bad news? They'd sat through supper, across the table from each other, and he'd not said a word. He'd left for bowling league with that information unexpressed.

"Dad, that's wonderful! I'm . . . I'm proud of you. You deserve it. I don't know anyone who's worked harder for that company." Ivy stopped herself. So many words. Too many words.

"The deal is," he looked toward the blank-faced television screen again, "the first thing I wanted to do when the boss let me know was tell you."

Did he hear the gasp caught in her throat?

"But I didn't know how."

Ivy pulled her blouse away from her belly. "Is that why you came home early from bowling?"

He leaned forward, forearms on his thighs, hands clasped together. "No. I quit the league."

"What?"

"The reason's not important."

She waited. His claiming it wasn't important hinted at the opposite. The sagging drapes at the window moved. She'd left the window open. Not that it helped any. The air was stifling, despite the promise of rain. Or storm.

This time, unlike the others, so many others, the silence forced an answer from him.

"The guys said . . . said something . . . about you and your . . . condition. And I . . . might have thrown out a few colorful words. Stupid gossip."

Where had the guys at the bowling alley heard about her? Was Jill making it her ambition to ruin her life? Wait. Her father stood up for her? Her evicting father. Her emotionless father.

"So I quit."

"I don't know what to say."

"Nothing to say about that."

Ivy let the moment swirl around her, knocking her equilibrium off but in other ways anchoring her to a thread of hope she didn't know was there.

"We're leaving this apartment."

The reality of her situation flooded in like blood swelling a hammered thumb. "I know, Dad. I'm looking for a place. I haven't found anything yet that I can afford. And I lost my—" She rehearsed his statement. "We?"

"I've always hated this place. Don't understand what you found so appealing about it." A rare smile broke the monument of his roughly sculptured face, bumpy, as if the sculptor had been interrupted before having time to smooth the clay.

"We?"

"There's a place out toward the fairgrounds that's been for sale longer than most. It's got some problems, but it's also got three bedrooms."

She held her breath until her eardrums started to bulge.

"I talked to a friend of mine. He thinks I can get it, with this raise and what I've been putting away every week, and still have enough to get a used car on credit, if it isn't too fancy."

His words died out then, the rush of them exhausted like a sudden air pocket in a bathroom faucet. Spurt and done.

He pushed himself out of his chair and angled for his bedroom.

At the doorway, he paused and turned to face her. "It weren't right that I meant to kick you out. House with three bedrooms? What would I do with all that space . . . without you?"

The tears she'd squeezed back rolled freely now—a hot, wide river on her cheeks.

He nodded toward the billowing curtain. "Don't forget to shut that window."

———

Anna spit toothpaste into the curved enamelware basin Ivy offered her. "He said, 'Don't forget to shut that window'?"

Ivy used the damp washcloth in her hand to wipe a remnant of toothpaste from the corner of Anna's mouth.

"I can do that myself, dear."

"Yes, of course, Miss Anna. And yes, that's what he said."

"To what do you attribute his change of demeanor?"

Ivy handed Anna her mother-of-pearl hand mirror. "I don't know. I stared at the ceiling all night asking myself a similar question . . . and praying I hadn't just dreamed his kindness."

"Praying, Ivy?" Anna stroked her hairbrush through her silver strands, dividing her attention between the mirror reflection and Ivy's reaction.

"Yes, praying. You've had a stronger influence on me than you know."

Thin silver eyebrows arched coyly. "Did you two talk at breakfast this morning?"

"Some. Fewer words. It's been a long time since things have been right between us." *Did Anna mean God or my dad? Either way, the answer stands.*

Anna drew a long, slow breath. "Sometimes you have to travel a long distance to get to where the real adventure begins. And sometimes the adventure is what happens along the way. Healing takes time. Wish I were going to be around to witness the fullness of yours."

Ivy gripped the steel footboard of Anna's bed. "You'll . . . you'll be around . . . for a long time."

"Neither of us has many more days here. Have they hired your replacement?"

Ivy's grip relaxed. "No. But Friday's my last day no matter." Just in time to save her from having to purchase maternity uniforms.

"I will miss you, dear Ivy."

"We're not done writing down your stories, Anna."

Was the mist in those dove-gray eyes for the loss of Ivy or for the incomplete stories? Ivy thought of all the after-hours moments they'd shared, filling the lined pages of the steno pad, Anna's aged voice blessedly slow enough for Ivy to keep up with the pace of her storytelling. The hope tucked between the lines. The light Anna's words shed on Ivy's shadowed existence.

"I talked to Dad about you this morning."

"Me?"

"About you moving in with us."

"Oh, glory, child!"

A noise at the door drew both women's attention. "Mrs.—I mean, *Miss*—Carrington, other patients are waiting for their sponge baths."

"Yes, Mrs. Philemon."

"What you do on your own time is your business. But while you're on duty—"

"Yes, ma'am. On my way."

Anna—1890s

Puff kept a remembrance key in his pocket. An orphan key. The lock into which it once fit was long gone, he said. One might think it worthless then. No. It spoke to him. When he dug his thick-fingered hands into his pants pocket and brushed against the cool metal of that key, he heard its singsong, "Puff, you're a free man. A free man. A free man."

When my mother's nerves troubled her, she fingered the tatted edge of a silk handkerchief given by her own mama . . . when they were still speaking to each other. Before I was born. I imagined those jittery fingertips engaged in a silent language perhaps even she didn't understand: "Oh, Mama, I need you! I need you!"

Aunt Phoebe's remembrance went to the grave with her. She asked to be buried with her silver locket around her neck . . . and the hinge open so the tiny tintype inside showed. The tintype captured Uncle Raif and Aunt Phoebe when love was young, their skin taut, their eyes bright, their future an unknown adventure. I believe she expected to be that precise age in heaven, and wore the locket as a means of introducing herself.

On Josiah's desk, at home among the files and papers and brass inkwell and marble paperweight, lay a feather—his reminder. Not an iridescent, showy, peacock feather. A simple drab-brown feather discarded by a common sparrow with one to spare. His cleaning woman dusted around it, except for the first time when she tried to treat it as garbage.

When Josiah leaned toward worry about his workload or his clients or his children, the feather would pipe up, "Consider the birds of the air! Not one sparrow falls to earth without the

Lord knowing about it. And are you not more important to Him than a sparrow?"

My reminders stay with me, a permanent part of me, to prevent me from misplacing them, I suppose. I run my hands over their pink, numb, erratic trails each morning when I pull my stockings over the scars.

They remind me that love always carries risk and not infrequently pain.

———

Ivy's pencil paused midair. She was about to hear the story of Anna's scars—the ones that showed.

———

From the moment I welcomed Marie into my home, I could sense her undercurrent of fear. A violent act had spawned the baby in her womb. She fought a constant, courageous battle to accept the child as it grew within her, without linking it to the attack and her attacker.

Marie was out visiting Lydia, taking piano lessons more for the diversion than for the music, the afternoon he showed up at my door. I recognized him from the pictures Marie had painted of him with her words. The snarling mouth of a hill badger. The evil eyes of one from whom all goodness had been extracted.

He did not actually show up at my door. He burst through it as if the place were a tavern party waiting for his arrival, rather than a home. My home.

"Where is she?" he demanded when I reached the front hall in which he stood, or rather staggered.

"Who?"

"Marie!"

How my heart pounded! "Not that it is any of your business, but she is not here."

"Not my business?"

"Sir, I'm going to ask you to kindly leave the premises." I straightened my posture but still failed to gain any height or power.

"I ain't going nowhere until she comes with me."

"You will have a great deal of difficulty convincing her of the wisdom of your plan."

"Don't have to convince nobody. She's mine. And that kid she's fixing to whelp. I'll kill anyone that tries to say different."

I gripped the sides of my skirt with my clenched fists to keep my hands from striking out at the beast that was fouling the air and curdling my blood. "She's not here. And she's not yours," I added, growling the last words.

The look he hurled at me was so venomous that I felt flush with the poison. "Take your argument elsewhere, sir. You're not welcome here."

What made me think the encounter was over? He exited, no less agitated than when he'd arrived, and I retreated to my office parlor, closing the tall double doors behind me, shutting out the stench of his presence. I collapsed into the chair at my desk, quivering with rage and concern. How would Marie's life ever be free of this man? Who would protect her and the child from his appearing at their door someday in the not-too-distant future, hissing and staggering and threatening?

It was many minutes before I stopped shaking. Puff and Marie were due back from town, and Josiah was expected to join us for our evening meal. Kitchen duties called to me. The chicken stew would not cook itself.

Would not cook itself. Those four words lodged themselves in my brain, stuck to the walls of it as though it had been branded with a hot iron. They were the last words I entertained before the rock shattered the window, before the flames danced up the drapes and raced across the floor toward me, before I discovered the doors to the office had been barricaded from the outside, before the smoke wrapped its vicelike hands around my throat and squeezed for all it was worth, before the darkness won . . . would not cook itself . . . would not cook itself.

God had a plan all along to protect Marie from her—and my—attacker. Prison bars. A hefty sentence . . . not for what he did to her, but for what he did to me and to my home. Even in my most desperate hours fighting off the spear-wielding demons of pain, Marie's freedom from fear soothed me.

Consciousness was not my friend in the days after the fire. I begged for it to leave. To be alert meant to feel, and I dared not feel. My throat and lungs were raw and soot-clogged. My palms were blistered as if I'd grabbed a roaster from the hot oven with my bare hands. Dr. Noel speculated that as the smoke overcame me, I slapped at the flames on my legs.

It couldn't have been more than a few minutes before Puff and Marie arrived. Only my legs were badly burned. My memories of that time are pieced together from snatches of nightmares, bits of conversation, reports I've been told, and mangled thoughts that blur the boundaries between truth and hallucination. Josiah said that by the time he arrived, Puff had the fire out. How he kept it from spreading to other rooms of the house is as much a mystery as the rest of him. As Josiah related it, Marie hovered over me as if she were already a mother—mine.

After Puff pulled me from the room and carried me to an oasis of shade, Marie tenderly picked charred fabric off the burned flesh on my legs. It was all she knew to do. Dr. Noel said that if she hadn't acted so quickly . . . or if they hadn't come home when they did . . . well, the scars are reminders that I am still here. Reminders, too, that the Lord was not inattentive, not unaware of the flames or of me in the midst of them.

Ivy—1951

"So now you know about the scars, Ivy."

Ivy choked out, "Do they still bother you?"

"Oh, yes. I had my heart set on becoming a Rockette dancer."

"Other than Drew, you're the first person who's made me laugh in a long time, Anna."

"Speaking of your Drew . . . "

She checked her wristwatch.

"Ivy . . . ?"

"I started a letter to him last night during a break from staring at the ceiling. I couldn't think."

Anna's chest rose and fell in an exaggerated sigh.

"I intend to tell him. It's hard to know what to say."

"Lies are complicated, Ivy. The truth is easy. It flows like maple sap on a warm spring day."

"Not this truth."

"Even this one."

It was Ivy's turn to sigh.

"Child, listen to me."

"I have been, Anna. And I don't want to stop. Please consider sharing the house my father hopes to get."

"Your father 'hopes to get.' And then you hope to convince him to share it with me when he's only just agreed to share it with you! Ivy . . ."

"Oh!"

"What?"

"This baby of mine must want to be a Rockette, too."

Anna's eyes teared up.

"What is it, Anna? Are you okay?"

"That's the first time I've heard you call the child 'baby of mine' and the first time you've talked about the little one with a smile on your face. How beautiful."

Ivy felt her cheeks flush, and something like warm syrup spread through her. So this is what it felt like to be a mother.

19

Becky—2012

Downsizing?" The word sounded like a disease that struck other families, not theirs. They'd never upsized, that she could recall.

Gil—once annoyingly absent, now annoyingly present for discussions like this—stated his case. "Do you see any other solution? I'm grateful for the work driving the school bus, but in a town this small, even if I volunteer for every out-of-town game and music competition, it still won't be enough. Wouldn't we rather downsize than face foreclosure?"

"I could get a job, too. Not back at Ellison, I'm sure, but something. There might be opportunities in Minneapolis or Mankato."

"Even if something opened up, Beck, who would Lauren get to babysit, to spend as many hours as you do caring for that little guy? And we certainly can't fork over money for child care. It would eat up your whole paycheck. Or mine."

She slit open another paper grocery bag, pressed it flat on the kitchen island, and stenciled red bells and green Christmas trees on what was once the interior surface. Presents were modest this year. She refused to spend more on wrapping paper than on the gift inside. Good thing the rustic look worked with their decor. "So, by downsizing, you mean . . . "

Gil poured himself a cup of coffee. Becky noticed he was drinking it black. Giving up cream and sweetener for the cause? Had it come to that?

"By that I mean, do you think we could get by with a town-house or condo?"

"You love this yard! This neighborhood!"

His look sobered further. "I love a lot of things that aren't possible right now."

"Already, Gil? Really? We're that bad off just a few weeks into it?"

He frowned into his coffee cup. "Trying to plan ahead. Do you know how hard it might be to sell this place? How long it might take us?"

"Where would we find a condo we could afford that has three bedrooms?"

"Three?"

Jackson wailed in the background, resistant to a diaper change or lost toy or some other little-boy crisis.

"Beck, under the circumstances, isn't Lauren going to have to work out her own solutions? We have to think of us."

Bell, bell, bell. Tree, tree, tree. Slam, slam, slam.

"I *am* thinking of us, all of us, the *whole* family."

"So, we're going to bear all the financial responsibility for Lauren's choices? Forever? Is that what you expect?"

Bell. Slam. Tree. Slam.

"You know I hate it when you go to the extreme, Gil. Forever?"

He sidled to the fridge and grabbed the half-and-half. Still unresponsive, he snatched two blue packets from the small bowl on the counter. The contents were well into dissolving in his coffee when he finally spoke. "Lauren has to pull her own weight in this. Especially now."

"We can't just abandon her."

"Asking her to take responsibility for her actions isn't the same thing as abandoning. She's going to have to act like a parent, a real parent, sooner or later."

"You're not thinking this would happen before the end of the school year, are you? I mean, come on."

A tiny sneeze brought the conversation to a halt. Lauren leaned against the archway between the family room and the kitchen. Jackson sat on her thrust hip, clinging with balled fists to her sweatshirt.

"Lauren, honey, we were just discussing—"

"I know. How much we're in the way. How much easier it would be for you if we weren't around. How tough we've made it on everyone."

Gil abandoned his coffee and rushed to put his arm around both of them. Lauren shrugged him off.

"No, Dad. I get it. We're a problem. As if that wasn't obvious."

"Lauren, we love you. And we love Jackson. It's just that—"

Gil! Say something brilliant! Say something day-saving, heroic, manly, correct.

"What, Dad? It's just that we're *inconvenient*? Tell me about it!" Lauren turned, the movement clunking Jackson's head against the doorjamb. Not hard. Enough to make him cry. She rubbed the spot and said, "Sorry, baby. Mama's sorry," as she stormed down the hall to her room.

Becky stamped a Christmas tree that bled clear through to the countertop.

Gil's laptop held his attention, all of it, for the next two days. Becky had to admire his devotion to job hunting, even if it did keep them from ironing out the wrinkles in their perspectives. She would have offered to help update his resúmé, but in the back of her mind lingered a bullet-point list she must have read somewhere: *How to Love Your Man through a Job Loss*. Writing his resúmé for him was not on the list.

On day three, Gil called her to the end of the couch where he'd planted himself. "Becky, take a look at this."

Bullet-point two: *Wait until he asks for help*.

She stared at the photo. "What is it?"

"A semidetached on Lexington. Looks promising. Priced to sell."

Becky gritted her teeth, then thought better of it. They couldn't afford a dentist bill for a cracked tooth. "A *duplex*? How many bedrooms?"

"Two."

"Bathrooms?"

"Just the one. It would be something we'd have to get used to."

"How many of us, Gil? How many of us would have to get used to it?"

"So we're supposed to go on as we always have, spending without even thinking, meeting everyone else's needs but our own?"

The cost of an ER visit for stitches in her tongue stopped her shy of biting down any harder on it. "They *are* our own, Gil. Lauren and Jackson are our own."

He closed the lid of the laptop. "I guess I expected that from you."

"You say it as if I disgust you because I care about what happens to our daughter and our grandson."

"You know that's not true."

"How would I know that?" She left the room in search of something—anything—to do with her hands. Fold laundry. Dust the top of the refrigerator. Alphabetize spices. Anything other than face the lump that sat on their couch assuming the answer to all their problems lay in miniaturizing the space in which they dwelled.

Vinegar-and-water-soaked rag in one hand, she held onto the top of the step stool and climbed the two steps that would enable her to see the dark unknown of the fridge's upper plateau. One swipe. She glanced at the rag. It had been too long since she'd done this. She folded the rag onto itself and took another swipe.

"Becky."

His voice, behind her, held something that faintly resembled an apology.

"What?"

"Look at me. Please?" Gil stood in the archway with his jacket on and hers over his arm. "Let's go for a ride."

"I'm in the middle of something."

"I can see that. This is important."

"Where would we go?"

"I called the realtor. He'll let us in to see the place tonight. They're pretty eager to sell."

Is it a crime to throw a vinegar-soaked rag at the face of your beloved? Is that considered domestic abuse in this state? Lord, I need an answer quickly.

She blew exasperation through her pursed lips in a whoosh. "I can't believe you called him before we'd had a chance to discuss it."

"Will you just look at it? Then we can talk?"

"Lauren—"

"—just left with Jackson. They're going over to hang out at Noah's for a few hours."

Great. Wonderful. Peachy. She tossed the rag in the general direction of the counter and climbed down to ground level. "Give me a minute to clean up."

"Sure. I'll start the car."

Married that many years and he still didn't know what "a minute to clean up" meant. He thought it was a literal minute.

Her jawed tightened. A duplex?

She ran a brush through her hair and spritzed a stubborn spot with hair spray. She changed from slippers to shoes, pulled a zippered vest over her turtleneck, and swiped at her mouth with tinted lip gloss. Certainly good enough to look at a duplex.

As she walked through the house to the back door, everything about their place seemed suddenly elegant and memory rich.

She found Gil in the driver's seat, a half gallon of fuel used up while she'd cleaned up, that detail fully visible on his face.

"On Lexington?" she asked as she buckled in and hunkered down for an excursion far removed from her idea of fun.

"It's not far from the bowling alley."

"Now, there's a plus." She vowed to drop the sarcasm a notch. Point three on the bullet list.

"And there's a unit just the reverse of this one on the other side," the realtor said.

On heightened sarcasm alert, Becky resisted saying, "Good grief, there are TWO of them?"

"Potential," Gil chimed in. "Think of the potential."

The realtor, black trench coat flapping as he breezed through the icy rooms, explained, "On foreclosures like this, unfortunately there's a tendency for the previous owners to . . . to express their dismay."

That would account for the cupboard doors hanging off their hinges, the graffiti on the living room wall, and the missing switch plates and baseboards. What would account for the South Sea Islands chain of stains on the bedroom carpet, or the putrid smell of undisciplined pets?

Becky put on her "I've always wanted to be a professional designer and remodel homes" hat. The potential still eluded her. All she could think about were the poor people who'd been foreclosed on and how they could not understand what kitty litter was for. "I'm not seeing it. The potential."

Granted, the location wasn't as bad as she'd thought. And the view from the sliding doors onto the patio must be pleasant enough in the warm months with the forest preserve abutting the backyard. The kitchen was surprisingly spacious, despite the loose-tooth cupboard doors. She tried to envision the smell of fresh paint overriding the current odors. Not a chance.

"I have time right now," Gil said, "to invest some elbow grease and carpentry skills. Fix it up nice."

The sarcasm clawed at her, begging to be given permission to speak. Captain Oblivious was happy to have time on his hands? And he thought he could turn the mismanaged pet motel into something habitable for humans? Not just humans. For her? Them?

The realtor rattled his keys and asked, "Would you like to see the other unit?"

"Sure," Gil said at the same moment Becky answered, "No need."

The three played three-way eye-contact tennis for a few moments, until Gil said, "I think we should look at it while we're here."

Becky considered the fine line between patience and lack of courage, between kindness and wimpiness. She wanted to run screaming to the car, pulling out her hand sanitizer as she ran. Instead, she followed the men to the other unit.

Mirror image. Except for the filth. This side was decidedly cleaner. No larger. No more homelike. But cleaner.

Gil clicked on the ceiling fan, then clicked it off. He checked the cupboard under the kitchen sink. He cared about leaks in a duplex she wouldn't be caught dead living in?

"How soon could we get in and start working?" he asked.

Becky swallowed her "I didn't have time to brush my teeth" gum. Her choking fit halted the conversation temporarily.

Assured Becky would live, Gil continued. "We'd have to make the purchase contingent on the sale of our house." He looked at Becky, as if for confirmation of her agreement, as if proud for having thought of that point. Her mind raced back home to her sewing machine and a satin costume with the words *Captain Oblivious* embroidered on the cape. No more than a three-day project.

"Gil!"

"What? Oh, of course, we have to have some time to talk about it."

"Of course," the realtor said. "But as I mentioned earlier, a place like this could go in a snap." His attempt to snap his fingers for emphasis failed.

Becky sniffed. Cat smell. But it wasn't coming from this mirror-image apartment. She sniffed again. The odor clung to her coat!

"You haven't said much, Mrs. Trundle. Did you want to see the closets? There's a stackable laundry pair in each unit, just down the hall here."

"Gil, I need some fresh air." She coughed twice for effect.

"Okay. I think we've seen enough for tonight, Ron. I'll get back to you as soon as we've made a decision."

The click of the key in the lock sounded for all the world like, "You've got to be kidding me."

———ⲟⲟ———

Gil split his attention between the snow-dusted road and sideways glances at Becky. Her peripheral vision could win awards.

"Talk to me, Beck, my paragon of patience."

What was that pain in her palms? Oh. Her fingernails.

"Beck, come on. What did you think? It's our answer, right?"

Naive? Desperate? Delusional? Depressed? Was he so depressed about losing his job that he saw "answers" in the ridiculous? And what was she supposed to do? Would she push him deeper into Delusionland if she told him how insane his plan sounded? Give up their home and move into half of a duplex that should be condemned for the smell alone? *Gil, honey. I think it's time you saw a doctor. The nice doctor will listen to you and help you, and if he can't, he'll prescribe something to make you think more clearly.*

"It's not ideal, granted."

"Gil. Seriously? You think I would seriously entertain the idea of moving into that . . . that . . . ?"

"Hovel?"

"You said it. I didn't. And leave Jackson and Lauren out in the cold?"

"It has heat." Was that whining in his voice?

"What?"

"The duplex. Heated. Air-conditioning, too. I think. Have to check on that."

"All four of us would live in a bedroom and a half? You'd let Jackson crawl around on that disgusting carpet?"

Gil swung the car to the side of the road and slammed the shift stick into park. He left the motor and the windshield wipers running. "Are you nuts? It's filthy!"

"At least we agree on one thing."

"What did you think I meant by—? Oh, Becky!" He reached for her.

She pressed her body against the passenger-side door. His chuckles confirmed her suspicions that he'd lost his ever-loving mind. As if she didn't have enough on her plate right now. Her husband was mentally deranged.

Gil raised his gloved hands, palms up. "You didn't honestly—? Oh, honey. I'm not a complete idiot."

Prove it.

"We'd fix up that side. Tear out all the carpet. Probably have to replace most of the subfloor, too. Paint would help. And switch plates. We'd pay for fumigation, if we had to. But the other side wouldn't need much. And there's our answer."

"The other side?"

"Beck, if we bought the whole building, both units, and let Lauren and Jackson live in half until she could afford for them to be on their own, and we lived in the other half until our financial situation improved, then we'd eventually wind up with two rental units and maybe a way to get back on track with our retirement plans. Providing, of course, I can get hired somewhere."

How long had it been since she'd blinked? Or breathed?

"Selling our current house would be critical. But Ron thinks he might have a lead for us already. And if we could make a strong enough profit from that sale, we'd have the funds for remodeling the disgusting unit."

Tears formed. "You . . . you think it's disgusting?"

"Are you feeling okay? Wasn't it obvious? I can't wait to get home and take a shower. And we were only in there a few minutes."

"I . . . I love you."

Gil tilted his head and ventured another reach in her direction. This time she allowed his hand on her shoulder, then his arm across both shoulders.

"Good to know. I love you, too." His voice had a question in it. He probably wondered if she needed psychiatric help.

Weren't they a pair?

20

Ivy—1951

She didn't expect a homemade cake or a card signed by the staff: *Best wishes on your new endeavors.* She didn't expect a baby shower with a pile of infant items from the Montgomery Ward catalog. But Ivy did think someone might say something, some little thing. *We'll miss you. Nice working with you. Good luck with, you know, the . . . um . . . the "in a family way" business.*

Nothing.

Girls in a family way usually disappeared for a few months to "help a sick aunt" or "recuperate from a curious illness." Or they got married quickly and had "premature" babies. Ivy could have handled things so many different ways and avoided the discomfort of coworkers who didn't know what to say or how to help.

Help? It was as if anyone who befriended Ivy would be in danger of catching what she had.

Even the lucid patients seemed withdrawn, skittish. Had the staff poisoned them against her, too? All except Anna.

Anna dabbed at her eyes with a handkerchief all day long. Her brave smile fought valiantly but couldn't dislodge the mask of sadness. Ivy fought back her own tears and clung to a thread of hope that their good-bye was temporary.

Ivy's shift ended uneventfully. One final task remained. The last good-bye for room 117.

"So . . . ," she said as she stood at the foot of Anna's bed.

"So . . . ," came the echo from its pillow.

"I'm not sure it's a good idea for me to visit. Not right away, at least."

"Oh, fiddle-dee-do on the whole silly world!"

"Anna!"

"You forget about the gossips and get on with the business of making a home for you and that baby and the baby's father."

Ivy sniffed back what was quickly turning into a steady stream of tears. "I'll come see you. Just not right away."

"So, we'd better make progress this afternoon then."

"I didn't plan to stay afterward to work on your story today, Anna."

"Oh, I see. You were going to rush off to—?"

An empty apartment. An unproductive session with the help wanted ads. "I guess I could stay for a few minutes."

"Good. There's something I need to get off my chest."

Anna—1890s

I wished I'd been born with more than two arms. I longed to embrace the brokenhearted parents who brought their daughters to me, without loosening my grip on the weak-kneed mothers-to-be.

I fought the urge to shake a few parents, to rattle the cages of the bitter and uncaring, the unkind and unforgiving. My heart caught in my throat, nearly suffocating the life out of me, the day a steely-eyed, steely-jawed father literally *kicked* his eldest daughter out of the back of his wagon. We tended to her skinned knees and forearms for weeks. We tended her bruised and tattered spirit every day she was with us.

Except for grace, I didn't believe she could ever be right. A person can't be treated like refuse without showing it somehow. Downcast eyes. A tic or tremor. An edge to the voice. Troubled dreams. I've gotten so now I can pick out of a crowd the people who have known no kindness at home. The pain of it shoots through me like a lightning bolt through a water-soaked willow, setting every nerve ending on fire.

Like a wave that retreats from shore for a moment, shivering as it gathers momentum, forgiveness should flood back in with more love and vigor than ever. I have seen it happen.

One mother—about to become a grandmother—swallowed her disappointment like a foul-tasting, but necessary pill. Rounder than she was tall, and well padded against life's jostling, she wore her arms too far forward, as though they were sewn in backward; but she was making do.

The lines on her face read like a map of her past. The tracks of wagon wheels that carried her family from the east to a not-so-long-ago uncivilized place. The still and forever visible trail of tears etched by grass fires and crop failures and a husband who didn't understand that she would never be free of the memory of a toddler son buried under a nameless, scrawny shrub on the unforgiving prairie.

And now this. Her third-born daughter of six—the one who had never given her a lick of trouble—her angel-child with flax-colored, silken hair and a face of tempting innocence was brought to my door with a swollen belly and the too-familiar downcast eyes.

The baby's father had been merely passing through town. The girl's own father didn't know how to rise above his hurt and embarrassment to continue to love her.

Amelia and her mother alone had the courage to face the crisis. Marielle, Amelia's mother, would not . . . could not . . . leave another child unattended. Against her husband's wishes, and no doubt at great emotional cost, she visited often during the months Amelia resided with me. She never came empty-handed—another similarity between the woman and her God. She brought soft flannel nightshirts and diapers for the baby, jellies or homemade breads and pies for our household, and carefully squirreled coins to tuck into her daughter's palm.

She spoke little, like Amelia.

"Marielle, would you care for some tea?"

"Yes, thank you. I'll get it."

"I'm happy to serve you."

"Please allow me, Miss Morgan."

When she returned with the tea, many minutes later, I knew she'd been at work in the kitchen while waiting for the water to heat. The skin on her fingers was pruned. I suspected the roasting pan I'd left to soak now looked like new.

Amelia and Marielle walked together on the property, their lips rarely moving but their hearts connected.

Who but God could have timed one of this mother's visits to coincide with the birth of her angel-faced granddaughter? I would have written the script that way, if the pen had been mine. With gratitude for the unexpected mercy, Dr. Noel and I stepped back from the bed and let this love-conquers-all woman with a deeply lined face and unspeakably kind eyes coax her granddaughter out of the womb. Love was the first thing that child knew of this world. Love's hands were the first to touch her.

I knew that Amelia and rosebud-lipped Aubrey Lillian would not flounder when the new grandmother asked Puff to retrieve from her wagon a beautiful hickory cradle that Amelia's thawing father made for the child . . . his pain-birthed grandchild. What it must have cost him to saw and plane and sand and carve and fit together the pieces of this forgiveness cradle! I prayed that his voice and arms would grow as skilled at expressing his love.

In the spring following the birth of her bright-eyed grand-daughter, Amelia's mother, Marielle, brought the dignity of a name to our home. She returned with a limp, scraggly-looking vine, and scratched a spot for it in the dirt along the foundation on the east side of the house.

"Morning glory," she said, as I watched over her shoulder.

The patch of ground she'd chosen did not look particularly fertile. And the scrawny vine held no visible promise. Marielle warned that morning glories resist being transplanted. But she worked with the confidence of one whose next task might be calling Lazarus from his grave.

I confess I had little hope that the vine would survive the afternoon, much less the season. As if amused rather than frustrated by my doubts, Puff smiled the smile of the knowing. He and Marielle listened to some voice of reason to which I was deaf.

Urged on by love alone, the nearly naked morning glory vine grew accustomed to its new home and to my sporadic watering.

I add this next detail so you can wonder with me at the odds against this tenacious plant. It was an exceptionally dry spring, as I recall. Other established plantings near Marielle's succumbed, their bowed, exhausted, parched heads tripping over their roots. But, with every element working against it, the vine—like the house and its purpose—survived.

Marielle returned one more time, in the early fall, with an armload of infant clothes her granddaughter had outgrown. Gifts for other too-young mothers.

We rarely had visitors so early in the morning. I guessed her secondary mission before she voiced it, following her out the back door, down the steps, and around to the east side of the house.

The morning glory vine had chosen to dress for company, for which I was as thankful as a proud mother on Easter Sunday. The profusion of blue, ruffled, translucent blossoms was a downright spectacle! A tight bud the night before, each flower had twisted itself open at the sunlight's invitation, even as the hearts of many of my girls twisted and wriggled their way open under the penetrating rays of God's Son.

Marielle didn't smile in response, as I assumed she would. Fresh tears pooled in her eyes as she quoted the Scripture that was her sustenance . . . and mine. "Weeping may endure for a night, but joy cometh in the morning."

Fingering the velvet of a sunlit blossom, she added her own commentary to the end of the verse: "And doesn't God get the glory in *that*!"

My home was first called Morning Glory Haven for Unwed Mothers that day.

———

Until now, I've not shared with you the battles I fought over the young men who left their seed in these girls and then walked away, with no more sense of responsibility than a male lion seeking not a family but an outlet for his urges—

———

Ivy—1951

Ivy's pencil stilled.

Anna coughed. "Dear, will you kindly erase that previous sentence? I need to edit out the bitterness. I'm still working on erasing from my *life* the remnants of bitterness that hover like a chronic case of indigestion."

Anna—1890s

I'm not unaware of or ungrateful for the young men who have humbly adjusted their lives to accommodate a change in their own timetable for fatherhood. My heart readily embraces the repentant, the contrite.

I'm painfully aware that God has set a standard of patience to which I have not attained. But I do understand—though I will never fully grasp—His promise from Isaiah 57:15: "I dwell in the high and holy place, with him also that is of a contrite and humble spirit."

How easy it is to love the contrite, those who understand the weight of their choices and their consequences. How freely the sympathy flows toward those who face their responsibility and let it propel them toward the sorrow that leads to repentance. And how much I am learning from observing that phenomenon.

To witness the birth of a child is to witness a miracle, even under ordinary circumstances. But within the walls of Morning Glory, the moment of birth was as holy a thing as earth can know.

"This! This is what God can do!" I said aloud whenever a young woman's heart was open to it. "Out of disappointment and shame, the Lord births life! In the womb of Grace, He nurtures an embryo of Hope. And when the time is right, Hope pushes its way out into the light. We catch it with grateful hands and gaze upon His handiwork with awe and gratitude."

I remember the words because I repeated them so often . . . to myself and to my girls.

Hope's labor pains. That's how I came to refer to the rejection and setbacks. They grabbed me around the belly and threatened to suffocate me. But I grew to look upon them with a measure of excitement, as a long-overdue mother greets with joy her first doubling-over pain. The baby—Hope—is about to be born!

It would do me no more good to scream in response to the distresses I faced than it would for my girls to react to their labor with thrashing and howls. What an unnecessary and counterproductive waste of energy!

When warning a laboring mother that her moaning and screeching would needlessly exhaust her and frighten the other residents, I knew I was speaking to myself. My own hysteria, if I'd allowed it, could have kept others from trusting that the Lord was more than equal to their need.

Morning glory sickness. In many ways, it looked and felt as morning sickness must everywhere else on the planet. Calling it morning glory sickness was perhaps a weak attempt at injecting humor into a humorless malady.

"Sharla has the morning glories," one of the residents might have reported about another. "She won't even touch the raspberry ginger tea I took her."

Some suffered more than others. Some not at all, which hardly seemed fair to the rest. We did what we could to ease morning glory's discomfort. Raspberry ginger tea. Dry toast at the bedside. Cold compresses. Patience. Prayer. But, like a pioneer confronted with the continent-splitting Mississippi, we, too, knew that the only way to the other side was straight through.

I have no proof, but I strongly believe that misery is intensified when the heart is not buoyed by joy. The girls did not need to hide their sick moments, as they often did before they came to live at Morning Glory, when their stories and babies were hidden. But they did need to learn to cope.

Empathy flowed through the halls of this home in abundance. Did it help? Doesn't it always?

We implemented nearly every home remedy whose reputation found its way to our ears. Not just for waves of nausea stirred by a babe within, but for whatever infirmity wandered through our doors.

Mild kitchen burns were tended with scrapings of raw potato. A tea of honey and vinegar calmed nagging coughs. Crushed onions for headaches. Onions roasted in ashes for colds. Onion juice and honey for croup. The garden was heavily devoted to onions.

But there is no antidote to bitterness, and no substitute for compassion.

I heard my mother's voice in my ears . . . and in my comfort. The silky voice she used as a birthing tool for all the women who called on her for help. How many births had she attended? And for how many did she insist I accompany her—so often against my wishes? It was books I wanted. An education. After too many truancies when called from the classroom to assist my mother, my education was up to me. Borrowed books and a listening ear. Stories from those who had been places and done things beyond the boundaries of my simple life. I thought my mother stifled my education. In so many ways, she formed it.

In the early days, I assumed she made me go with her because we were alone, the two of us. She couldn't very well leave her little girl home alone in the middle of the night when a furtive knock at our door sounded the alarm that she was needed . . . that *we* were needed. I was her "assistant." The mothers-to-be accepted me as part of the package. Mother and I were a team.

If I'd had a father, as a child I could have stayed snuggled under the covers until morning. He would have taken care of me, listened for me, and tended to my needs until Mother returned. If morning had dawned and she still had been holding a laboring hand, I could have made breakfast for Daddy. He would have been so proud of my talents in the kitchen, for such a young thing. I could have learned to make his tea and surprised him with its morning-defining aroma.

"Pumpkin!" he'd have called me. Or "Princess! How kind of you! What a sweet girl you are! Come give your papa a hug." And that's how we would have started our day.

But if I'd had a father, how would I have learned all I needed to know to fulfill what was asked of me? How would I have learned the stages of labor and their transitions, having no children of my own, if I had not attended nearly every birth my mother attended?

How would I have gained the stamina to endure if I'd not practiced at my mother's knee? From what source could I have gathered the insight to know when the path of labor was leading to a life-threatening precipice, when a doctor's expertise was required, when and how to prepare a woman's heart to bear the unconscionable agony of miscarriage, the twisting pain of stillbirth?

God knew what comforts I needed to go without.

Ivy—1951

Ivy's pencil disengaged with the page once more. Anna's voice always took on a poetic quality when she spoke of the past. When not reminiscing, even at eighty-six she talked like any young woman of the 1950s. A "cool cat," some might say. But when her memories took over, the storytelling that flowed from her wrinkled lips and love-smoothed heart held an almost Victorian elegance.

Although mesmerized by the rhythm of the words, Ivy remained glued to the stories themselves, often rereading them at night in her room, catching bits of wisdom she'd missed when focused on committing it all to paper.

What would happen to Anna's words once the story was complete?

Ivy couldn't imagine God meant them only for her.

And she couldn't believe she'd just considered that God had given her even a moment's intentional thought. What was happening?

"Ivy?"

"I . . . I need to sharpen my pencil." She pulled the small sharpener from her purse, bent over the wastebasket, and twirled the pencil to a fine, fresh point, leaving curls of yellow-edged wood shavings in the basket.

"Turn to a new page, would you please?"

Ivy complied, anticipating a new chapter, maybe more about Mr. Grissom and where he fit.

"Jot this down please, Ivy." Anna cleared her throat. "'My dear Drew. It's time I told you a most amazing story about the life we've created and ask you to forgive me for not including you in the miracle before now.'"

Ivy's pencil shook as it hovered over the paper. "I really need to get home. It's getting dark earlier these days."

Anna lowered her gaze. "Then write fast."

21

Becky—2012

Becky's best imitation of aerobic exercise was bending into some lesser-known yoga shape and holding her breath while she plugged the Christmas tree lights into the outlet buried behind the donated tree. Only four something in the afternoon, but the room needed the lights. It got dark so early these days.

The donated tree—thanks to a sympathetic tree farmer from church—wasn't at all the kind she liked. She loved the smell of balsam fir and appreciated their softer needles. This one was as prickly and pale as a bleached-out cactus. But it was free. At the moment, *free* scored top points with her.

Becky vacuumed twice a day to keep the family room from acting like a minefield of prickles. With Jackson no longer an inanimate object, rolling off the play blanket and to interesting locations like under the coffee table, keeping the minefield effect to a minimum grew more important by the hour.

As he played now with a stuffed penguin that mere months ago had been Lauren's, Becky studied the tree. The lights disguised a lot of imperfections . . . as long as she focused on the glow. When her eyes drifted to the bare spots on the branches or to the crooked top—Angela, the homemade angel, leaned a little left of center—Becky felt the bare spots as if they were crusty scabs on her skin.

Jackson giggled, apparently responding to the joke the penguin told, blissfully unaware of the family and financial dynamics swirling around him, unaware of the national debt, the health-care debate, the cost of education, the starving children in Africa, the melting polar ice caps, and the fact that the Korean War never really ended.

Oh, to be unaware.

Becky couldn't picture their traditional Christmas tree resting anywhere other than that spot in front of the sliding doors to the patio. Couldn't imagine leaving the room that once was Mark's. Couldn't imagine squeezing twenty-plus years of married life into half a house. Couldn't imagine how Lauren would keep her half clean.

But after the shock waves subsided, she did see the wisdom of the plan. In theory. And in theory, even though it felt as if they'd given up so much in the aftermath of Lauren's one-night stand, two-night stand—*Oh, Lord, I don't want to know how many nights' stands there were!*—and even though more sacrifices were on the way, the shining light covering the bald spots was Jackson.

Unto them a child was born. A precious, well-loved, happy child. Joy to their world.

Becky scooped Jackson sans penguin into her arms, snuggled him close in the valley where lies a grandmother's heart, and thanked God for him in the shadow of an imperfect tree.

The phone interrupted the reverie. Didn't phones always interrupt?

"Becky? It's Monica."

"Hi. I've been meaning to call you. How are you doing?"

"Better. Then not. Comes and goes."

Becky hugged Jackson a little tighter. "What helps?"

"You always could read my mind."

"What?" *And no, not always.*

"It helps to get out and do something for others."

The tentative bridge they'd begun to repair made Becky double think every word. "Win-win, huh?" She should have thought three times on that one.

"I'm doing so much volunteering, between church, the library, and the women's shelter, that it's . . . it's created a problem I . . . I wondered if you could help me solve."

Becky set her grandson back on his play blanket. If Monica asked her to volunteer nonexistent time . . .

"I know you and Gil are going through some money struggles."

And the gap widens. In a corner of her mind, Becky heard the whisper of a high-end dishwasher in someone else's kitchen.

Monica drew a noisy breath. "And I wondered if you'd consider working part-time for me? Cleaning?"

Was four seconds considered dead air? Becky rushed to fill it. "Hey, Monica. Love to talk about that sometime, but there's someone at the door. Can I call you back? Thanks. 'Bye."

It wasn't a complete lie. Disappointment stood in the doorway, sticking out its tongue.

⁕

"Any responses to the résumés you sent out, Gil?" Becky turned down the covers on her side of the bed while Gil sat on his side, rubbing heel healer into his winter feet.

"You mean, in the six hours since you last asked that question? Nope. Nothing." He switched to the other foot. "I imagine there's a bidding war for my talents, lawyers constructing pro-posals I can't walk away from. No phone calls yet. I wonder if I should see if there's something wrong with our phones." He rolled into bed like a clown might roll out of a basket. Ta-da!

Becky slipped between the sheets, regretting their decision to crank the furnace down so low at night. Did blanket sleep-ers like Jackson's come in her size? She pulled the comforter under her chin and shivered for good measure. "I wasn't trying to be a pest about it. Just hoping."

"Yeah," he said, no longer the clown. "Me, too."

"It was snowing the night we looked at that duplex."

"Right."

"Was there a yard? I don't remember."

Gil turned on his side to face her. "Kind of a bad news/good news thing. Not much of a yard, but it will only take one pass with the lawn mower. Imagine the time we'll save on weekends."

"Captain Lame-o?"

"Yes, ma'am?"

"Can I have a little spot to plant morning glories?"

"Boom! We just cut the mowing time in half."

"Oh, Gil!"

"Laugh or cry—our only two choices."

Becky pulled the sides of her pillow over her ears as she lay on her back, focused on the textured ceiling. A bug smudge, likely from the summer, held her attention. "We have a third choice."

"Go crazy?"

She dropped her grip on the pillow. "Okay, four choices."

"What's the fourth?"

"I can call Monica back and tell her I'd be honored to be her scullery maid."

The call came at nine the next morning. Ron had an interested party who wanted to see the house.

"Christmas week? Gil, come on. Really?"

"The place looks . . . festive."

"No, really. This is impossible. They want to see the house today?"

Gil jiggled Jackson on his hip while Becky brushed her teeth. "I'm going to go wake Lauren. She'll have to help with the cleanup."

Becky spit and rinsed. "I'm serious, Gil. This is worse than impossible. We can't have this house ready for a viewing today. Have you seen Lauren's room? The garage? The basement?"

"In this kind of market, I don't think we have much of a choice."

She had stooped as low as she thought she could go, an emotional limbo-dancing champion. The tropical music beat in her head even now as she bent over backward and slid under the ever-lowering bar of life challenges. "Seriously? Christmas week? Better idea. Let's put an 'as is' sign on the front door and hop a flight to the Caribbean. Seems appropriate."

A shadow crept over Gil's let's-make-the-best-of-it face. "I wish I could say, 'Yeah, let's escape for a while. Lie in the sun. Walk on the beach and let nothing knock us flat but the waves.'" The shadow deepened. "This isn't where I thought we'd be at this stage of life."

Ah, this "stage" of life. All ad-lib. No script. No teleprompter. All made up as they went along. She could pull the shades lower or let in a little light. "If we have company coming, we'd better get busy. You grab the shovel. I'll grab the garbage bags and the air freshener."

22

Ivy—1951

Ivy stood in the doorway, one hand clutching a newly composed letter to Drew, the other waving good-bye to what would have been her last choice, but her best choice, of a friend. Anna waved back, her arthritic fingers splayed in odd directions but as gentle as they must have been when easing babies into the world.

"I'll be back, Anna. As soon as I can."

"I would hope so. You haven't heard my love story yet."

Ivy smiled in spite of the tightness in her throat.

"But, dear child . . . ?"

"Yes?"

She nodded and pointed toward the letter. "Don't come back before you've done the repair work on your own love story. Deception breeds deceptive success. A false front. An imitation of a true answer."

"Yes, ma'am." She'd overacted the obedience gesture and bowing, but believed Anna's every word.

Anna sighed. Every line of her face filled with compassion. "That baby's name is not Remorse."

Ivy stood before the post-office building, its tan bricks lined up, not staggered, speaking of order and neatness—two things patently missing from her relationships, especially the one represented by the letter in her hand. Written. Stamped. Risky.

Oh, so risky.

She'd prayed every day for Drew's safety, not confident of her skill in prayer or of any obligation on God's part to listen to her who'd given Him so little thought. And yes, it lent an undertone of guilt to her prayers. But Anna's persuasive history pushed Ivy to venture into new prayer territory—making a request for herself.

She pressed the envelope to her heart and asked God, who seemed to care far more than she knew, to prepare Drew for the news it held.

Was He listening?

She asked for one thing more. A miracle. That Drew would still love her.

A stirring in her belly changed her prayer. That Drew would love the child.

She kissed the envelope and slid it into the after-hours mail slot. The truth was long overdue.

The four-block walk from the post office to the dry cleaners felt uphill, though Ivy knew it was flat as the prairies that drew Anna's ancestors to the area. Her last day at work. Maybe the beginning of her last hope of a future with Drew Lambert.

The storefronts held little notice, except for how her reflected profile in the plate-glass windows had changed. Tomorrow she'd take a few dollars to the secondhand store and look for a couple of maternity blouses and a skirt with an elastic panel. The rash of babies born nine months after the Second World War ended a handful of years ago might mean the racks of no-longer-needed maternity wear would hold an ample supply for her choosing.

Before long, she'd have to concern herself with baby clothes, too. The "Help Wanted" sign in the front window of the dry cleaners could *not* be a sign from heaven. *No. Please, no.*

She stood at the base of the stairs to the apartments above, exhausted by life's uncertainty. She gripped the handrail and pulled herself from step to step, hesitating on the landing. Their apartment door swung open. The shock of it slammed her against the wall of the landing. In the oppressive heat from the cleaners, flakes of plaster stuck to the backs of her arms.

"Ivy! You're home. Come on."

Her dad shot past her down the stairs before she could explain how badly she needed to collapse on her bed and cry out the remains of the day.

She followed him. Her apron waited behind the apartment door. Whatever her father had in mind automatically held more appeal than making—*what day was it?*—pork chops and applesauce, maybe cabbage slaw for a change.

"We'll stop at the diner for supper," her dad called over his shoulder, his traditionally emotionless voice bearing a faint hint of excitement.

The echo of her footsteps stopped.

He turned back to her. "Now don't get yourself used to that. It's a special occasion."

"Yes, sir."

At the base of the stairs, he paused until she caught up, then wordlessly walked out into the deepening dusk and climbed behind the wheel of a raven-black and chrome Oldsmobile with faint fringes of rust.

Ivy took in the scene. Her dad behind the wheel, beckoning through the open window for her to get in. The Andrews Sisters and Bing Crosby harmonizing on the car radio—"Have I Told You Lately That I Love You?"—a song that had never meant as much to her as it did at the moment. Ivy grabbed the chrome handle of the passenger door and pulled. The interior—two-toned black-and-white vinyl—showed surprisingly little wear compared to the exterior rust. From a home with no garage? The victim of many Midwestern winters? She wanted to capture all of it, every detail, to tell Drew and Anna.

Her dad's driving technique was smooth, as if it hadn't been years since he owned an automobile. The town looked different at driving speed than it did at walking speed. Less intimidating. Friendlier. Normal people rode in cars with their dads.

But a second heartbeat pulsed a few inches lower than hers, and it partially belonged to a soldier who didn't yet know, but who would soon know, it existed. She'd slipped her fate into a mail slot, said good-bye to her truest friend, been evicted from her source of income, and now rode beside a man who had fathered her but who barely talked to her and couldn't even point to the radio when it sang, "Have I told you lately that I love you?"

Life was far from normal.

"This is it." Her dad pulled to the curb in front of a squat, pale yellow bungalow. It wasn't the best light to get a good look, and her dad made no move to turn off the motor or get out of the car. Ivy did what she could to assess the property from that distance.

Set back from the street. A long, broken, weed-choked side-walk led to the front door, centered between two twelve-paned windows. A living room and dining room? The lawn, unlike that of its neighbors, hadn't been mowed, perhaps all summer.

Wildflowers and what looked like prairie grasses towered over the crisp lawns on either side. The smallest of the homes on the street, it gave the sense of having shrunk with age, as had so many of the patients at Maple Grove Nursing Home. Anna.

She kept her gaze directed out the window. "How many . . . how many bedrooms?"

"Three. They're small. The largest has an alcove. Might work for the crib. Room for both of you in there. Might want to paint."

Her dad made allowance for the baby. Everything above her neck pinched to staunch the tears that threatened. He'd used a baby word—*crib*. The child had a home.

Dad tilted his head and leaned her way, as if getting a better view of the house. "We'll have to buy one more bed. But I think I have a lead on one from a guy at work. His mother-in-law lived with them the last few months until she died."

Where were all these words coming from? They didn't flow naturally. It was as though he squeezed them out through a corroded pipe. Flat and emotionless, they told the facts, just the facts. But hidden behind the statements lay hope of a change Ivy didn't see coming, a change that glowed like the anemic streetlight on the corner of the block, a light that eased to life as the Olds pulled away from the curb.

She felt the trees arching over the street as if snugging the neighborhood. As the breeze rushed through the open window, she took a deep breath. Not a hint of dry-cleaner fluid or steamed wool. She smelled freshly mowed lawns, night-blooming jasmine, and an outdoor grill's contribution to a family's supper.

A bedroom she could share with her child. A place at the table.

She turned toward her dad, his face now reflecting the odd greenish light of the dash instruments. "Buy one more bed?"

231

He cleared his throat of years' worth of congestion. "For that Anna."

Ivy tried but couldn't suppress the one-beat sob or the tears that blurred her vision.

"Make sure you know I'm not responsible for taking care of that woman. You'll have your hands full with"—he nodded toward her belly—"those two. But they're not my responsibility. Got that?"

"Got it."

"They can have a room and food. Anything else, you're all on your own."

"I got it, Dad. Thank you."

"I don't know how you're going to work and manage taking care of—"

"Dad. I got it. I don't know, either. But I'm pretty sure God does. And I'm . . . going . . . to have to . . . trust Him."

As if agreeing, the baby leapt in Ivy's womb.

—⁂—

Plowing through the paperwork to get Anna Grissom released to Ivy and her father's custody took as long as wading through the legal details for the purchase of the house. Anna had outlived Josiah's children, which both complicated and uncomplicated the matter of legal custody.

The remains of late summer took down the last of its decorations to allow room for autumn's before Ivy and her father closed the door to the apartment and moved their possessions to the bungalow. Ivy had done all she could to clean and patch, emptying box after box and canister after canister of various cleansers, painting all the bedrooms, scrubbing the hardwood floors—wishing for the luxury of carpeting but knowing Anna's wheelchair would fare much better on the hardwood—

sewing curtains for the kitchen window, and finding drapes for the front windows at the secondhand store.

The alcove in Ivy's bedroom remained empty, but there was time. A little time.

Anna's room overlooked the side yard on the east. Ivy positioned the bed, made a space for the wheelchair, and added a small table for a view out the window. After two days of unpacking Carrington boxes and moving furniture, which went slower because of the restrictions the baby placed on her involvement in heavy lifting, they transported Anna from room 117 to 329 Cottonwood Drive. It took some fussing to get her settled in and to convince her that her excessive gratitude made Ivy's dad claustrophobic. He spent most of that evening raking leaves in the backyard, as if there wouldn't be a far larger collection before the season ended.

Anna directed where her few possessions should rest. A very long life. So few possessions. But it seemed as if Anna had held onto what mattered and had discarded the rest.

"I don't know how to talk to him." Anna refolded a handful of embroidered hankies for Ivy to place in the smallest drawer of the dresser along the north wall of the room.

"My father?"

"Yes."

Ivy chuckled. "You'd think asking me would get you at least a handful of answers, wouldn't you? You've known him an afternoon. I've known him all my life and I'm no farther along—" The choice of words halted her. No farther along. She laid her hand on the shelf of her belly.

"I don't want to offend him."

"Oh, Anna. If you discover that secret, please tell me."

"Has he always been this tightly curled upon himself?"

Somewhere in an unpacked box was a thick black photo album, with scallop-edged photos tucked into neat black corner triangles that held them in place, that held her childhood in place. Wagon rides. A toddler-sized rabbit fur coat and hat. Ivy on her daddy's shoulders. Perched on the back of a carnival pony. Standing between her parents. Neither parent wore definable expressions. No one would caption the photos with the word *Joy*. And three-quarters of the way through the album, the remaining pages held black triangles with emptiness where pictures had been removed, followed by pages with nothing at all.

"Ivy, forgive my prying. I forget sometimes that others aren't as eager to share their stories as I am."

Ivy closed the dresser drawer and turned toward Anna. "We should decide where you'd like your lamp. How about here?"

Anna reached for the chain. Ivy scooted the lamp closer.

"I'll get an extension for that chain this week. Dad can bring one home from work."

"Much appreciated."

Too tired to tell stories that night, Anna retired early, which left Ivy to rearrange things in her own bedroom, imagining the crib in the alcove, a rocker near the window, an additional dresser for baby necessities. All those thoughts wove their way through the ever-present thread of concern.

She'd received one letter from Drew. It arrived the day after she sent the truth winging its way toward South Korea. Nothing since then. Maybe nothing ever again. Her hand moved to the mound of her child. "We'll be okay, little one. But I wish you could know your daddy."

Ivy slept that night with a wet pillow.

When she checked on Anna in the morning, she found the woman wiping her own tears.

"Anna? What's wrong?" Ivy rushed to her side. "Are you in pain?"

"Far from it. Are those what I think they are?" She squinted and pointed out the window.

A vine partially obscured her view. Ivy would have to get out there later in the day to cut it back so Anna could see the—. No. A handful of azure and raspberry-pink blossoms nodded at the sun.

"Morning glories, Anna." Ivy pulled her chenille robe tighter across her budding body.

Anna's smile—all her own teeth—widened. "I'm home, Ivy. We're home."

The cramped bungalow didn't resemble the house Anna once named the Morning Glory Haven for Unwed Mothers. But the love did.

"Yes. We're home."

Anna—1890s

"A mother was born last night, Puff. Not a baby only. A mother, too, was brought to the light of life."

"It's a wondrous thing, Miss Morgan."

Puff and I shared tea at the worktable in the kitchen. The sun was an hour from checking in for the day, as was Puff. I had yet to go to bed from the night before.

"Do you want me to set a fire under the copper boiler for washing up the sheets and such?"

"Puff, I believe the hot water would be ready before I am."

"Wait a bit?"

"Please. I have them soaking in cold water."

"You might want to get some sleep."

"Maybe. You know how unpredictable these first hours of life can be."

"The new mama's resting well?"

"Reba is an amazement to me. For such a young thing, she bore her labor with courage. When the babe was laid in her arms, I saw in her eyes a maturity that must have entered just as the child left her body. Some new mothers act as if they've birthed a doll, a plaything. Reba seemed to sense she cradled the essence of life."

He studied my face and the way I rubbed my knees. "You hurting?"

"My legs ache, that's all. They don't like working long hours without being pampered. They're rebelling against what I asked of them last night."

"Swolled up?"

"A little."

"Can't push too hard without paying a price somewhere."

"You're right."

"You want I should ride in and ask Miss Lydia to spell you today?"

Fatigue couldn't prevent the smile that overtook me. "Her own little one is putting up a fuss in the mornings, Puff."

"She in the family way?"

"Some would call it a miracle."

"Aren't they all?"

I learned to think of sleep as a luxury—like white sugar and silk stockings and oranges at Christmas. A treasure, when I could get it. Savored as if it were chocolate lingering on my tongue.

Sleep had its seasons. When the house was quiet, the spare bedrooms empty, I slept deeply, the sleep of a carefree child. As the rooms filled, sleep grew thinner, like soup watered down to accommodate extra guests at the table.

I listened for the tears my girls cried in the night. My senses stood sentry through the darkness, ready to respond to their distress, if necessary. It often was. I followed indigestion down the stairs and fed it bicarbonate of soda and words of comfort. I massaged cramped calves and pressed my fist into knots in young backs. I opened the Word and poured its healing balm over the wounds of raw rejection. Over midnight tea, I listened as the stories spilled out, stories that were too ashamed to show their faces in the daylight.

The ribbon of stairs gracefully connecting the first floor with the second creaked brazenly with every footstep on its polished treads. On damp days and nights, however, the boards swelled tight and grew silent. One could fairly accurately report the weather conditions according to the squawking the floorboards and stairs produced.

Would-be intruders would surely abort their mischief after having planted but one villainous foot upon an alarm-sounding step.

"Better than any barking dog," Puff said when asked to oil them or tighten them or whatever one does to correct such an annoyance.

I only asked him once. After that, I resigned myself to appreciating the clear signal that my girls were prowling about. Many a night, a creaking stair roused me to follow a troubled heart to the kitchen for warmed milk with honey.

Call it a gift or a curse, I was often awake, alert, and half-dressed for battle long before one of the young women informed me that her labor had started. I heard every suckle, every sweet breath, every delicate, life-assuring sound of the newborns.

I view it as concern, but I suppose God would call it worry, that kept me listening, too, for horses' hooves and footsteps and pebbles tossed at upstairs windows.

Morning Glory was not a prison. It was a haven. That was my intention, at least. But some of the girls saw bars on the windows and locks on the doors, though there were none. They considered house rules confining, stifling. They plotted escapes and rendezvous with past or present lovers.

Most were thwarted by my half-alert sleep state or Puff's uncanny ability to sense trouble, coupled with his chameleon-like countenance. Sweet spirited and calming by nature, he became vigilante-like when the girls' honor, safety, or common sense were threatened.

I repeatedly lectured, "If your young man is motivated by adventure and risk, by deception and mischief, he will arrive in the cloak of night. Love shows its face in the daylight."

For years, the majority of the rounds I made at night were not for bed checks but for what I considered the better portion of my responsibility to the women—prayer.

How many nights did I wander the shadowed halls? How many times did I stand at a closed door, my hand pressed silently against the oak panel, my heart pressed hard against God's throne in agonizing prayer for the troubled young woman in fitful sleep on the other side?

It's a wonder there were not salt stains on the floorboards outside each door, for all the tears spent there.

Why did I cry? For some, the tears fell because of their naïveté. They had no knowledge of how difficult the road they'd chosen was going to be. While still within the protective walls of Morning Glory, they remained safe. But none of them could stay forever. All eventually left that place, where, like it or not, they were loved.

"Look at the birds of the air," Jesus said. "Look and learn."

He provided for the birds of the air, even the ones that made unwise choices.

On a warm summer day, we left the doors at the front and back of the house open, so the wildflower-scented breeze could blow through. A misdirected bird flew into the house, but couldn't find its way out.

The girls living with me at the time fell into two categories—those who screamed and locked themselves in their rooms until the "crisis" passed, and those who were determined to help rid the house of the intruder.

The bird—a common brown sparrow—showed its utter fright in its erratic flight, bumping into furniture and lamps, and eventually flying full bore into the panes of a window.

"Stupid bird," one of the residents said as the sparrow lay flopping on the floor beneath the window.

"That was its problem a few seconds ago," I told her. "Now, its problem is pain."

In that moment, I gained an answer for those who wondered why I would show mercy.

When young women from the Morning Glory Haven for Unwed Mothers walked out through the front doors, they stepped into a world that felt no obligation to care that they were precious, only that they were fallen.

The world they faced did not know that the sound of our falling is the call that sends Him to catch us.

Was it any wonder my heart for those young women would press me—strong in other respects—to tears for them? Some would be rejected by prospective suitors who viewed an unwed mother—no matter how beautiful and desirable—and her fatherless child—no matter how charming and bright—as too great a responsibility. Some would be turned away from many a door, many a job opportunity, and even—sadly—many a church because of the child, the product of passion they once mistook for love.

Night after night, in that moonlit hall, I wept for my girls and for myself—for the nightly faith-struggle to surrender them completely to the God who followed them when I could not, to the God whose relentless love never stopped pursuing, to the God who was and is a better protector than I could ever hope to be, the God whose love dwarfed my own, the God who—unlike me—was never unaware of where they were or what they needed.

I cried, too, for the childless mothers. Some came to me with a babe in the womb and left empty-armed and empty-hearted. I cried for babies who died, and for their mothers who died a little, too. For the mothers with love enough to spare but no resources with which to raise a child. For the agonizing moment of deciding to let someone else adopt their own flesh and blood.

Would I have been brave enough for that? No matter how wise or rational or necessary, could I have kissed the doeskin newborn's head and chosen to "labor" immediately again, wordlessly bearing the heart's death-grip contractions as the child with my eyes and chin was delivered into the waiting arms of an adoptive woman with nothing but longing in her womb? Could I have been that selfless?

Could I have been as selfless as my own mother?

Ivy—1951

"Your mother didn't give you up for adoption, Anna. You worked with her."

"Until the fall of 1885, when I was sent away." She angled her head to the window, sadness etching deeper lines into her face.

"But, you would have been twenty years old by then."

"Yes."

"I don't understand."

"If it weren't for love, I wouldn't either."

Ivy's heart rhythm lurched forward. "Please. Tell me."

"We worked hard, my mother and I. Long hours. Difficult conditions. Too few doctors. Too many babies. We lived as sparsely as we could and served as often as we could."

"I can't imagine how rewarding that must have been for you."

Anna drew the blanket around her arms as if the room weren't already toasty. "It became all the more so in my memories when she died."

"How did it happen?"

"I should have known what she intended. I should have known. I should have stopped her."

Ivy slid her chair closer. "Stopped her from what?"

"She sent me away for a holiday. A month at Aunt Phoebe's. I couldn't understand why she wouldn't come with me. We were never apart. She loved her aunt."

"*Her* aunt?"

"Phoebe was my great-aunt. My mother's aunt. Hadn't I said that before?"

"I don't think so. Why did your mother stay behind?"

"To save me."

The color faded from Anna's complexion, what little color remained after a lifetime of labor.

"We can talk later, if you'd like, Anna. Is this too much for you?"

She patted her hand on her chest. *Tap. Tap. Tap. Tap. Tap.* "It's lived in here too long." *Tap. Tap. Tap.* "No one alive remembers what she gave. Except me."

Ivy laid the notebook aside and watched for evidence that Anna's breathing was suffering from squeezing out a long-tamped memory.

"While I frolicked at Aunt Phoebe's, taking tea every afternoon in the parlor that would one day become my office, while I slept until the sun was high and stayed out late with young people who Phoebe had enlisted to see that I was sufficiently entertained—me, who had skipped most of my childhood—"

The words stopped.

"What happened while you were gone?"

"My mother gave up her life."

"What? Why? Oh, Anna!"

"A mother with four young ones and another on the way. Three of them with the sickness—smallpox. No one would go near the home when her time came. My mother knew no one would help. And she knew if I were at her side, as I always was, I'd either stop her or enter the house and the danger with her. So she sent me away, 'gave' me to someone who would love me when she couldn't."

"And you never went home again."

"Once." Anna's chin quivered. "For her funeral."

Anna—1890s

You can see how the path of my life helped paint with delicate strokes the exquisite gift of adoption, the true meaning of a mother's sacrifice.

You can see why I mourned over those who spat on the sacrifices made for them.

Like a deep, untouchable bruise, my heart ached for women who, despite our best efforts, left Morning Glory pregnant with unresolved doubts.

Mamas and papas sent me their shame-shrouded daughters. Unable to shrug off their own embarrassment, parents sent their unwed children to me.

I cried for the stony-hearted, who refused to cry for themselves. I cried for the young mothers with no mother-heart, who coldly announced their distaste for the child they carried, their indifference about its future, and their eagerness to rid themselves of their "problem." As I consider what I have just spoken, it sounds as if I had a joyless life, that the task assigned to me was one of crushing heaviness and unbearable concern. Forgive me for sketching the picture with excessive shadows. Light beat back the shadows. Joy was a daily companion.

Ivy—1951

"Joy?"

"You didn't miss that part, did you?" Anna twisted her hands over each other. "Oh, that would be my fault. I've been so intent on explaining the heart-wrenching and the miraculous that I may have given too little attention to the joys."

"I've been guilty of the same, I suppose." Ivy laid a hand over her child and waited for it to acknowledge its presence. A child, curled on itself now, cushioned in a sea of warmth that pulsed with its mother's pulse. A child that already kept her awake at night as it rolled in the sea and stretched its limbs, practicing for life outside the womb. A baby. A joy-maker.

"You know the details about that first dinner party. We made fund-raising an event for the social calendar. Picnics and potlucks, holiday gatherings. Christmas at Morning Glory became a tradition for local society. Not right away, mind you." Anna waved her hand as if dismissing a misconception. "Over the years, the ice melted and charity won another heart or two, then three. Buggies and wagons filled the yard. Then a mix of cabriolets and automobiles."

"Cabriolay?"

"Fancy word for buggy."

"Christmas at Morning Glory. I wish I could have seen that."

"What a sight! A fire in every fireplace. Tables of food— our own Morning Glory handiwork plus donated goodies. Pine boughs cut from the trees that lined the property. Josiah's contacts in the cities meant we always had musical entertainment—a harpist, a string quartet, a vocalist who eventually went on to make a name for herself in radio."

"And people were more charitable at Christmas?"

Anna's eyes danced with the light and warmth of a long-ago hearth. "Something about the babe in the manger—a child born to an unwed mother, but a child who changed the world—made people pull their hands out of their pockets and give."

"I can't imagine how hard you worked. But how much fun it must have been."

"Oh, my legs ached at the end of those nights. Throbbed clear through the next day sometimes. But I soaked them then sat with them propped on pillows with a muscle-cramping smile on my face."

"It's still there."

"Not because of the festiveness or the way the house glowed. Not because of those divine aromas—pine and brown sugar and ginger and pumpkin. But because of the people—some of the very people I least expected to care, I'm ashamed to say.

Do you know that Mrs. Witherspoon volunteered to direct the Ladies Aid Society in sewing layettes for the newborns?"

"None were born during the fund-raising parties, were they?"

Anna's smile widened. "Only one. Dr. Noel spent the latter part of the evening upstairs with Lydia and a laboring mother. We fully anticipated a long labor for that wisp of a girl. The celebrating carried on. As was our custom . . ." Her voice quavered.

Ivy waited, feeling in her own body empathetic twinges.

"As was our custom, Josiah concluded the evening with the reading of the Christmas story, including Isaiah, chapter nine." She leaned closer. "Can you imagine the thrill that rolled through the parlor when he read, 'For unto us a child is born,' and a baby's first cry pierced the night?"

"Oh, Anna!"

"Half the crowd dropped their teeth and the other half burst into applause."

Ivy sobered. Who would applaud when her child was born? She alone. And the woman with more stories than time. "Was it a boy or a girl?"

"A darling, red-haired, red-faced boy. The mother named him after Dr. Noel."

23

Becky—2013

Becky set her purse on the boot mat inside Monica's back door. "If asked how I thought the New Year would begin, I can't imagine it would have occurred to me to answer, 'Working a mercy job.'"

Monica stopped sliding her laptop into the glove-leather shoulder bag lying on her granite countertop. "It's not a mercy job. I really do need help."

Friend of mine, you need a little practice in authenticity. "And I really do appreciate it."

"How did the house showing go?"

Becky draped her coat over the back of a bar stool. "They weren't interested."

"That's too bad."

"I'm okay with it."

"Really?"

"Lauren was still on Christmas break then."

"Brianne, too."

"Oh. Right. So, we weren't sure when would be the best time to talk to her about the whole idea of selling our house and moving to the duplex."

Monica zipped her shoulder bag closed. "You haven't told her?"

"We did. Right after the realtor called and said he wanted to bring someone over. Are you familiar with the term *hissy fit*?"

"Seen a few." Monica smiled. "Thrown a few. Lauren wasn't happy about it?"

"When the realtor called back to confirm a time, he could hear her in the background. He offered to try to set up a different day."

"How kind of him."

"Christmas week? Really? I don't know how he could have imagined that was a good idea. But desperate times call for—" Would conversation ever be devoid of dangerous topics, pain-inducing catch phrases?

Monica shrugged into her coat and tucked a too-stylish-to-be-warm scarf around her neck. "Is Lauren more comfortable with the idea now?"

"She's gone from hostile to mildly irritated that she wasn't brought in on the initial discussions, since it's 'her life' and all. Not her money, but her life. I can't blame her, I guess. She was so close to expressing gratitude that we'd be willing to do something like that to help give Jackson and her a head start, but then . . . "

"Then what?"

Becky sighed, well practiced at it. "Then she heard that the duplex doesn't have a built-in dishwasher and . . ."

With her hands gripping the ends of her scarf, Monica said, "I don't think God intended life to be this complicated."

"Agreed. Well, I'd better get busy and you'd better get moving."

"Everything on the list make sense?"

Becky scanned the spreadsheet of cleaning chores that her best friend had created for her. "Makes sense."

"So what do you think? Four hours? That's about all I can afford to pay, and about how long I'll be at the women's shelter annual meeting." Monica hiked the strap of the shoulder bag higher. "With Brianne back at school, you can feel free to . . . um . . . use the sound system if you want music. There's bottled water in the fridge. Leftover quiche."

"I brought a sandwich." Becky rattled the lunch bag in her hand as if to prove the point.

"Is Gil watching Jackson?"

Yes. Instead of job hunting. "He has me on speed dial for emergencies, like losing the pacifier." *Bad example! Becky, can you never say anything right to this woman with whom conversation used to flow like a chocolate fountain?*

Monica laughed more loudly than the situation called for. "Well, there's a cure for that." Monica's face blistered.

Awkward. Their debates about the merits of pacifiers and Brianne's history of finding a "cure" for an unwanted baby fogged the air between them.

"So, have a great meeting, Monica. Don't worry about anything here. If I can't get it done in the four hours, I'll make a note on the spreadsheet."

"Great. That's . . . thank you. See you in a bit."

Becky took a deep breath the moment the door closed behind her friend. *Awkward, awkward, awkward.*

What was there to clean? She had a list, but from all appearances the kitchen, at least, was photo-worthy. Nothing out of place. Not so much as a water spot on the faucet or a dot of burned-on mac and cheese on the stovetop. She tucked her lunch bag onto one of the sparkling clean refrigerator shelves and turned back to the room and the list.

Arms extended, she leaned over the granite-topped island and laid her cheek against its cool, impossibly smooth surface, not out of island-envy or granite-envy, but with the exhaustion that comes from holding it together when everyone around her was falling apart. She stood like that—bent at the waist with her cheek pressed into the granite—until her neck protested.

Upright, and with the stark winter sun flooding the kitchen as if it owned the place, Becky noticed the smudge her cheek had left on the stone surface.

Finally. Something to clean.

—◦◦◦◦—

Having more than two bathrooms had a downside, apparently. They all needed cleaning.

Had Monica mentioned that each of the five bedrooms had its own bath, plus the powder room by the front entrance and the half bath in the finished basement? Becky couldn't remember hearing Monica complain about an excess of toilets and tubs. But she wondered now how her friend had managed to get anything else done before hiring a scullery maid.

With four second-floor bathrooms sparkling and one to go, Becky hauled her bucket of cleaning supplies to the door at the end of the hallway and bumped it open farther with her hip.

A caterpillar of discomfort crawled up the back of her neck, every hair disturbed by the action. Something wasn't right. Her stomach clenched. It was odd enough being alone in her friend's house, moving possessions that weren't her own, rearranging microscopic dust molecules and praying she was putting the magazines back exactly as Monica had artfully splayed them on the coffee table.

She wasn't about to use the sound system, as Monica suggested. She touched only what she had to in order to do her job. But here, in Brianne's room, something made her want to go digging. Trouble had an odor. Acrid. Sulphurus. She smelled it now.

Becky hadn't been quiet while scrubbing, flushing, and vacuuming. Any intruder—hiding—would know she was there. The thought did not bring even a dust bunny of comfort. Someone knew. Waited. Lurked. Hidden.

If she were going to make a career out of cleaning houses, she'd have to conquer the squirmies. Ridiculous.

She steadied herself and made each footstep solid, WonderWoman-like, as she moved deeper into the sunlit room. She swung her bucket of supplies and contemplated whistling, but couldn't think of a whistleable song.

A wave of outright envy replaced the silly ruffling she'd felt. Brianne's room didn't need vacuuming. Not even a gum wrapper or fleck of potato chip on the floor, much less the Lauren piles Becky was used to. Nothing on the floor.

Except Brianne.

On the window side of the bed, Becky found Brianne sitting on the floor, her back against the eyelet dust-ruffled bed, her bare feet straight out in front of her, eyes locked on emptiness.

"Hey, Brianne. You scared me. I thought . . . your mom thought . . . we thought you were at school."

No answer. But the girl drew her thin arms around herself.

Becky slid to the floor beside her and assumed the same position, back against the bed, feet in front of her. "Not feeling well today?"

Nothing.

Kids playing hooky didn't scare Becky. But the utterly blank look on Brianne's face did.

"Hon, I know things have been rough lately." *Lord God, if You ever had words to spare, I could use some!* She waited.

Brianne's toes must have been cold. They were almost blue.

"Do you want me to call your mom?" *I'd like to call mine.*

Becky rubbed her hands on the knees of her jeans. "I'm here if you want to talk. Even if you don't. I'm . . . here."

Several moments passed, each more awkward than the previous.

"Look, Brianne, why don't we go down to the kitchen and make some tea. Do you drink tea? We can talk down there. I'm getting too old to sit on the floor for too long."

Brianne's arms fell limp into her lap. Her left fist unclenched, releasing what she'd been holding—an orange plastic bottle with a white childproof cap.

Becky grabbed for it. Empty. "Oh, Brianne!"

———

By the time she'd called both Monica and Gil, the paramedics were flying up the stairs. Becky shook and paced as they checked the girl's too-faint vitals and tried to stabilize her enough to get her loaded onto the collapsible gurney.

"I made her throw up," she coughed out. "But I don't know if that was the right thing to do. It's all here in the bucket." She pointed to the repurposed cleaning bucket with a pool of stomach contents and partially dissolved pills. "I'm sorry. I'm so sorry. And I just sat there with her when I found her. Probably five minutes. I should have called right away when I saw her sitting on the floor that way. I just never thought . . . I didn't think . . . "

"Mrs. Trundle, it's going to be okay. We need all of our people working on Brianne right now. Why don't you give her mom another call and tell her we'll be transporting Brianne to Memorial."

"I think she knows that. It's the closest hospital." She circled the huddle of paramedics.

The female paramedic nearest her laid a hand on Becky's forearm and gave a comforting squeeze. "Just call to confirm, okay?"

"Okay."

Memorial Hospital. Where Lauren and Brianne were born, three months apart. Where life began for them, in a way. *Life, Lord. Please, spare this life.*

No mere cry for attention, the doctor said. Brianne took enough painkillers—leftovers from Monica's hysterectomy a year earlier—to completely silence whatever voices screamed inside her head.

Becky couldn't hear what screamed inside Monica's, but she could imagine.

Motherhood isn't for sissies. She'd read that somewhere. She'd lived it. Still did.

How many nights would she relive the scene in Brianne's bedroom and everything she'd done wrong? She'd cleaned four bathrooms while a young girl suffered in silence down the hall, slipping closer to the edge of eternity. She'd shaken off the unease rather than listening and acting sooner. She'd thought she could *talk* to Brianne and make her feel better. She'd suggested *tea* to a young woman an inch from death.

Not exactly impeccable mothering instinct.

"It's my fault." Though softened because of the crowd in the hospital cafeteria, Monica's voice shook so much that it sounded like a choir member with excessive vibrato.

Becky sipped her coffee and temporarily suspended her own guilt. "Monica, this is not your fault."

"Yes, it is. I . . . I didn't say it aloud, but I thought it." Her gaze registered as blank as Brianne's a few hours earlier.

"Thought what?"

"How . . . lucky we were." She huffed. Monica no longer exhaled. She sighed her way through life. "Blessed. I used the word *blessed*."

Becky's mind wandered close to the edge of what Monica might have meant, then shrank back. "What do you mean?"

Monica tore her napkin into scraps of discomfort. "My grandchild is gone. That will never be okay. But few people knew . . . or will ever know. Life . . . life was going on as if nothing ever happened." She swept the scraps into a small pile. "But look at you and Lauren." Her eyes flicked to Becky, then quickly away. "It's always *with* you. The problem. The history. The fallout."

The debt. The sleepless nights. The smell of sour milk. Smeared diapers. More diapers. A ceaseless echo of concern for Lauren's and Jackson's futures.

The smell of baby lotion after Jackson's bath. The sight of his only-for-Grammie smile. The bubbling giggle that was worthy of YouTube. The feel of his hand on her cheek, no heavier than a birthmark.

"Jackson's life may not have started the ideal way, but that's what grace is for."

"And I think I was secretly grateful, in a twisted sense, that Brianne and I didn't have to deal with it anymore. It was over. Done. Sad, but . . . behind us. You know?"

The look on Brianne's face a few hours earlier said it was anything but behind them.

"Beck, I brought this on, thinking thoughts like that. It's a miracle Brianne's alive, considering what an idiot I've been."

Becky's next swallow of coffee tasted especially bitter. Or maybe that was the taste of sorrow.

"I've been thinking about this since the moment Lauren came to me a year ago, broken. I've wrestled with the question, desperate to know an answer that would make sense."

Monica sniffed. Twice. "What question?"

"What comes after remorse?"

"A constant, relentless, throbbing pain."

"That's all true—the relentless, throbbing, piercing pain. And mercy when we've blown it. And grace for the next step."

"Lauren, what are you doing here?" The sight of her daughter alive, upright, and standing in front of her in the hospital hall brought Becky within a hair's breadth of tears.

For the first time in a long while, the hug Lauren returned was at least as strong as her mother's. "I had to come. Dad said he'd watch Jackson longer so I could . . . be here. Is Brianne . . . ?"

"It's not good, honey. But the doctors are hopeful. The paramedics were there so fast."

Lauren's chin quivered. "I should have been there for her."

"We all have our regrets. Every one of us."

"Brianne and I used to be so close. Jackson kind of changed all that."

"Changed a lot of things." Becky put one arm around Lauren and squeezed.

"Yeah. Like teaching me the meaning of love."

Whoa! Where had that come from?

With a mittened hand, Lauren swiped at her eyes. "Can I see her?"

"We'll ask Monica."

"I need Brianne to know I get it. I understand."

Becky's vision blurred. It happened a lot lately.

When Monica's ex-husband arrived from Colorado Springs, the hospital shrank. Lauren and Becky stepped back, promising the hurting ones that they were a phone call and five minutes away, if needed.

Becky considered asking Lauren to drive them home. Her eyes hurt and a headache flashed across her forehead like an electronic tennis match, all service aces.

But Lauren seemed just as shaken, and she blinked her eyes as if fighting a dislodged contact lens.

Tragedies without explanation provoke either copious amounts of speculation or complete silence. The Trundle car remained a vacuum chamber of silence on the ride home, until they pulled into the driveway.

"It'll be all over school in the morning," Lauren said, face forward, hands pressed between her knees.

"I imagine it will."

"That's one of the hardest parts."

Becky steered into the garage, put the car into park, and turned off the engine. "Was it the hardest part for you . . . with Jackson?"

"No. I mean, there's always gossip, even if kids are getting pregnant on purpose."

"What?"

Lauren looked at her. "Not me. That was a total accident."

"The *dare*?"

"Could we save that for later?"

"Later comes eventually."

Lauren quieted. "I know. The hardest part was telling you and Dad. What was the hardest part for you?"

"You've never asked that before, Lauren."

"I know. Mature, huh?"

Oh, that girl has her father's sense of humor. Great. "I guess the hardest part for me was lying awake that first night after you told us. Okay, the first week. All I could think about was how much harder things were going to be for you than they had to be. How many things were changed now. How much narrower your choices, and how much it would cost you."

"You and Dad have paid for most of it."

"Not in dollars."

"Oh. Right. You didn't lie awake thinking how stupid I was?"

The temp in the car quickly plummeted with the heat off. But this was too important to hurry. "If Jackson rolled off the couch and bumped his head on the coffee table . . . "

"Mom!"

"Stay with me. If he did, despite the fact that you told him to stay put, and he got a concussion . . . "

"Good grief, Mom! That's a horrible thought!"

"*If* that happened, would you lose sleep over his not staying put or over his pain and the consequences?"

"Is it okay if I say both?"

"Good answer."

"But mostly, I'd worry about the bump on his head."

"Another good answer. A very motherly thing to say." Becky patted her daughter on her knee. "Now, let's go inside before we get frostbite in our own garage."

Lauren reached for the passenger-side door handle, then hesitated and turned back to face Becky. "Mom?"

"Yes?"

"Is Brianne going to be able to live with herself?"

"For now, let's focus on praying she lives, honey."

24

Anna—1890s

Yes, the days—the years—were laced with both work and joy. With concern that often ended in celebration. But how can I describe the depths of the pit into which I fell when Robyn Anita stood on Morning Glory's threshold? A slip of a child, with her decidedly unhappy newborn in her arms. She held the bundle awkwardly, as if the babe were flour she'd been enlisted to haul from a barrel in the cellar.

"Is this the place where you take in people like us? Even if we can't pay?"

"This is the Morning Glory Haven for Unwed Mothers. You're welcome here. What's your name, dear?"

She shifted from one foot to the other, not rocking gently, rhythmically, as most mothers instinctively do, but nervously, as if she'd not taken care of "necessary" things far too long and her bladder was about to burst. She flinched as the baby's cries escalated. When she spoke, she labored through the revelation of her name. I had the sense she was inventing it, syllable by syllable.

"Robyn . . . with a y . . . Anita. Robyn Anita."

"And your baby?"

"Got no name yet. She's a girl."

"How old?"

"Three days."

"Goodness, child! You've been walking? I didn't hear a carriage."

"I rode some . . . with different people."

"Where's your home?"

"I'd rather not say."

"Well, we can attend to those matters later. Let's get your baby quieted before all three of us lose our minds. There's a rocker here in the parlor. A quiet spot for you to nurse her. I'll get you something to eat while—"

"I can't nurse her. I'm . . . I'm dried up like a raisin."

"Perhaps your milk hasn't let down yet. If you'll allow, I can help you learn ways to—"

"Won't happen. Have to feed her by bottle. I must be . . . deformed . . . or something."

I'm not one to easily give up when I believe there is hope, but the baby's distress grew more severe. "Come with me to the kitchen then. We'll get a bottle of milk warmed."

Robyn Anita's relief matched that of the infant, once they both were fed. "Robyn, can you tell me why you've come here? Are you looking to find an adoptive home for your daughter?"

"Give her to some other family? No, I couldn't do that!"

"How old are you?"

"Almost four— um, fifteen. Fifteen and a half, actually."

"Do you know how difficult it will be for you to raise your baby by yourself? I assume the father is not around."

"Oh, he's around." Her eyes grew dark with something akin to rage.

"But not . . . involved?"

"Not if I can help it. He won't touch this child if I have any breath in me and any say-so at all."

Robyn Anita was a deepening mystery that I wasn't sure I had the strength or energy to solve.

"Let's get you settled upstairs. Your daughter could sleep for hours, from the looks of it. And I am concerned about you being on your feet so much this soon after delivery."

"I'm all right." She dropped her eyes. "Yes, I . . . I should probably lie down."

I gave them the room nearest mine, certain the path between would be well worn before the mystery resolved.

Rattled, my spirit wouldn't let me sleep. Ironically, every welcome was tainted, not just this one. It always disturbed me to open my door and find on my threshold a young woman in trouble. I found joy in being able to help, but my heart broke every time.

Robyn Anita brought with her a restlessness that affected us all.

"Something's not right, Anna." One of the other residents at the time, a repeat customer, I'm grieved to say, voiced her own concerns two days into the saga. "That girl's not being honest with us."

I'd grown to love and appreciate Lily, having had more time with her than with others—short-termers—who made better choices after they left Morning Glory. I didn't yet trust Lily's decision making in regard to men, but I did value her sensitivity and insight on other planes. She gave voice to what I'd already suspected.

"I'll tell you something odd," she continued. "When I dumped the commodes this morning, I noticed hers was . . . well . . . there wasn't any . . . you know . . . blood. You ever know a woman just five days a mother who wasn't still bleeding like a—"

"Lily! Please. These are private matters."

"I'm saying—"

"I know."

"What do you make of it, Miss Anna?"

I didn't want to confess aloud the conclusions I drew. Whose baby, if not Robyn's? Where was the grieving mother, breasts aching to feed her absent child? Was my first move to send Puff for the sheriff or to confront the girl, a possible kidnapper?

I opted to ease the truth out of her, if possible.

We worked together folding sun-bleached diapers before attending to a bucket of hickory nuts Puff had collected for us that afternoon. "Dr. Noel will stop by tomorrow to examine you, Robyn Anita."

"What?"

"He cares for all our residents. He'll check your daughter, too."

"No!"

The widening of her eyes told me most of what I needed to know. "Don't worry, dear. It's his gift to our residents. No charge. We want to make sure you're both healthy before the next leg of your journey. Birthing babies may be as natural as breathing, but it takes its toll on a woman. And your daughter's cord has me a little concerned. Does it look weepy to you?"

"No doctor. Please. It's not . . . not necessary. And I . . . I'm not fond of doctors. You can understand."

I took the stack of folded diapers from her lap and set them on the table near us. "Would Dr. Noel find that you've never had a child in your womb, Robyn Anita? Would he be able to tell that this little girl isn't your daughter?"

Tears flowed like the milk she should have had.

"She's my . . . sister."

"Oh, honey. What have you done?"

"It's what *he* done."

"Who?"

Fear knotted the cords in her neck. They stood out as prominently as the first pass of a new plow on a virgin field.

I stroked her hair, though it needed a good washing, and asked again. "Who?"

Her story sickened me. A father who beat his children nearly senseless. She wasn't about to let the same fate befall this newest little one after her mother succumbed in childbirth. While the older children cared for their mother's body, Robyn Anita overheard her father talking to himself about dealing with this newborn as he would an unwanted litter of kittens, with a burlap sack and a ditch full of water.

I might have broken a tooth, as hard as I clenched my teeth with fury against a man not fit to live, much less parent. If she now spoke the truth—and all evidence pointed in that direction—Puff had all the more reason to run for the sheriff.

And I had all the more reason to pray for an answer to another impossible situation.

To what lengths would I have gone to save those sisters from having to be returned to their father? I wouldn't have the chance to find out. They were gone by morning, slipping past the creaking stairs and my alert senses. If I'd thought Robyn Anita capable of caring well for that helpless infant, I wouldn't have worried myself sick over where they disappeared to.

———

When Robyn left, Lily's demeanor changed, as if she had matured overnight, her latent mothering instincts kicking in with her discomfort over what had brought the girl to our doors and what had made her flee.

"She's endangering that baby!" Lily protested.

"Yes. And there's little, perhaps nothing, we can do about it. The law is looking for them. I pray they find them before her father does."

Lily snapped beans in two as if they represented a man's neck. "Putting seed in a woman doesn't make a person a father."

I would have asked her to express it more delicately, but she spoke truth.

"And holding a child in your arms or pushing one through your legs—"

"All right, Lily."

"—doesn't make you a mother. It takes more than that."

I took the pan of beans from her hands and gave her a bowl of yeast dough to knead. "We've both lived long enough to know the truth in that."

She didn't talk much the rest of the day. The furrows in her brow said her mind kept pace with how hard her hands worked.

As pleasant as she'd been to that point, she changed somehow. I don't believe I heard a hint of a complaint from her about any of the aches and pangs, about the chores she took on, about the short but intense labor that brought her son into the world. This child she kept. His almond eyes and thick tongue spoke of hardships ahead. But she didn't complain.

I was the one who cried.

———

I could not then, nor can I now, abide whining, even my own. It galled me, as it galled the Almighty to hear His children complaining about the wilderness fare that not only smelled and tasted of heaven but also saved their ungrateful lives.

I must add that the food I prepared for my girls could not be accused of having either the odor or flavor of heaven in those early days. But it was tasty, filling, and similarly provided as manna. A wild turkey laid at our doorstep by a shy but generous hand. A box of necessities—flour, salt, molasses—tucked in the back of our parked wagon while we worshiped. A venison flank offered humbly by the father of one of the girls.

On occasion, when his wife was otherwise occupied, Mr. Witherspoon would slip into my order a double portion of sugar or rice or beans. My eyebrows questioned his actions. His wink and smile answered. I knew to silently thank him and praise my God, who had softened a withered prune's heart.

It is my studied opinion that those who have known genuine hunger—raw, vacuous hunger—experience a shriveling of the part of the brain from which complaints are generated.

When one of my girls wrinkled her pert nose at the thinness of the stew or the sameness of repeated potato suppers—when potatoes were what we had—I knew without asking that the young woman had nothing in her memory to tell her what true hunger felt like.

I was not assigned the task of correcting all the flaws in the girls who came to me. If so, who would the Lord assign to correct the ocean of my own failings and weaknesses? He asked, rather, that I love and provide for them. It was my hope, sometimes realized, that the love itself and the overtness of my own gratitude would create a hothouse in which discontent would wilt and appreciation thrive.

Learning gratitude proved a more challenging lesson for some than others. I was too often the floundering student. It didn't take me long to discover that my lack of appreciation almost guaranteed we would have lack in our house. An interesting connection that almost never failed.

Every meal, however pale or pitiful, was served on a platter of gratitude. Gratitude was, in fact, a more certain element than the presence of meat. We learned to celebrate the simple joy of herbs, which Puff encouraged me to plant near the back door of the kitchen—sage, mint, rosemary, parsley . . .

And when Puff brought Melody to Morning Glory, both the flavors and joy increased.

∞

Ivy—1951

"Puff was a musician, too? I love music."

"A musician?"

"He brought melody to Morning Glory?"

"Melody, his sweet-faced, darling, song-in-her-heart bride! And oh, could that woman cook!"

"All that time, Puff had been married?"

"What? No, dear. All that time Puff had been single. Then one day, he came home from town with more than just the flour and salt we needed. Sitting on the wagon seat beside him was a beautiful woman with clear black eyes and flawless skin the color of a rich walnut stain. She floated down from the wagon, a wisp of a thing, like the feather of an exotic bird, shining in every way."

"I can see it."

"From a distance, I surmised she was a woman in need of shelter. But she appeared past childbearing age and the exuberant smile on her face told a different tale. She was a woman in love. And Puff! Oh, I'd never seen him so overflowing with life."

Ivy set aside the notebook and drew her chair closer to Anna's wheelchair for more details.

"You don't want to miss recording all this."

"I won't. I'll remember. I just need to sit for a minute in the middle of someone's love story."

264

Anna patted her friend's hand. "We don't know the end of the Ivy and Drew love story yet. But someday, someone will sit in the middle of yours."

"You have more hope than I do."

"I don't mind sharing a commodity like hope."

"Where did Puff find Melody?"

"It was the other way around. She found him. They'd been childhood sweethearts fifty years earlier but lost track of each other. The war."

"Wars do that to people." Ivy's thoughts drifted six thousand miles from where they sat.

Anna readjusted her position, then pressed her hand to her heart.

"Are you feeling all right?"

"A little catch is all."

Ivy waited a moment. Should she press for more details? "So Puff had never married?"

"He claimed he couldn't. His heart belonged to someone already."

"That's a long time to wait, to hope, to pray that your true love will come back into your life."

Anna laid her head back against her chair. "He had a knowing."

"A knowing."

"Deep in here." Anna tapped her heart with a reverence equal to the longing. "It carried him through one season after another—barren winters, springs and summers without her, autumns that hinted of yet another barren winter ahead."

Ivy rubbed her hands together as if they were cold. "Winter's coming."

"And so is that precious baby of yours."

"I may be all she or he ever has. That's not enough."

Anna chuffed. "Your baby's name is not Regret. You've still so much to learn." She folded her hands. "Dear Lord, please keep me alive long enough to walk this child all the way to wisdom."

"How many of your girls got married, Anna? How many had whole families, more children? How many found grace?"

"I don't know. I understood most would not return after they left Morning Glory. Some did, to say thank you or to bring a contribution to the needs of other girls as hurting as they had once been. But we understood that even as a city of refuge might be held as a tender memory, we would not be a destination to revisit. We were no tourist stop. We were there for a time of trouble, a time that most hoped would remain locked away from prying eyes and from the future they worked hard to construct."

"A secret? You advocated that?"

"No, dear. I always encouraged the truth. But I did not encourage my girls to maintain a connection with Morning Glory. They needed to move on, to leave that season of pain and remorse in their past."

"Didn't that make you curious about what happened to them? You poured such love into their lives."

"I did. But I wasn't asked to keep them. The task I faced was to love them, help them heal, and then let them go. What happened after that was between them and God."

Ivy thought of the months she'd cared for Anna at the Maple Grove Nursing Home. She'd had no visitors, no family members. She had been alone. Yet never alone.

"I did ask one thing of them." Anna slapped her palms together as if anticipating a Christmas gift.

"What was that?"

"As they left me, I gave them each a small brown envelope of morning glory seeds. My hope was that those seeds would be planted wherever the women landed. And I asked that when the day came that their morning glories bloomed in their yards and in their hearts, when they understood the grace they'd been shown and were given the opportunity to show it to others, they'd harvest seeds from those *blossuns*—sorry, that was Puff's word for them—seeds from the blossoms and send a handful to me."

"And did they?" Ivy mentally traced through the possessions they'd moved from Anna's room at Maple Grove to their bungalow. So few possessions for a woman who'd lived so long. Either too few of those she helped remembered her kindness or the way Anna remembered the stories was heavily laced with imagination.

Anna smiled and tugged at the engraved book-shaped locket at her throat.

On Sunday nights, *The Ed Sullivan Show* proved a shared interest between Anna and Ornell. They laughed together as Ivy repaired tiny garments collected from the secondhand store. She edged cotton diapers and stacked them in neat piles in the top drawer of the dresser in the bedroom she would soon share with a child.

Somehow Anna and her father had conspired behind her back on a project that tugged at Ivy's heart as much as it frustrated her. Her father had brought home what he called an early Christmas present for her—a heavy black Remington typewriter.

"Thank you?"

Anna shot her a look pregnant with meaning.

"Thank you. I appreciate it."

The gift was too heavy for her to manage in her current condition, so her dad hauled it to her bedroom and set it up on the small desk that he once had claimed.

"Dad, thank you, really. But I don't type."

"Not yet," Anna called from the spot in the hall where she'd wheeled herself. "Not yet, dear."

"You're gonna need some more skills for after—" Ivy's father nodded toward her child-sized belly. "Merry Christmas, and I'd suggest you practice now, before that clacking noise wakes up my grandson."

"Grandson, Dad?"

"Might be." The faintest hint of a smile on his weathered face warmed her all the way to her unpracticed fingers.

"Anna, please, now that Ed Sullivan is finished for another week, can we get back to Puff and Melody's story?"

"It's almost bedtime."

"Can we talk while I help you get ready for bed?"

"Not tonight, Ivy."

Ivy laid the back of her hand against Anna's pale forehead. "Are you feeling okay?"

"You're not the only one missing her beloved. All that talk about Puff and Melody, about the girls and their babies who came into my life and left again . . ."

"I'm sorry. I shouldn't have pushed."

"Oh, it's silly of me. I've had my share of wonderful. And now God's given me another burst of joy watching what He's doing with you. Can't wait to hold your little one. Look at that!"

"What?"

"I think that was an elbow making its presence known there."

"Elbow. Knee. Here." Ivy took Anna's hand in hers and laid it on the spot where the baby had last kicked. It wasn't long before the little one responded with a healthy prize-fighter punch.

Tears filled the crevices on Anna's face. "Such a beautiful thing. What that must feel like for the mother!"

Anna had never known.

25

Becky—2013

Quiet grace speaks louder than noisy blame." The flip calendar was right again.

Then Lauren blew into the house and had to be reminded to shut the door behind her, despite the single-digit temps of a late-winter Arctic blast. "Sorry, Mom. But when I tell you what I have to tell you, you'll forgive me for being a little distracted."

Becky tucked her feet underneath her on the couch and wrapped the chenille throw tighter around her shoulders. The surge of cold air would dissipate before it tried to slither under the closed door behind which both Jackson and Gil slept in the master bedroom. Both had been whining entirely too much lately. A nap would do them good. She hoped.

"Is Dad here?"

"He's sleeping off the dregs of driving the fourth-graders on their field trip to the capital."

"Ooo. Brutal. Can I wake him up?"

"Not without waking Jackson, too. They're napping together. Your dad volunteered to lie down with him for a few minutes. That was an hour ago."

Lauren's mouth formed a series of smooth, cursive *w*'s. "Hmm. I wanted to show you at the same time." She bounced on her toes, her hands stuffed in the pockets of her thank-you-Goodwill coat.

"Show us what?"

"This!" She pulled her left hand out of her pocket and stuck it under Becky's nose.

"A . . . a tattoo?"

Lauren sighed. "It's a ring!"

"A tattoo of a ring."

"Right. Brilliant, isn't it? Can never get lost. Won't catch on sweaters. Doesn't need insurance. Don't have to take it off when I do dishes."

"Oh, honey! You're going to start doing dishes? I'm overwhelmed. This is so unexpected."

"Mother, you're so funny. Look at it. It's an en-*gage*-ment ring. Isn't that the most outrageous thing?"

What was that disease where a person's eyes bugged out? Former first lady Barbara Bush struggled with it for a while. Graves' disease. That was it. Lauren had the power to induce Graves' disease. Becky pressed her palms against her closed eyelids to push her eyeballs back into their sockets.

"Mom, I'm engaged!"

Which, oh which, question to ask first? *Are you kidding? Are you insane? You got a tattoo? You're engaged? To whom?*

"Mom, say something. It's perfect, isn't it?"

"In . . . what . . . way? Could we start at the beginning?"

Lauren huffed her exasperation and plopped on the floor in front of Becky. Cross-legged and almost audibly screeching the brakes of her emotions, she said, "Okay, so, Noah and I were at the mall, and I thought he was just kidding, but he wasn't, when he said we should look at rings."

Becky shook the loose synapses in her brain. "Wait a minute. Noah and you are that serious?"

"Uh, yea-uh!" She wiggled her ring finger in Becky's direction.

"Is he Jackson's father?"

"That is so not the point, Mom. Will you just listen to the story?"

Hot flash? Heart attack? Stroke? Aneurysm? Her vision skewed as though she were viewing the scene through waxed paper. Her hearing fogged. Incapable of speech, she nodded.

"So I thought, of course, he meant the jewelry store, but we headed to the Skin Art Gallery."

"Oh, lovely."

"Do you know how much money we saved? Once the redness and swelling go down, you'll see how gorgeous this ring is. I'll have to go back for the wedding band part after the wedding. It wraps right around the diamond over on one side like a vine. Kind of like your morning glory vines. See how it sparkles? They put a special additive in the pigment to make it glisten like that. Kind of like glitter. Look." Lauren held her hand out flat under the lamp on the end table and wiggled her hand back and forth so the "diamond" could catch the light.

Blinded by its brilliance, Becky turned away, blinked, and called out, "Gil? Gil, come on out here."

"Noah proposed right there in the store. It was so sweet. I mean, we'd talked about it, but I thought he'd wait until we graduated."

"At least."

Lauren sank onto the couch beside her mother, causing a tidal wave of cushions and emotions. "But, then, we realized that we both turn eighteen before the end of the school year, so . . ."

"So . . . ?"

"Legal age."

"I realize that. I wasn't making the connection between the number eighteen and the wisdom of getting married the next day."

"That would be dumb."

Becky allowed herself a tiny, controlled exhale.

"That's a Thursday. Who wants to get married on a Thursday?"

"Gil, honey? This is important." *Blood pressure, somewhere in the two hundreds.* "Lauren, let me go get your father. He'll want to hear all this."

"We can talk later. Noah's picking me up in a few minutes. His aunt has a cupcake shop—SweetCheeks. She runs it out of her house. He thinks he can get her to give us a cupcake tower wedding cake for our present. See how financially responsible we're being?"

The speed of Lauren's recitation—well beyond warp speed—didn't allow Becky to think in sync, much less form a response.

"But, Mom, we can't take Jackson with us to a place like that, so, could you, like, watch him for a few more hours? Thanks a bunch."

"No."

Now on her feet, rezipping her coat and gingerly pulling on her mittens as she left the room, Lauren turned. "What did you say?"

"Can't watch your son tonight." *I have a nervous breakdown scheduled in five, four, three, two . . .*

—❦—

Gil padded into the family room, staring down at his cell phone then up at his wife. "Did you just text me? My phone started to vibrate and the text said, 'Come here. I need you.' That was you, right? Not a Watson/Alexander Graham Bell thing?" He grinned as if considering making a living as a stand-up comic.

Becky's eyeballs throbbed in synch with her heartbeat. She opened her mouth, but nothing flew out.

"Hey, you'll get a kick out of this. While Jackson was trying to find a good position for his nap, I flipped through my *Learn a New Word Every Day* paperback. Today's word is *mammothrept*: '*n.* a spoiled child raised by its grandmother.' Great word, huh? *Mammothrept*. Not that . . . not that it applies here . . . at all . . . because you're not . . . spoiling— Becky? What's wrong?"

Becky raised a robotic left hand. "What do you see here?"

"Your wedding ring?"

"No. This one."

"Your engagement ring."

"Right. Lauren has one, too."

"What?" He sank to the couch beside her. "No."

"Oh, yes. Only hers is—" Becky gulped like melodramatic actors did in the 1950s when they were acting scared. "Hers is tattooed."

"Have you been sniffing too much ammonia on your cleaning job?"

She punched him in the arm with the back of her non-ringed hand. "Gil, I'm absolutely serious. She's in her room calling Noah to tell him they can't go look at cupcake towers because I refused to watch Jackson for them so they could perpetuate this ridiculous—"

"Wait. Noah? Is he the father of—?"

"She didn't say."

"What's a cupcake tower?"

Becky swiveled to face him more directly. "That is not the main issue here, Gil. They're planning to be *married*."

"When?"

"About ten seconds after they both turn eighteen."

Gil leaned into the drooping couch back. "And we feel horrible about that, right? I mean, Noah's a nice kid . . . "

"The operative word is *kid*."

"But if he's Jackson's father, wouldn't the best thing be for them to be married and to raise him together?"

Becky bent over until her chin touched her knees. "I don't know. You'd think so. But they're so immature. That's no way to start a marriage."

"That's how *we* did it." Gil rubbed her turtle-shell back. "We got married pretty young."

"That was different."

"And immature."

"Only one of us." She nudged his foot with hers.

"And we survived."

"By the grace of God."

The phrase laid a blanket of silence over the room, interrupted by a squawk down the hall. The door to Lauren's room opened, then the door to the master bedroom—different hinge sounds. In less than a minute, Lauren and a Jackson-shaped hip attachment headed for the kitchen and a premade bottle in the fridge.

Becky stood. "Want me to get that? So you can show . . . your dad your ring?"

"Stupid ring."

"What?"

"Noah can't go look at cakes tonight," she said in what could only be described as her snottiest tone. "He's grounded. His parents are so strict, it's sickening!"

Five, four, three, two . . . "What was the offense?"

"Get this. He's grounded because he spaced on picking up his little sister from school. So his dad had to leave work early, and his mom was all freaked out wondering if Noah's sister had been kidnapped or something, and Noah wasn't answering his phone because we were, like, in the middle of something."

Becky caught the twitch in the skin around Gil's right eye, even from across the open-concept great room/kitchen.

Lauren looked from one parent to the other. "Oh, get your minds out of the gutter. We were in the tattoo parlor!"

Gil stood then. "Lauren, watch your tone."

"Why can't anything ever be simple?"

Becky handed her the warmed bottle and warmed her voice to match. "Honey, you gave up simple about nine months before Jackson was born."

Lauren stumbled into the kitchen the next morning with evidence of a night of crying all over her face. She poured herself a bowl of cereal and told her mother that she couldn't go to school that day. Would Becky call it in to the school office?

"Why? What's wrong?"

"You'll laugh."

Becky thought back to all the reasons not to laugh in the last year or so. "No, I won't."

Lauren sniffed then grabbed a paper towel on which to blow her nose. "Promise?"

"I promise. What is it?" Becky stuck her coffee mug into the microwave for a reheat, pulling off nonchalance as well as she could under the circumstances.

"I think my ring's infected." Lauren held out her delicate left hand, which had a swollen, beet-red, blistered ring finger.

For the first time she could recall, Becky broke a promise to her child.

"It's not funny!"

Becky choked. "Oh, I know. I'm s-sorry, honey. Not funny at all. Here, let me get a closer look. This isn't good. We need to get you to the doctor to check this out."

"It really hurts."

"Don't touch it! I'll call the clinic." *And thank the Lord Gil's work insurance still has a few more weeks on it.* "Your dad has a job interview today, so we'll have to take Jackson with us."

"Yeah, uh, the baby's awake, but . . . "

"But what?" Becky pulled open the cupboard door on which was tacked a list of important phone numbers.

Lauren brandished her infected hand. "I don't think it's a good idea for me to change a dirty diaper right now."

Becky considered suggesting latex gloves but instead tapped the spot of the clinic number on the list and handed Lauren the phone while she headed down the hall to the messy diaper.

Will there be a time, Lord, when things aren't this complicated? Now we're in perpetual survival mode.

She followed the sound of her sweet grandson waking to the day, burbling and chatting in an indecipherable baby language despite the foul odor he gave off. "Oh, Jackson!"

Oh, Lauren! What had she done? She wasn't just crying all night. She must have also been cleaning by flashlight while Jackson slept. Cleaning while crying was a trick Becky might have passed on to Lauren without knowing.

"Come on, baby boy. Let's get you ready for the day." He reached for her and smiled as if he'd reserved a batch of joy just for her. It was a scene Becky wouldn't experience if Lauren were twenty-five, married, and living in Wichita.

As she worked to make Jackson smell good again and tugged him into an outfit he'd soon outgrow, she focused on enjoying the opportunity while she had it.

Sprawled across Lauren's unmade—*some things never change*—bed was the latest issue of *Brides* magazine.

26

I feel the press of time, the relentless ticking of the clock, the exhausted beating of my heart, surely using up its allotment of pulses like a sieve with too-large holes.

So, yes. I'll tell you more about my Josiah.

It wasn't Josiah's words as much as the timbre of his voice that I found soothing, as comforting as a fire-warmed brick at the foot of my bed midwinter. His voice was silken, yet wakened within me a sweet quickening of life, as I imagined the first flutters of a babe's womb movements must feel within a grateful mother-to-be.

The subject of his conversation didn't matter. The rhythm of it, the rise and fall, the gentleness and gentility stirred within me an emotion I hadn't known. Truthfully, I'd never experienced the gently lapping waves of soul peace that washed over me when Josiah spoke.

And when he breathed my name! The pace of my heartbeat responded like a horse to the tap of a whip.

I read respect in his eyes and voice. And affection. Who could want more?

It was by firelight that he first broached the subject of my past, a past that carved my future as surely as rivers carve can-

278

yons. I was confident enough of his friendship by then to risk telling him the truth about my beginnings. He listened attentively, as he always did, but uncharacteristically dropped his gaze mid-story. I don't know why, but I was led to push past his discomfort and tell it all. I gambled that Josiah would flinch but not crumble, that he would accept what he was hearing without finding it necessary to distance himself from me, the unsophisticated, uneducated, too often ungrateful.

My few residents at the time were in their rooms upstairs trying to recapture some of the sleep they'd lost the night before in false labor or caring for a newborn. The sound of Josiah's carriage wasn't uncommon. And not unwelcome.

He stood in my doorway that evening with a sheaf of papers. "This," he said, waving the stack, "is a pretence, I must admit. There's no hurry to get them signed. I confess I made the trip purely for the pleasure of your company, Anna."

He waited then, as if there were any real chance I would turn him away. My wide-swung door and wider smile invited him in.

Providentially, the evening was cool enough for a fire. Fire no longer frightened me as it had for long months after the attack. I saw it once more as a source of heat, light, fuel. No longer a weapon. That, too, was redeemed for me.

Josiah built and stoked the fire in the front parlor while I cut thick slices of apple pie for us and heated water for tea. The fireplace flames were well established by the time I returned to the parlor with our tray.

Yes. The flames were well established.

His hand brushed mine when he took the cup I offered. So brief a contact, but it rearranged all my internal organs— my heart into my feet, my stomach into my throat. When I extended a plate of pie, his hand intentionally engulfed mine. "Thank you, Anna." The moment lasted a split-second lifetime.

The firelight was all we wanted or needed for illumination. Josiah's sideburns showed flecks of silver in the fire's amber glow. We both acknowledged the fair difference in our ages. But he never treated me like a child. Now that I think about it, I don't believe I ever was one. I graduated much too quickly from babe-in-arms to adult, skipping the innocence and unconcerned days of childhood altogether. I'm sure it registered in my countenance. The lines on my face brought our ages closer together.

It occurred to me that Josiah Grissom could teach a thing or two to many of the young men who were the absent fathers of Morning Glory's children. Professor of responsibility, with doctorates in kindness, gentility, godliness, and strength of character. I could gather the irresponsible, and the unkind, the uncouth, the harsh, and the weak-willed in a room, set Professor Grissom before them, and tell the reluctant students, "Watch this man! He will show you how to live."

I am aware that Mr. Grissom, for all his gifts and purity of heart, was saddled with humanness. I'd seen him angry, but had never failed to see him ask forgiveness and make amends. I'd witnessed his irritation with the addlepated, the foolish of this world, but not without an accompanying repentance and a turning from agitation to prayer for the fool's soul. And isn't that the difference between those who please God and those who do not?

Unlike Josiah, for so many people failings are the pavement on the road they walk, not an occasional pebble quickly tossed out of the way.

Did he ever disappoint me?

No more than I disappointed him.

Dinner and a concert, he'd said a few weeks later, when the house began to fill again. A traveling musician I'd longed to hear, one my memory can no longer name.

Anticipation served as one of my long-suffering companions in that endless night of waiting for him to arrive. Anticipation sat with me in my lamp-lit office, twisting my stomach into a thick braid. She and I were like schoolmates at recess—she plaiting my stomach while I chattered about my fairy-tale dreams for the future.

But Anticipation grew tired of the game. As the evening wore on, Concern took her place.

Had I misunderstood his invitation? Not likely. One can wonder, in a busy week, is it Tuesday or Wednesday? One can get so caught up in the living of it that one fails to flip the calendar page from July to August, the days being so similar. But one does not misplace the particulars of something for which one has so long waited.

He was simply, unavoidably detained. That was all. An unexpected visit from an important client. A pressing matter that could not wait. I would not allow Concern to voice her well-reasoned opinion that it was unlikely anything in his caseload would be so pressing as to keep him this long beyond the close of the business day.

Having read *The Strange Case of Dr. Jekyll and Mr. Hyde*, it didn't surprise me when Concern grew ugly, convulsing and contorting herself into a hideous, sinister monster called Worry.

Picking up the gauntlet of the wait, Worry tormented me with thoughts of his body caught beneath the bulk of his overturned carriage. Or of a disgruntled client holding a derringer to his throat. For what earthly reason, Worry couldn't elaborate. She spoke in clipped, disjointed sentences and seemed unbound by laws of reason and logic. *"What if he—?"* she taunted, then left it to Imagination to fill in the blanks.

Imagination possesses a fair working knowledge of disasters and is a skilled artist. She sat musing at the easel in my mind. She painted him hurt, deathly ill, already dead, or worse—disinterested.

He'd changed his mind about dinner, the concert, me. He hadn't sent word because he couldn't find any that seemed appropriate. He tried them on—one at a time—like hats or ties. But none felt or looked right.

> "Anna, I'm sorry. This was not a good idea. Best we keep our relationship strictly professional."

> "Anna, I don't know what I was thinking when I invited you to accompany me for the evening. Surely you, too, can see that it would be in our best interests not to pursue this further."

> "Anna, I feared that my attentions might mislead you into thinking I care more than I do."

Now watery thin, the evening once held the cream-rich potential of changing everything in my relationship with Josiah. From friendship to . . . to an indefinable something, the very thought of which tasted sweet. We'd shared many a dinner together. Always business. That night there was to be no business on the menu. That night was for us.

Us. A coarse-sounding, wholly unlyrical word for a concept so soul-satisfying. How easy it is to invent a future from a mere possibility! The fact that all my dreams starred a gentle, refined, intense man with blue-delphinium eyes and spring-water laughter did not guarantee that *my* face had ever appeared in *his* dreams.

He was flawlessly kind to me, true. But he was kind even to his opponents in court or business. He seemed to enjoy my company, but wasn't he at ease in almost any circle and circumstance? Debating politics, theology, and literature with both conviction and grace.

Attentive to the ailing widow neighbor—whose conversations knew no other dimension than a recitation of her pains and menu of current treatments—and to the senator who wielded career-disabling or -enabling power.

When the situation called for it, he addressed the court with authority.

Your Honor, gentlemen of the jury, I direct your attention to . . .

I'd seen his legal finesse stop objections mid-word. And yet, he could sit in my parlor and listen with endless patience while I wrestled with one paltry crisis or another. He could be enraptured, as I, with a butterfly's effortless flight pattern above the wildflowers at the creek's edge. He could sip chicory-thinned coffee at my kitchen table and never let on that he noticed. Of course he noticed. His palate had been treated to the fare of the governor's mansion just the evening before.

In our working relationship, I stiffened at some of his counsel. But I never doubted his wisdom. His presence was as calming to me as a cello played by a skilled muse with long, sonorous draws of the bow.

Could I have merely imagined his affection for me? No. But my mind may have exaggerated the depth of his caring. That's what troubled me most that long evening of waiting—that I had perhaps *invented* the dream.

The mantel clock I'd always found comforting became a spine-wrinkling irritation as I waited for him that night. Its once dulcet tones stung like vinegar on an open wound. Six o'clock. Seven. Eight. Too late for dinner. Nine. Too late for the concert. Ten. Too late for us.

To the young women in my care, I had preached until I was hoarse that good men kept their promises. Always. Would I now have the courage to follow my own counsel and let Josiah go . . . or rather, let my imagination-fed infatuation with him fade? The girls were watching. I would discipline my heart not to race when he drew near. I would sit with him across a desk, across a room, and not ache with what might have been if he had loved me in return.

How could I blame him for shying away from me? I was inextricably packaged with the work to which God had called me. We were inseparable. A heavy load for any man to consider sharing.

Reason spent but a few brief moments with me that night. She argued that since Josiah had never intentionally disappointed me in the past, his absence could be explained. I chased her and her opinion from the room with the groaning sound a heart makes when it is breaking.

What a sight I must have made. Bent inside. Ladder-straight in posture. Perched stiffly on the front edge of the settee facing the window through which I hoped to view his approach. I watched in vain.

My long-fussed-over attire was dismantled as the time slipped by. The wool cape was laid aside, my gray felt hat and Lydia's lavender gloves summarily removed. The brooch at my neck—which I surmised interfered with my breathing—joined the pile of discards. My breath still felt pinched and strained.

Frugality finally pushed me to action. I could not justify letting the lamps burn for a lost cause.

My girls were long abed. Alone, I walked the halls of my suddenly hollow home, turning down the lamps with theatrical solemnity, as if each vanishing pool of light represented the snuffing of hope.

Ivy—1951

"Anna, that must have broken your heart! Even now, as you're telling the story, you're crying."

"I'm not crying as much for that long-overcome disappointment as I am for how close I came to giving up on a good man because I couldn't believe he could love me as much as I needed. Does that sound at all familiar, Ivy?"

Ivy leaned back.

"What is it about Drew that makes you so certain he won't still love you?"

"I haven't heard anything since I told him the truth."

"And has the postal system always been prompt in getting mail from the battlefield to our doors?"

"I should have heard by now."

"You're assuming he will walk away from you and from the baby, that he'll abandon his responsibilities and that his love for you will dissipate as soon as he reads those words. That's a cad, Ivy, not the man you've described to me. Maybe you're better off without him."

"That's not who he is."

"No?"

"Drew is kind and generous, brave, strong but tender. He's like no other man I've met."

"Then what makes you so certain he won't marry you?"

"Oh, he'll offer to marry me. But will he do so out of obligation, because he is such a fine man, or because he loves me?"

"Can it be only one or the other? Or can love and responsibility blend to form something exquisitely beautiful?"

Her notebook never far out of reach, Ivy smoothed ointment on the scars on Anna's legs as she and Anna talked. The strokes grew slower, lighter. "He . . . will . . . leave me."

"Why would you dishonor him by saying such a thing?"

Ivy's throat tightened. The room with solid walls shimmered. "This isn't my first child. My mother left us the night she found me in our bathroom in the midst of a miscarriage. I was sixteen. Love had nothing to do with that one. And love wasn't enough to overcome my mom's disappointment in me."

"That wasn't it." Ornell's coarse voice, though subdued, stopped the shimmering. "That's not why she left us."

Ivy turned toward the doorway where her father stood, but she avoided his gaze. He took one step deeper into the room.

"She didn't walk away because of you, Ivy. How could you think that?"

Ivy searched the ceiling—as she had for years—for some other explanation. "Because of me, your marriage broke up. Because of me, she abandoned us. Because of me, you were saddled with a soiled daughter who even after she grew up couldn't survive on her own."

"Ivy, stop!" his voice commanded now. Then softer, "You never were very good about recognizing the truth."

She glanced from her father to Anna. Two sets of eyebrows arched high.

"What mother in her right mind would run away from her child in trouble?" He whispered the words, but they echoed in the room.

"Dad?"

"In her right mind. She weren't in her right mind, Ivy."

It took him hours to give birth to the rest of the story—a difficult labor. The women waited as the words crowned, then retreated, to crown again.

"You weren't meant to be an only child, Ivy."

And after a few more contractions, "Your mother would have had dozens, if she could have."

With the next wave, "Instead, she had dozens of miscarriages."

"Dad, I never knew."

"Some of them, even I didn't know about. But I guessed. She'd slip into her own world and I couldn't reach her, couldn't stop the pain."

Ivy splayed her palms over her live, hiccuping child, cradling it. "I only knew she was sadder than other mothers. Until now, I thought it was her disappointment with me."

"It was the others—the sons and daughters who refused to stay with her long enough to be born. With each one, she moved a few more inches away from me, until we lost sight of each other." He inhaled a labored breath. "Then, that night, with you losing a child you hadn't longed for, hadn't prayed for, hadn't begged the heavens for the privilege of holding . . ."

No more.

"What happened to her, Mr. Carrington?" Anna braved the breach of speechlessness.

Ivy watched her father's whiskered chin quiver. Then he turned and left the room.

Anna and Ivy sat in silence, the evening deepening around them, though a splinter of light had dawned.

Inhale and exhale. Breathing in the slivers of truth. Breathing out the shards of pain. A cricket in the basement sang a rusty tune with no meaning. Then her father stepped back into the room.

"She asked me to take her to the bus depot. So I did. Helped her purchase a ticket to Des Moines, where her grandmother lived. She got lost somewhere along the way."

The slap of metal on metal signaled the mailman had tucked something into the narrow black box that hung near the doorbell, letting the lid drop shut.

Ivy made a pretense of taking time to dry her hands on the dish towel before racing to the mailbox. Nothing looked, smelled, or felt like Korea.

It was possible, she reasoned, that her letter had fallen on the floor of a mail room between here and there. So she wrote another, saying all she'd said in the first one and more, sketching a poor representation of the bungalow and of the crib she'd found at a late-season rummage sale. Ivy hand delivered it to the postmaster at the iron-barred window downtown and stood sentry while he postmarked it and slid it into the proper canvas mailbag along the wall behind the counter.

She asked again if her mail—all her mail—were being forwarded to the new address. No new mail carriers who hadn't heard of the change? No stockpile of undelivered letters? No news?

How desperate she must have looked.

How desperate she was.

⸎

The fire of Anna's life once roared and snapped, from what her stories revealed. Ivy watched now as the flames grew mellow and sparks became embers. If anything, her spirit glowed brighter, but Ivy found herself pausing at Anna's door each morning. Would she find Anna smiling? Or gone? She adopted the habit of whispering, "Lord, help me accept whatever I find behind this door today."

Anna would call that a habit worth keeping.

"Good morning, Ivy. How are you and the little one today? Did you sleep well?"

"I was up three times to the bathroom."

Anna used her fingers to fluff her sleep-matted hair. "I am happy to have lived long enough to see the introduction of indoor plumbing for occasions such as this."

Who would make Ivy laugh like that when Anna had drawn her last breath?

"Let's get your morning routine done as quickly as we can. You left the story unfinished last night."

"Which one?"

"Anna, you know very well which one."

"My beloved . . . on the night he wasn't. Or so I thought."

"Let's get some breakfast in us. The little one is especially hungry this morning. Then we'll talk."

⁂

When Anna finally felt up to talking, Ivy risked asking, "Where was he? Where was Josiah that night?"

Anna smoothed the blanket on her lap. "He was detained."

"I suspected that. I couldn't for a minute believe he stood you up. What detained him?"

"Not what. Who."

Ivy set her dust rag aside and picked up the notebook, the third one since she'd started writing midsummer. "Who?"

Anna smirked. "The local law enforcement."

"Josiah was arrested? For what?"

"Not arrested. Detained. They weren't sure what to do with him, prominent attorney and all."

"What did he do?"

"Speeding."

"Speeding? A hot-rodder?"

Laughter filled the small room. "Hardly. Josiah's motorcar was one of the few on the roads in those days. It was to be my first ride in it. He was . . . he was in a hurry to reach me that evening. Clairmont had a speed limit for horse-drawn vehicles but had yet to implement one for motorized vehicles."

Ivy made a note in the margin of the page. "How fast was he going?"

"Ten."

"Ten miles an hour over the speed limit?"

"Oh, no, dear. The speed limit was six miles an hour. He raced along at ten, the law enforcement officer estimated, and spent the night in the hoosegow, although we didn't call it that at the time. No charges were filed because no one knew what to do without an adopted motorcar speed limit."

"Anna! You forgave him, I hope. That's so romantic. Racing to see you."

She clutched the locket at her neck. "Eventually. I forgave him eventually. The law was in a greater hurry to do so than I was."

⸙

Anna—1890s

So many of the young women sent to me arrived because they'd taken their relationships too far too fast. As Josiah and I grew to consider each other more than business partners, we talked about our responsibility to present an example to the residents. Patience. Self-restraint. Decorum. Purity. We were not children. But we lived our relationship under the scrutiny of those who had made unwise choices in their relationships. That put an additional restraint on our growing affection for each other.

The affection nearly flamed out before we gave it voice.

The conversation began innocently. Josiah and I walked in the orchard, under pretense of checking on the harvest readiness of the Yellow Transparents, as if Puff were not daily on the case. Truth be told, it was togetherness that drew us to the top of the hill. That and the impeccably blue canopy overhead, the autumn freshness and intoxicating fragrance in the air, and the joy of feeling comfortable and appreciated whether speaking or silent.

"This is a good place."

I assumed he meant the property as a whole, not just the tiny square of it on which we stood. "Yes. I'm grateful."

"Anna, have you ever considered having a family of your own?"

A bolt of lightning skittered recklessly through my body, exiting through my toes, though the sky remained cloudless and unthreatening.

"I have a family, Josiah. So many daughters and grandchildren that I find it increasingly difficult to name them all accurately."

Did his silence mean he was considering the validity of my answer or constructing a response?

"Have you . . . thought about . . . marriage? About sharing your life and your future and your passion for this work . . . with a man who would love and cherish you and meld his efforts and his heart with yours?"

He had not specified *which* man.

"The work is so consuming," I said. "It takes all my energies to love and care for these girls, to teach them how to be good mothers and godly women."

"But, Anna, it's also important to show them what godly husbands and wives are like, how a man and woman can build a relationship that knows His blessing. Don't they also need to be taught what pure love looks like when it stumbles, when it grows?"

My inability to answer became a wedge between us. At least, that's how I saw it. And felt it. I would have longed to tell him point-blank that his was not a new thought, that I'd heard the murmurings crescendo. But to admit so would have been to confess that I needed him. Josiah Grissom. Not *a* man or *a* husband. Those I felt no need for. It was Josiah with whom I longed to share life.

Was it fair of me to obligate his heart with my admission? And if he were merely speculating, merely proposing a theory rather than proposing, I couldn't bear the humiliation. I knew I'd collapse from the inside, piece by piece, until the shell of my body lay shriveled on the ground, limp and lifeless and worthless as the too-far-gone windfall apples at our feet.

"I'm grateful," I finally managed to respond, "for the Kinneys' example. We would be hard-pressed to find a stronger testimony to the wonder of God-pleasing love."

He lifted his chin, as if freeing an obstruction from his throat. How his countenance reacted after that point, I don't know. The grass at our feet drew and held my attention.

"That is true, Anna. But they have only occasional contact with the young women. Sunday services. Afternoon visits to Morning Glory. Community activities. Hardly the realities of day-to-day living, the constant give-and-take of compromise, the tender moments between a husband and wife as they sit by the fire, the wrestling with crises . . ."

Memory fails me now, trying to recall if he spoke more than those words. I was lost in the dream of Josiah at my side, not for an evening near the fire, but for a lifetime. And then I woke with a start. He was not courting me. He was counseling me. With the wisdom of years beyond my own, he was undoubtedly taking the opportunity to advise me to look for a mate.

Perhaps he even hoped that if I succeeded in finding a man willing to care for me, Josiah himself would be relieved of many of the roles he played—listening ear, companion, problem-solver, heart-mender.

Tears stung my eyes. I'd grown to depend on Josiah's presence, his attention, his strength. And now he was asking me to wean myself from him. I did not even pretend to be ready for that. But I respected him too much to ask more of him than he had already given.

"I will give your counsel consideration, Josiah."

It must have been the response he was looking for. He smiled and reached over to squeeze my hand. He didn't intend it, I'm sure, but his touch squeezed the life out of my heart.

Ivy—1951

"You couldn't see that he was in love with you?"

Anna's silver eyebrows arched. "Like others I have known"— she slowed her words and leaned toward Ivy—"it took me an excess of convincing to believe someone could love me that completely. A man like that."

Ivy shook her head from side to side and made the *tsking* sound she'd heard Anna direct toward her in the past. "Oh, Anna. How could you have doubted—?"

"And you are so certain your Drew can't love you enough to forgive your silence and embrace the child you share?"

"I would have heard from him by now."

"Oh, my dear." She scratched the top of her head with a gnarled hand. "And you criticize my naïveté with Josiah?"

"You did marry. Anna Morgan became Anna Grissom."

"Yes. Not soon enough."

Ivy's heart fluttered. "What? Did you . . . did you and he . . . have to get married?"

"Ivy! After the misery I'd seen? After the remorse I'd felt in my own bones for the young women who paid such a high price for letting themselves be carried away by passion? Ivy, really!"

"I'm sorry. I don't know what you mean that you didn't marry soon enough." Her baby kicked as a friend would sock someone in the arm.

"I mean simply that it took me too long to believe he loved me as much as he did. We had only ten years together as husband and wife before I was alone again."

Ivy drank in the sobriety of her words. *Took too long. Alone again.* "I wonder if I could contact the army directly to ask about Drew. I wonder if I could write to his chaplain and ask him to intercede for me."

———

Anna—1890s

In that weariness-drugged moment before sleep captured me, when feathers pillowed my head and invited me to release my hold on the day and its concerns, I often wondered just how far back my girls—or any of us—would have to trace to stop the flow of regrets.

"If we hadn't let our guard down . . . ," one might confess. But history no doubt contained many pages before that moment. Leaving thoughts unchecked. Challenging the edges of danger, not recognizing that the cliff edge is not solid granite but crumbling sandstone. Entertaining, if only for a flash, risk's possibility. Opening the door to opportunity. Not looking away when sin's bribe was offered, as if the agreement held no consequences.

How far back would we have to go to find the blink of time in which a wiser choice—a different choice—would have changed everything?

I learned and taught that a person doesn't burn to death by falling on the fire, but by staying there. I learned, too, that grace heals scars, massages the stiffness out of losses, creates purpose out of pain. And that the deeper the mine of shame, the richer the vein of gratitude.

Ivy—1951

The white aluminum tree—bare except for clumps of tinsel, per her dad's request—crowded the corner of the petite living room. But the way it sparkled as the sun hit it in the morning, or as the rotating red, green, and blue spotlight illuminated it at night, made it mesmerizing, if untraditional. Anna appreciated the aluminum more than Ivy did and asked that her wheelchair be positioned to face the tree as she told her stories on the days she felt up to sitting. It gave her an unobstructed view of the cardboard nativity set at its base.

"Did you find purpose in the pain of losing Josiah?"

Anna fingered the locket at her throat, as she so often did. It rested lower on her chest than it must have when she weighed more than a flyswatter. "Some distress"—she drew a breath—"has no end point this side of eternity."

"I don't know that I can live without Drew."

"And if you have no choice?"

A band of tightness radiated across Ivy's abdomen and around to the small of her back. "I'm not ready."

"We never are, dear."

"For any of this. I'm not ready for metal Christmas trees. For giving birth. For raising this child without his father. For living indefinitely with mine. For getting to the end of your story."

Anna closed her eyes and didn't open them.

"Anna?"

"I want so badly to meet your Drew. It makes an ache inside of me that I think will crush me. It's as if I feel in my own body a hint of what you must feel in yours. That's what love does." She opened her eyes then, glassy, glistening, tired-looking. "Time's running out for both of us, Ivy."

"I think I have my answer already."

"Which one?"

"I think the only glimpse I'll ever have of Drew is in the face of this child." She caressed the mound that held her baby, soothing it as she would if rubbing the little one's back while she or he slept in the waiting crib in the other room. The lullaby of the circles she traced were as much for her as for the baby she cradled. Another wave of tightness stretched across her muscles. She rubbed it away.

"Ivy?"

"Yes, ma'am?"

"Are you now willing to talk to Drew's family?"

She curled the corner of the notebook paper. "I wrote to them."

Anna leaned forward in her chair. "You did? I'm proud of you. You told them everything?"

"I asked if they'd heard from Drew. I said that I was concerned about him and needed to get in contact with him."

"Skirting the truth."

"It didn't seem fair for them to know about the baby before Drew does. And yes, it's another twisted consequence of not being honest from the beginning."

Anna tilted her head to the side. "Did they write back?"

"Just one word."

"One word?"

A sour taste flavored the saliva that pooled between her tongue and teeth. "It starts with a *w* and rhymes with *more*." She swallowed hard. "They already know."

"Rhymes with—? Oh. Oh, dear."

What was it about Anna that made it so easy for Ivy to spill her soul? "I can only think of two ways they might have found out. Someone from here in Clairmont told them. Or . . . "

"Or . . . ?"

"Or Drew told them after he found out." Gripped by a pain that flashed through her like lightning, she paused to let its intensity fade before finishing her thought. "And that would explain why I haven't heard from him."

Morning dawned with new snow and no new contractions. They'd passed in the night, unlike other kinds of pain.

Anna begged for another hour's sleep, commenting that the heavy crop of pinecones and the amount of black on each end of the wooly worms portended a harsh winter ahead and misery for her *ar-thur-itis*. So Ivy and her father shared the breakfast table alone. The newspaper headlines drilled the ongoing dangers in Korea, despite the peace talks. Celery on sale at the Piggly Wiggly. Holiday bazaars at several local churches. More MacArthur hubbub.

Ornell folded the paper and set it beside his glass of tomato juice on the yellow Formica table. "You have plans for Christmas Eve?"

A ready-to-be-born baby kept Ivy from sitting close enough to the aluminum edge of the table. She held her breath, waiting for the cramping to start again. Maybe today. Maybe next week. Maybe Christmas Eve. "I don't know, Dad. Do you have plans?"

"Could we maybe have deviled ham?"

"Okay."

He pointed to the folded paper. "Candlelight service at Trinity Church that night. Thought about going."

Oh, Anna. You've gotten through to him, too!

Ivy took a deep breath to slow her heart rate. "Anna would say I've more than approached my time of confinement."

"What?"

"That's what they used to call it when a woman was ready to give birth."

"Now?"

"No, not now, Dad. Soon."

His gaze darted around the room, as if searching for a safe place to land. "Well, then."

27

Becky—2013

There was no joy in Mudville . . . but there was neither joy nor mud at all in Monica's household. Becky's once-a-week cleaning job still felt like a mercy hiring, and the discomfort about what they both knew about each other's daughters—a link that should have drawn them together—stood between them like a thick acrylic barrier. See-through, but impenetrable.

Becky suspected Monica intentionally timed leaving the house before Becky showed up with her knee pads and cleaning supplies. She often saw Monica's SUV rounding the corner toward downtown when pulling her own car into Monica's drive. Too coincidental to be coincidence.

This day, though, Monica sat at the kitchen island, worrying a cup of tea into dizziness when Becky entered the rear-of-the-house kitchen.

"Oh, you're home! Sorry, I would have knocked."

Monica looked up, a tight smile fighting for legitimacy. "Yes, I wanted to talk to you."

"Great," she said, depositing her coat, boots, and bucket of preferred cleaning supplies near the door. *Ooo. New hall tree for coats. Antique. Nice. Fits the place.*

Monica pushed a cup of tea toward her.

"Thanks. Is that the ginger peach I like so much? Smells like it."

"Comforting."

"Soothing."

"Smooth." Monica's line of sight seemed somewhere beyond where Becky stood.

Becky turned to look. Nothing. Windows. A well-maintained but now snow-covered backyard. A handful of apple trees on the rise at the far edge of the property, their branches clothed in individual late-winter snowy sweaters with sequins sewn in for sparkle. She pivoted to face her friend. "I'm glad we'll have a chance to talk. I've missed you. How's Brianne?"

"Better. Her counselor is helping us both."

"Good. Good." She sipped the fragrant tea. *How many cups of tea or coffee had they shared over the ye—*

"Becky, I can't afford to have you clean anymore."

Funny. Becky's first thought wasn't the cost to her own budget, but sympathy for whatever financial crisis threatened Monica's. "Honestly, your house is always immaculate. I've felt guilty for taking your money. You know that. If your finances can't afford it anymore, that's probably the Lord's way of—"

"It's not the money. I can't afford it emotionally." Monica stared into her teacup.

Wasn't Becky the one who should have been embarrassed? Scrubbing toilets for her best friend to make gas money for her husband's job interviews?

"I can't afford the . . . the friendship."

"What?" A nerve ending in her brain twitched. Then another. She pressed two fingers against her right temple. "I'm sorry. What did you say?"

"I love you, but every time I see you all I can think about is *that* moment. The day Brianne— You were here for her when I should have been."

"Monica, you couldn't have known. None of us suspected the depth of her pain. Neither of us knew she'd skipped school." Becky drew closer and gave Monica a sideways hug. "Does it matter which of us was here that day? We're just grateful she—"

Monica shrugged off her embrace. "Don't. I can't . . . can't be around you. It's too hard."

"You don't really mean that." She hadn't felt this nauseous since her last confrontation with her own daughter.

Stiff as a posture expert, Monica planted her palms on her thighs and resumed staring into the barren backyard.

Words, Lord. I need words!

"Your pay for today is there in the envelope. But I don't want you to . . . "

"I understand. Well, I don't understand. I think we need each other now more than ever. But I won't try to tell you how to feel." *Wish I could, but I won't.*

"Thank you."

Becky picked up her teacup and brought it to her lips. She hadn't noticed earlier how tepid it was.

As Monica drew circles with her fingertip on the spotless granite countertop, Becky angled for the door. "I guess I'll go home, then."

"Thank you."

What? You're grateful I'm going home? Oh, Monica! I'd better step up my prayers for your counselor. And get the phone number. I may need it, too.

Gil had rigged a bouncy-swing in the archway between the kitchen and the family room. It looked like something from the 1950s. But Jackson didn't seem to care about style. He was happy bouncing, no matter the apparatus.

301

Gil pointed to the cell phone in his hand when Becky walked in. "Yes, sir. Certainly. I understand." He shook his head side to side for her sake. He had no idea how well she understood that yes-with-my-lips, no-with-my-heart concept. "I'd appreciate that. Thank you."

"Tenneson?"

"Second interview scored high, he said. But they went with someone else."

She dropped her coat and kicked off her boots—hadn't she just done that in another home?—and kissed Jackson's head on her way past him to where Gil sat in his couch cockpit. "I'm sorry, Gil. What's still out there?"

"I hear the cleaning business is good, my dusting queen."

She'd let him think that wasn't the dumbest thing he'd ever said to her until she got control of the tears that threatened.

"No?" His face showed some of the puzzle pieces slipping into place. "What are you doing home this early?"

She sat beside him and slid her hand into his. "The last time I asked you that question, you'd been let go."

He chuckled. "Yeah, but best friends don't fire—"

"Not so much fired as divorced."

"What?"

"The ultimate pink slip. Not only am I not welcome to clean her mirrors, she also let me go as her friend."

"Come on. That's nuts. You saved her daughter's life."

"Part of the problem, apparently. Do we have any of those brownies left?"

"Beck, it's nine-thirty in the morning."

She patted him on the thigh and stood to go look. "It's been that kind of day."

"Hon. They're gone. I ate the last one for breakfast."

Sympathetic as she was to his futile job hunt, she might never forgive him for eating the last brownie.

Gil joined her in the kitchen, Jackson still drooling and bouncing as the scene unfolded. "I don't understand, Becky."

"Chocolate is comforting. And chocolate in the form of a brownie is—"

"That, I totally get," he said. "I don't understand what happened at Monica's."

Becky gripped the counter, then snatched a paper towel from the holder, dampened it, and swiped at the sticky spot she'd found while looking for stability. "I'm an anathema to her."

"You give her asthma?"

"Oh, Gil! Sometimes humor is . . . is . . . an anathema!"

He wrapped his arms around her. "Sorry. I'm not a hundred percent sure I know what that word means, but if it's any comfort, sometimes you make it hard for me to breathe, too, but not in a bad way. You know?"

"Gil. Not only is the baby watching, but also if there were ever a time I was not in the mood . . . "

He loosened his grip. "Bad timing. I know. I have a Sidam touch."

She pressed her hands against his chest and looked up into his scruffy face. "Sidam?"

"It's the opposite of Midas. *Nothing* I touch turns to gold. Or dollar bills, either. Or electronic deposits."

Cry or laugh. It could go either way.

"Good news, though," he said, his normally rock-solid voice more like the loose skree on which they lost their footing while hiking on their honeymoon. "Ron has a tentative offer on our house. He called right after you left. It's not a great offer, but we should probably take a look at it."

Cry. Definitely. Cry.

28

Ivy—1951

It had all gone so wrong.

No Christmas Eve service. No deviled ham. And no Christmas baby, either.

The first wave of doubled-over pain hit with blinding fierceness a few minutes after Ivy finished the lunch dishes on the 24th. Intent on lowering herself into the tweed chair for a few minutes, instead Ivy skinned her knees on the hardwood floor in the living room as she fell. She stayed there, on all fours, an hour-long thirty seconds before the pain subsided. So different from the bands of tension she'd felt over the past week, this condensed education about the realities of labor stole her breath and her courage.

Anna called out from her bedroom, "Ivy! Ivy what happened? Dear one, are you okay? Answer me, please!"

"Oof. I'm okay."

"Is it the baby?" Her voice drew closer. How had she maneuvered out of bed into her wheelchair without assistance?

By the time Anna wheeled into the room, Ivy was seated in the chair, dabbing at her raw knees with a handkerchief.

"Oh honey, you're bleeding."

"I didn't expect my knees would take the worst beating during labor." Ivy worked up a smile that she hoped would reassure her friend.

"I'll dampen a kitchen towel for them."

Ivy placed her hands on the arms of the chair to lift herself out. "I'll get it."

Anna's glare could sear meat. "You sit! I'll get it. The way this is starting, you will need every ounce of strength you can spare. How soon before your father gets home?"

Ivy leaned back in the chair, closed her eyes, and massaged her abdomen. "He went to the post office. To check. For me."

"Why are you crying? Have your pains started again?"

She choked back a belly-deep sob. "Anna, I wanted this child to bear Drew's name. We've run out of time."

Anna bent as well as she could and laid the cold compresses against Ivy's knees. "Carrington is a fine name."

"It's not his."

"I know. I know, dear."

"Oh! And my dad will be so upset."

"That you prefer Lambert to Carrington? He understands more than you think, Ivy."

"Not that. About the chair. My water broke."

⌒∞∞⌒

Bright light. Too bright. Marrow-deep pain. Crushing. Bruising. *Who is that tearing at me, pressing on me, smothering me?*

White and noise. Smells. So foreign. Alcohol. She smelled alcohol. And blood. Hers.

Ether. Dark. Too dark. Pain breaking through the darkness.

Whispers.

Silence.

305

———∞∞∞———

Eight women in the ward. When the curtains were opened, Ivy counted eight women and ten beds—two empty, five on each side of the room—and feet facing a wide aisle for the medical staff. The crushing pain had fled, replaced by a stinging pain and a weariness that forced her to use both hands to grip the bed rail to pull herself onto her side.

The woman in the bed to her left had babies suckling at both breasts. Twins. The woman to her right had given birth to her seventh child in seven years. Tired. She looked as tired as Ivy felt.

A woman Ivy couldn't see from where she lay complained that her husband—her *husband*—read magazines until midnight while she labored, then went home so he wouldn't miss his mother's Christmas morning brunch with his family. Her bitterness soured the ward. If Ivy had had the energy, she'd have shut her up. The mother of twins shushed the woman with a word that held the power of an industrial floor fan.

The twins' suckling sounds made her have to go to the bathroom and created an odd tightness in her breasts.

"Miss Carrington?"

Miss. Did she have to say it so loud? Women on the ward might have had to get married, but no one would know. Their names started with Mrs.

She rolled to her back, her arms empty, a soup of darkness, whispers, and pain swirling in her mind. She hadn't heard a tiny cry before the darkness engulfed her. Now some Nightingale had been sent to tell her.

The nurse's crisp white hat, banded with a thin black velvet ribbon and held to her Lucille Ball curls with white bobby pins, loomed large in her vision as she stood beside Ivy's hospital bed. Her face was as kind as Anna's had ever been.

"Miss Carrington? Are you with us? You had a pretty rough time of it."

"I'm here." Her voice scratched across a dust-dry throat.

Someone's baby mewed. The sound was so close. In the nurse's arms.

"Ready to meet your daughter?"

It had all gone so wrong. And so right. No Christmas Eve service. No deviled ham. And no Christmas baby, either.

Joy Elizabeth Anna was born a Carrington, not a Lambert, eight minutes into December 26th.

Joy to the world.

<hr />

How could something so tiny and beautiful have caused so much distress?

Joy of my heart, welcome to the world.

Ivy stroked the downy skin of her daughter's forehead; miniature ears; full, flushed cheeks; and perfect chin. She ran her finger along the now-closed eyelids. So soft. While the noise of the ward swirled around her, Ivy remained in a cocoon of Joy. The ache of Drew's absence pulsed strong. But hope lay content in her arms. Hope grabbed her finger and held tight in its small but tenacious grip. *My strong girl. Do you know how much I love you? You will.*

"Eighth Army?" The voice came from somewhere above the cocoon. The Nightingale.

"Excuse me?"

"Daddy's in Korea?"

"How did you know?"

Nightingale held a stethoscope to Ivy's heart, put two fingers on her wrist, and pushed rudely on Ivy's shrinking abdomen as she talked. "You said a few unkind things about Korea during labor."

"I did? I'm sorry."

"Not unexpected. We OB nurses have heard a few choice words on a few dozen subjects over the years. Joy's daddy will be proud to hear how valiantly you fought when he gets home."

The bundle of warmth in her arms pushed back against the cramp of longing.

"Now, I think it's time for you to take a nap and for me to get this little one back to the nursery. Your father's been waiting at the viewing window for an hour."

"My father?"

"I think he may have rubbed the brim off his hat by now, twirling it in his hands while he waits."

Ivy buried her face between the receiving blanket and Joy's ear.

"Are you okay, dear? Your emotions may be in upheaval for a few days. That's normal."

Ornell's first grandchild. No. That wasn't true. The first he'd get to hold.

Her arms shook as she lifted the bundle toward the nurse, but she couldn't help smiling when her eyes focused on the name tag—*Gale*, the Nightingale.

"I'll bring her back."

"When?"

A laugh punctuated Gale's final sentence. "When she's hungry!"

From now on, never a day without Joy.

———

Ivy lowered herself into the passenger seat of the Oldsmobile, grateful her father had left the motor running so that a wave of heat waited for her and the baby so carefully shielded from the New Year's wind and laid into her arms.

She noticed every pothole in the road, every train track on the way from the hospital to the bungalow. The patches of ice on the road—patches she would have ignored before Joy was born—flashed danger.

So quickly she'd changed from woman to mother.

Anna must have stretched out her arms the minute she saw the car turning into the driveway. She sat just far enough inside the door to allow them to enter, a pillow on her lap to help support and cradle little Joy. Both were mesmerized—the older staring down into the angelic face, the younger staring up into no less of an angel. Ivy steadied herself with the back of a kitchen chair and enjoyed the moment.

"Let me get your coat." Her dad slipped it from her shoulders as if she were the breakable one, which too many times she had been.

"Thank you."

"I made soup," he said.

"You did?"

Anna looked up. "With a little backseat-driving help from me." She winked. "You might want to keep the salt shaker handy."

"I think I'd like to sit for just a minute before lunch, if that's all right with you two."

Anna winked in her father's direction this time. "You do that, dear. Go on into the living room. Ornell will wheel us in to join you."

The tweedy chair gone, in its place stood a chintz-covered padded rocker. The pink and rose peonies in the fabric matched nothing else in the room, but the sight of the chair

309

and its meaning to the situation brought her again to the edge of an emotional downpour. "Oh, Dad! It's wonderful!"

"You can't tell anything until you sit in it." His eyes gleamed.

The arms were the perfect height and width for resting her elbow when nursing Joy. Her head nestled comfortably against the upholstered back. And the rocking motion, smooth as her daughter's breath, spoke of future naps and storytelling.

"Ornell, get her a drink of water," Anna commanded. "She needs to drink plenty. The way this little one is squirming, I'd say she'll be hungry before her mother is. The soup can wait."

Her mother. Two simple words made Ivy's tear ducts fill.

Her dad would have looked more comfortable holding a bowling-ball bag in the crook of his arm than he did transporting his granddaughter from Anna to Ivy. But he lingered a moment at Ivy's side, as if drinking in the wonder of life in a small package.

"She's a beauty, Ivy."

"Thanks, Dad. For everything."

He leaned down and kissed Joy's forehead, as if blessing her. The tears Ivy had held back flowed unhindered when she felt the same kiss on her own forehead.

For all the agony that child had caused her during labor, Joy made up for it by keeping her fussing to a minimum. She woke at night with a sweet call for attention and returned to sleep quickly after nursing and a diaper change. Ivy lost more sleep listening to her daughter breathe, grateful for the sound, than she did with the feedings.

When Ivy slept, her dreams reflected her physical and emotional exhaustion. Ether mixed with the odor of gunfire. Drew cradling a Korean child, then their child, then a fallen soldier, helmet askew, with a face too much like Drew's.

She woke shivering, her bedcovers thrown to the floor as she wrestled with the darkness. Weariness soon claimed her again—a few minutes, it seemed, before the little one realized her tummy was as empty as her mother's hopes.

It was time to let Drew go.

Joy Elizabeth Anna Carrington deserved her full attention and a happy mother—stable, forward-looking, strong. Their life together would confront enough challenges—a fatherless child and an unwed mother. They couldn't live with Ivy's dad forever. Anna slipped closer to eternity every day.

Somehow, they'd muddle through. But not if Ivy dragged an anvil of impossibility behind them.

The early days of 1952. Time to let Drew go.

29

Becky—2013

Gil, I can't help plan a wedding, take care of a near-toddler, pack this entire house, and move!"

Gil took a bite from his apple and mumbled, "I'm here to help."

"I can't help plan a wedding, take care of a—"

He bumped her in the ribs. "Becky, we don't dare ignore this offer."

"It's thousands less than the house is worth."

"But it still leaves us enough for a down payment on the duplex."

She wondered how a simple six-letter word could feel so heavy. "We won't need the duplex if those two get married, will we?" Things were happening too fast. Where was the time to process?

"Seriously? Nice thinking, but exactly where will they find an apartment that takes cheese doodles for rent money? Or Purse Suedes?"

"New plan."

"What?"

"Lauren has a new plan. She's talking about opening a day-care center."

Jackson protested the idea with a string of screeches, no longer content to bounce. Becky started toward him, but Gil reached him first, freeing the baby from the fun that had become an "unbearable" constraint.

"Hey, little buddy. What's up? Ooo. What's down? That is one heavy diaper you've got there, bud." He shot a look Becky's way.

"'I'm here to help,' you said."

"I did, didn't I?"

She followed as the boys headed toward the changing table. "There are too many changes."

"Tell me about it," he said, holding the squirming boy with his forearm while he tugged at the diaper's tape tabs.

"Not diaper changes, you goof. All these"—she gestured with her hand as if including the world—"insane choices. I don't want to leave here. I don't want to live in the duplex. I want to be a normal grandma, not half grandmother, half mother. I want you to find a job that makes you feel fulfilled and makes our mortgage. I want to—" Her thought spontaneously aborted.

"To what?"

"To see my daughter happy. Is that not . . . not possible anymore? And if you use the term 'new normal,' you'll have more than a diaper to clean up."

She retreated to the master bedroom. Where else did she have to go? She sat at the foot of the bed, her hands propping her upright, her head bowed. *Oh, God. How did it all go so wrong?*

The pain in her soles originated in the lining around her heart. She rubbed her feet back and forth on the aging carpet until the static electricity stopped her. Winter, glorious winter. The air so dry that she could spark a fire with her socks.

"May I come in?" Gil stood in the doorway. He held Jackson on his hip who was drinking from a bottle Gil held like one would for a calf.

"It's your room, too. Until the new owner takes over."

"Come here." He took her hand and moved her to the head of the bed. They propped Jackson between them on the center pillow and lay on either side of him, leaning on their elbows, facing the baby as he drank, one chubby, dimpled hand wrapped around Gil's bottle-holding thumb, the other clutching the collar of Becky's denim shirt.

It would have been peaceful if not for the chaos.

"Move the clock back two dozen years," Gil whispered, "and this was us with our son between us."

The memory clamped its hand around her throat. *It's too much, Lord. Too much.*

"We've been through utter misery before, Becky."

She smelled hints of the baby lotion left over from Jackson's bath. His toes wiggled as he drank, just like his uncle's had when he was a boy, not a Marine.

Yes, they'd known utter misery. A flag folded in a thick triangle. A precision guard bearing a military casket. Death and life and death and life.

Jackson's eyelids fluttered then closed, his lips still moving. His suction-hold on the nipple released with a gurgle. Mouth pursed, he sucked as if eating, but only in his dreams.

"Gil?" She barely breathed. "Gil, are you sleeping?"

Her husband didn't open his eyes but breathed back, "Praying, hon. Praying."

———❧———

It had been years since Becky fell asleep in the middle of the day. She woke to a puddle of drool on her pillow, unsure if it were hers or Jackson's. Where Gil should have been was his pillow laid sideways, like a bolster to keep the baby from rolling toward a grandfather who was no longer in the room.

She eased off the bed and made a similar bolster on her side.

Where had Gil gone? Captain Optimism snuck off. Out ridding the world of negativity, no doubt.

No, he was making himself a sandwich.

"Your grandpa would have called that a Dagwood."

"Too much?" he said, peeling off a layer of ham and a layer of cheese.

"Oh, go for it," she said. "We're about to sell our house. That calls for a . . . celebration." A word reserved for birthdays and weddings, graduations and baby showers, sounded rough and coarse.

"Even with the sale of the house, we won't be able to get a loan for the duplex if I don't have a job. One of us, at least, needs to have a job."

"Do you want me to call the magazine and see if they have an opening now?"

Gil sliced his sandwich on a slant. He must have watched a little of the cooking channel before they canceled their cable. "They would have called you, wouldn't they? If they'd had the funding, they would have taken you back in a heartbeat."

She jerked open the fridge and pulled out the plastic container of leftover spaghetti. "Maybe they heard I was fired from my last job. Oh, was that just this morning?"

"I love you, my sarcasmalicious one."

"Love you, too."

"We're in this together."

"Knee-deep."

He took a bite of his sandwich, his eyebrows colliding as he chewed. Sour pickle or deep thought?

"I have an idea," he said when his mouth was almost empty.

"I hope it's brilliant."

"Maybe we could get the duplex on a rent-to-own basis."

"Still have to have a job to pay rent."

"Oh. Right."

Brilliant.

He chewed another thought. "So, tell me honestly, would it be so bad if we moved in with my mother?"

———※———

"Here. Eat this spoonful of peanut butter. Eat, Becky. It'll stop the hiccups."

"How (*hic*) do you (*hic*) know these things?"

Gil put the spoon in her hand and wrapped her fingers around the handle. "I don't have a job. I watch more morning TV than I should."

"Blog."

"What hon? Oh, here. I'll get you a drink."

She smacked her lips. "Blog. You should start a blog. (*Hic*) 'Gil's 'Net: When You're Fishing for Answers.'"

He pursed his lips and wiggled his backward hands near his cheeks in a reasonable facsimile of a fish.

"Of course, you'd need to sell ad space (*hic*) to make that profita—(*hic*)—ble."

The warmth in his embrace did more to stop the hiccupping than her mouthful of peanut butter.

"You, my creamy protein-ness, are the one with all the answers."

"Gil, we both ran out of answers a long time ago."

He held her a long moment. "Then we are perfectly positioned for the spectacular, aren't we?"

The morning brought a phone call from the realtor—the offer was withdrawn—and with the flip of a switch, expect-the-spectacular Gil became as sullen as a teenager with PMS *and* a baby. And . . . the circle was complete.

If it weren't for their shrinking reserves and the distress it would have caused her husband, Becky would have admitted that the news made her ecstatic. There was still time for a real answer to show up.

Still time, too, for Lauren to show up. She hadn't come home the night before.

Becky took her anger out on the pan of oatmeal she made for Gil. Mr. Cranky couldn't afford irregularity. While he sat watching her from his self-imposed Time Out stool at the breakfast bar, she stirred the bubbling cauldron with a vigor usually reserved for hand-whipping meringue.

In her frenzy, she almost missed it. But moms hear things like the faint click of a key in a lock.

Lauren thought she could sneak in the front door? At nine thirty on a Saturday morning?

Impeccably cued, Jackson alerted the world that he was awake.

Roused from his catatonic state by the concurrent crises, Gil pointed down the hall to signify he had dibs on the boy. She could have the girl.

"Lauren?"

"Mom, don't start. I'm not in the mood."

"Excuse me? Young lady—"

"I'm really tired. I'm going to bed."

"No, you're not. Sit. Sit!" Becky's blood pressure fluctuated wildly when she saw the look on Lauren's face. "Honey, sit down. What's going on? Where were you?"

"The wedding is off."

The gasp heard 'round the world.

"You broke up?"

"Noah is such a jerk!"

To talk or not to talk—that is the question.

Lauren flinched when her son let out a man-sized holler.

"Your dad's taking care of it, Lauren. Now, talk. What happened? Maybe it's cold feet. A lot of grooms get—"

"Oh, Mom. Give it up. There's no hope. We're done."

"Is it worth it to get some premarital counseling, Lauren? Jackson needs his daddy."

"What?" Lauren's forehead creased like a sideways pleated skirt. "Noah's not Jackson's father!"

"He isn't?"

She scrunched her nose. "What's burning?"

Oatmeal!

Becky ran to clamp a lid on the saucepan and slide it off the stove. The stench still billowed into the room, so she took the pan outside and stuck it in a snowdrift. When she returned to the house and the bizarre conversation, the other half of the conversation had disappeared.

To her bedroom, no doubt.

What was Becky going to do with that daughter of hers?

She knew the answer to that one. Keep loving her . . . and step up her prayer labor.

⁓

"You can't give back a tattooed engagement ring."

The Lauren Trundle Book of Modern Proverbs. There was a job for her—writing how-not-to books.

"No, dear. That's true. But maybe"—was she really going to say this?—"maybe you could go back to the shop and have something tattooed on top of it. A flower or something."

Lauren rolled onto her back on her perpetually unmade bed. "What did you say?"

"Trying to help."

"Mom, you're amazing. How can you keep loving me?"

Becky swept the too-long bangs off Lauren's forehead. "It's in the contract."

"Your daughter gets pregnant on a dare—"

"What?"

"Yeah. We'll talk about that later. But, I mean, how many ways can I mess up my life?"

I'm keeping a ledger. I'll go get it.

"And yours? And what are the odds I won't totally mess up Jackson's life too? Poor kid."

"Parents pretty much all feel that way, no matter how old they are."

"No they don't."

"Trust me."

Lauren's facial expression shifted. "Not you and Daddy. What have you two ever done wrong in raising us?"

I'm keeping a ledger. Let me get it. "Well, let's see. Earlier today . . . "

"Come on. I'm being serious."

"So am I, Lauren. Do you really believe you'll never be any smarter about parenting than you are today? No smarter about relationships? That you won't learn anything useful over the next few years? That mistakes are practice for the next big goof-up rather than life lessons?"

Lauren shook like a toddler coming down from a tantrum. "I . . . I really do love him, you know."

"Noah?"

"NO! That jerk. I'm talking about Jackson. I really do love him."

"I know, honey. It shows . . . sometimes."

"It's supposed to show all the time, isn't it?"

"Parenting 101."

Lauren sat up and hugged her mom sumo-style, and with sumoferocity. "Will you help me?"

What do you think we've been trying to do for the last year? "Absolutely."

"A dare is a superdumb way to make a baby." Lauren tugged Jackson's sweatshirt over his belly. He sat in her lap, facing out, as she sat cross-legged on the couch next to her mother. The recliner Gil rescued from Goodwill was his new office and crisis-management center.

Becky glanced at him, then focused her attention on her daughter. "I think we can all agree there."

"Lots of things start out ugly, Lauren." The pace of Gil's words held as much meaning as their multiple definitions.

"That chair, for instance."

"Hey, it's comfortable."

"Mom, you're okay with it messing up your design scheme?"

Becky leaned in conspiratorially. "It's temporary. There's no way it'll fit in the duplex."

Lauren giggled, a far too infrequent sound. "Yeah, but if you're staging a house with hopes of selling it . . . "

"Gil! She's right! Quick! Haul it out to the yard. We'll have a bonfire. We can throw in your ratty hooded sweatshirt too."

"Ladies," he began, pounding his feet on the chair's footrest to bring the monstrosity to its pseudo-upright position, "I've worn dress shirts and ties almost every day for twenty-four years. Cut me some slack on the unemployment dress code, all right?"

Lauren stroked the pulsing soft spot on her son's head. "Slack? It's called grace, Dad. And thanks for sharing it so generously with me."

What was that sound? Gratitude? Becky held her breath, afraid the gossamer bubble would burst if she exhaled.

"I'm ready to listen to you guys."

Can't exhale yet!

"What do you think I should do?"

Gil and Becky exchanged invisible, inaudible, parental Morse code. *You take this one, Gil,* she tapped.

"Bullet points or lecture?"

"Bullet points, please."

Come on, Unemployed Dad of the Year. Do your thing!

"First, focus on getting your diploma. A given."

"Agreed."

Becky raised her hand. "May I add some color commentary here? As intriguing an idea as was the Purse Suede business . . . "

"Yeah, Mom. You can save your breath. I can't even sew. Someday maybe. Might make a nice hobby when I'm old."

Why is she looking at me?

"Okay then." Gil used one index finger to point to the other. "Second? Look into any financial help offered to single moms for online learning so you can at least get an associate's degree."

"More school?" She wrinkled her nose.

"More possibilities," Gil countered.

"You don't know," Becky offered, "if you'll need to support the two of you on your own for two years, five years, or ten years, so you'll need marketable skills."

"Way to be supportive, Mom. 'You may never find a guy who loves you, Lauren, so . . . '"

"That's not what I meant."

The sound Gil's chair made when he scooted forward would have delighted a gaggle of fourth-grade boys. "Back to our bullet points. One more. Love that son of yours and lean on God."

"That's two points."

"Not exactly. They're so closely tied together, it's hard to separate them."

Jackson arched his back and squirmed as if he were old enough to slide from Lauren's lap and run outside to play. Too soon, that would be true.

Becky's muscles tensed. Her instinct was to reach for him, settle him, and relieve her daughter of the awkwardness of an unhappy child. Instead, she smiled at the scene taking place inside her brain. Her breaths came in hee-hee-hee-whoo patterns as she mentally took her hands off the moment and let a mother be fully born.

Excellent grandmother was enough of a goal. Jackson already had a mother.

"Oh, sick!" Lauren held her son at arm's length. "He peed on me!"

She left the room to change both of them.

Gil called after her, "Love that son of yours and lean on God." Becky raised her hand for an across-the-room fist bump.

30

Ivy—1952

You going to be okay if I'm gone for the day?"

Her dad's words landed somewhere just beyond his bowl of corn flakes, but she knew they were meant for her. "We'll be fine. I'm feeling stronger every day. Anna's holding her own. You know Joy. She's always fine."

One corner of his mouth twitched upward. "Sleeps a lot."

"That won't last forever. We should enjoy it while we have it. But are you sure you want to go out in this? Snow piled up overnight." She nabbed her dad's second piece of toast—not his norm—from the toaster and glanced out the window while she buttered it. "Doesn't look like it's letting up, either."

He slurped his coffee, then adjusted the bow tie at his throat. "I've driven in snow before."

"Where are you going?" She set the toast plate in front of him and sat to peel her hard-boiled egg. A breakfast without protein was unacceptable for a nursing mother, Anna would say.

"I have an errand to run." His words were tight and sober. Anything but casual.

An errand? Dress shirt and tie? "Can't it wait until the—?" She stopped herself before his look did. Dad was still Dad.

"Be back before dark. You call Gert and Roy if you need anything."

Ivy couldn't imagine how neighbors older than Anna would be much help if any of the women in the household—a newborn, a new mom, and a near invalid—faced something they couldn't handle, but nodded. "We will. But—"

He ran his tongue over his top teeth, as he often did when thinking too hard. "We'll talk about it later. Please, Ivy. Just stay put and lay low today. Okay?"

"Dad?"

"I don't want to worry about you while I'm . . . out running errands."

"I thought it was just one errand."

"Don't get mouthy."

Ivy never pressed, never poked at the hornet's nest of conversation with her father. He'd been quiet for the last day or two, reminiscent of the days before, when he struggled to look her in the eye. She didn't want to go back to that season in their relationship. "It's your business. We'll 'lay low' and have chicken and dumplings waiting for you when you get home. From that Betty Crocker cookbook you got me for my birthday."

He lifted his head. The line of his jaw was still lumpy and cementlike, but a tear caught in his lashes. What was going on?

"That'd be nice, Ivy. I like your chicken and dumplings." Flat, even words.

"Then pray your granddaughter behaves herself today."

He left the crust of his toast—another first—and stood. "I already did."

Stormy days crawl forward. The wind turned the new snow into a blizzard. Never too late in the season for a blizzard in the upper Midwest. Watching the frozen white swirl around the house and down the street fascinated all but the youngest of them, but the hours slogged along anyway for Ivy and Anna.

The cold always made life harder for Anna. Her joints. Her breathing. Ivy warmed a blanket on the radiator and tucked it around her, shoulders to toes. Anna rested uneasily, seemingly as worried about Ornell as any mother would be.

An ideal day for storytelling. But Anna and Ivy had formed a silent covenant to wait until the baby didn't need so much of Ivy's time.

The typewriter sat silent on the desk in the bedroom. Someday, someday like this molasses-slow one in the future, she'd commit Anna's stories to typewritten form. Preserving them might turn out to be Ivy's life's work. Someday.

Her father's promise to get home before dark sneaked under the wire like a teen getting home thirty seconds before curfew. The streetlights glowed, creating an eerie backdrop for the still-blowing snow, when the Oldsmobile crept down the street and stopped near the curb. Ivy watched from the front window as her father drudged up the driveway, then headed back to the curb with his snow shovel. An hour later, he'd cleared enough of a path to drive the car into the driveway.

"Wicked cold out there," he said, stomping his boots on the mat inside the kitchen and shaking drifts from the shoulders of his gray wool coat and hat.

Anna called from the living room, "About time you got home."

Ivy's dad looked at his feet. His socks made damp marks on the linoleum. He stripped them off and laid them near his boots, then picked up a small brown bundle wrapped in string, the size of a pound of hamburger from the butcher.

"Supper's almost ready," Ivy offered.

"I need to get into some dry clothes first. Then, you and I need to talk. Can supper wait?"

"Sure."

When he returned from his room, slippered and sweatered and still rosy-cheeked, Ivy was still standing in the same spot.

"Where's Joy?" he asked as he dragged his chair away from the table and motioned for her to sit.

"Sleeping in her crib. Anna's sleeping in her chair. I think maybe we need to have Dr. Simons take a look at her one of these days."

He raised his chin as if acknowledging what she said but not interested in pursuing that subject. "Ivy, I got some news. About your Drew." He set the brown bundle on the table and nudged it toward her.

Her pulse no longer a soft thud barely noticeable, it now banged like hardheaded mallets on a bass drum in an erratic marching band. "What's this?" She reached toward the packet, then drew her hand back. "What is this?"

Her father laid his hand over hers. "Your unopened letters to Drew. His half-written, undelivered letters to you. Some of them."

"W-where did you get them?"

"His folks had them."

"How did they—? Why would they have—?" Worms of bile crawled up her throat.

"Ivy, since the middle of October, Drew's been missing in action."

"Put a cold compress on the back of her neck!"

Anna's orders broke through the fog. The room hadn't gone black, but it had faded to gray flannel. The color crept back into Ivy's vision, hesitant as a Minnesota spring. Their kitchen. Supper on the stove. The table set. Anna leaning on the arms of her wheelchair. Her dad folding a damp washcloth this way and that. And a tightly swaddled brown paper bundle on the table.

"Why wouldn't they have told me? Why would his family keep that from me?"

Ivy traced back through the months since mid-October. All that had happened. Always with a sense of foreboding. She thought his love had disappeared. But *he* had.

"Was he captured?"

"He's not on the P.O.W. list. The army doesn't know what happened. We may never know. *Missing in action. Whereabouts unknown.*"

Ivy twisted the hem of her blouse. "That's not what the government said, is it? 'Missing in action. Presumed dead.'" Anna pressed her hands to her lips. Ivy's father scooted his chair closer and laid his arm across Ivy's shoulders.

"Not you, nor me, nor the military, nor the president knows the answer to that. And we can't speculate."

"How did you find out?"

Ornell tugged at a thread in his shirt cuff. "I called around. Talked to some people in Westbrook who knew Drew's folks."

"They've known all this . . . all this time?"

The thread gave way and his cuff button spurted onto the floor. He kicked at it with his foot. "Didn't know right away. But knew too long."

She still hadn't touched the bundle. "How'd you get the letters?"

"I planted myself in their front room and told them I intended to camp there until they let loose of any information that rightfully belonged to my daughter." He cleared his throat. "I aimed for persuasive, but it might have come across as intimidating."

Oh, Daddy!

"I told them how sorry we all were for their loss, but that you and his little girl deserved to have them letters back—and any he meant to send you if he could have . . . before . . . "

"I can't read them right now."

"There's time."

Anna cupped her hand around her ear. "Do I hear the little one squirming? She'll work herself up into a fit if someone doesn't go get her as soon as she's awake. Ornell?"

The ploy was too obvious for words. Ivy thawed a degree or two inside. "Thanks, Dad."

Anna's gaze followed him as he left the room. Then she stretched out a beautiful, gnarled hand and cradled Ivy's chin. "Look me in the eye, child."

She obeyed.

"You hear me. This story isn't over yet. All we know is that we don't know anything."

A sniff replaced the words Ivy wanted to speak.

"Hear me. This isn't the end of it. Ends come. They do for all of us." Anna paused long enough to draw a deeper breath. "But this can't be it. It can't be the end of it."

Biblical "fountains of the deep" opened, with both women feeding the stream with their tears.

More than once, over the next few hours and days, Ivy thanked the Lord for the gift of Joy Elizabeth. Someone needed Ivy to be strong. The child snuggled into her neck as if the world were a safe and peaceful place. She fed and slept and learned how to coo. The weight of her in Ivy's arms comforted like a hot-water bottle wrapped in lamb's wool.

Ivy changed the baby's blankets more frequently than normal because they were dampened with a mother's grief.

Her father changed the television channel when the news came on. No one in that household wanted to hear how the peace talks were going, what was taking so long, or the clever name of the most recent battle. Heartbreak Hill had been enough.

The paper bundle held only two unsent letters from Drew. The rest were Ivy's—he'd saved them all, it appeared—and the undeliverables, packaged by some army clerk to return to the soldier's parents along with any other mail. Her dad said Drew's family had waited months for his possessions to be returned—everything except his dog tags and the fatigues and boots he was wearing when the hill exploded. She wanted to feel sorry for his family. She had to. She did.

Drew's two letters took up permanent residence on Ivy's nightstand, tucked into her Bible, as if the book of holy words could influence the words he'd written. She'd not opened them. Was it pure foolishness to leave them unread and let her imagination invent what they held?

His understanding. His forgiveness. His excitement about the baby he hadn't even known had been born already—a girl with his thick hair and chin dimple. Sketches of the house he'd build them on a shady street with a big backyard that linked to others peppered with children. A place where they could blend in like any other family, the past a matter of record but not regret.

In time, she'd be strong enough to read what must have been his response to her confession. Not now. Ignorance allowed her a wisp of hope that he'd loved her anyway.

—∞∞—

No ring. No rights. She had no rights regarding news about the search, if any, for a missing soldier with thick, tawny hair and a chin dimple like the child she rocked to sleep at night.

No ring, no word, no reason to believe he would be found. The gruesome tales of what happened to American soldiers caught behind enemy lines hadn't improved with each new war. The word *missing* merely prolonged the inevitable, prolonged the slow, rusty, burred scalpel-pull through the flesh of her heart.

It wasn't a matter of giving up hope. On the first day of spring, she sliced through the cold ground behind the garage with a garden shovel, dug a shallow grave, and buried a token—one of the scalloped-edged photographs Drew had sent in one of his first letters to her. She buried *false* hope.

Longing drained her energies for parenting, and for caring for the family she did have—her father, Anna, and everpresent Joy. She needed all the strength she could muster. The bungalow was too small for longing.

"Anna, how did you go on after Josiah died? I know you'll answer 'By God's grace' or 'In His strength alone' or 'Because of Jesus.' But how? What does that look like?"

Anna flinched as Ivy turned her on her side to rub lotion on her back.

"Did that hurt? I'll be gentler next time."

With her head turned back over her shoulder, Anna said, "Not much left of me that doesn't hurt, dear. It's the way of it."

"Do you want to sit up for a while? I can wheel you out to the front room. The sun's so warm coming through that window. You'd be amazed how the recent rain greened up the grass."

"Not today. I'll have to trust your eyes to take it all in for me."

Ivy bit her lower lip to keep it from quivering. She took a deep breath. She could mourn Anna's death before she was gone, or she could enjoy the moments they had left and thank the Lord for the time they'd had together.

A woman with a hundred and twenty-seven daughters. Ivy massaged lotion into the bony, age-spotted back, grateful to be counted among those women. A hundred and twenty-eight.

"I went on," Anna said, her voice jiggling with the movements of Ivy's hand on her back, "because that's all a person can do with a broken heart. If you don't keep going, it gets brittle. Pieces break off and get lost in the carpet or under the sofa. I only had ten years as his wife, but so many more as his friend. And I learned not to discount the healing power of tender memories. So many memories."

"I have so few."

"Intensifies them, doesn't it?"

"What do you mean?"

"The fewer the memories, the richer, sometimes. Like when you make that Swiss steak and cook it down until the gravy is so thick and flavorful. I used to do that with apple butter. The longer it cooked, the more the water evaporated, the lower the volume. But oh, it was sweet!"

Ivy rolled Anna onto her back, tucked her pillow under her neck like she preferred, and rubbed the lightly scented lotion on the translucent skin of Anna's hands and thin arms. "I feel badly for you, that those you helped aren't here for you now to tell you how much you meant to them, what you did for them."

"I have you." She smiled. All her own teeth. "And I have these." She reached with her unlotioned hand and touched the locket at her neck.

These? One locket. No doubt a picture of her beloved Josiah. Anna had never offered to show it to her. Ivy had never asked.

"Would you open it, sweetness?"

Ivy wiped excess lotion from her hands. "Are you sure you want me to see it?"

"Them," Anna corrected. "It's time."

She dug a fingernail under the clasp. With no small effort, the book-shaped locket opened. A tiny photograph looked out at her from the left pane. A man and woman on their wedding day. Anna in her youth. Josiah Grissom by her side. The look of love unmistakable.

Pressed into the hollow of the other part of the locket was a tiny key. When she touched it, the key dropped into her hand.

Anna nodded. "Take it. And get that wooden chest from my things we put in the hall closet, would you?"

On her way, Ivy peeked in at Joy. Sleeping like the angel she was, her rosebud lips moved as though she were thinking about her next meal. Ivy held an arm across her chest until the drawing sensation eased.

The box weighed little more than the wood it was made from. Ivy slid it from the shelf and carried it to Anna's bed.

"The key. There," she said, pointing to an adornment that swung to the side to reveal a small lock.

The lid opened, releasing the fragrance of cedar and earthiness. Lined up four across and dozens per vertical column, two-inch by three-inch yellow-brown envelopes filled the box. Each had a single name written in flowering script in the upper right-hand corner.

"Look," Anna encouraged. "Take a look."

Ivy fingered through the envelopes in the first column. Women's names. Meg. Dania. Marie. Amelia. Reba. Lily . . .

"Your daughters."

"Yes. Most of them."

Ivy tugged one envelope from its position. "May I?"

"Yes, of course! Open it."

The envelope she chose—*Olivia*, identical to the others— was sealed with a pair of cardboard disks, around which was woven a thin red thread. Inside the envelope, a waxed square held a half dozen chestnut-brown seeds, each smaller than a faith-sized mustard seed.

"Morning glories?"

Anna beamed.

"They sent them to you after their own morning glories bloomed."

"After they knew, in their heart of hearts, that they were loved and forgiven. After they'd seen the grace of God"—Anna caught her breath, or it caught her—"and found a way to show it to someone else."

The waxed paper, smooth to the touch, warmed in her hand. Life in the seeds. Forgiveness. Freedom.

Anna reached for the back of the last column. "These few are unmarked. Empty." She pulled one and handed it to Ivy.

"For me?"

"Ivy, they're all for you, now. But this will be the one with your name on it."

Joy stirred.

"Bring her in here. I can't get enough of that child."

Ivy left the box open on the bed beside Anna. There was plenty of room for both.

Freshly diapered and eager to eat, Joy grabbed handfuls of her mother's blouse as the two settled into the chair in Anna's room. Ivy drew her daughter to her breast, fully conscious of the double meaning of *Joy* pressed to her heart.

———∞∞∞———

Ivy's tennis shoes sank into the rain-softened lawn. The added weight of Joy on her hip, bundled against the still-chilled early spring air, guaranteed the shoes would need washing or polish when her deed was done. Hyacinths bloomed in a yard nearby, heavily perfuming the air. Intoxicating.

Moving late in the season and late in her pregnancy left no time to tend to the neglected flower beds. The tiny grape hyacinths and daffodils struggled for recognition among the tangle of last year's deadfall and bleached weed growth. She'd find a way to borrow a buggy for Joy and fix the mess as soon as the weather warmed a little more.

When the two reached the side of the house by Anna's window, Ivy tapped on the glass. Propped in her bed, Anna waved. Yes, she saw them.

Ivy tugged at the papery pods left on the spent morning glory vines. They crumbled in her hand, the chaff of the pod gone with a breath, leaving glorious dark seeds. Working one-handed, she slipped seeds into the pocket of her jacket, collecting more than enough. She looked up periodically, sharing the moment with Anna.

Content that they'd gathered enough to plant and enough for memories, Ivy hoisted Joy higher and waved the baby's mittened hand at Anna.

No!

Anna's face blanched. Eyes wide and looking past Ivy, she clutched her hands to her chest.

No! Oh, Anna, not now!

No fear painted Anna's face. She smiled and pointed beyond Ivy, like a pool shark defining which billiard pocket he targeted.

Rooted to the spot outside the window, Ivy froze.

Anna clapped her disfigured hands.

"Ivy?"

Joy's bonneted head turned at the sound. Ivy followed.

Limping, but alive, he approached as fast as his limp allowed.

"Drew!"

31

Becky—2013

Mom?"

"In here." Becky climbed out of the cardboard box in which she was digging for a roll of paper towels or her oven mitts. Both items were missing.

"Hey, is your air conditioning working on this side?" Lauren walked into Becky's box-strewn kitchen hunched over, holding Jackson's hands as his pudgy sandaled feet slapped the vinyl tile in a pseudowalk. "Whew! Guess I have my answer. No."

"Dad suggested we not crank it up until the guys are done coming in and out with furniture."

"That explains your side. What about mine? We're roasting over there."

Becky stood and stretched her back. "Check"—she scanned the room—"that big green tote. I think there's a tabletop fan in there."

"Can I have it?"

"Borrow it? Sure. Just put it up high enough that—"

Lauren and Jackson penguin-walked toward the tote. "I know. I know. He's into everything."

"And make sure the cord is—"

"Tucked out of the way. I *know*, Mom."

It was the heat making people cranky. Living side by side was going to work out swell, just . . . swell.

Lauren dug out the fan and an extension cord. "I made chocolate chip cookies for your movers. Want one?"

"You did? Yes. Absolutely. Thanks."

"Just being neighborly. I'll bring them over when I get Jackson down for his nap. And before you say anything, I already checked. Yes, the baby monitor works all the way over here."

Her daughter's laughter had always been infectious—in a good way. Becky didn't realize how much she'd missed that element of their relationship.

"So, Dad starts work Monday, huh?"

"Yup." Becky resumed pawing through the box marked "Odds and Ends."

"Kinda stinks that he won't have as much time to spend on the remodeling."

She surveyed the unfinished drywall repairs, the still cock-eyed cupboard door, the capped wires where a ceiling light should be. "Kinda stinks. But I'm not complaining. Work is work."

Lauren snatched an unidentified object out of her son's hands on its way to his mouth. "I hope he likes the job."

"Me, too. He'd grown so fond of that recliner." Their laughter harmonized this time.

Lauren hiked Jackson onto her left hip. "Well, I'd stay and help, but this is a hazmat zone at the moment. Not exactly child friendly." She peeled another something out of Jackson's grip.

"Understood. I need to focus on making the best use of space here and figure out what will have to go to storage."

Lauren stood at the edge of leaving an extra moment. "I'll get the fan when I bring the cookies."

"Okay, hon."

"And Mom?"

Becky hoisted two oven mitts from the dark recesses of the box. Victorious!

"Thanks."

"For . . . ?"

"A chance. A place to live. Options. Hope. Pretty much everything."

The smudge Becky made when she swiped at her eyes must have been more than Lauren could stand. She licked her thumb and said, "You got a little something right . . . there," and wiped it away. Just like a real mom.

Eww.

But endearing.

Two men and a bed frame slid past them on their way to the bedroom.

"Okay, we're leaving." Lauren coached Jackson to wave bye-bye to his grandma. "Hey, I met one of the neighbors this morning."

"You did? That's great. Once I get settled in, I'll have to get out and do that." *Pancake flipper. Nutmeg rasp. Lemon zester, which come to think of it looks a lot like a nutmeg rasp.*

"Nice enough lady. Ivy Lambert. She looked like a hundred but said she was only eighty-five."

"Only."

"So, that makes her kids, like, sixty-five and her grandkids forty-five. Can you imagine?"

Paper towels! Another victory. Ooo, and the can opener. "How many children does she have?"

"She lives with one of her daughters in that little house across the street. But get this. When I asked her how many kids she had, she looked all proud and said, 'Four sons and sixty-nine daughters.' I don't think she's all there, if you know what I mean. But she was real nice. Overdosing on stories. But Jackson took to her right away. She gave me this." Lauren pulled something from the pocket of her shorts.

A small brown envelope tied with a red thread.

"Seeds from her garden. Mom, the whole side of her house is covered in morning glories."

Discussion Questions

1. Anna, Ivy, Becky, Lauren, Monica, Brianne. With which character did you most closely identify? Was it her personality, her circumstances, or her faith issues that resonated with you? In what way?

2. Morning glories play an obvious symbolic role in the book. At what point in the story did you make the connection to their meaning for the main characters? Did that meaning differ for any of them?

3. Even in light of forgiveness and grace, consequences often linger. How has that shown itself true in your life or the life of someone close to you?

4. In what ways were community reactions similar in each of the eras—the 1890s, the 1950s, and today? How were they different?

5. At first glance, Ornell may have seemed a cold, heartless father. By the end of the book, when you know more of his story, how would you characterize his initial emotional distance? Did your attitude toward that character change? How?

6. How far back would Ivy need to trace to find the root of her insecurities? The story doesn't show everything. Share a scene from your own imagination that isn't expressed in the book, but one that would have shaped the woman she was in 1951. What, if anything, in your own history led you to imagine that scene?

7. Smells were dramatic emotional triggers for Ivy. With which ones did you most closely identify and why? Why might the author have used a sense of smell to bring life to Ivy's character?

8. Describe your reaction to Anna's friend Puff. What was it that made him essential to the story? In what way was Puff's presence a reflection of a larger truth?

9. Anna's wisdom was hard-earned. How did her mother's sacrifices set her up for her life's work but also throw shadows across her path?

10. Who has played the role of "Anna" in your life?

11. Best friends Becky and Monica experienced a major breakdown in their relationship. Do you hold out hope for their restoration? Why or why not?

12. Gil and Becky worked hard to maintain their sense of humor in the face of family crises. Some would say it was their saving grace. Relate a time in your life when keeping your sense of humor in a difficult situation had that effect for you.

13. Becky struggled to know the difference between helping and enabling. If sitting across the table from her, what advice would you give her?

14. In what ways did the concept of "home" mean something very personal and unique in each era, for each character?

15. Which scene in this novel most clearly defines your impression of the book's theme?

16. Which child in *When the Morning Glory Blooms* would you most want to hold? What would you whisper in that child's ear?

If you missed Cynthia Ruchti's first adventure, check out this sample chapter

—⁂—

They Almost Always Come Home

1

From the window [she] looked out.
Through the window she watched for his return, saying,
"Why is his chariot so long in coming?
Why don't we hear the sound of chariot wheels?"
—Judges 5:28 NLT

Do dead people wear shoes? In the casket, I mean. Seems a waste. Then again, no outfit is complete without the shoes.

My thoughts pound up the stairs, down the hall, and into the master bedroom closet. Greg's gray suit is clean, I think. White shirt, although that won't allow much color contrast and won't do a thing for Greg's skin tones. His red tie with the silver threads? Good choice.

Shoes or no shoes? I should know this. I've stroked the porcelain-cold cheeks of several embalmed loved ones. My father and grandfather. Two grandmothers—one too young to die. One too old not to.

And Lacey.

The Baxter Street Mortuary will not touch my husband's body should the need arise. They got Lacey's hair and facial expression all wrong.

I rise from the couch and part the sheers on the front window one more time. Still quiet. No lights on the street. No Jeep pulling into our driveway. I'll give him one more hour, then I'm heading for bed. With or without him.

Shoes? Yes or no? I'm familiar with the casket protocol for children. But for adults?

Grandma Clarendon hadn't worn shoes for twelve years or more when she died. She preferred open-toed terrycloth slippers. Day and night. Home. Uptown. Church. Seems to me she took comfort to the extreme. Or maybe she figured God ought to be grateful she showed up in His house at all, given her distaste for His indiscriminate dispersal of the Death Angel among her friends and siblings.

"Ain't a lick of pride in outliving your brothers and sisters, Libby." She said it often enough that I can pull off a believable impression. Nobody at the local comedy club need fear me as competition, but the cousins get a kick out of it at family reunions.

Leaning on the tile and cast-iron coffee table, I crane everything in me to look at the wall clock in the entry. Almost four in the morning? I haven't even decided who will sing special music at Greg's memorial service. Don't most women plan their husband's funeral if he's more than a few minutes late?

In the past, before this hour, I'm mentally two weeks beyond the service, trying to decide whether to keep the house or move to a condo downtown.

He's never been this late before. And he's never been alone in the wilderness. A lightning bolt of something—fear? anticipation? pain?—ripples my skin and exits through the soles of my feet.

The funeral plans no longer seem a semimorbid way to occupy my mind while I wait for the lights of his Jeep. Not pointless imaginings but preparation.

That sounds like a thought I should command to flee in the name of Jesus or some other holy incantation. But it stares at me with narrowed eyes as if to say, "I dare you."

Greg will give me grief over this when he gets home. "You worry too much, Libby. So I was a little late." He'll pinch my love handles, which I won't find endearing. "Okay, a lot late. Sometimes the wind whips up the waves on the larger lakes. We voyageurs have two choices—risk swamping the canoe so we can get home to our precious wives or find a sheltered spot on an island and stay put until the wind dies down."

I never liked how he used the word *precious* in that context. I should tell him so. I should tell him a lot of things. And I will.

If he ever comes home.

⸺◦◦◦◦⸺

With sleep-deprived eyes, I trace the last ticks of the second hand. Seven o'clock. Too early to call Frank? Not likely.

I reach to punch the MEM 2 key sequence on the phone. Miss the first time. Try again.

One ring. Two. Three. If the answering machine kicks in—

"Frank's Franks. Frankly the best in all of Franklin County. Frank speaking. How can I help you?"

I bite back a retort. How does a retired grocery manager get away with that much corny? Consistently. One thing is still normal.

"Frank, it's Libby. I hate to call this early but—"

"Early?" he snorts. "Been up since four-thirty."

Figures. Spitting image of his son.

"Biked five miles," he says. "Had breakfast at the truck stop. Watered those blasted hostas of your mother-in-law's that just

344

won't die. Believe me, I've done everything in my power to help them along toward that end."

I don't have the time or inclination to defend Pauline's hostas. "I called for a reason, Frank."

"Sorry. What's up?"

I'm breathing too rapidly. Little flashes of electricity hem my field of vision. "Have you heard from Greg?"

"He's back, right?"

"Not yet. I'm probably worried for nothing."

He expels a breath that I feel in the earpiece. "When did you expect him? Yesterday?"

"He planned to get back on Friday, but said Saturday at the latest. He hates to miss church now that he's into helping with the sound system."

"Might have had to take a wind day. Or two."

Why does it irritate me that he's playing the logic card? "I thought of that."

"Odd, though." His voice turns a corner.

"What do you mean?"

Through the receiver, I hear that grunt thing he does when he gets into or out of a chair. "I had one eye on the Weather Channel most of last week," he says.

What did you do with the other eye, Frank? The Weather Channel? Early retirement has turned him into a weather spectator. "And?"

"Says winds have been calm throughout the Quetico. It's a good thing too. Tinder-dry in Canada right now. One spark plus a stiff wind and you've got major forest fire potential. They've posted a ban on open campfires. Cookstoves only. Greg planned for that, didn't he?"

"How should I know?" Somewhere deep in my brain, I pop a blood vessel. Not my normal style—not with anyone but

Greg. "Sorry, Frank. I'm . . . I'm overreacting. To everything. I'm sure he'll show up any minute. Or call."

From the background comes a sound like leather complaining. "Told my boy more than once he ought to invest in a satellite phone. The man's too cheap to throw away a bent nail."

"I know." I also know I would have thrown a newsworthy fit if he'd suggested spending that kind of money on a toy for his precious wilderness trips when I'm still waiting for the family budget to allow for new kitchen countertops. As it stands, they're not butcher block. They're butcher shop. And they've been that way since we moved in, since Greg first apologized for them and said we'd replace them "one of these first days."

How many "first days" pass in twenty-three years?

His *precious* wilderness trips? Is that what I said? Now *I'm* doing it.

Frank's voice urges me back to the scene of our conversation. "Hey, Libby, have him give me a call when he gets in, will you?" His emphasis of the word *when* rings artificial.

"He always does, Frank." My voice is a stream of air that overpowers the words.

"Still—"

"I'll have him call."

The phone's silent, as is the house. I never noticed before how loud is the absence of sound.

It's official. Greg's missing. That's what the police report says: Missing Person.

I don't remember filing a police report before now. We've never had obnoxious neighbors or a break-in. Not even a stolen bike from the driveway. Yes, I know. A charmed life.

The desk sergeant is on the phone, debating with someone about who should talk to me. Is my case insignificant to them? Not worth the time? I take a step back from the scarred oak check-in desk to allow the sergeant a fraction more privacy.

With my husband gone, I have privacy to spare, I want to tell him. You can have some of mine. You're welcome.

I shift my purse to the other shoulder, as if that will help straighten my spine. Good posture seems irrelevant. Irreverent.

Everything I know about the inside of police stations I learned from Barney Fife, Barney Miller, and any number of CSIs. The perps lined up on benches along the wall, waiting to be processed, look more at ease than I feel.

The chair to which I've been directed near Officer Kentworth's desk boasts a mystery stain on the sitting-down part. Not a chair with my name on it. It's for women with viper tattoos and envelope-sized miniskirts. For guys named Vinnie who wake with horse heads in their beds. For pierced and bandanaed teens on their way to an illustrious petty-theft career.

"Please have a seat." The officer has said that line how many times before?

Officer Kentworth peers through the untidy fringe of his unibrow and takes my statement, helping fill in the blanks on the Missing Person form. All the blanks but one—Where is he? The officer notes Greg's vehicle model and license plate number and asks all kinds of questions I can't answer. Kentworth is a veteran of Canadian trips like the one from which Greg has not returned. He knows the right questions to ask.

Did he choose the Thunder Bay or International Falls crossing into Canada? What was your husband's intended destination in the Quetico Provincial Park? Where did he arrange to enter and exit the park? Did he have a guide service drop him off? Where did he plan to camp on his way out of the park? How many portages?

I should have sent Frank to file the report. He'd know. Greg probably rambled on to me about some of those things on his way out the door seventeen days ago. My brain saw no need to retain any of it. It interested him, not me.

Kentworth leans toward me, exhales tuna breath—which seems especially unique at this hour of the morning—and asks, "How've things been at home between the two of you?"

I know the answer to this question. Instead I say, "Fine. What's that got to do with—?"

"Had to ask, Mrs. Holden." He reaches across his desk and pats my hand. Rather, he patronizes my hand. "Many times, in these cases—"

Oh, just say it!

"—an unhappy husband takes advantage of an opportunity to walk away."

His smile ends at the border of his eyes. I resist the urge to smack him. I don't want to join the perps waiting to be processed. I want to go home and plow through Greg's office, searching for answers I should have known.

Greg? Walk away?

Not only is he too annoyingly faithful for that, but if anyone has a right to walk away, it's me.

———

I thought it would be a relief to get home again after the ordeal at the police station, which included a bizarre three-way conversation with the Canadian authorities asking me to tell them things I don't know. We won't even mention the trauma of the question, "And Mrs. Holden, just for the record, can you account for your own whereabouts since your husband left?"

Home? A relief? The answering machine light blinks like an ambulance. Mostly messages from neighbors, wondering if

I've heard anything. A few friends and extended family—word is spreading—wondering if I've heard anything. Our pastor, wondering if I've heard anything.

I head for the bedroom to change clothes. The cotton sweater I wore to the station smells like tuna and handcuffs. Or is that my imagination?

Quick census. How many cells of my body don't ache? You'd think I'd find this king-sized bed and down comforter impossible to resist. But it's another symbol that something's missing. Something's wrong and has been for a long time. Moving from our old queen-sized mattress to this king represented distance rather than comfort. For me, anyway. I needed a few more inches between us. A few feet. I guess I got my wish.

I throw the sweater in the wicker hamper, which ironically does not reek of Greg's athletic socks today. On the way from the hamper to the closet, I clunk my shin on the corner of the bed frame. The bed takes up more of the room than it should. Old houses. Contractors in the 1950s couldn't envision couples in love needing that much elbow room. My shin throbs as it decides whether it wants to bruise. That corner's caught me more than once. I ought to know better. About a lot of things.

I pull open the bifold closet doors. Picking out something to wear shouldn't be this hard. But Greg's things are in here.

If he were planning to leave me, couldn't he have had the decency to tidy up after himself and clear out the closet? For the ever-popular "closure"? How long do I wait before packing up his suits and dress shirts?

One of his suit jackets is facing the wrong way on the hanger. Everyone knows buttons face left in the closet. Correcting it is life-or-death important to me at the moment. There. Order. As it should be. I smooth the collar of the jacket and stir up the scent of Aspen for Men. The boa constrictor around my throat flexes its muscles.

With its arms spread wide, the overstuffed chair in the corner mocks me. I bought it without clearing the expenditure with Greg. Mortal sin, right? He didn't holler. The man doesn't holler. He sighs and signs up for more overtime.

Maybe I'll find comfort in the kitchen. This bedroom creeps me out.

———

Greg has thrown us into an incident of international intrigue. Melodramatic wording, but true. We're dealing with the local authorities plus the Canadian police.

Staring out the kitchen window at the summer-rich backyard proves fruitless. It holds no answers for me. I'm alone in this. Almost.

Frank's my personal liaison with the Canadians—border patrol, Quetico Park rangers, and Ontario Provincial Police, the latter of which is blessed with an unfortunate acronym—OPP. Looks a lot like "Oops" on paper. I can't help but envision that adorable character from *Due North*, the Mountie transplanted into the heart and bowels of New York City. Sweetly naive as he was, he always got his man. Will these get mine?

Frank will be much better at pestering them for answers. My mother-in-law would be better still. Pestering. Pauline's gifted that way.

I'm no help. Big surprise. When I spoke with the north-of-the-border authorities, I either tripped over every word and expressed my regrets for bothering them or shouted into the phone, "Why aren't you doing something?"

They are, of course. They're trying. Analyzing tire tracks. Interviewing canoeists exiting the park. Looking for signs of a struggle. The search plane they promised is a nice touch. Under Frank's direction, they'll scan Greg's expected route to check for mayhem.

While I wait for yet another pot of coffee to brew, I brush toast crumbs—some forgotten breakfast—off the butcher shop counter into my hand. Now what? I can't think what to do with them.

The phone rings.

It's Greg's district manager again. He's the pasty-faced, chopstick-thin undertaker hovering just offstage in a lame western movie.

No, no word from Greg yet. Yes, I'll let you know as soon as I hear something. Yes, I understand what a difficult position this has put you in, Mr. Sensitive, I mean, Mr. Stenner. Can we request a temporary leave of absence for Greg or . . . ? Of course, I understand. Not fair to the company, sure. Only have so much patience, uh huh. God bless you too.

Right.

Oh, and thanks for caring that my life is falling apart and my husband is either muerto *or just fine but not with me and either way he's a dead man.*

I slam the phone into its base station, then apologize to it.

The sweat in my palm reconstituted the bread crumbs during the call. Wastebasket. That's what one does with crumbs.

How long will it take me to figure out what to do with the crumbs of my life?

And where will I find a basket large enough for the pieces?

Want to learn more about author
Cynthia Ruchti and check out other great
fiction from Abingdon Press?

Sign up for our fiction newsletter at
www.AbingdonPress.com
to read interviews with your favorite authors, find tips
for starting a reading group, and stay posted on what
new titles are on the horizon. It's a place to connect
with other fiction readers or post a
comment about this book.

Be sure to visit Cynthia online!

www.cynthiaruchti.com